# A Face in the Sky

Greg Jenkins

Harvard Square Editions
New York
2016

*A Face in the Sky*

ISBN 978-1-941861-14-1
Printed in the United States of America

Published in the United States by
Harvard Square Editions
www.harvardsquareeditions.org

To my brother Phil and my buddy Joe Smith

*The future's uncertain, and the end is always near.*

—The Doors, "Roadhouse Blues"

BOB STALLINGS WAS SCARED. Though he didn't know how or why, he understood that death was bearing down on him.

It was bearing down on everyone.

He was outside on a clear bright day, moving through the downtown. He seemed to be walking, but he couldn't have been; he was careering along at too great a speed. Was he on a motor scooter? A Segway? A moving ramp? For some reason, he was unable to tell. Yet this strange uncertainty about his locomotion didn't disturb him.

What was happening around him, however, bothered him keenly. In front of him, orange flames engulfed the top three floors of a tall building, making it look like a huge torch. To either side of him, people he didn't know were stampeding like misplaced cattle up and down and across the streets. The cause of their panic was a mystery to him, but he knew it wasn't the burning building. It was something even larger, immeasurably more threatening. A few of the people were yelling and screaming; most were hurrying ahead in stone-faced silence. His heart tightened into a knot as he sensed their adversary was closing in on them—closing in on him as well. The thing could speak and it could calculate and it could destroy. Though he jerked his head left and right, he was helpless to see it.

From out of nowhere a gorgeous young woman grabbed him, seizing both his shoulders, her black-as-night hair flowing and sparkling in the sun. She ranted at him, but her words held no meaning for him; they were gibberish.

"What?" he shouted at her.

"China!" she shouted back.

"What?"

"Des Moines!"

He shook his head in confusion, but something in her violet eyes, those intense beautiful eyes, broke through to him....

Stallings groaned in misery on his sofa. Gradually, as if riding an elevator up from some dark underground floor in his muddled life, he was coming awake, shaking off the dream.

As usual, his hangover was pretty rough. Then again, over the preceding months—the past year—he'd had others that were much worse. Hangovers that could fell a rhinoceros, upend a bulldozer. Hangovers that would not only torment him physically but assault him spiritually. *Who do you think you are?* they'd taunt him. *What's your purpose? What's your worth? Why don't you just go away somewhere and be done with it all?* While this particular hangover was nowhere near as ferocious as one of those unholy beasts, it was no toy poodle either. And it would keep him poor company for the rest of his day, which was just now commencing.

Rolling over, he groaned again. The sofa was L-shaped, and the angle of his beefy shirtless body was suddenly in geometric conflict with the crook of the L. His lower back pinched him. "My God," he mumbled, and rolled back to his original position.

Out of old habit, he reached over to touch his wife. Touching her warm body, especially at bleak moments like this, always gave him reassurance that everything would be all right, even if he knew it wouldn't be. He reached over, and felt nothing. Then he remembered that he was not in bed but on his living room sofa. He also remembered that his beloved Jenny was dead, having been torn from him more than a year ago. These thoughts did little to salve his hangover. How long would it take him, he wondered dimly, to adjust to life without her? Before he fully accepted that the warm smooth body he yearned to touch was gone forever, no matter how far he stretched? Another year? Five years? Ten? Would it *ever* happen?

Despite himself, Stallings tried to recall what exactly he'd done last night, where he'd done it and with whom. Aha. Yes. After putting in another long and trying day of teaching roomfuls of zombielike students at Harris Community College, he'd gone to Johnny's Place downtown. It was a swank but friendly saloon made all the friendlier by Stallings' connection with the colorful owner, the legendary Johnny 'Jet' Black, former major league pitcher. Decades before, the two had grown up together, gone to high school together. Now, once in a while, they drank together, as they'd done with some gusto last night.

Long retired, Johnny still retained his star status, a status that Stallings had never enjoyed at anything, ever. All Johnny had to do was swagger into a room like a buccaneer on the deck of his galley, and heads would swivel, eyes would focus. Voices would grow hushed at first, then become high and excited. People liked Johnny, wanted to be near him. They wanted to savor his breezy happy-go-lucky style that always went down lightly and bracingly, like a cold beer after work. Even those who insisted they had no use for the man found themselves beaming when he granted them an autograph, which always consisted of a single brash word, his ultimate nickname: 'Perfection.' For though his baseball career had been uneven at best, tainted and retainted by scandal, no one could ever forget the glory he'd achieved that one magnificent Sunday afternoon in the Bronx against none other than the New York Yankees. No, like 'Jet' before it, this final nickname had been earned, if only for a moment.

Last night, Johnny's charisma had been operating at full force. Things had begun quietly enough with some freewheeling conversation at the bar, followed by a few games of nineball among Johnny, Stallings and a handful of others in a back room. A slate table with drop pockets, the piquant aroma of cigar smoke, and every game won by the gabbing laughing owner, who, showing off a hand-eye coordination that was after all professional caliber, played perfectly ...

"Why don't you miss one now and then," Stallings had needled him, "just for the sake of variety?"

"Variety's overrated," Johnny said. "Unless we're talking about bed partners."

When they returned to the bar—Johnny sometimes behind it mixing drinks, sometimes on the other side mixing with the patrons—the pace of the partying seemed to accelerate. Women entered the picture, as they often did with Johnny, whose dense dark hair and roguish handsome face made him appear ten years younger than his calendar age of forty-four. These were attractive women too, and young (they could've been students at the college), and they pressed as close to Johnny as his golden suntan. He didn't seem to mind. One of them insisted on teaching him a new dance called the Countdown. "Well now, hold on just a second," Johnny joked. "Just what the hell are we counting down *to?*" But he went along with her, music pounding, and soon everyone, Stallings included, was out on the floor, arms and legs flying, dancing the Countdown. Drinks, plenty of them, began appearing for free—though the cost next morning was steep.

Sprawled sideways on his sofa, hairless belly protruding round as a small planet, Stallings slowly became aware of a soft voice in the room. Two voices. Surely he hadn't brought someone home with him! Toward the tattered end of the night, he'd been in very close quarters with a curly-headed young creature whose hair jounced and quivered at him as she spoke in an extremely earnest tone about ... something. The notion that aliens had been visiting Earth, or that sex and not math was the universal language, or that we were all sinners and deserved to die ... Something. Surely he hadn't ...

With an effort, he opened both dull eyes into filmy slits, lifted his lead head and blinked around the room. Seeing no one, he thanked God and sank back.

He did notice, however, that the TV was on and that it was the source of the unwelcome voices. He could see the wide screen, even now with his aching head in recline, and, though he didn't want to, he began paying limited attention to what was evidently a movie. A gruff unkempt balding man in a white A-shirt was bullying a woman; he was cursing at her, shoving her. Stallings was reminded of the classic scene in *The Public Enemy* when an irate Jimmy Cagney crams a grapefruit into Mae Clarke's hapless face. But this movie was more current. "Why are you doing this?" the woman wailed. The man then flung her to the floor, and the camera angle switched to her point of view as she stared up at her attacker. Filling the screen completely, the man's grubby face loomed down, pressed down, at both her and Stallings. Neither of them seemed to appreciate it. "Because I can," he answered with a snicker. "And because I don't like you."

The feeling being mutual with Stallings, he found the remote control somewhere beneath him—it'd been a painful bump in his ribs—and clicked the dreary world of the movie into silent oblivion. His attitude improved instantly. Actually, he'd been rather amused by the man's heartless comment and might've even smiled had he felt more like his usual peppy self. "And because I don't like you." The words closely resembled those offered way back when by Henry Ford, Jr. in dismissing his cocky underling Lee Iacocca. *But why are you firing me?* Iacocca had wanted to know. *Because, Lee,* the reply came, *I just don't like you.* As a Professor of Business, Stallings sometimes used this anecdote in class to illustrate the vagaries of life in the business world. One day you're up; the next day you're out. The students, of course, never got it.

His left arm dangling clear to the floor, he felt immensely grateful that he wouldn't have to deal with students today. It was the weekend. He was off. Yes!

Wait a second, he thought. A moment passed uncomfortably, his ravaged mental circuitry attempting to fire. What day was it? It wasn't the weekend, not even close. Today was *Tuesday*, for crying out loud, and he did have to work! Dear God, what had he done to himself? He frowned down at his watch, which not only confirmed the day but gave him terrible news regarding the time.

Coughing, grimacing, groaning once again, Stallings worked himself to a sitting position and then, after a long deliberate pause, launched himself to his bare feet. To his surprise, he felt fairly stable. He was a big bulky man who shambled gingerly toward the bathroom in a pair of khaki chinos that, despite what they'd doubtless been through during the night, still looked sharp. Kneading his forehead gently, he wondered what had become of his shoes, socks and shirt; he didn't see them about. Well, they'd turn up sooner or later, he supposed. Parts of his economy-size body jiggled as he lumbered onward.

Halfway to the bathroom, he did something that even he couldn't have explained. He changed course, went to a window and looked outside. It was as if the window, or something beyond it, had beckoned him. Gazing left and right, he saw what he'd expected to see: a scrubbed residential neighborhood beginning to brighten with the day and with the pert fresh greenness of another spring. A woman was walking her dog, a bouncy little brown-and-white terrier, and a yellow-helmeted man on a bicycle passed by, gliding in the opposite direction. It was quiet out there. Normal as could be. Stallings had no idea why he was standing at the window.

On impulse, he lifted his gaze toward the sky and saw ... nothing unusual. The color was a morning's pastel blue, a few wispy white cirrus clouds adrift at a majestic height. Though the sun was hidden behind a stout red-flowering maple, its light nevertheless pricked his raw eyes, and finally he pulled away from the view, went about his business.

2

IN CONTRAST TO STALLINGS, Johnny woke up this morning feeling quite lively. He too had washed down more alcohol last night than he'd planned, and indeed he'd stayed up even later than the professor. (The dance teacher had wanted to continue her lessons in a more private setting—Johnny's condo—and he was inclined to show her some moves of his own.) But alcohol tended to agree with Johnny, as did late hours and misbehaving women. His body seemed to require a regular quota of each, and on the rare occasions when he fell short of his minimum dosage, *then* he would wake up feeling pained, enervated and out of sorts.

Showered and shaved, Johnny was making his rounds of the city, the young lady a sweet but already sketchy memory. From a gym he'd recently bought, he phoned his longtime agent George 'Buzzy' Bilkman. Buzzy was a chain-smoking suspendered old wheeler-dealer of consummate skill. Back when Johnny'd been playing, it was the wily, unscrupulous and fast-talking Buzzy who'd squeezed all those gilt-edged contracts out of the White Sox' front office. Nowadays Buzzy, who was still as wily, unscrupulous and fast-talking as ever, worked for Johnny on other matters. Personal appearances, memorabilia, product endorsements. Whatever came along. The two men had known each other for many years and appreciated each other's talents. But even Buzzy, with all his gray hairs and seasoning, was perplexed and amazed by what Johnny was telling him now.

"You're comin' back!" Buzzy squawked like a Mynah bird in Johnny's ear. "You're comin' back to what, for Chrissake?"

"Baseball," Johnny said.

"Baseball! Whadaya mean, baseball, for Chrissake? You mean—"

"I'm making my comeback," Johnny said.

"Comeback!" There was a pause, not a long one, while Buzzy presumably took another drag from an unfiltered Camel and exhaled a feathery stream of smoke. "You're talkin' about bein' a baseball *commentator*, right? On TV? Just sit there—"

"No."

"Sit there in a booth, eat your chilidogs and run your yap all night—is that what you mean?"

Johnny chuckled. "No, dude. I'm talking about playing the game again." Despite Buzzy's skepticism, Johnny was calm and upbeat. He had a vision of the future he'd come to believe in. "I'm gonna climb back on the mound," he said. "I'm gonna show 'em this left arm's still got some K's in it."

This time the pause from Buzzy was considerable. "For Chrissake," he said.

They kept jawing. Arguing from what sounded like self-interest to Johnny, Buzzy claimed that the public was fond of the ballplayer the way he was—retired. An ill-conceived comeback attempt could make him look foolish, and maybe even jeopardize some of the current business deals Buzzy had labored so hard to arrange. As things were, people could remember Johnny selectively, focus on the luminous performances he'd put on when he'd been at his crowd-wowing best. But if he tried to come back, fans would then be seeing him as he was today, which might not be so good. Buzzy supported his argument by citing other well-known athletes who, past their meridian, had tried and failed to recapture the old magic. Mark Spitz. Muhammad Ali. Bjorn Borg. Michael Jordan.

"Not a baseball player among 'em," Johnny said dismissively. "Listen, Buzz. I can do this. My arm feels super."

"You're too damn old," Buzzy told him.

"I'm thirty-eight."

"You're forty-four. And you was over the hill, for Chrissake, when you *was* thirty-eight."

"I'm in shape. I been working out. Where do you think I

am right this second?"

Another pause from Buzzy while smoke was either inhaled or exhaled. "I dunno. Some goddam cathouse somewhere, I guess."

Irrepressible, Johnny chuckled again. "I'm in a gym. I went out and bought my own fitness center." It was true. Johnny was in a gym, and he was the sole proprietor. Perfection Fitness. "I work out here every day." That part of his statement wasn't true.

Buzzy made a sound that was somewhere between a wheezing sigh and a tortured moan. He then brought up a difficult and delicate subject. Although Johnny did have his partisans, he also had a number of detractors, many of whom were influential in Major League Baseball. Owners, for example. General managers. Managers. Coaches. Players. Journalists. Johnny'd quit baseball under a cloud—a dark churning thunderhead at that. Over the years, Perfection hadn't always been so perfect. He'd been arrested twice for DUI (convicted once), fought with teammates, had his name linked to a gambling ring, and been accused by several women of having fathered their children. (One daughter, Sarah, he admitted to. With varying degrees of vehemence and believability, he denied all other charges of fatherhood, and nothing was ever proven in court.) The final outrage occurred one blustery night in Chicago when, miffed at a called ball four that Johnny insisted had painted the inside corner, he tugged down his pants atop the mound, mooned the home plate umpire and then, using a bent-over spin-move, mooned the entire stunned and flabbergasted crowd.

"So what's your point?" Johnny asked.

"Point is," Buzzy said, "I dunno if there's a market for you, I don't care *how* good you pitch. You may be what they call persona non grata."

Johnny told him to save his French for when he was visiting Paris. He also told him that Buzzy had misjudged the situation totally.

"You forget the times we live in," Johnny said. "These days, bad is good. People like things with a little spice, a little bad-boy irreverence. I come back today, I'll be bigger than ever."

Dutifully he waited for the sarcastic swipe Buzzy was sure to deliver within the next two seconds. None came.

"Real soon," Johnny went on, "I'm gonna have a scout watch me throw. Frank Dutwell? He's gonna check me out. If he likes what he sees ..."

"Bad is good," Buzzy murmured in a distracted faraway voice. He seemed intrigued with the notion. "For Chrissake."

They talked for a while longer, and when he hung up, Johnny felt as if he'd eked out a hard-fought victory in the conversation. Or at least he'd staked himself to a slender lead in the game, with more innings yet to be played.

* * *

Wearing an American Eagle T-shirt and a pair of loose-fitting faded Levis, Johnny looked and felt comfortable. In another minute he'd look and feel even more comfortable.

He ambled over to the refrigerator—it had a see-through door so the patrons could peer in and observe what sort of beverages were available—and opened it. Nudging aside the various energy drinks, protein shakes and bottles of vitamin-laced colored water, Johnny located a can of Lite beer in the back and happily brought it out into the soft fluorescent light, the fan-driven air of the gym. Keeping beer in this public fridge—and in a commercial fitness center, no less—was probably a debatable idea, but so far no one had complained. And where else could he store it, if he wanted it both cold and close at hand? Besides, he didn't sell it; he drank it himself, so he doubted he was breaking the law. Then again, maybe he *was* breaking the law. More important to him than any hair-splitting legal niceties was his firm moral resolve that before noon (like now) he would never consume even a drop of 'real' beer, only the more civilized low-cal low-carb stuff.

He ambled back to the front desk, cracked open his beer and treated himself to a lengthy and satisfying draft. "I woke up this morning and I got myself a beer," he crooned. It was a line from an old Doors song. Johnny was a rock 'n' roll kind of guy, he told himself.

Idly, he allowed his gaze to roam the interior landscape of Perfection Fitness. To his left was a long metal rack of dumbbells, from light to very heavy, running toward the rear of the gym. A series of benches, flat and incline, stood near the dumbbells. Directly before him rose an array of exercise machines that looked like medieval torture devices—and felt like them too. To his right was a free-weight area replete with Olympic barbells, squat racks and even a deadlift platform. At the back of the spacious room, up on an elevated stand, was the cardio area where people could ride bikes that never advanced, climb elliptical stairs that went nowhere. Clients doing cardio faced the front of the gym, and it sometimes spooked Johnny to have all those blank humorless eyes staring down at him as their owners struggled on, puffing, sweating.

While being a gym owner had its plusses (the music was agreeable, the spandexed babes were a delight to ogle), Johnny frankly could've done without it. He didn't understand gyms and didn't care for them, especially his own. Yet from time to time he was more or less obligated to be here. The only reason he'd acquired the facility was to buff up not his body or his wallet but his public image. Everyone knew he owned a saloon, and that blunt fact, coupled with his well-cataloged history of personal shenanigans, projected a negative karma. Bad was good, but too much bad was bad. A gym, on the other hand— a place where folks could improve their health and quality of life—was positive. It brought his controversial image a hint of balance, permitting people to say, *Yes he's a rake, yes he's a rascal, but let's weigh both sides, OK?* It was a factor that might prove crucial to a guy hoping to return to professional baseball.

Johnny gave his Adam's apple a ride up and down with

another satisfying draft of beer.

He mulled whether he should undertake one of his rare workouts today. He was due, and he was overdue. Or he could give his buddy Bob Stallings a call, make sure he survived the 86-proof night. Neither idea swayed him just now.

Instead, he snatched up his phone and took a moment to compose his thoughts. He'd heard lately that his nomadic ex-girlfriend Wanda, who happened to be the mother of his daughter Sarah, was back in town. Back from God knows where. From the dead maybe. He'd also heard that Wanda, who in her own way had been every bit as flaky as Johnny, was in dire need of money and that she expected him to donate to her cause. Meant to persuade him to, at any rate. He'd paid her a small fortune in child support while Sarah was growing up— he was no deadbeat dad!—but those days were over. Sarah, wherever she was, was in her twenties and independent. Wanda was supposed to be independent as well. Phone in hand, he continued to concentrate. He was selecting his words precisely.

Abruptly he punched out a number. "Wanda?" he said. "Johnny. No."

Without another word he hung up and lifted the can of beer to his mouth, tilted back his handsome head.

3

THE REPORTER FROM THE *TIMES*, Laura Kennedy, was struggling with the interview. Despite her thorough preparation, which included watching some of the most explicit porn movies imaginable, she was much more skittish than she'd anticipated. She kept stumbling over her own questions, trying to frame them so they sounded candid but not vulgar. (They sounded vulgar anyway.) Then too, her offhand comments seemed stilted, forced. Not only that, but a large portion of what she was hearing simply failed to register, so she repeatedly found herself saying, "Excuse me?" or "I'm sorry?" or sometimes just plain "Huh?"

She'd come to this sumptuous Mediterranean-inspired house in the hot dry San Fernando Valley to interview the celebrated porn star Zoey Zanders. ("We've got to do it," she'd urged her editor. "Porn is a multi-billion dollar business, growing all the time. It permeates our culture. And the stars are ... well, they're *stars*.") Zanders, who owned the house, was pleased to talk in ear-singeing detail about her work. A raven-haired knockout with big deep vivacious eyes and a wide collagen-lipped grin that sometimes erupted into laughter and sometimes didn't, she was remarkably open and straightforward. She would speak about giving a blowjob in the same matter-of-fact tone that a contractor might use to discuss laying a section of PVC pipe. Perhaps it was her very lack of reserve that had Laura rattled.

That, and some of the breathtakingly immodest characters Zanders had cavorting around.

They were all situated behind the house, which blazed red and white in the hot sun. Not far from where Laura and Zanders sat, a raucous pool party was underway. About a dozen multi-ethnic types, mostly young, mostly nude, splashed and shrieked in the heart-shaped pool, the noisiest of them playing volleyball, others kicking along on fruit-colored rafts, and still others making uninhibited love. Outside the pool, a few people lingered at the tiki bar, sipping exotic drinks, and a few sat chatting at the shaded tables. More people wore sunglasses than wore swimsuits or any other form of clothing. From a source unseen, rock music thumped and blared.

"Would you care for a drink?" Zanders asked. In her turquoise bikini, Brazilian-cut, she qualified as relatively demure.

"Excuse me?"

"Would you care for a drink? You look a little tense."

"A drink," Laura said. "Well, yes, thank you."

She'd been staring off at the towering white picket fence and the purpleleaf plum trees that encircled the yard. She didn't think anyone could see in. Of course, if anyone could, this group wouldn't have cared.

Then she reversed herself: "No, no thank you. I better not."

"Oh, a teeny one won't hurt." In her deck chair, Zanders wrapped her sensuous lips around a straw that plunged down into a Naughty O'Pear: Belle de Brillet, Stoli Vanilla, pear nectar and champagne. "You should try one of these," she said, smacking her lips.

"Well, I'm not—"

"Derek!" Zanders' voice, when she called out to someone, was clear and robust. "Derek, c'mere!"

A young bronze-skinned man in a black Speedo brief stepped toward them. He'd been standing just a short distance away, much like a sentry, talking to no one, keeping the majority of his attention on Zanders and her visitor. He was very muscular; when he strode toward them, the chiseled grooves and ridges in his shoulders, midsection and thighs rippled rhythmically. His brown hair had been buzzed down to a tight bristle, and his lean face, which was defined by his dark predator-style Ray-Bans, was well-shaped but unpleasant to look at.

"Be a good boy," Zanders said, "and fetch Ms. Kennedy a drink, won't you? One of these," she added, holding up her own drink for inspection.

Quietly but sullenly Derek said: "You know I ain't your puppy dog. Don't you?"

"Of course you're not."

"I shouldn't have to run these stupid little errands."

This time, if Zanders agreed, she didn't say so. "What are you?" she asked.

Derek shrugged. "Your fiancé."

"And would you care to retain that august status?"

He said nothing.

"Do you want to keep on being my fiancé?" she clarified.

He nodded.

"Really," Laura put in, more flustered than ever, "you don't ... There's no need—"

"It's all right," Zanders said. "Derek, do be a dear boy and fetch Ms. Kennedy a drink. Please. Do it now, and we'll both be exceedingly grateful."

After a brief hesitation, Derek nodded, turned and went to the bar.

Zanders favored Laura with a brilliant smile and said: "Where were we?"

"Let's see." The reporter made sure her digital voice recorder was still running and checked the notes she had on her laptop computer. "Uh ... You've been called the Princess of Porn. How do you feel about that?"

"Princess, huh? Like royalty? Like maybe a royal pain in the ass?" A peal of wind-chime laughter that managed to soar far above the other competing sounds before quickly dying off. "I've been called worse."

"And you've made your name in just a few short years— three? Four? What's your secret?"

"Raw talent, honey. In this business we've got a saying. 'The cream always rises to the top.' "

Leaning back in her chair, Laura worked up the nerve to ask a question that hadn't been scripted. "Are your boobs real?" she blurted. Melonlike but gravity-defying, Zanders' eye-popping breasts strained the thin fabric of her overmatched halter, threatening to burst free.

"Course not," Zanders said easily. "I had a boob job, along with everyone else out here." She grasped her own breasts, hefted them up even farther, and let them go. There was a slight rebound effect. "If you're interested, I can fix you up with a primo plastic surgeon."

Politely, Laura indicated she had no desire to have her breasts enhanced.

She did, however, hope to hear Zanders' observations and insights concerning a sampling of sex scenes Laura proposed to play on the laptop. Zanders was amenable, so Laura slipped in a DVD, and, seeking a better view, the actress sat forward.

"Just walk me through this, if you would," Laura said.

Lurid fleshy images began to move and moan on-screen. Zanders and a lithe shaggy-haired man, both nude, were caressing each other lustfully. Abruptly she turned around—they were on a picnic table in the woods—and assumed the doggy position. He pushed into her smoothly and adroitly, began pumping her.

"That's Peter LeMan," Zanders said. "One of the best dongs in the industry. Notice how he's got one hand on his hip, there, and he's leaning backward instead of hunching over me. It's an unnatural posture, OK? But he needs to accommodate the camera."

Laura absorbed these fine points and asked: "Didn't the picnic table hurt your knees?"

"It did. I raised holy hell about it when we were done, but what can I say? Too little, too late."

"What's this guy, Peter ..."

"LeMan."

"Right. What's he like away from the set?"

Zanders shook her raven hair, sending off a sparkle or

two, and had a sip of her frothy drink. "I have no idea," she said. "We had sex five times on-camera, but he never bothered me, never said a word to me, off-camera." Her tone was one of sincere respect. "He's a real pro."

Cradling a fresh drink, small boy's pout on his face, Derek returned to the table. He handed the drink to Laura.

"Oh, look here, Derek," Zanders said. "We're playing a scene from *A Boff in the Woods*. What do you think?"

With little success, he fought to control his irritation. "I think," he said, "that you shouldn't be out here in the sun."

"Derek isn't overly partial to Peter LeMan," Zanders told Laura, loud enough for Derek to hear. "Are you, Derek? Seems that Peter is better-looking than Derek, better endowed, and does a better job of fucking me."

"We've gotta shoot first thing on Friday," Derek said, holding his voice steady, "and you know what the sun does to your skin."

Zanders looked at him sharply, and her own voice took on an edge. "Am I in the sun, Derek? Truly? Or am I in the shade?"

The entire table was protected from the sun by a giant umbrella.

"There's sun out here," he said, waving his hand generally around.

"Oh, go away, Derek. Please. Just walk away."

He stood still for a moment, looming over them, then resentfully marched to a spot twenty or thirty feet away. He turned to face them once again, gold-brown sinewy arms crossed on his carved gold-brown chest, and silently glared at them. His right hand clenched into a blocky fist, he looked as if he wanted to attack Zanders; maybe attack Laura too.

Discretion! Laura thought, and shut down her laptop, closed it.

"Actually, Zoey," she said, "I think I've got more than enough now to do my story."

"Sure?"

"Oh yes." Standing, Laura felt somewhat self-conscious at being the only fully dressed person in sight.

Zanders stood as well. When she did, her body seemed even more imposing—almost cartoonishly erotic, but at the same time hinting of athleticism.

" 'Zoey Zanders,' " Laura mused. "That's an unusual name."

"It's a stage name. Most of us have stage names."

They began walking toward the gate.

"I heard a rumor," Laura said, "that your father is a former major league baseball player. Johnny Black, the pitcher."

Zanders stopped as if she'd bumped into a palm tree. She stood motionless, her lips parted in mild shock.

"I heard," Laura continued, "that your given name is Sarah Black. Is that so?"

Several seconds passed, filled with mindless music and squeals and splashes from the pool.

"Ms. Kennedy ... Laura," the answer came at last, "I'm perfectly willing to talk about my work. You want to ask me about fellatio, about double penetration, about anal intercourse—fine. But please, let's not get into an area I consider personal."

Laura was abashed. "I'm sorry," she said. "I didn't mean to ..."

"It's all right." Warmly, Sarah took her hand. "It's OK. No problemo."

The noise from the pool reached a giddy crescendo, and now a wet volleyball came bounding toward the two women. Showing some rapid reflexes, Laura freed her right hand, bent over and caught the ball in mid-hop. A dark extravagantly hairy man, wearing not a thread, came loping over to her. He was dripping water from every extremity.

She tossed him the ball.

"*Gracias*," he said, and loped away.

* * *

Far overhead, three small globes of light appeared in the sky. The first shone amethyst, the second saffron, the third candy apple red. Bright and pulsing, they swirled silently around each other as if being tossed by a master juggler. Earthly science could not have explained their color, their movement, their nature or their existence.

The dazzling spectacle continued for several minutes, but no one at the house noticed.

4

OWLISH READING GLASSES perched on his broad fleshy nose, Bob Stallings peered out at his class, then jotted some notes on his seating chart. The classroom was kin to a holding cell in a border town police station. The ceiling, walls and floor were all the same washed-out gray, and a solitary window admitted only enough light to accent the dust motes in the air. A poster taped to the wall facing the professor delivered the school's quixotic slogan in black block letters: EXPERIENCE. EXPLORE. EXCEL.

He was taking attendance. As usual, about half his students were missing. A couple of the missing were no doubt sick or otherwise genuinely indisposed, he guessed. But most of them were absent purely because their desire to be somewhere else outweighed their desire to be in class. Any class.

At this instant, Stallings shared their desire to be somewhere else. His night on the town still dogging him, he felt a steady Tylenol-resistant pressure on his skull, and his stomach was queasy, gurgly. Still, he was a paid professional, a man of principles, regardless of how battered and bent some of those principles had lately become. He understood he had a job to do.

"All right," he sang, twisting his pale lips into a gutsy smile, "how we doing this afternoon?"

No one answered him. Some of the students stared off dazedly into space, while others managed to focus on Stallings, but with such an empty exhausted look that one might've thought they'd just survived some natural disaster, having lost most of their family and friends.

"That's good," he said. "Now—how many of you had a chance to read the assignment for today?"

No hands went up.

"How many of you did *not* get a chance to read?"

No hands went up.

A less experienced professor might've fretted over the illogic in these two nonresponses, but Stallings, a battle-toughened warrior, forged on.

"How many of you," he inquired, his voice serene, "can tell me what the reading assignment for today was?"

A noise at the door behind him alerted him that a late student had arrived. Turning to see who it was, Stallings caught a glimpse of his own face in the dark screen of a TV monitor used for showing videos, web info and whatnot. He looked ghastly.

The student was six-foot six-inch Jamal Jameson, one of the school's basketball players. Stallings was always encouraged anytime an athlete actually made it to class. Wearing pants that appeared too long to be shorts—they extended to the young man's calves—and yet too short to be full-blown trousers, Jamal was wending his way to the back of the room.

"Jamal," Stallings called out, "can you tell us what today's reading assignment was?"

After wedging himself gamely into a wooden desk that'd been designed, decades ago, for a much smaller person, Jamal furrowed his brow, stroked his chin. "Somethin' 'bout business," he said. "Somethin' 'bout economics."

Stallings nodded noncommittally, a motion that had the unfortunate effect of increasing the pressure on his skull. He had mixed feelings about Jamal's answer, which, while essentially worthless, was at least an answer of sorts. And it'd been delivered in English, not by means of a scowl, a moue, a head shake or a hand-flip.

"Let me be a little more specific," he said to the group at large. "Last time we met, I asked you to read some excerpts from a certain book. Can anybody name the book?"

Suddenly a hand—it belonged to a plain-faced wide-bodied girl named Amber Glotfelty—shot up.

Stallings nodded at her, once again intensifying his cranial distress. His head felt like a walnut that someone, using a crude instrument, was trying to crack. "Amber?"

"Mr. Stallings," she said, speaking so hurriedly that she sounded like a youthful auctioneer, "Andrea wanted you to know she isn't gonna be here today she's having a problem with her car she wanted me to tell you."

Another timid noise behind him indicated another late arrival, but, reluctant to move his head too much, Stallings kept his bloodshot eyes on Amber.

"OK ..." he said uncertainly. "Thank you, Amber. But what about the reading assignment?"

"What about it?"

"Can you name the book?"

"No."

One of the countless fascinating things about students, Stallings recognized, was how they all looked basically alike. Not as individuals, of course; every individual student was unique and distinctive. But taken en masse, they presented a striking and oftentimes misleading visual sameness, so that merely observing a classroom of students as they sat there breathing at you disclosed only the most superficial of facts about them. Students were mostly young. They dressed casually. They carried book bags and cell phones. A snapshot of students at Harris Community College, therefore, probably wouldn't look too different from one of students at some brutally competitive Ivy League university. No, it was only when you asked your charges to *do* something—when you urged them into some sort of intellectual activity—could you see and gauge what you had.

At this stage of the semester, and indeed of his career, Stallings knew what he had.

"Let me see if I can jog your memory," he offered. "I asked you to read from a book written by Adam ..."

He waited for someone to fill in the blank. No one did.

"C'mon," he said. "Adam ... What comes along with Adam?"

From the back of the room, someone said: "Eve."

Two seconds of stupefied silence, and then irreverent laughter went rippling from desk to desk.

Stallings, whose own humor was in short supply today, waited stoically for the laughter to cease before saying: "Smith. Adam Smith."

Yet another late student entered the room. Privately, Stallings granted that attendance was improving even if punctuality wasn't.

"And the title of the book," he said, "was what?"

Someone said: "*Wealth of Nations*," and the response, being correct, nearly caused Stallings to stagger.

"That's right," he said finally. "Now—did you understand what you read?" Pause. "Did you?" The faces that tilted up at him were themselves unreadable. "If I gave you a quiz on the material right this second, could you handle it?"

He knew, and the students did too, that it was unlikely he'd burden them with a pop quiz. If he did, most of the students would fail it. But then most of them were already failing his class as it was. Failing an absurd number of students, even if they deserved it, could raise some discommoding questions not about the students' deficits, which were a given at HCC, but about the professor's apparent inability to reach out and motivate those students, inspire them, uplift them.

"Any questions about the reading?" Stallings asked, allowing the threat of a quiz to just slide away. "Any questions at all?"

Surprisingly, a student over near the window, Danny Pepper, his uncombed red hair swirling around his head with such vigorous abandon that it looked like a miniature forest fire, did have a question. "What do you make," he asked, "of that building in Iowa?"

"Building in ..." Stallings was lost.

"Iowa. That building that just, you know, disappeared. In Cedar Rapids."

"I don't ..."

"It was in the news this morning."

Stallings allowed that he'd missed the news that morning. He noted too that he saw no obvious connection between some building in Iowa and Adam Smith's book *Wealth of Nations*. Probably, there wasn't any. Nevertheless, acting on the unproven theory that any kind of class participation was better than none, he invited Danny, who, like the others, seldom said a word, to be a shade more expansive. A building had disappeared? What was he talking about?

"One second it was there," Danny said. "Next second— poof. Nothing."

"Man, that's what I heard," Jamal spoke up. "Bank buildin' or somethin'."

"It blew up?" Stallings asked.

"Insurance buildin' or somethin'."

"No," Danny said. "It's more like, the building was there, OK?... and then it wasn't there. That's what they said on the news."

"Maybe a gas main exploded," Stallings suggested.

Amber shook her head. "No explosion, is what they're saying. The building just ..."

"Disappeared," Danny said.

Hoping to reduce his physical discomfort, Stallings wandered over to his lectern, rested his forearms on it. The tactic didn't work.

"Do they think it might be terrorism?" he asked.

"Man," Jamal said, "what kinda terrorism gonna disappear a buildin'?"

"Touché."

"Huh?"

Stallings, who knew full well that HCC students were quite capable of distorting the facts or even inventing them outright, was beginning to suspect that the story might be just a fairytale. Perhaps one that'd been deliberately concocted to sidetrack, if only for five minutes, his impending lecture on Adam Smith.

"Here's what I think happened," Stallings said. It was to be his first and only attempt at levity for the day. "I think an enormous hand swept down from heaven, took hold of the building and plucked it away. A gigantic Invisible Hand ..."

No one was remotely amused by this comment; in fact several students, brows knit, mouths agape, seemed violated and appalled.

"I'm kidding!" Stallings tried to soothe them, spreading his arms. "It's a concept from your reading. Adam Smith and the Invisible Hand."

A clumsy segue to what would prove a subpar lecture, but it'd served its purpose. For the next half-hour or so, before pleading illness and cutting the session short, Stallings held forth in a tired raspy voice concerning Smith's seminal vision of how a society functions. There *is* a God, the great economist maintained, and that God is benevolent; He wants us all to be happy. But, as lowly human beings, we're interested mainly in ourselves. That is, we're not out to enhance the common good so much as our own individual good. Yet our self-interest, according to Smith, works out for the best. Because in pursuing our personal goals, we're led, through the division of labor and the workings of a free market, to behave in a way that inadvertently benefits society as a whole. And we're guided in this mysterious process by an agency that Smith pictured as an Invisible Hand, subtle, crafty, ineffably powerful—maybe the hand of God Himself....

To be sure, some critics took issue with Smith's simplistic vision. Even with government intervention, society didn't run faultlessly, and no sane person was always happy. Could it be that God wasn't benevolent after all? What if the atheists were right, and there was no God? Perhaps the Invisible Hand was invisible because it didn't exist!...

\* \* \*

Class finished, Stallings went to the nearest men's room where he stooped over the sink and splashed some cold water on his wan face. He hoped the sting of the cold water would make him feel more alive, or less dead anyhow. It didn't.

While the pressure on his skull was holding firm at about 100 psi, the pressure inside his roiling stomach definitely seemed to be mounting. Uh-oh. It occurred to him that he ought to relocate to a stall in case he had to vomit—which might not be a terrible outcome; it would likely bring him some relief. But no sooner had he stepped inside the ill-lit cubicle, one hand fumbling for his spiffy Donald Trump silk tie, ready to yank it out of the way if need be, than his fluttering nausea pulled back a notch.

It was still there, however.

What to do? Stick a finger down his throat and hope to get it over with? Wait, and see what happens? The rancid yellow bowl beneath him, unflushed in ages, was disgusting but not quite sickening. He hadn't the strength to flush it. Lifting his eyes, he spotted a graffito on the wall next to the toilet:

Here I sit, wise and prudent.
I just made a Harris student.

He exhaled. Exhaled again. The minutes crawled by as if wounded. His face and hands were moist, clammy. More than once as he stood there fidgeting, dithering, suffering, he thought *This is no goddam way to live*, and honestly meant it.

*This is no goddam ...*

*This is no ...*

Slowly he raised his hand to his mouth, thrust his index finger to the very back of his throat and began to retch.

5

IT WAS EARLY EVENING when a small birdlike man named Dunkin Helbig parked his bicycle outside the Your Town Theatre, a neighborhood playhouse. The sun's orange face hung low and warm in the sky. Traffic had been light, and, earlier, his day's work (he was a trainer at Johnny's gym, Perfection Fitness) had been only a hair worse than usual. By rights, he could've and should've been in a decent mood.

But he wasn't. Decent moods were for other people, not for Dunkin Helbig. Others—women especially—would've killed for the access Helbig had to the renowned Johnny Black. He and Johnny sometimes hung out together, went places together, had long and frank conversations with each other. But young Helbig, a malcontent for the ages, took no delight in these experiences, and in fact he labored to tolerate them.

Today Johnny had called on Helbig to guide him through a workout. Johnny 'Jet' Black, aka 'Perfection' ... If you didn't know he was a celebrity, Helbig thought, all you had to do was check out the framed blown-up photos of him that hung all over the gym's walls. One shot caught the former pitcher at the peak of his windup, the high leg kick, all that coiled energy; another showed him in street clothes posing, big smile, with his Cy Young trophy. Inescapably, there was a photo of him being mobbed by delirious teammates at the conclusion of that one lightning-in-a-bottle game he'd pitched at Yankee Stadium.

Other gyms displayed pictures of famous bodybuilders, Helbig sighed. Arnold Schwarzenegger, Dorian Yates, Ronnie Coleman. This gym had pictures of a baseball player.

Helbig had worked with Johnny before, so it wasn't a first-time event. And he despised Johnny less than he despised most people. But today the ex-ballplayer had, in Helbig's view, made a mockery of the training session and, by extension, of the trainer. To begin with, Johnny drank not one but *two* beers while working out. Outrageous. Then he either made or accepted six—Helbig counted them—*six* cell phone calls while he should've been exercising. No priorities. He topped everything off by signing a baseball for some teenage hottie who'd approached Johnny as he was grinding out a set of leg presses. While Helbig stood by stewing, Johnny interrupted the set, yukked it up with the girl for a while and signed the ball with his typical brassiness and panache. 'Perfection,' he wrote.

Annoyed by Johnny's cavalier attitude, Helbig worked him as hard as he could. Which, the way Johnny dawdled, wasn't all that hard. "C'mon," Helbig barked at him, clapping his hands briskly. "Pick it up! Pick it up!" It annoyed Helbig further that Johnny, who wasn't exactly in supreme condition these days, was obviously capable of outperforming Helbig, who, though undersized, was in tiptop condition. The unfairness of it! The inequity!

When they finished, Johnny dropped off a good-natured joshing remark about the T-shirt Helbig was wearing and took him aside. (The shirt was adorned with a cartoon rendering of an aged and fantastically woolly George Bernard Shaw. "That's you in ten years," Johnny said.)

"What's up?" Helbig asked.

Johnny had a last swallow from his second can of beer. "Listen," he said. "I don't mind when you ride herd on me. Hell, I probably need it. But the way you treat some of the others ... Dunk, you gotta use some ..."

"Some what?"

"Some restraint, some judgment."

"Whadaya mean? Somebody say something? Somebody complain?"

"Well ..."

"Who was it?" Helbig asked. "Schnitzer? He say something? Bubba Schnitzer?"

"Him, for one." Shielding his mouth with the back of his hand, Johnny belched. "Said you called him a 'huge hill of flesh.' "

"So? You seen him lately?" Helbig was indignant; the epithet was from Shakespeare's *Henry IV*, and it fit.

"I've seen him."

"The man is beastly big. He looks like something Ahab would go after with a spear."

Johnny crushed his beer can, searched for a place to throw it. He resisted the temptation to throw it at Helbig. "There you go again," he said.

"Whadaya mean?"

"I mean I expect you to use a little diplomacy with the paying customers, OK? 'The gentleman has a weight issue'—all right? Choose your words."

Helbig stood up straight, cocked his head. He resembled a bantam rooster. "What I'm doing," he said, "is called 'tough love.' "

"What you're doing," Johnny came back, "is called chasing away my business, and it's gonna be 'tough shit' if you don't cut it out. You hear me?" For emphasis, he chucked his mangled beer can—with some force—into a trash receptacle.

Well, Johnny and his fat customers, Helbig groused to himself. He guessed they were fat, or had 'weight issues,' down at Johnny's bar too; he'd never been there. But one of these days he'd show them all—Johnny Black, the beefballs and everyone else. He'd make his mark in this world, by damn....

Outside the theatre, Helbig secured his bike and glanced around. No sign of Ben Temple's 'Your Town'–decorated van. Would the contemptible old son of a bitch bother to show up at all? Helbig had arranged to meet here with Ben, the theatre's artistic director, this evening. He was hoping— irrationally, he supposed—that Ben might have some good news for him, but the missing van hinted otherwise. He glowered down at his Timex, clamped his bony jaw.

For Helbig, any and all news was routinely and predictably bad. Bad news, of course, was bad in and of itself. But good news was bad as well, once his acid pessimism had gotten done with it; he was certainly no starry-eyed Pollyanna. Indeed, he took pride in being able to pierce through the false veneer of any person, thing or situation that others might deem good news to discover the ugly tangled knot of problems that invariably lay writhing and festering underneath.

As an artist, he was *perceptive*.

Helbig made his way to the front door, his movements quick and erratic. His lean triangular face was highlighted by a pair of gray darting eyes that seemed to notice everything and nothing, and by a taut flat line of a mouth that grimly signaled resistance, resignation or bitterness. Occasionally he sensed that something in his face or manner had the effect of distancing people, of bringing them a weird chill, but he couldn't have stated what it was and wouldn't have changed it even if he had the power.

Let the others change, was his attitude. The hell with them.

Arriving at the door, he fished down into his pants pocket and brought out a key, inserted it into the lock. As always, the door refused to open for him. So he jiggled the key, wrestled the doorknob, rammed his shoulder into the door, kicked it once or twice and muttered imprecations aimed at the door, at life and at God almighty. (Not that Helbig believed in God.) Locked or unlocked, the damned door frequently stuck, and it seemed to stick more often for Helbig than for anyone else, as if it bore him some special grudge.

Finally, miraculously, the lock yielded, the door opened and Helbig, swearing, pushed into the building.

Inside it was dim, but for now he refrained from turning on any lights. He didn't mind dimness, or even darkness; a lack of light suited his nature. Sometimes he would tell people that, like Poe's character C. Auguste Dupin, he was "enamored of the Night for her own sake," after which he would take rich satisfaction in the looks of puzzlement the comment reliably drew. Ordinary people, Helbig knew, slopped around in a mucky pool of ignorance miles below his own supernal level of cultured learning.

Silently he drifted through the lobby, past the box office

and the little canteen that sold M&M's, Almond Joys, Reese's peanut butter cups, red shoe string licorice, popcorn and soft drinks. The theatre was a timber-frame structure that featured a lot of wood both outside and in. While this setup did have a strong aesthetic appeal, as even Helbig would've admitted, it had also resulted in several instances of dry rot, black mold, termites and powderpost beetles, as he also admitted, and loudly. Wafting along, eyes darting, he wondered what new problems might be launching themselves all around him at this very moment.

When he entered the theatre proper, with its tiny stage and the cramped area where the patrons sat when any attended, Helbig was obligated at last to turn on a light. The light he chose was a weak one, and did little more than fill the space with black eerie shadows. But that was fine. He could see well enough, he could move about readily, and as he did so, he could feel himself relax. Somewhat. (He never relaxed more than partway.) He always felt better here—enfolded, as he was, in the intense intimate embrace of theatre—than anyplace else in the world.

He'd been associated with Your Town for three years now, almost four. During that span, he'd helped with publicity, stagecraft and general upkeep. Now and then, he'd directed. He'd also done some acting, and not just minor roles, either. He'd played Willy Loman in *Death of a Salesman*, confronting at painful length the mystery of success. In *Picnic* he'd played Hal Carter, a young man who agonizes, fists clenched, over his lack of *patience*. And he'd played the slobbish but loveable Oscar in Neil Simon's *The Odd Couple*. Curiously, it was in this last role that he'd achieved his highest acclaim, such as it was, with two or three playgoers noting how he'd enlivened Oscar with a strange and compelling fieriness: "If you want to live through this night," he'd roared at Felix, "you better tie me up and lock your doors and windows!" Being recognized for his portrayal of Oscar pleased Helbig, sort of, but it also disturbed him. Though popular, *The Odd Couple* was a mere comedy; it wanted substance. Helbig's talents, he felt, should be savored in a grander context.

Perhaps that day was coming.

He flopped down in one of the stone-hard chairs meant for the audience, stared up at the darkened stage.

Helbig had written what was, in his own estimate, a world-class playscript that he'd respectfully submitted to Ben Temple for consideration. Why not get it produced here first, at his home theatre, before letting it storm triumphantly across the globe? In his turn, the pokerfaced Temple had respectfully submitted the script to the theatre's governing board for their reaction. Quite some time had elapsed with no verdict from anyone, and Helbig didn't know how to read the silence. On the one hand, if they liked the play, it shouldn't be taking them this long to green-light it. On the other hand, if they didn't like it, it shouldn't be taking them this long to shoot it down. What the hell was going on?

There was an excellent chance he'd find out soon, if Ben Temple ever showed his kindly albeit contemptible old face. He was fifteen minutes late already! If Helbig had to guess, he would've calculated that the answer was no—what else could it be? the philistines!—and that Temple, the old son of a bitch, was off somewhere rehearsing how he'd break the news to the temperamental Helbig. Or, short on guts, he'd decided to stay away altogether—to avoid the young playwright for as long as possible.

"Goddammit," Helbig said out loud to the assembled shadows.

Life was always so *frustrating!*

Sitting there seething, he reached down into his pocket and pulled out a plastic cigarette lighter. A Bic. He didn't smoke—never had—but he always carried a lighter. For while he liked darkness, he absolutely loved fire, and he loved it most of all when he was tense. Like now. Like usual.

With a flick of his thumb, he lit the flame, watched it dance before him. It was orange and yellow and beautifully pure. He could sense its heat. By breathing on the flame, he could make it dance more.

Fire gave him a thrill. Once, at a rock concert, the band began to play a power ballad—was it "Fly to the Angels"? "House of Pain"?—and everyone held up lighters, flames atremble, thousands of hot little flames dancing brightly in the cool darkness of the evening, and Helbig could feel himself becoming sexually aroused. As he could now. The sheer beauty and potency of a small controlled flame like this one were enthralling, and when you multiplied it by thousands, or ... or when you considered something like a full-scale conflagration, oh God, the involuntary wood and metal groans rising from a fire-struck building, the wild play of searing heat and blazing light, tongues of flame licking feverishly, hungrily, at the black heavens above—

"*Fiat lux!*" came a familiar crackly voice from behind him. "Let's shed some light on the subject, shall we?"

Igniting a whole bank of overhead lights, Ben Temple, his white hair a bramblelike mess, blue eyes crinkled at the outside corners, strolled toward Helbig carrying a meerschaum pipe in one gnarled hand and a sheaf of papers—the script—in the other. He moved with some spryness, as did Helbig, who snapped shut his Bic, jumped to his feet and dropped the lighter in his pocket.

"So what's the verdict?" Helbig demanded.

"And a very pleasant good evening to you, Dunk," Ben said mildly. "I'm just fine, thank you. And you? I trust you're in the pink of health."

"C'mon, Ben, you know how long—"

"And my family?"

"—how long I've been —"

"They're all fine too. My wife, my kids, my—"

"Dammit, Ben, what the hell did they say?"

Ben, who stood calmly and benignly within spitting distance of the hyper Helbig, put his unlit pipe in his mouth and chewed on it. He regarded Helbig with a mixture of curiosity, distaste and grandfatherly indulgence. Then he took the pipe out, smiled and said: "Dunk, we're gonna produce your play."

For one shivery instant, Helbig felt ecstatic—and terrified too; never having experienced ecstasy before, he thought he might be suffering a heart attack. But the sensation passed swiftly as he picked up on something, some thorny clue, some discordant message in Ben's crinkly face or maybe in the tone of his words that seemed to echo still in Helbig's ears.

What was it?

"What?" Helbig said, his normally aggressive voice reduced to a harsh whisper. "What is it?"

"What's what?"

"There's something you're not telling me."

"Not a thing," Ben said. "We're gonna do your play." He put his pipe back in his mouth, held it tightly with his bridgework. He leafed thoughtfully through the unbound stack of papers. "Just as soon as we get 'er in shape."

"Get 'er in shape?"

"Sure. A script is always subject to editing and polishing, you know? Everybody's."

"Editing?" Helbig said. He was rather pleased with his script the way it was. "Polishing?"

Ben nodded. "We'll get 'er in shape."

"What sort of changes we talking about?" Helbig felt as if a hand made of living ice was about to grip his bare genitals.

Ben cleared his throat, shrugged, waved his pipe. "We'll have plenty of time to talk about it."

Then he seemed to remember something, and he assumed the look of a man spellbound with wonder.

"Say," he said. "Did you hear about that building in Iowa? The one that just disappeared? Isn't that the damnedest thing?"

"Building," said Helbig. "No, I—"

"Just totally disappeared! It's all over the news." Ben's eyebrows were cruising at maximum altitude. "Like, abracadabra! Gone! Isn't that the damnedest thing?"

6

FRIDAY'S SHOOT, which took place in a rented apartment in Van Nuys, went superbly. No shock there, since Sarah—or Zoey Zanders—was not just a sex kitten but a dedicated and disciplined professional. She always arrived on time, knew what she had to do, got along well with her colleagues and put on a spectacular show, one that ran the full spectrum from schoolgirl teasing to gasping shouting quivering orgasms (most of them convincingly faked) in assorted positions. Moreover, she had a gift for bringing out the best in those around her.

That gift came in handy today since she'd had to do two guys, one after the other, and neither had been at the top of his game. The first guy, a veteran known as Tom the Bomb, was too overheated for his own good. He'd craved to work with the sultry Zoey Zanders since she'd first exploded on the porn world like a bomb herself a few years before. The prospect of realizing his satyr's dreams was almost too much for him to contain. The other guy, a rookie whose name not even the director seemed to know, was having the opposite problem. Like Tom the Bomb, he knew Zoey by reputation, but in his case the knowledge proved intimidating. Deflating. Yet somehow the Princess of Porn, who understood male psychology better than most, conjured a powerful performance from each.

Not helpful to the second guy's mental state was a one-sided conversation he'd had just before the shoot. Sculpted delts and pecs flexing visibly beneath his black second-skin T-shirt, Derek walked up to him and said:

"You know who I am, don't you?" Minus his Ray-Bans, Derek looked less villainous but no more amiable.

The guy shook his head.

"I'm Zoey's fiancé. And I know how this stuff goes. So I

want you to do your job, OK? But don't let me see you enjoying yourself. Not for one fraction of a second. You just do what you gotta do and be done with it. Dig?"

The guy bobbed his head.

"I'll be watching, motherfucker."

What most of them didn't know, and what made her own performance all the more extraordinary, was that Sarah, too, was feeling a surplus of stress. They didn't know it because she didn't advertise it. But the pressures on her had been mounting for some time, and yesterday they'd soared to a new level of discomfort.

Late that morning, following a call from her lawyer, she'd shaken free of Derek—a feat in itself—and driven straight to her lawyer's office. She could've continued the discussion by phone, but for matters like this she wanted to see him, study his body language; as a porn star, she believed in body language.

Her lawyer, a swarthy middle-aged man named Ernesto Cruz, was a freethinker who made a lucrative living in and around the porn industry. He held the odd distinction of being the only man ever, soaking wet and stark naked, to accept a runaway volleyball from journalist Laura Kennedy. This he'd been happy to do at the pool party just two days before. Today, as circumstances had it, he was wearing clothes—white Oxford shirt, gray tie, gray slacks. Even Cruz would've ruefully conceded that he looked better in clothes than he did in the raw.

He liked Sarah—he was both a fan and a friend—and he welcomed her with a gap-toothed grin and a warm hug.

"Coffee?" he suggested.

She nodded.

"I've got Britt," he said, and went to a credenza along the wall where he poured them each a steaming mug. "Direct from Costa Rica."

With a sweep of his hand, he guided her to a cushy chair in front of his broad gleaming desk. He sat on the edge of the desk next to Sarah and blew on his coffee. Then he set the mug down beside him. His face, almost coffee-colored itself, had become abstracted, as if he were measuring how best to resume their dialog.

"Is it bad?" she asked him. She was referring to her latest predicament.

Cruz tilted his head one way and then the other. "It could be better."

Like her father, Sarah had accumulated some unfortunate legal history. Delicately, for he had no wish to offend her, Cruz recounted the highlights of that bumpy history. There'd been a shoplifting incident (inexplicable, since she had scads of money), several incidents involving illicit drugs, and several incidents involving moving vehicles. To Cruz's dismay, the shoplifting fiasco, in which Sarah had raced away from the crime scene, a handbag boutique, in a cherry red ZO6 Corvette whose bucket seats were littered with crystal meth, managed to combine all these issues. A legal trifecta, he mused, but the payoff had been unlucky.

"So those occurrences," he said blandly, without passing judgment, "serve as a kind of backdrop for what happened on Mulholland Drive."

It was on Mulholland Drive, two weeks ago, that Sarah, having been pulled over for speeding, physically assaulted a state trooper. This time, enraged, she bounced out of her 'Vette and struck the trooper in the head with a glass meth pipe containing traces, once again, of crystal meth. The assault was captured on videotape by the victim's partner.

Cruz lifted his coffee mug, had a sip. "Zoey, of all the crazy things you've done in front of a camera ..."

"The guy reached through the window and felt me up!"

"It's not on the video," he said. "I checked. You whacking him in the head is."

She made an impassioned speech about a woman's right to defend herself, but Cruz, who stood up and meandered around his office, hands in pockets, didn't appear to be listening. He could've been a worn-down father whose daughter had found trouble for the umpteenth time in high school.

"Two small pieces of advice," he said when she stopped talking. "First, stay the hell away from cars. Especially fast cars. They get you in trouble. Or get someone to drive you, OK? Hire a chauffeur. Hire me."

"C'mon, Ernie."

Usually he bridled when someone called him "Ernie" rather than "Ernesto," but with Sarah he let it go.

"Second," he said, "stay the hell away from that goddam ice. You addicted or what?"

"No." She gave her lustrous black mane a toss. "I like it, is all. It gives me a lift."

"You want a lift, take an elevator. Drink coffee, for God's sake. That other shit's no good. It's poison! Stay away from it."

"I don't shoot it," she objected. "Or even swallow it. I only smoke it."

"Chasing the white dragon, huh?" He stood in front of her, and for the first time his voice had a sharpness to it. "Zoey," he said, "I don't care if you've been shoving it up your ass." Some users did, in fact, take it in suppository form. "You need to find a new hobby."

"Derek doesn't mind when I smoke just a little every now and then. He says I've got a right—"

"Ahhhhh." Cruz slapped contemptuously at the air, as if he were slapping some delinquent's face, and set himself in motion again.

"—I've got a right to my recreation."

With some animation, Cruz said: "I'll give you a third piece of advice; you can ignore it along with the other two. Get rid of that guy. What's his name? Eric?"

"Derek. We happen to be engaged."

"Yes, you're engaged in a lot of nonsense. He's a loser, Zoey. You know it and I know it."

"Has it occurred to you—"

"He probably knows it himself," Cruz said. "If not, it just

shows what a loser he is."

"Has it occurred to you," she asked, "that we might be in love?"

"No," he said flatly. "It hasn't, and it won't."

If he thought perhaps he'd gone too far with this last volley, that she might fire back in self-righteous anger, he was mistaken.

"Ernie," she said, "you're so cynical."

He circled around behind his desk, sat himself in his swivel chair. "I *am* cynical," he said. "I'm also concerned." He put on a pair of reading glasses in preparation for scanning through some papers he'd arranged neatly on his desktop. Then he rethought himself, removed his glasses and flipped them on top of the papers. "Zoey," he said, "I'm afraid that fairly soon they're gonna want you to do some time."

"Time?"

"In jail."

Now she rose, moved about in a desultory way. She was wearing a pink Piquant Pictures T-shirt and a pair of Armani jeans that might as well have been spray-painted on. She had the ability to look naked even when she was clothed.

"I don't want to go to jail."

"Nothing's for certain yet. I'll do what I can." He stood up. A hint of an impish smile flickered across his dark face, a face that was not yet jowly but headed there. "You whacked that trooper a helluva shot, you know? Roundhouse right. *Boom*." He mimicked the way she'd done it.

"I don't want to go to jail."

Cruz came around to the front of his desk, melancholy and cheerful at the same time. He placed a gentle supportive hand on her shoulder. "Nothing's for certain yet," he repeated.

Sarah raised her large long-lashed eyes as if seeking help from above and locked stares with a portrait of an important-looking man who was unknown to her. He stared down at her, his expression severe and searching, and it seemed for an instant that he was about to speak to her, to tell her something that would startle her. The face was very old and very judgmental; for a moment it caused her to feel lost within herself.

"We'll see what the future holds," Cruz said.

* * *

Next evening, after the shoot, Sarah sat brooding in her kitchen while, nearby, Derek whipped up a protein drink in the blender. The blender screamed at them for what seemed to Sarah like an hour.

Finally Derek shut it off, popped the top and drank straight from the carafe. At this point in the day, he wanted to present himself as content, civil and irenic, but his natural testiness seeped through anyhow.

"That shower scene today?" he said, swallowing.

"Yes?" Some of the sex had been shot in a shower stall.

"That was fantastic. Historic. Made the shower scene in *Psycho* seem tame by comparison."

He laughed. She didn't.

"Whatsa matter?" he said. "You don't think that's funny?"

"It was funny," she said, "the first four times someone else said it."

He had another swallow of protein goop; it was strawberry-colored and had the same texture as quicksand. "I always liked Albert Hitchcock," he said.

Expressionless, she debated whether to correct the misnomer but in the end decided not to. You correct one error, you feel compelled to correct another, and another, and another. Where do you stop?

"You know who I'd like to kill?" she said suddenly.

"Who?"

"My father."

Talk of killing always stimulated Derek. "Why?" he said.

She roused herself from her chair. "Because he made me what I am today."

"Don't forget me. I helped out too."

"You're part of the picture as well," she said, leveling her dusky violet gaze at him. "But my father was the one ... right there in the beginning. He gave me the push."

"So why do you want to kill him?" He held the half-empty carafe out to her. "This ain't bad," he said. "Want some?"

She shook her head.

"If he gave you the push," Derek said, "you should thank him. He put you on your way to being a star."

Standing close to him, she was never more remote. She said nothing.

"I mean look at this place," Derek said. "Look at the kitchen." In his own fashion, he indicated the recessed mahogany dome in the ceiling, the solid mahogany cabinets. There were rose-veined granite countertops, a Thermador wall oven. The stainless steel refrigerator, which Derek visited regularly, cost in excess of $10,000. "This place is so cool," he said.

"If they put me in jail, how cool will that be?"

"You ain't going to jail." He reflected. "If you do, ol' Cruz'll have you outta there in two shakes." Then: "You gotta learn how to drive."

Absently, she walked over to the kitchen's island, laid her hands on its beveled edge, leaned against it. "That reporter the other day ..."

"Yeah?"

"She's about my age. Has a normal job."

"So?"

"Probably has a normal family, normal friends. Probably goes to church on Sunday ..."

"Baby, you wanna go to church, go to church," Derek said. "Sunday or any other day. Hell, I'll even take you."

"I don't want to go to church." She refrained from biting her lip. "But I wish I did."

"How about this then." He slurped down the last of his pink glop and came up behind her, put his bronze arms around her, nuzzled her neck. It was like being nuzzled, she thought, by a horse. "How about we go to bed."

"Not now," she said. "I don't want to."

"C'mon, Zoey."

"Not now, I said." And she pushed away from him.

"You serious?" He looked genuinely incredulous. "You can't be serious." He reached for her again.

"Stop it," she said.

Fists on his narrow hips, he stood eyeing her for a long moment in an attitude of deep bafflement and rising irritation. He was like a man who suspects he's been hoodwinked but can't quite figure out how or even if.

"I'm not in the mood," she said. She raked her hand through her hair, straightening it, and moved farther away from him.

"But ... but you're a fucking *porn* star!"

"I've got things on my mind," she said.

7

FEELING MUCH PERKIER after a few days' sobriety, Bob Stallings strode down the skinny hallway known as Faculty Row. It was the area that housed offices for most of the instructors at Harris Community College, Stallings included. He was headed toward the far end of the passage where a couple of the fluorescent lights overhead had burnt out, rendering the atmospherics there shady and mysterious, and where Professor of English Jeff Jenson had his cubby.

Among the problems Stallings' students were displaying was an inability to write at the college level. Or sometimes at the high school level. They confused 'then' and 'than,' 'their' and 'there,' 'affect' and 'effect.' Punctuation was hit-or-miss, and commas were a particular source of vexation not only to the writers but to the increasingly cranky reader. Often sentences that should've been separate were yoked together improperly, while other sentences, when closely examined, turned out not to be sentences at all. Most gratingly, Stallings commonly read paragraphs—even entire essays—that made no sense; what the hell was the student attempting to say?

Stallings was no elite writer himself, but surely folks should be doing better than this! Maybe Jenson, as an expert in English, could offer some insights, share some techniques that would help these students improve.

On that note, Stallings was determined to make some improvements in himself—in his lifestyle. While nothing catastrophic had come from that last drinking bout, it'd left him feeling ridiculous and ashamed. As had all the others. He guessed that maybe it was time now to set off in a new direction, one that would take him back to being the mature and levelheaded fellow he used to be.

Used to be ... back before his wife died.

Not a day went by that he didn't repeatedly think of Jenny. He visualized her pretty face, recalled the timbre of her voice, remembered all they'd done together, had imaginary conversations with her. Long conversations in which he probed, gossiped, rambled, swore, laughed and wept. He recognized that after a while such obsessive behavior was hurtful to him, self-defeating. It accomplished exactly nothing except to make him feel worse than he already did. (It made him feel like drinking.) But he couldn't help himself. Jenny had been the lambent love of his life, and he couldn't just shunt her aside after a year's worth of grieving. She wasn't an old flannel shirt that'd finally worn out, or a favorite car that he'd sadly traded in on another. No, she was the one person who, more than any other, had blessed his life with meaning, and her ghost would linger with him for the remainder of his own days, however many he'd been granted.

Which was fine, he figured. But he needed to do a better job of managing his emotions; he needed to put himself and keep himself on a more healthful and productive path.

To that end, he'd drawn up a new business plan: starting today, he'd conduct himself in a way that would earn Jenny's approval. What would *she* want him to do? It didn't take him long to realize that basically she'd want him to quit moping, take command of his life and spend more time looking forward, not backward.

Obviously a big key to the plan would be to stop thinking so much about her. About how she'd been perfectly alive and well one second and perfectly dead the next courtesy of a hit-and-run driver who knocked her halfway across a rather large asphalt parking lot. She'd gone to a drugstore to buy her husband some corn cushions for his tender right foot (it hadn't been all that sore; he could've gone himself), and as she was approaching her parked car to come home, some lunatic, some bastard, slammed into her killing her instantly. The guy—it *was* a male—was never apprehended or even described apart from his gender. His vehicle was said only to be a compact blue or black sedan of indeterminate age. The fuzziness of the eyewitness reports, both of them, left Stallings bewildered since anytime he'd done something wrong, the entire world seemed to know about it, and know in microscopic detail.

What he wouldn't give now, imagining that piece of dung behind the wheel—the murderous creep must still be around somewhere!—what he wouldn't give right this very second, right here in Faculty Row—

Ah, but there he went again, dwelling on the whole hideous episode. Dwelling ... obsessing. Come on, he told himself, stick to the plan.

Poking his head in Jenson's doorway, Stallings saw him sitting there at his cluttered desk, pellet eyes fixed on his glowing computer screen. He appeared rapt. Jenson wasn't a bad guy, Stallings judged. Not for a liberal arts type anyhow. Slim and intense-looking, Jenson sported a carefully clipped gray-flecked beard that lent him the exotic sophisticated air of a pen-and-ink sketch artist working the Champs Elysees. As a rule, Stallings took a dim view of beards, even trim ones, all of which tended to strike him as vaguely Marxist or Trotskyite. Like Popeye's girl Olive Oyl, he preferred a man to be freshly shaven, a condition that squared more readily, in his mind, with sound capitalist values.

I want a clean-shaven man!
I want a clean-shaven man!
Oh, how I'd behave
When he takes a shave!
I want a clean-shaven man!

Still Jenson, who'd reputedly published a handful of creative pieces in lit journals, came across as bright, collegial and reasonably mainstream.

Noticing Stallings at last, Jenson waved him to a chair. "Bob," he said, "what's up?"

Hating to plunge right into a substantive discussion,

Stallings gestured at a framed photo resting on top of a filing cabinet. The photo depicted a handsome square-chinned man with dark hair and a dark mustache; he was seated outside on a veranda, grinning wryly and cupping a tumbler of what must've been whiskey.

"Is that your father?" Stallings asked.

Jenson glanced up at the photo and chuckled easily. "In a way," he said. "Metaphorically. That's a shot of Ernest Hemingway."

"Oh."

Having thus established that he was no rival to Harold Bloom or George Steiner in his knowledge of English, Stallings proceeded—sheepishly—to outline his concerns about all the students who knew even less than he did.

"Sometimes I'll be reading an essay," he said, "and it's as if the student were grappling with English as a foreign language. Everything strained and tortured ..."

"You just now noticing this?" The comment was more merry than sarcastic.

"No. But I think it's gotten worse, don't you? I'm seeing a pretty scary decline in skills."

Jenson agreed that writing skills, never first-rate at HCC, were probably tumbling further downhill through the mud.

"I went into my classroom the other day," he said, "and these two guys were having an argument—about a word."

"A word?"

"And they wanted me to settle the dispute, right? So the one guy says: 'How do you spell the word "hisself"? One ess or two?' "

"Hisself! Was he serious?"

"As a stroke. Both of 'em."

"What'd you tell 'em?"

"What *could* I tell 'em?" Jenson said. "I told 'em two esses. I tried to explain that the word was nonstandard, but I don't think they caught my drift."

The two sat silently for a moment, contemplating. During

this time, Jenson's aggie eyes traveled sideways once more to his computer screen where they settled briefly. Then he shifted back to Stallings.

"These are Intro to Lit papers," Jenson said, waving his hand at the sand dune of essays that sloped across his overburdened desk. "*Othello*." They didn't seem to be in any logical order, but with an English professor, Stallings wouldn't have wanted to bet. Jenson grabbed a paper and held it up. "This guy's got the Venetians fighting a flock of turkeys."

"Huh?"

"He meant to say 'Turks.'" Jenson dropped that paper and seized another. "This one's a pretty solid analysis of *Macbeth*, which we haven't covered. Totally different play. Where this essay came from—why it's here—I haven't a clue."

"Huh!"

Warming to his task, Jenson discarded the last paper, found yet another. "Now this one," he said, "is excellent. Everything impeccable. Content, structure, grammar, style. Well researched, well documented."

Stallings, who was beginning to feel sorry for his colleague, said: "Well, that should give your spirits a boost."

"Not really. It's plagiarized. Copied word for word off the Net."

"Oh my."

As before, the two sat there in the same kind of forced heavy silence that fills a dentist's waiting room. As before, Jenson's eyes sneaked over to his computer screen.

"So what do we do?" Stallings asked after a decent interval.

Jenson laced his hands behind his head. "Summer vacation pretty soon," he said. "I'm gonna play some golf."

"No, I mean —"

"You play?"

"I don't. But I mean beyond vacation. What do we ..."

"Beyond vacation we've got retirement. It'll be here before either of us knows it." He linked his hands together down near his belt buckle as if manipulating a putter. "Then I'm *really* gonna play some golf."

Unlike Jenson's students, Stallings *was* able to catch his drift—apparently there wasn't much to be done. He slumped back in his seat, allowed his breath to escape his lungs in a slow mournful sigh.

"Listen Bob," Jenson said, "I like your moxie. But students spend the first eighteen-twenty years of their life learning pidgin English, you're not gonna straighten 'em out in a semester or two."

"Mm."

"The ones that seem marginally capable, send 'em to the Writing Center. Or get 'em a tutor. The rest, the hell with 'em. Fail 'em."

"Been a long time—"

"Sometimes," Jenson broke in with a trace of frustration, "I'd like to fail the whole damn lot of 'em, you know? Exercise godlike power."

Stallings smiled. "Been quite a while," he said, "since I've had a student who could flat out write."

"I hear you."

"Or truly think, for that matter. Think with some real depth and agility. Last one I had—"

"Been years. I know."

"Last one comes to mind, three, four years ago ..."

"Sarah Black," Jenson said.

"That's it. Sarah." Stallings felt a pleasurable tug of nostalgia. "Very capable student. Independent thinker."

"Quick. Strong-willed. Not bad-looking, either."

"Whew!" The exclamation was one of fervent support.

"Whatever happened to her?" Jenson wondered.

"I dunno. Went to California, I think. I sometimes rub elbows with her father—"

"Yeah? Perfection?"

"But he won't talk about her," Stallings said. "Sore spot, I gather. Some sort of falling out they had ..."

"Hmm. Life's never quite what we hope for, is it."

The conversation winding down, Stallings' agenda having gone nowhere, Jenson gave his computer screen a steady uncompromising stare.

Stallings rose to his feet with a grunt and stretched. "What's so fascinating on your computer?" he asked.

"The news. You been following that story about the building that disappeared?"

"In Iowa? Not really." Spend your day following every screwy story in the news, Stallings thought, and that's all you'd get done.

"They've confirmed that some people are missing. Supposedly they were in the building when it just ..."

"Uh huh."

"Now it seems another building has vanished. A restaurant."

"In Iowa?"

"Amarillo, Texas." Jenson clicked his mouse. "Look at this."

Peering over Jenson's shoulder, Stallings saw a still photo of—nothing. A shadowy cavity surrounded by cityscape. Some people huddled there pointing and gawking.

"What is it?" Stallings asked.

"That's where the restaurant used to be. Wild, isn't it?"

Stallings didn't answer, but he observed the scene closely for some time. He could feel himself growing more interested than he wanted to be. "Any explanation?"

"No. None." Jenson also mentioned that reliable witnesses, hundreds of them, had seen an unaccountable play of whirling multicolored lights last evening in the twilit sky over Cincinnati.

"Any connection between the lights and what happened in Texas?"

"I don't know." Jenson turned his chair around and faced up at Stallings. "What do *you* think?"

Stallings had no opinion. "You think all this ... strangeness means something?" he asked.

"Must mean something." Jenson touched his chin lightly. "One of my students claims we're facing the end of the world."

Stallings guffawed. "If a student said it, we're probably safe. Right, Jeff?" He slapped Jenson's shoulder.

Rocking back in his chair, Jenson brought his hard pebblelike eyes to bear on Stallings. He didn't seem too optimistic. "I don't know," he said.

8

MOTORING ALONG FASTER than he should've been in his Ford F-150 pickup (jet black, the custom license plate reading PERFECT), Johnny was having one of the less conventional conversations of his life. He was chatting with Dunkin Helbig, who was riding shotgun and who'd just made a snide comment about the music twanging out of Johnny's radio.

"Dude, that's Garth Brooks," Johnny defended his musical tastes. "One of Nashville's all-time greats."

"Glorified hillbilly," Helbig said.

"And that song is 'Friends in Low Places.' A country classic."

"Dreck." Helbig arched a captious eyebrow at the driver. "I thought you were a rock 'n' roller anyhow."

"Well, I am. But it doesn't—"

"Not that some three-chord mating song from the Dark Ages would prove any more impressive."

"Doesn't hurt to keep an open mind, Dunk."

Feeling guilty about the way he'd come down on Helbig at the gym a few days before, Johnny was trying to make amends now. He reached over and clicked off the radio.

"There," he said. "That better?"

"Infinitely."

"We aim to please. Now—you were saying a moment ago that you don't believe in little green men."

"Certainly not," Helbig said. "By the way, these days extraterrestrials are most often described as little *gray* men."

"So how do you explain all those funky lights over Cincinnati?"

The alleged event, which lasted for about ten minutes, had been videotaped and was being shown on TV everywhere. Most of the experts (military types, ufologists) were saying they hadn't yet had time to study the tape carefully. Air traffic controllers, whose radar had evidently detected nothing, were saying just that: nothing. Yet rumors abounded that air traffic had been prudently routed around some unprecedented disturbance in the sky. Was this the case? Pilots were tight-lipped. Some of the passengers who'd been on aircraft in the vicinity, however, were willing, even eager, to speak out. "It was bee-yooooo-tiful," one blue-haired old lady gushed. "I believe those lights were God's angels shimmering and dancing all around us. The colors were marvelous, purple and green and scarlet.... God's angels." Members of the public who had no direct involvement with the incident seemed either amused by the story or unaware that anything had happened, if indeed anything had.

"I *don't* explain it," Helbig said. "I don't even acknowledge it. Could be a hoax for all we know."

"What about the video?"

"C'mon, man. Video gets faked every day. Ever hear of 'special effects'?"

"What about the eye witnesses?"

"People see things all the time. Meaningless."

Unlike most drivers, Johnny didn't slow down for railroad tracks but instead automatically sped up. He took them as a gut-level challenge to his own constitution and to that of whatever vehicle he happened to be driving. Without warning, he gunned his truck over a vast minefield of raised rails, and it sounded and felt as if the truck were being jolted by explosions. Helbig's head hit the roof twice.

"So you think the only intelligent life in the universe," Johnny said, "is right here on our planet. Is that it?"

"I see no evidence to the contrary." Helbig rubbed the top of his head. "And I'm not positive 'intelligent' is your best word choice."

"But what about the pyramids? The Greeks didn't put them up all by themselves, did they?"

"Egyptians."

"I'm saying—even with help from the Egyptians, there must've been some aliens in there somewhere."

Helbig gazed out at the rapidly passing scenery.

"All those Steven Spielberg movies," Johnny went on. "Dude, you don't make a movie like *E.T.*, unless you're onto the truth."

"The truth comes in many guises," Helbig replied, trying to sound sage. "Where are we going?"

Johnny glanced over at him. "You mean in life? In our conversation?"

"I mean in this truck. What's our destination?"

With a chortle, Johnny took a left-hand turn on two fat tires, hurling Helbig up against his door. "You'll see."

Returning to his theme, Johnny cited the countless people who'd claimed to've been abducted by aliens, taken aboard fantastic spacecraft—sometimes levitated from the security of their own bedrooms!—to be subjected to all manner of bizarre and invasive medical examinations. "One of these days they're gonna get *you*," he said. "Find out what the hell's the matter with you."

"I'd stand a better chance of being struck by lightning. Getting burned to a crisp."

"And then there's the Bible," Johnny said, saving his trump argument for last. "Even the Bible talks about UFO's." Drawing on a PBS special he'd recently watched in his bar and largely committed to memory, he enlightened his passenger about the strange 'clouds' that appear throughout the sacred text, about the flying 'thrones,' about the airborne 'chariots,' about the spinning 'objects' in the heavens, about 'Nahum's Freeway' (on which Johnny seemed to be navigating even now). "All that stuff's in the Bible, Dunk," he said. "You can't argue with the word of God."

"The Bible's a bunch of hooey," Helbig said shortly. "On a par with *Grimm's Fairy Tales*."

"Man, how can you say that?" Johnny's tone was one not of anger or resentment but of sheer astonishment. He could

never tell if Helbig really meant some of the heterodox things
he said or, like a kid copping a pose, was simply trying to shock
his elders.

"I can say that," Helbig answered, "because I'm an
atheist."

"An atheist!"

"Along with many others. Kit Marlowe was an atheist.
Noel Coward, Jean-Paul Sartre ... George Bernard Shaw—the
gentleman who was on my T-shirt the other day ..."

Johnny's lower jaw had swung down like a drawbridge, and
his bugged-out eyes were attached to Helbig, a condition that
didn't favor his driving any.

"Please," Helbig said nervously, flailing his hand at the
twisting lurching road before them. "Please."

"An atheist ... Wow."

At least once a week Johnny asked himself why he
tolerated the likes of Dunkin Helbig. The young trainer-actor-
dramatist was rude, arrogant, argumentative, insecure, self-
centered and nowhere near as clever as he pretended. By his
own admission, he was also an atheist and was probably,
Johnny suspected, gay to boot. Strictly from a business angle,
Helbig surely repelled more customers from the gym than he
brought in. Even the T-shirts he wore, often featuring images
of effete playwrights or obscure theatres, were, from the
standpoint of an ex-jock, peculiar and off-putting.

Well, Johnny tolerated him, he'd decided, as a means of
proving to himself and to the world that Johnny wasn't such a
ne'er-do-well after all. Pretty much the same reason he'd
bought the gym. Some would argue that Perfection was, and
always had been, too much into himself—his own goals,
interests, carnal satisfactions; his ex-girlfriend Wanda and
estranged daughter Sarah would be singing soprano in that off-
key chorus. But acting as an uncle-figure to Helbig would, if
not end their song, maybe lower the decibel count a notch.
Besides, Johnny felt that his easygoing influence could
humanize Helbig slightly, make him more palatable. With all

his gifts and shortcomings, Johnny Black was nothing if not human.

For his part, Helbig was slouched there asking himself why he habitually agreed to go off on these periodic mini-adventures with Johnny. He guessed it was because they gave him something to do, and because no one else ever invited him to go anywhere, except go to hell. (He was convinced he did have his share of personal charm, but it was so subtle and low-key that most people, being knotheads, overlooked it.) Ultimately, he hoped he could persuade Johnny to become a financial backer of the Your Town Theatre.

The last time they ventured off like this, they went to a television studio downtown so Johnny could shoot a commercial. Helbig had been allowed to hang around the set and observe as Johnny, a pitcher of some note, pitched a brand of iced tea, which was ironically one of the few beverages he refused to touch unless he was being paid. The script called for him to pour himself a tall glass of the tea and say: "Hipsley's Iced Tea. On a hot summer's day, it'll shut out your thirst." He would then treat himself to a delicious lip-smacking gulp, wink at the camera and say: "Ahhhhh. Perfection." To everyone's delight except Helbig's, Johnny came through splendidly, nailing his performance on the first take.

A champion of method acting, Helbig immediately charged over to the exultant director and raised a fuss. He slammed what he'd just witnessed as plastic, artificial and inauthentic. "He looked like a guy doing a TV commercial!" Helbig ranted. "Which is precisely what he was!" the director retorted, not too graciously. Helbig questioned whether Johnny had made full and proper use of his 'instrument,' much to everyone's puzzlement, and supposed that Konstantin Stanislavsky and Lee Strasberg were both rolling madly in their graves even as Helbig battled on their behalf. "Who—is—this—person?" the director shouted, and an apologetic Johnny quickly hustled Helbig, without even being asked to do so, away from the set and outside to the waiting truck.

His memory of that woeful day all too clear, Helbig surmised they were highballing now to some different location where Johnny would shoot another commercial; from a safe distance, Helbig would be allowed to watch.

Not for the first time ever, Helbig was wrong.

\* \* \*

Johnny drove them to the Harris Community College baseball field, where they were met by Danny Pepper, a stocky kid with hair so blindingly red it seemed to be delivering a warning. An HCC student, Danny was also catcher for the college baseball team; today he'd be catching Johnny 'Jet' Black.

"I don't understand," Helbig said. "You two are going to play catch? You want me to watch?"

"That's the bare bones of it," Johnny said.

He explained to Helbig what Danny already knew: that Johnny was planning a return to professional baseball, but first he'd have to work himself into condition. Today's workout was to be part of that conditioning program. Like Danny before him, Helbig was sworn to secrecy since Johnny, though brimming with confidence, wanted to be further along in rebuilding his skills before he stirred the world by announcing his comeback.

Without enthusiasm, Helbig stood near the first base coach's box and watched as Johnny, wearing a Chisox cap and street clothes, went to the mound and began to throw, softly at first, then a mite harder. At the receiving end, Danny, all abubble with the excitement of a college jock, seemed well up to his task, bouncing around behind the plate like Carlton Fisk in his heyday.

As a youngster, Helbig had been no athlete. While he'd won a measure of praise in the classroom, especially in subjects such as English, art and music, he always felt lost and confused when it came to sports. Baseball was exceptionally challenging,

mainly because of that hard little fast-moving ball that clearly
had a devious mind of its own. Whether he was trying to hit it,
throw it, catch it or avoid it, the ball had a way of defying him.
It mocked him, stultified him, seemed to hold some personal
bias against him. The other guys, most of whom were more
physical than he was, weren't too kind to him either. He
grasped from an early age that sports, aside from lifting weights
to add a few ounces of meat to his scrawny frame, were to be
shunned and dreaded.

Seeing Johnny atop the mound, then, the tall rangy
southpaw unfurling toward home with a fluid graceful motion
that some said whispered of Spahn and even Koufax, was
intriguing to Helbig. Not awe-inspiring or overwhelming, since
he wasn't given to those feelings, particularly in response to
athletics. But intriguing. For here was a man, Johnny Black,
who'd once risen to a level in baseball that Helbig couldn't
have attained even in his most fervid dreams. No, and with
that one blazing gem of a game Johnny had fired at the New
York Yankees, he'd soared to a celestial height reached by only
a smattering of players in the long and fabled history of the
sport.

Johnny was throwing full-speed now, and to Helbig's
untrained eye, the ball appeared to leap from his fingers in a
ghostly white blur; it plowed into Danny's mitt with an audible
smack. If Helbig was thankful for nothing else in life, he was
thankful at this moment that he was standing far off to the
side, a mere spectator—that he had no duty to participate in
this ... intriguing demonstration of Johnny's pitching prowess.

But suddenly Johnny paused in his workout, walked
toward Danny and signaled that Helbig should join them. This
turn of events didn't sit well with Helbig. Pulse rate climbing,
uncallused palms moistening, he slowly trudged across the flat
dry dirt to home plate.

"Here's what I want you to do," Johnny told him. "Take
this bat"—Danny produced a Louisville Slugger—"and stand
in the batter's box like you're a hitter."

"Why?" Helbig asked.

"You don't have to swing. Just stand there."

"But why?"

"'Cause I wanna get a sense of what it feels like pitching with a guy standing in there holding a bat. Now c'mon."

Helbig tried to weasel out of it, but his arguments were lame, and he soon found himself staring out—and up—at the imposing sight of Johnny Black with a baseball in his hand. Johnny stood almost six and a half feet tall, and on the mound he appeared about ten feet tall. With the bill of his cap pulled down in his eyes casting a shadow across his face, he looked daunting. And never more so than when he launched into his windup—there was the high leg kick, the overhand delivery— and *sssssmack!* the ball colliding with Danny's mitt. Though Helbig never actually saw the ball in flight, he heard it as it buzzed by; it sounded like a crazed hornet, a hornet that'd been dosed up on a mixture of steroids, adrenaline and Jack Daniels, and then deeply offended. He almost dropped the bat.

And it occurred to him that he wasn't wearing a helmet.

He hoped they'd be done soon but knew in his gut they wouldn't be. Johnny intended to throw for a while.

The day was hot, and Helbig, who didn't often sweat, was sweating freely now, partly from anxiety and partly from the oppressive heat. He decided to let his mind drift—it might help him survive if he could exit the scene mentally—and he began to recall another occasion, perhaps a year ago, when he'd been made to feel awkward and uncomfortable.

On the sidewalk outside his bank he'd found a signed personal check made out to 'cash' in the amount of six thousand dollars. Without hesitating, he took the check into the bank and tried to cash it. The teller, after studying the check and studying Helbig, refused him. He went to a different teller, and she refused him as well. No reason was offered, and he didn't press for one. He went to another branch and was turned down again. At this point he went home and cleaned himself up—shaved, put on a laundered shirt—and went to a third branch where the teller, a chopped-haired cold-eyed woman, once again declined to cash the check. Exasperated, Helbig demanded to know why.

"This check is made out to 'cash,' " he said. "You should cash it. There's no reason not to."

"Sir," she came back at him, looking him straight in the face, "I don't want to get you in trouble, but if you persist—"

"Cash the check!" he yelped.

"If you persist," she said with striking firmness, "I'm afraid you *will* wind up in trouble. A great deal of it. Please leave."

Helbig left and came back sometime later with several jugs of gasoline. He drove around to the rear of the bank (this was before he gave up his smart little Kia Spectra for a Schwinn) and parked in the lot, which, in the early evening, was mostly deserted of cars. Deserted of people too. The building was made of brick and cinderblock, and aside from some bushes, he saw nothing there that was likely to burn, but that irksome fact didn't keep him from emptying the jugs, one after the other, along and against the bank's rear wall. He would send a message regardless. He returned the jugs to the trunk of his midnight-blue Spectra and brought out his Bic lighter. It was still light outside, and when he set the fire, it became lighter still.

Pleased, he stood in place and observed his handiwork. As he'd expected, the fire was minimal, but its mere existence brought him an intense almost orgasmic thrill. And the pungent chemical smell of flaming gasoline was intoxicating, empowering.

Gradually, and then abruptly, Helbig realized he'd committed a stupid act. Not immoral, but stupid—he could be caught. He could go to jail. Panic washed over him like an ice-cold ocean wave and propelled him helter-skelter to his car, and even as he grabbed at his door and fumbled with his keys, he understood he was a very poor arsonist. As dopey and inept as they came. But what he lacked in know-how he made up for in ill will, and next time, he vowed, tromping on the accelerator, he'd do a better job of it. Next time, they'd best watch out.

Yeah, they'd best watch out, he thought.

"WATCH OUT!"

The words, screamed by Johnny and Danny at the same time, scalded Helbig's ears just as the baseball whizzed beneath his chin, ever so lightly brushing his throat. A four-seam fastball had gotten away from Johnny, and if it'd sailed up and in just three inches more, the daydreaming Helbig, who hadn't moved even a hair, would've been mangled—possibly killed. As it was, he had a pink spot on his throat.

"What," Helbig said. "Whatsa matter? What happened?"

Rushing in from the mound, Johnny arrived as Danny motioned at Helbig's throat with his mitt.

"Close shave," Danny said.

"Dunk," Johnny said, "my God, you OK?"

"Sure, sure," Helbig said. He had no idea what he'd done, or hadn't done, to cause a ruckus.

"Goddam," Johnny said. Sweating even more than Helbig, he gripped the shorter man by both shoulders, bore down on him. "Wake up," he said. "Get in the game." His stern face was only inches away from Helbig's, and their noses almost whopped together. "When something bad's coming at you, man, you gotta do your damnedest to get the hell outta the way."

"Sure."

But Johnny stayed in his face, kept his hands on him, shook him roughly.

"You hear?" Johnny said.

9

WHEN THE SITUATION CALLED FOR IT, Derek could be conciliatory. It was one of his better qualities. Standing in the kitchen he loved and admired so much, an uncooperative Sarah glaring at him, he tried some conciliation.

"OK, OK," he said, moderating his voice. "I know how it is. We all get heavy stuff on our mind now and then, and it can ... darken our mood."

"Do you get 'heavy stuff' on your mind, Derek?" She said it sarcastically, but her tone eluded him.

"Sure I do." He offered an example. "Sometimes it bothers me that my upper body is slightly better developed than my lower body. My calves could use more shape and size. This is the kinda issue that can turn me into a very sour guy."

"You're a cretin."

"I do believe in creatine," he said, misunderstanding her completely. "But that's not the point I'm trying to make. Lemme say this. One of these days, and it may happen sooner than you think, I'm gonna take you clean outta porn."

"Are you?"

He nodded, pressing his lips together in a semblance of rumination. "I can tell you're getting restless in the biz. And you got talents and abilities that go way beyond ..." He searched for the word.

"Fucking."

"Right."

"May I ask: how are you going to accomplish this?" She was near the refrigerator, which was speckled with yellow sticky reminder notes. None of them helped her now.

"Leaving porn?" He shrugged. "We'll just walk away. From that time on, I'll provide for us."

"How?"

"Whadaya mean, how? I'm gonna be the breadwinner."

"But how? You don't *do* anything, Derek."

He blinked a few times as if she'd just bopped him on the nose with the flat of her hand. "I'm a manager. I manage you."

Yes, you manage to hang all over me, she thought, like a dress that's three sizes too big. "How are you going to manage me," she said, "if I'm out of porn?"

He took his blender to the sink, squirted some blood-red detergent in it and followed that with a blast of hot water. He liked to watch the iridescent bubbles foam to the top.

"You know," he said, "I been hearing some real negativity outta you lately, and I ain't sure why. Let's just say when we're married, I'll take full responsibility for everything."

" 'Fool' responsibility?"

"You heard me."

She began to move randomly around the room; she had an inkling that movement lay in her near future, even as it marked her past.

"Derek," she said, "we're not getting married. And as for leaving porn—"

"Whoa. What the hell's that mean?"

"As for leaving porn, what am I supposed to do with all my 'talents and abilities,' as you put it? Start up a knitting club?"

"What the hell do you mean—"

"Take up golf?" Still moving. "Take up bridge?"

"What the hell do you mean, we ain't getting married? We're engaged." He advanced toward her.

"We are," she admitted, "and we can represent that to the world. But no way are we ever gonna take the ultimate step of matrimony; that can't happen."

For the moment, he stood within arm's length of her. "Why not."

"Oh, Derek." She lifted her hands, then let them flop down to her sides. "Various reasons. Number one, you're a moron. You remind me—"

"You bitch," he said.

"You remind me of the troglodytes I knew back at Harris Community College."

He'd never heard of HCC, or of troglodytes, but he knew he'd been insulted yet again, and he struck her hard across her face with his open hand—a sharp sweeping blow that spun her halfway around and into the wall beneath a softly ticking clock. He always hit her in the same spot, high on her left cheekbone, and it was a marvel he'd never fractured it. The ringing sound of the impact hung in the air for several soft ticks.

"I gotta watch you all day," he said, "with these ... these other guys, and then you got the brass ..." With both hands he jerked her around to face him. Her violet eyes were wide open. "Just what the hell do you take me for?"

"How many times do I need to tell you?" And she rocketed her knee up into his groin. Her aim was off, but she still caught him squarely enough to drop him to all fours, and she sprang away from him, stumbling, scrambling, flinging herself headlong into the next room where she bowled over a tall stand-alone teakwood birdcage containing a parakeet named Beanie. Flapping wildly in the overturned cage, the bird squawked and shrieked.

Derek rose in time to see his fiancée bolt up a flight of stairs toward the bedrooms. Hobbling after her, he judged that this misadventure might yet resolve in his favor.

It was a judgment that appeared doubtful when he located her in the master bedroom, her back to the wall, holding a nine-millimeter Beretta Cheetah at his hardening face. A patient man whose patience had all but drained away, he couldn't help but wonder where was the respect? Where was the love? After all he'd done to make the relationship work, where was ...?

"Stay back," she warned him, "or I'll kill you."

"This is what I've earned?" he said. "After all the sacrifices I've made? After all the horseshit I've had to put up with?"

"I'll kill you." She was gripping the gun with both hands,

thrusting its terrible maw up at his raging eyes.

"You stupid bitch," he said, and moved toward her, clenching his fist. "You stupid fucking idiot bitch. You think I'm so dumb, but lemme tell you something, bitch. Are you listening?"

"I'll kill you," she said.

"You got no bullets." He shook his fist at her, came closer. "I TOOK THE MAGAZINE OUTTA THE GUN, BITCH." He came toward her slowly and confidently; she had no escape route. "You think you're so smart." He planted himself six inches in front of the gun, fist raised, arm quivering. "I TOOK THE FUCKING MAGAZINE—"

The shot hit him precisely between the eyes, driving him backward with such a violent hammer-blow that he looked like a man attempting to do a backflip and failing spectacularly. He crash-landed ten feet from where he'd stood, face-up, arms and legs splayed crookedly, his shattered head leaking blood. He didn't move even to twitch.

Eventually Sarah lowered the gun. "I put it back in," she said.

\* \* \*

Sitting on the edge of the bed, she fingered the gun as if it were a set of prayer beads. She felt neither good nor bad, but rather numb and hollow. Apart from her hands and fingers, she was nearly as motionless as Derek.

All her life she'd been in trouble; was this so different? She'd been born to Wanda Sue Lease prematurely, a three-pounder, and for months no one, certainly not the doctors, would've bet on her survival. But survive she did. In grade school, she got sent to the principal's office on a weekly basis for fighting, usually with boys. Then, in junior high, her outlook on boys did a one-eighty, and now she got into trouble for being too nice to them. Twice she was busted for possession of illicit drugs (marijuana and Ecstasy back then), and the count would've been higher had people been paying closer attention. She drank, but so did everyone else, her parents included, and little concern was voiced about the alcohol. Concern *was* voiced when she became pregnant at fifteen—the culprit was the school's guidance counselor, a married man in his grizzled fifties—but fortunately a miscarriage solved that problem.

From a distance, her parents took note of her difficulties. But Wanda couldn't help, and Johnny (in Sarah's view) chose not to. Wanda had problems of her own, depression and diabetes chief among them, and her most consistent reaction to any of Sarah's escapades was to break down and cry. And not just cry for an hour or two, but for upwards of a week, depending on the offense. Great sobbing mindless jags that filled her days and nights, overruling any need to eat or sleep. It was a tendency that, at a minimum, hindered communication, hampered progress. What scant strength Wanda had was often spent relocating from town to town, dragging Sarah with her; Wanda and Johnny never did live together for an extended period. Why she moved so much, no one knew, maybe not even Wanda. Later on, Sarah would theorize that the movement was a way of attracting Johnny's attention—a sort of blinking light—though it seldom worked.

Typically, Johnny was somewhere else. Even when he was physically present, his attention was somewhere else. For most of Sarah's life, baseball meant he was away for long stretches. A mildly intoxicated voice on the phone. After he retired, he was apt to be off chasing business deals or chasing women. It didn't much matter since by that time Sarah and her mother were bouncing around haphazardly themselves, like a pair of silver balls in a pinball machine. Johnny often referred to Sarah as a 'spirited girl' who would 'do all right for herself' once she decided what she wanted to do. "She reminds me of myself at the same age," he'd say. "Except I had baseball." Almost always, he was pleasant and cheerful when he saw her, but he rarely saw her, and after she dropped out of HCC and went off on her own, he didn't see her at all. She'd had enough of his laissez-faire approach to parenting.

But she hardly left her troubles behind. In recent years, Sarah had made her presence felt in the California judicial system with a knotted string of brazen boneheaded violations. (Interestingly enough, her work in porn was absolutely within the scope of the law; she was OK there.)

So—was her current mess all that different from what she'd experienced before? Well, maybe it was, actually. Because now she had a dead man on her floor, and she'd put him there. Anxiously she stood up and peeked at the body, sat back down again. Around his head was a widening pool of blood that looked, perversely, like a large crimson halo.

What to do. She knew she should call her lawyer, Ernesto Cruz, but she also knew he wouldn't take this latest piece of news with bubbly good cheer. Though he'd urged her to 'get rid' of Derek, she guessed he'd disapprove of her method. Ernie could wait.

A dozen other names and phone numbers flashed through her churning mind, all of them linked to porn. She even thought of contacting Peter LeMan, the enigmatic actor who'd co-starred with her in *A Boff in the Woods* and who'd never spoken to her. Could he have been saving all his wise words for this very crisis?

She doubted it.

Now she stood up again, found a suitcase, opened it on the bed and threw some things in it. Maneuvering around the room was somewhat awkward with the body sprawled there and all the blood. When she finished packing, she carried the suitcase downstairs and set it by the door.

Behind her, her pet parakeet Beanie was still squawking in his overturned cage. So she righted the cage and cooed to him till he settled down. What must Beanie have thought to see her face, so immense and overpowering to a trapped bird, hovering over him? The face of an alpha creature whose intentions not even the smartest bird could begin to decipher?... Then Sarah took the cage to the door, whispered "Bye bye, birdie" and set him free. Though he hadn't flown in a while, he still remembered how; he flapped away in a feathered frenzy. She didn't know if a parakeet could survive in the outdoors, but for some reason she wanted him free and not caged.

In the doorway she paused, thinking. She was forgetting something; what was it? Recalling, she hurried up the steps, circled around the body and went to the bed.

Charcoal gray—such a sullen brooding color—the gun was lying on the white chenille bedspread where she'd left it. Derek had told her it was a reliable weapon, and for once he'd been right. She picked it up and flipped the thumb safety on. Then she grabbed a blue Louis Vuitton purse and slid the gun down inside it.

Back down the steps she went, out the door with the purse and the suitcase and into the warm evening air.

10

IT WAS THE WEEKEND, and, in his home office, Bob Stallings stood frowning down at the neat rows of facts and numbers glowing silently at him from his computer screen. Stood, not sat, because he was fidgety. Reading glasses at half-mast on his blob of a nose, he was clad in a loose linen shirt, shirttail out, and baggy cargo shorts. He was studying his stock portfolio and mulling the possibility of doing something with it. Maybe something radical.

He'd been in the market for many years and, as a business professor, felt confident that he knew more about investing than most people. He was a 'value' investor. That is, he liked to pursue stocks that he believed had been wrongly underpriced and were therefore due for an upturn in fortunes. To this end, he operated by a strict set of rules, showing interest only in companies he felt he understood in depth, that looked sound for the long haul, that had stellar management, and that had the all-important cheap price tag. In this regard, he'd been influenced by some of the shrewdest thinkers in the history of Wall Street. Men like Ben Graham and David Dodd, who co-wrote *Security Analysis*; men like Warren Buffett and Charlie Munger of Berkshire Hathaway fame.

Trouble was, Stallings hadn't enjoyed the kind of dazzling success that would allow his name, Robert Earl Stallings, to be added to the gold-lettered list of all-time investment greats. In fact, he hadn't made much money at all. Hadn't lost much, but dammit, despite all his theory and discipline, he simply hadn't made much. This fact was another keen source of frustration to him (of which he had a few).

He reached down and had a sip from the glass of Hipsley's Iced Tea he'd placed on a coaster next to the computer. Setting the glass down again, he tugged pensively at his lower lip. His expression was exceptionally focused, his mental machinery humming along at top speed and efficiency.

Something was wrong with the economy, Stallings had noticed. Indeed, any number of things were wrong. Unemployment and inflation had crept up; consumer confidence had fallen off. Housing and energy prices had escalated, while the dollar had dwindled. A metastasizing credit crisis had thrown the banking community and everyone who dealt with it into confusion. Hedge funds had gotten out of hand, and international reserve positions had ballooned. The Beige Book had lost what faint color it had. More to the point, stocks were clearly overbought, selling at multiples that were historically scary. To Stallings' mind, all those angry growling noises he heard in the distance were the sounds of an approaching bear market.

But he also saw and felt warning signs out there that went well beyond mere indications of economic turmoil. His wife's death, for example. (Here he stole a glance at a photo of him and her laughing and holding hands at the beach, the framed five-by-seven image not far from his glass of tea.) It wasn't just the fact that she'd died; it was the manner in which she'd died—struck by a craven hit-and-run driver and left to breathe her last in an empty parking lot. What did it say about society? Then there was the decline of literacy, a disease he saw every day at school. No one read anymore; TV, the Internet, music and electronic games reigned supreme. People were turning into dopes, and what did this portend for the future? For that matter, what about the ascent of porn in our culture? Time was, Stallings guessed, when women especially had to be tricked or coerced into the business. Now they lined up for blocks—young beauties!—begging to have sex with strangers on camera. What could it mean?

Nothing good, he'd concluded.

Yet there was more. On a tiny round table next to him lay today's newspaper. The front page was packed with stories about the remarkable phenomena that had allegedly been occurring around the country and around the world during the last week. People had supposedly disappeared. *Buildings* had supposedly disappeared. Lights that no one could explain had been seen in the sky, and not just above Cincinnati; apparently they were being witnessed all over. And videotaped. And here was a garish new twist: now a scattered handful of people had come forward to claim they'd seen a face in the sky, an enormous human face, and that this face had spoken to them! What it had supposedly said they would not disclose. While the stories were all just a crock in Stallings' opinion, they still played into his thesis.

He paced around his office, picking up small objects— pens, paper clips—handling them, putting them back down. Pondering.

As he was aware, a sophisticated investor could benefit handsomely in a market sell-off, like the rout he sensed was coming, by using the right strategy. That strategy was known as 'short selling.' With this technique, the investor would borrow shares from a brokerage firm and then sell them in the overextended market. Later, after their value had shrunk, he would repurchase them at the reduced price and return them to the lender's account. Obviously the profit, which could be hefty, consisted of the difference between the proceeds from the initial sale and the subsequent cost of buying back the shares. The more stocks fell, the bigger the profit. Though sometimes criticized as unseemly or un-American by the touchy-feely crowd, short selling was perfectly legal and aboveboard.

It was also risky as hell. Because what if stocks didn't go down after all but unexpectedly went up? Nothing was ever certain. When going 'long,' the investor risked a worst-case scenario of having the price of a stock shrivel to zero, and the loss incurred would be equal to the cost of the investment. But when going 'short' as Stallings was now contemplating, the investor faced the alarming possibility that the stock price might not only rise, but keep on rising and rising. And rising some more. In that case, the loss sustained could be greater than just heavy or even total; it could be stupendous. Unimaginable. Potentially, it could be infinite!

Jaw set, he placed his hands on the back of his leather-and-oak captain's chair and stared down intently at the computer screen. It was as if he were hoping the data there might actually speak to him—do this or do that.

But he knew full well already what he should do; he should go short with a vengeance.

Was he psychologically ready, though, to take the plunge? It would require a boldness of the type he'd never displayed in the past. Did he have the courage of his convictions? Did he even have real convictions, or were they just notions or velleities?

In a soft murmurous voice he said out loud to himself: "Are you ready?..."

The question recalled a discussion he'd had only a couple of days before with the Associate Dean of Academic Affairs, a man named Bill Yommer. Stallings was just finishing his chat with English Professor Jeff Jenson when Yommer stuck his balding pate through the dim doorway and said:

"Bob, I thought I saw you headed down this way a while ago. Do you have a minute?"

Unable to come up with a valid-sounding excuse that quickly, Stallings accepted a look of sympathy from Jenson and followed Yommer up the hall, into the light. As an administrator, Yommer had his office in the next hall over, and they moved automatically in that direction without speaking.

Walking a pace or so behind the tall lanky Associate Dean, Stallings couldn't help but wonder what he wanted. It was bound to be something problematic—it always was—and it was also bound to be something minor and technical and yet disproportionately irritating to Stallings. It always was. Maybe Yommer had a question about some quirk he'd discovered in one of Stallings' syllabi; Yommer was probably the only person at the school, faculty and students included, who spent more than thirty minutes a semester thinking about syllabi. Or maybe

Yommer wanted him to attend some pointless meeting out-of-town that would accomplish nothing other than to waste Stallings' time and energy. Or maybe he meant to quiz Stallings on why he'd failed to attend the last such meeting. (Yommer was madly in love with meetings. He'd meet anytime, anywhere, for any purpose. One time he held a meeting to argue that they should hold more meetings.) Or maybe he wanted Stallings to serve on yet another committee, bringing the total to a hundred and fourteen, which of course would result in still more yakety-yak meetings.

In his early seventies, Yommer was the oldest employee at Harris Community College. To his credit, however, he had the springy energy of a much younger man. Whether his energy level was a desirable thing was much debated behind his back; a good percentage of the faculty wished he'd wear out some so he'd stop bothering them as much as he did. Yommer also dressed like a much younger man, though his sartorial style was difficult to classify. Even in winter weather, he favored these silky short-sleeve fashion T-shirts, which he usually wore with jeans. Oddly, he wore not one but three or four thin gold necklaces and, on his right wrist, a similar number of thin gold bracelets. To Stallings, who rarely went to work without a tie, Yommer looked like a Columbian drug kingpin who'd fallen on hard times.

They sat down at a conference table in Yommer's office, and Yommer, resting his forearms on the table, tilted forward and fixed his twinkling brown eyes on Stallings. As was often the case, Yommer's mouth was open in a half-smile that was partly indulgent, partly accusatory; partly supportive, partly skeptical. With no preliminaries whatever, he increased his tilt toward Stallings and said:

"Amber Glotfelty."

It dawned on Stallings that he'd just been asked a question, though the thrust of the question was unclear to him.

"Amber Glotfelty ..." Stallings repeated stupidly.

"Do you know her?"

Ah: a crisp lucid question that Stallings could address.

"Yes, she's a student in my Intro to Business class."

Yommer nodded as if this information squared with information he'd already collected.

"Bob," he said, "she's filed a complaint against you."

Stallings, sitting straight up to begin with, sat up even straighter. "A complaint!"

"That's right." Calm but alert, fatherly, methodical, Yommer kept his eyes on Stallings as if he were examining some new species of life in a test tube. "And at this stage I'm just trying to find out what actually occurred."

"OK."

"Complaint has two parts. First, she's alleging that you made a speech in class the other day arguing against the existence of God. Is that true?"

Flustered, Stallings scanned his memory furiously for whatever may've given the girl this false impression. "No," he said, "I don't think it is."

"You sure?"

"Well ..." There *was* that Invisible Hand lecture; could that be what she was referring to? "I did give a lecture on Adam Smith," he admitted, "that made some allusions to God."

"Did you deny God's existence?"

"No. Most of the lecture was pro-God. Adam Smith was a believer. Now, toward the end of the lecture I may've ..."

"Yes?"

"Raised some ..."

"Doubts? About God's existence?" The energetic Yommer, who'd begun the discussion tilting toward Stallings, was now tilting in a variety of directions, one after the other. He resembled a weather vane in a swirling squall. Despite his movement, he still seemed more relaxed than Stallings, who continued to sit bolt upright.

"I suppose so. Bill, is that wrong?"

Yommer probed his right ear with his index finger. He was either scratching his ear or adjusting his hearing aid. His bracelets jangled softly. "Amber seems to think so."

"But does that make it wrong?"

"Well," Yommer said, his voice restrained and professional, "we're talking about a business class. Reasonable people might wonder why you're commenting on God at all in a business class."

Stallings knew that, given the context, he could justify what he'd stated and how he'd stated it. But feeling he didn't have to now, he didn't. "There's a second part to this complaint?" he said.

"People can be pretty damn sensitive, Bob, when it comes to God."

"I'm sure. What else did Amber say?"

Yommer crossed his long right leg over his long left one and tilted straight back. "That most recent test you gave the class—I'm told it was about two weeks ago?"

"Yes."

"Amber informs me she received an F on it."

"She got an F on it, all right," Stallings said. "She didn't take it."

"Why not."

"She refused to. Said she hadn't had time to study for it, so she wasn't going to take it. Said I should allow her to take it at a later date when she'd be better prepared."

Stallings rolled his eyes and chuckled at the girl's audacity, but Yommer seemed more curious than amused.

"Did you consider granting her request?" he asked.

"Hell, no!" Stallings fairly shouted. Though not angry, he felt as if his sense of outrage, locked in a steel cage, were being poked at with a stick. "I can't give tests to students on their individual schedule, at their convenience."

"No one's asking you to." His voice calm, the infuriating half-smile still warping his mouth, Yommer was apparently relishing the exchange. "But in this instance, why not make an exception?"

"Why should I?"

"The student said she wasn't ready."

"But it was her job to *be* ready," Stallings said with some emphasis.

"But she wasn't. And who knows? Maybe something in her personal life had come along and distracted her."

"Who knows, is right."

"Did you ask her?"

Doing his best to ignore the caged prowling beast inside him that was roaring to be turned loose, Stallings gritted his teeth. He ungritted them long enough to say: "No."

"I didn't think you had," Yommer said. "Bob, sometimes life throws things at us, and we're not ready. Happens to students, happens to all of us." He stretched and stood up, signaling that their talk, at least for now, was nearing an end. Thank God, Stallings thought. "For example," Yommer added, "were you ready for this?"

"Ready for ..."

"This. Our little tête-à-tête. Did you see it coming? Were you ready for it?"

Stallings slid back his chair, stood up. "No."

"I rest my case," Yommer said, not unkindly.

Two days later. Same theme, different setting.

Eyeing his computer screen, sipping his tea, Stallings had finally decided he *was* ready. He was ready to reconfigure his stock portfolio utterly, going short on everything. And not in a timid way, either; he'd put as much cash to work as he could. When the market tanked, as he was convinced it had to, he'd make himself a pile of money. No half-measures this time, he thought. Let's go for broke.

He just hoped he wouldn't wind up *going* broke.

"The readiness is all," he said, borrowing a quote from Jeff Jenson. His rounded jaw as firm and resolute as he could make it, Stallings sat himself heavily in his captain's chair and took his mouse in hand, began doing the deed.

\* \* \*

Afterwards, he stepped outside, stood in his backyard. Stallings was no outdoorsman, but he'd learned that getting outside now and then could be soothing. He liked the feel of some mild sunshine on his face; of a gentle breeze against his skin. Indoors, he tended to sink down within himself; he became mired in his own boggy world. But outside there was a freshness, an openness, that brought him a better perspective on life. A simple but genuine pleasure could be had in observing the shape and texture of a tree or a cloud.

Outside, people seemed relatively small.

Every year, Jenny had planted a vegetable garden along the edge of the yard. Her favorite, and his too, had been tomatoes, but she might also plant squash, cucumber and even watermelon. Stallings wondered if he should continue the tradition this year. Knowing almost nothing about gardening, he'd have to get someone to show him what to do and when; he figured he'd have to plant pretty soon. He'd probably have to buy some plant food—was that its proper name, 'plant food'?—and where was the garden hose? Out in the shed? But if he could master the basics of gardening, he mused, it might prove an agreeable hobby. Jenny had certainly enjoyed it.

Still sipping his tea, Stallings made his leisurely way toward the strip of ground that'd served as a garden. Might as well take a gander at it, he thought.

He was about halfway there, strolling across his newly mown lawn, when he heard something from directly overhead. Or he would've sworn he did. A faint distant rumbling noise, possibly thunder. Had there been a flash of white light as well? He paused and looked up at the sky, which was clear, cloudless and powder blue—not the sort of sky one associated with storms. Seeing nothing out of the ordinary, he nevertheless felt he should stay where he was, keep his gaze turned skyward. Keep watching ...

Now he did see something. It was ... he couldn't tell what it was. Directly overhead, it looked like a black dot, far, far up in the sky. It seemed to be growing larger, or drawing nearer.

Or both.

Was something falling out of the sky? A satellite? A meteor? It didn't look like an airplane....

Fascinated, Stallings continued to watch as the thing zoomed closer. It never entered his mind to run. Where could he have gone if he'd hoped to escape anyhow? As he could now see, the thing was monstrously big, moving extremely fast and coming straight at him. It took him no more than a few seconds to discern what the thing was, or what it appeared to be.

Except ... it couldn't be what it appeared to be. Could it?

It was a face, a human face, a face in the sky. It was masculine, evenly featured and inconceivably large. Its race was impossible to determine since it almost seemed to encompass *all* races, melded together. Its brown eyes, clear and steady, were trained on Stallings' eyes, and its expression, while not hostile exactly, was profoundly serious, bordering on stern. An intelligent authoritative face, it was topped by a generous shock of dark brown hair, long and luxuriant, and it wore a trim brown mustache and beard as well. No neck was visible. Just the face.

Soon, very soon, the face filled most of the sky, then the entire sky, reaching from horizon to horizon. The eyes were as big as cities, the mouth—lips parted as if in preparation for speech—the size of a canyon.

To Stallings' dismay, the face continued to stare at him, and at him alone. It looked vividly, stunningly real. It looked alive. Terrified, he dropped his tea, collapsed on his back and screamed without shame.

Now, suspended over him, the face did speak to Stallings, in a firm articulate booming voice. Breath from the vast mouth hit him like warm and powerful gusts of wind.

Neither a brave man nor a coward, Stallings was ill-equipped to deal with this. His hands held up in a clawing defensive posture at the uncanny apparition above him, he lay flat on his back, screaming and screaming.

11

NEWSPAPER SPREAD CAREFULLY on the table before him, Dunkin Helbig sat in a coffee shop, The Daily Grind, and awaited his visitor. As usual, Helbig was ahead of everyone else's schedule. At his elbow stood a pale pink smoothie, a Strawberry-Banana Explosion. He would've preferred a beverage with more bite—an espresso or a hot cup of fresh-roasted coffee—but the caffeine always blitzed his nervous system, made him more hyper than he already was. A smoothie would have to do.

Like others, Helbig was finding plenty of diversion these days in the news. Today, there was the usual flurry of claims about lights in the sky and disappearing buildings. (Readers were now being informed of a library that had existed, but didn't anymore, in Schenectady, New York.) In addition, increasing numbers of citizens were claiming to have seen in the sky some sort of vision that went beyond mere lights. A vision involving a gigantic living face that'd tormented them with a doomful message. Interestingly, some of the claimants were local, and one of them, Trevor Null, was a well-respected County Commissioner of twenty years' standing. "We're all in a helluva lotta trouble," Null was quoted as saying.

Ludicrous, Helbig snickered. Chicken Little and his flock. It just went to prove that some people would spew all kinds of malarkey to attract some attention. And in an age when newspapers were losing their importance, some of them would print even the smelliest baloney if it promised to sell a few more copies.

Helbig couldn't have explained why the other media, not just newspapers, were covering the same stories, but he would've dismissed their efforts as so much humbug as well. In his mind, this was all a smokescreen designed by someone, probably the United States government, to mislead the public away from the real issues of the day. The unfair distribution of wealth. Corruption at the highest levels of government and business. A loss of moral principles. The exploitation of the weak by the strong. And perhaps most intolerably, a general lack of recognition for working class art and working class artists (such as Helbig). He was a big believer in conspiracy theory, particularly when the theory coincided with his worldview. The fact that conspiracies had to be carried out by large networks of smart dedicated people while Helbig deemed most people stupid and lazy didn't faze him.

He had a sip of his smoothie and checked his Timex. Where was Abdul?

For that matter, *who* was Abdul? Helbig had connected with this Abdul person by chatting with him on the Internet— they seemed to share some of the same fringy opinions—and they were supposed to meet in person for the first time any minute now. Since both men were exceedingly cautious, Helbig knew very little about Abdul, just as Abdul knew very little, Helbig felt confident, about him. They were moving ahead slowly. But it was possible, Helbig presumed, that Abdul could in time develop into a ... not a friend, since Helbig didn't believe in friends, but an ally perhaps. A partner. A co-conspirator.

Finished with the paper, Helbig folded it crisply, laid it in front of him and placed a slim softcover book on top of it. Entitled *Rogue State*, the book was a ripping critique of the United States that had actually drawn an endorsement from Osama bin Laden. While Helbig had barely glanced at the book himself, he guessed he agreed with it anyhow and hoped it would make the right impression on Abdul. With that moniker, the man had to be a Muslim, right?—and maybe a radical one at that. Wanting to underscore that Helbig too had problems with the Great Satan, he turned the book around so that when Abdul arrived, he could see the cover clearly.

Although an atheist, Helbig had given due consideration to

radical Islam. If he were going to believe in God (which he wasn't), any God that took a harsh view of the fat jaded diseased West was his kind of God. Death to America! Hadn't he been fighting his own personal jihad against mainstream American values for most of his young life anyhow?

Then again, there was much to be said for the God of the Old Testament—Yahweh, the name so sacred that many refused to say it out loud. Not Helbig, though. "Yahweh," he muttered to himself in the coffee shop. Sacred name or not, Yahweh too was a kickass God. This was the highhanded and wrathful God who'd abused Job to win a bet with the devil; who'd destroyed Sodom and Gomorrah; who'd killed the 185,000 Assyrians at Jerusalem; who'd called down the Great Flood that devastated the entire world. Man! Now there was a God that even Helbig could've respected—if He existed, which of course He didn't—and it crossed Helbig's mind that perhaps he should embrace Judaism.

Either Judaism or radical Islam. One of the two ...

For the moment, Helbig was content to think about theology if for no other reason than it beat thinking about the cultural war he was waging against Ben Temple and the others over at the Your Town Theatre. Pressured by the Goody Two-Shoes governing board, Ben was insisting that, from top to bottom, Helbig's script be 'adjusted.' Meaning ripped to shreds, as Helbig saw it. Even the play's hardcore grabber of a title, *Death and Destruction*, would have to be 'adjusted.'

"Why?" Helbig had demanded.

"Too negative," Ben said.

"Why does everything have to be positive?" Helbig complained.

"Everything doesn't have to be positive," Ben said. "But that title is way too negative. Let's see if we can adjust it."

Trying to show some flexibility, Helbig had offered to essentially cut the title's negativism in half by calling the play either just plain *Death* or just plain *Destruction*, but kindly white-haired Ben rejected those alternatives as well. The old son of a bitch.

Another point of contention between Helbig and Ben was the front door to the playhouse, which continued to stick, especially for Helbig. What had been a nuisance before had now turned into a crisis since it was Helbig's play and not someone else's that was about to see production. How could people get in to watch his masterwork if they couldn't get through the damn door? "Let's do something about that door, Ben!" Helbig urged him. Ben said he would, though both of them knew he probably wouldn't.

Most frustrating of all was the unenthusiastic response Helbig's play was receiving from the ragtag crew of local actors he'd called in to begin reading—before the script had been completely 'adjusted,' before it even had an acceptable title. Many of those reading said they simply didn't 'get' the material; for starters, they couldn't discern a plot. Patiently, Helbig explained that his drama was a postmodernist mood piece, and it was the atmosphere, not the plot, that counted. But then some of them said they didn't get the atmosphere either.

"I ain't no expert," said Buck Winters, who, when he wasn't acting, delivered the mail, "but this thing's got atmosphere about like the *moon*'s got atmosphere. There ain't any."

"Buck," Helbig began.

"And some of these words you got in here. 'Athwart!' What the hell's 'athwart' mean?"

"It means 'across,' " Helbig said.

"Well, then why," Buck wanted to know, "can't you just say 'across'?"

"Because I wanted to say 'athwart.' Melville used the word all the time. Have you heard of Melville?"

"I've heard of him," Buck said, scratching his head and biting his tongue.

Jabbing his straw repeatedly into his smoothie, Helbig labored to tame his anger. What the hell did Buck Winters know about theatre? he asked himself. Anything? If Buck Winters knew beans about theatre, then why the hell was he a mailman?

Just then a tall square-shouldered man entered the coffee shop. The man had glossy black hair and a close-cropped black beard. His expression was solemn, almost black itself, and he wore a black shirt, black slacks, black shoes.

There could be no question—it was Abdul.

His severe appearance matched the description he'd provided Helbig, and Helbig, who was wearing his prearranged *Waiting for Godot* T-shirt, met and held Abdul's dark gaze for a single charged second. The men nodded to each other briefly, almost imperceptibly. Abdul then went to the counter to order coffee.

As he did so, Helbig watched him quietly but feverishly, letting his torrid imagination run amok. What must it be like, he wondered, to be recruited for a terrorist mission, an operation that might lead to glorious martyrdom? He tried to picture himself as a young man living in the Middle East, in Libya, say, in the mystical city of Darnah. There, in the shadows cast by the massive limestone bluffs that surround the city, amid the crumbling futureless concrete tenements, filled with angst and sexual ambiguity and a razor-edged desire to make his meager presence felt, Helbig might seek to become a small but significant part of the resistance movement. He could see himself meeting with someone in the marketplace or in a mosque or perhaps even in a coffee shop, not too unlike the one he was in. A dark mysterious man would approach him and, after some polite exploratory conversation, ask if Helbig was willing to lay down his life for a holy cause in which they both believed.

Could such an experience be all that different from what was happening at this very instant?

Steam rising like a genie from his coffee, Abdul came toward Helbig, stood before him. At this moment, the man could've been a limestone bluff himself.

"I am pleased to meet you," Abdul said, his words inflected by some exotic unidentifiable accent. He offered his hand.

Helbig rose and shook it. "And I am honored to meet you," he said, gesturing that they should both be seated.

With boyish zeal, Helbig immediately took command of the conversation. He reminded Abdul of the ground rules they had agreed to prior to this meeting: that for now they would speak only of general or ideological matters; that neither man would have an obligation to discuss personal or biographical details. Those details could come later—or not—depending on how the two parties felt. Abdul nodded his assent.

Then, ignoring the ground rules and surprising even himself, Helbig abruptly went off on a lengthy spiel about his own life, his own struggle. He spoke of how he'd been born and raised not far from the very coffee shop where they presently sat. His parents divorced when he was quite young (he remembered them only through old photographs), and when neither expressed a wish to raise their son, Helbig found himself being raised first by one aunt and then by another. Martha and Edna. Hair piled up on top of their heads like lacquered monuments to mediocrity. The two aunts didn't much like each other (or favor Helbig, from what he could tell), and he didn't care for either of them. They baked pies, sang in choirs, belonged to clubs. It was nothing that Helbig, who was iconoclastic even as a kid, could relate to.

Unpopular in school, he devoted himself to his studies. This predictably had the effect of making his classmates dislike and mistrust him all the more. He was unafraid to disagree with his teachers and occasionally proved them wrong, rendering him unpopular with them as well. Some observers noticed, or claimed to notice, signs of effeminacy in Helbig. His wrist, they said, had a hint more play in it than did most guys'; his hips had an inch or so more swing in them than was strictly necessary. Some of his classmates mocked him as a closet, or not-so-closet, homosexual, while others threatened him or physically assaulted him. Though Helbig was certainly no XYY supermale type, he was no pushover either, and when someone threw a punch at him, he'd fire back with a couple clumsy shots of his own. Often, to the dismay of Martha or Edna, he'd come home sporting a blackened eye or a busted lip, but he was able to live with it. Inevitably, his self-reliance was growing, along with his alienation and radicalization.

"I think you'll agree," Helbig said to Abdul, "that one is not born a radical. One must become radicalized by events."

"Mm," Abdul grunted, his dark motionless eyes peering down through the mist rising from his jet black coffee.

"One sees cruelties and inequities and feels a desire to lash back. And I happen to've been blessed with, or cursed with, a rather sensitive soul. So I feel more deeply than some do."

"Sensitive," Abdul said.

"Well, I *am* a playwright, you know."

Abdul slowly shook his head, indicating he *didn't* know.

"Nothing frivolous," Helbig clarified. "Hard-hitting stuff. Edgy. Raw. Oppositional." He wondered if his pinkish smoothie might not be undercutting his rhetoric. He also wondered if maybe Muslims didn't disapprove of theatre altogether; he thought maybe they did. "You're familiar with this book?" he asked, hoping to steer the conversation in a different direction.

Abdul let his coallike eyes fall with a thud on the paperback, *Rogue State*, that lay on the table. Once again, he shook his head—slowly, stolidly.

"Is it good?" he asked.

Helbig was unsure how to answer the question, and not just because he hadn't read the book. "It's a polemic," he said. "Isn't supposed to be good or bad. It's supposed to be … provocative."

Slowly and deliberately Abdul raised his eyes and again fixed them firmly on Helbig. "Oh," he said.

"You see, it's a kind of scholarly—"

"Words are fine," Abdul broke in, showing for once a burst of animation. "Plays. Books. But sometimes one must resort to real action."

Helbig bobbed his triangular head while sipping from his smoothie. It made sipping difficult. "Of course," he said. He told Abdul about how he'd begun stockpiling jugs of gasoline in the garage behind his apartment.

"Gasoline," Abdul said.

"I appreciate fire. I appreciate what it can do, and how it does it."

"You've dabbled in arson?"

"I've dabbled," Helbig said. "And I've participated in ... other activities."

Swallowing some coffee, Abdul said nothing, but gave his eyes an inquisitive cast.

"Last year..." Helbig was inclined to boast, but was also wary of saying too much. "There was a person who had to be ... removed from the picture."

"Removed?"

"Yes."

A pause. "And you ... removed this person?"

"I did. I ran her over with my car."

"Her!" Abdul said. "A woman?"

"It couldn't be avoided. She—got in my way."

Running his thick hand through his thick black beard, Abdul seemed reflective, like a man weighing an offbeat but tempting offer from a car dealer. "Mm," he said.

Helbig sat back in his chair, tried to unwind a tad. He felt good about the way the meeting had gone so far; about the way he'd presented himself.

"Now," he said. "I've told you quite a bit about me as a person. I didn't have to, but I did. I'd like for you to reciprocate. I'd like to know about the personal side of Abdul."

Abdul's face, already dark, darkened further. "I'm afraid not," he said.

Helbig blinked. "Why not."

"Because I choose to stick to our agreement. Nothing personal today. Only general matters and ideology."

"But I already know about that," Helbig said. "I want to

know about *you*. Who are you?"

Abdul folded his thick square dark hands on the table. "Sorry," he said.

"You don't understand." Helbig's voice was up in both volume and pitch. "I told you some things; you should tell me some things."

"Mr. Helbig, it is you that fails to understand." Abdul tilted his big body forward. "When I make an agreement, I stick to it. Very simple."

"But I insist."

"And I decline."

Helbig scrambled out of his chair, pointed his finger at Abdul. Around the shop, people had taken open-mouthed notice of him. "Who are you?" he shouted.

Immobile, Abdul said nothing.

"Where are you from?" Helbig shouted. "What do you do?"

Abdul said nothing.

"You a cop?" Helbig shouted. "You CIA? FBI? Who the hell are you?"

Abdul said nothing. Behind the counter, the shop's aproned manager appeared and gave Helbig an unhappy stare.

"Everything I told you I made up!" Helbig shouted, still pointing. "It was all a lie!"

"Mr. Helbig," Abdul said soberly.

"This meeting never happened!" Helbig shouted. "I never talked to you! You never talked to me!"

Wildly he flung himself out the glass door, almost knocking over an elderly woman whose expression would've been no more horrified had she ordered a pricy lunch only to find it crawling with fat white maggots, and then he disappeared up the sidewalk.

When the manager gingerly approached the scene, Abdul, still in his chair, a puzzled and innocent look on his face, simply held up his palms as if to say *Hey, I'm just sitting here having                    some                    coffee.*

12

FORCING A SMILE, Laura Kennedy said a final goodbye to her tiresome visitor from work, closed the door to her matchbox of a Woodland Hills apartment and turned the deadbolt lock. She leaned back against the door, arms dangling, and released a luxurious world-weary sigh.

Woodland Hills. It was ironic, because one of the reasons she'd chosen to live in this town, and in this particular apartment, was the closeness of fabled Ventura Highway. It was so close she could hear the bustling hum of its traffic. Before she was born, a group called America brought out a song romanticizing that California roadway as a place of sunshiny days and 'no despair.' The song found her, and, rightly or wrongly, stayed with her like a fragrance, teased her, inspired her, led her on.... Well, there was an ample supply of sunshine out here; that part of it was true. But alas, there were moments of despair as well, and they were liable to grab ahold of you, work you over, anytime you slowed down enough in your daily routine to allow for a quiet period of reflection. Like now.

Her life was anything but a parade of kicks and thrills. No, it was mainly a repeating cycle of work, one small-time meaningless assignment after another. Journalism fascinated her, but not at the mundane level of covering social events, ribbon-cutting ceremonies and retirement speeches. What a load of crap. Now the porn story, which had been Laura's own brainchild, had been different. This was an assignment she could sink her underused teeth into. But her editor's response, to this point at least, had been less than enthusiastic. She'd written the article, apparently, with a shade too much zest.

"My God," he'd said, "this is all about *sex*."

"It's about porn," she answered.

"Porn is fine," he said. "But keep the sex outta there, OK? My God, you wanna get us all arrested?"

The piece would have to be rewritten drastically. Bowdlerized. Probably, it would never see the light of publication.

Of course, her social life was no more exciting. Most of her family were back in Minnesota (had the tall drifts of snow melted there yet?), and she rarely saw them anymore. She and her mother talked frequently by phone, but these calls gave her scant satisfaction. For one thing, her mother, who still owned just an outmoded landline, couldn't afford to make many long-distance calls. So the duty to call usually fell on Laura, causing her to feel like a pest. Then too, the content of their conversations, while certainly well-intended, was always so humdrum and boring. Faithfully, her mother would report on any new physical ailments she may've incurred. A sore back, bouts of psoriasis, a funky-looking mole, numerous head colds (confirmed by her snuffly nasal voice) had all been recently reported; migraines had been around for a while. Laura's taciturn father, she was told, was still working for Social Security; still watching a lot of baseball on TV. Oftentimes, her mother would ask her if she'd eaten yet. If she said she hadn't, her mother would immediately urge her to go eat something. Laura found these automatic reminders to eat intensely annoying. "I'm twenty-four years old," she'd say curtly. "I know enough to eat." Yet sometimes she did forget.

In fact, it occurred to her just now that she might grab herself a quick bite. So she trudged over to her undersize kitchen and rummaged about. Not much there: some frozen dinners, some cinnamon-raisin breakfast bars, some peanut butter. Without conviction, she decided to make herself half a peanut butter sandwich that she enhanced, or tried to, with three slender slices of banana. Then she poured herself a small glass of skim milk.

Peanut butter. Banana. Skim milk. For the love of God— even the food she ate seemed drab and bereft.

One topic Laura could depend on her mother to bring up in any and every conversation was Laura's ex-boyfriend, a young man named Bryson Dimmer. Bryson was a CPA ("a good-paying job," her mother always noted) who not only felt comfortable with numbers but actually reveled in their company. A pear-shaped fellow with Woody Allen glasses and soft white hands, he spent large portions of each day playing Sudoku and adding columns of figures in his head just to keep his math skills sharp. He had favorite numbers, among which were 3, 5 and—oddly—89, and he encouraged Laura to 'adopt' some numbers as well. He harbored a particular fondness for prime numbers and Fibonacci numbers, and regarded any number that was both prime and Fibonacci as 'holy.' For her part, Laura wasn't even sure what a Fibonacci number was. And after a while she realized she didn't know exactly what Bryson Dimmer was either, except a kook. So to her mother's and Bryson's keen disappointment, she performed a mathematical feat of her own by subtracting him neatly from her life.

Remarkably, her life seemed slightly fuller to her, or somewhat less barren, without him. Could he have been a walking negative number?

Munching her sandwich, Laura began to shamble aimlessly through her miniature apartment. Its dimensions being what they were, she was limited in how far she could shamble in any one direction. So she'd shamble a few steps, pause, turn, shamble a few more....

Despite herself, Laura began to relive the painful ordeal of spending the last two hours with that motor-mouthed dullard from work, Tammy Spickler. The idea had been that Tammy would drop by with her recipe for tuna casserole and, after a brief interval, leave. Well, she forgot to bring the recipe—no matter, it was a bland boring dish anyway—but managed to hang around blathering for most of the evening regardless. Basically a secretary with a much jazzier title, Tammy knew most everyone connected with the newspaper and was pleased to discuss them from all angles. Since Laura didn't gossip much, or not as much as Tammy, she had little interest in her chum's windy monologs. This person was demanding a raise, that one was threatening to quit, and this one, having demanded and received a raise, was threatening to quit because the raise was so puny, so degrading, that it amounted to a bigger slap in the face than being rejected for any raise at all.... And make no mistake, absolutely everyone was jumping into bed with absolutely everyone else. On and on.

Tammy did, however, deliver one nugget of information that struck Laura. She said that earlier today Laura's sister had called to check Laura's address; the sister, whose name Tammy didn't quite catch, wanted to send Laura a gift for her birthday, which was coming up next week.

What made this tidbit striking to Laura were two facts. First, her birthday wasn't next week at all but instead seven months from now. Second, and even more to the point, she had no sister; she was an only child. A bewildering message, then, but one she chose not to follow up on since at that stage she was trying desperately, without being rude, to bring Tammy's strong-lunged visit to a merciful end.

As she often did of late, Laura found herself mulling that porn star she'd interviewed, Zoey Zanders. Or what was her real name? Sarah Black. What a contrast in lifestyles we had here, she thought. Jet black and skim milk white. While Laura was no particular fan of porn, she did try to keep an open mind about it (and about various other dark-edged curiosities that life presented). Despite her conservative upbringing, she couldn't help but feel, on some level, a hint of envy for this infamous, rebellious, not to mention rich chick who was likely two or three years younger than Laura herself. What must Zoey/Sarah be doing at this very instant? she wondered. Dining at some exclusive gourmet restaurant maybe ... or raising pure hell at some raucous rock 'n' roll sex and cocaine party ... Chances were she wasn't just pacing around, mumbling forlornly to herself and eating a peanut butter sandwich.

On a whim, Laura stuffed what was left of her sandwich into her mouth and stood hipshot before the full-length mirror fastened to her bedroom door. She eyed herself critically. If she'd been so inclined, could she've become, she asked herself, a porn star? Leaving aside the harsh reality that her sexual experience (and skills) were thus far pretty minimal, she felt confident that her looks were ... at least average. Her abbreviated brown hair was not without sheen, and her wide-set brown eyes, while not terribly mischievous or alluring, were large enough and clear enough. A defensible nose. Although her mouth may've appeared a trifle lopsided, that was mostly due to the peanut butter.

Her body was ... Well, why not have a better look at it? With that bold thought, she kicked out of her suede flats, shrugged out of her buttery top and dropped her gray twill slacks to the floor. After some hesitation, she stripped off her support bra and her Jockey panties as well. Laura didn't especially like being totally naked, even when alone, and she supposed that such modesty could certainly prove a drawback to anyone even remotely imagining a career in porn. Nevertheless ...

She'd seen worse bodies, she guessed. After studying herself head-on, she turned her slim figure slowly to one side and then slowly back to the other. She resisted any mild temptation to shake or shimmy. The boobs could definitely use more size, she judged. Same with the butt. But she did have a kind of overall sleekness to her that, in theory, could be seen as appealing. By some, anyhow. And not counting that faded scar on her reasonably tight abdomen—some years ago she'd had her appendix removed—she displayed no undue deformities. Nothing hideous, at any rate, and that was a plus. Besides which, as her mother constantly reminded her, she was as healthy as a newborn colt.

Turning away from the mirror at last, Laura shrugged indifferently. The hell with it, she decided; I'm an acquired taste. Like tofu. Like spinach. (Two more of her favorite foods.)

She wrapped herself in a white lacy calf-length robe and went to what passed for her living room, flicked on the TV. Very quickly she discovered that the news was being dominated by two stories, neither of which gladdened her.

The first story was national in scope—or international, actually, since reports seemed to be coming in from everywhere. Evidently there was a slow-moving but steadily mounting panic afoot. Some were using the term 'mass hysteria.' For nearly a week now, bizarre and inexplicable events had been happening, and people were becoming distressed. Several buildings, for example, many of them made of steel and concrete, had outright vanished. Most of them had contained people, who of course had gone missing along with the buildings. To be clear, the buildings had not been destroyed by a bomb blast or the like; they had simply ... ceased to exist, leaving behind a sooty residue at the site. Moreover, strange lights had repeatedly been photographed and videotaped in the sky, and no one could say what they were or what they meant. (Here now, as Laura stood watching her TV, was another clip of an unaccountable—and rather beautiful—lightshow. Broad day, and the multicolored things surged, swirled and snaked through the heavens. They made no sound.)

Were the disappearing buildings somehow associated with the eerie lights? No one seemed to know.

At the same time, increasing numbers of citizens were coming forward to speak of the almost supernatural experience they'd had with a face, an immense human face, that they'd seen in the sky. One such citizen, a chunky crinkle-browed wheat farmer in Kansas named Herb Bellview, peered earnestly at Laura from her TV now. Wearing bib overalls, he kept a thick arm around what was presumably his wife, a pale and quivery woman who bore the sunken anguished look of one condemned.

"I was out in the field," Bellview said. "I was on my

tractor. All of a sudden, I seen it." He raised his eyes and his free hand, his fingers spread like the spokes on a wheel. "My garsh," he said. "It started off little-bitty. But then it got big. Real big. It swole up like a balloon. And it was still up in the sky, you see, but I felt like I could reach out and touch it. Or like it might touch me. I almost wrecked my tractor."

"What'd it look like?" someone asked.

With a blinking effort, Bellview brought himself to focus on whoever had asked the question. "I done told you," he said. "It was a face."

"But what kind of face?"

He took a moment to consider. "A damn scary one."

"Did it say anything?" someone else asked.

"It did," Bellview said. "It surely did."

"Can you tell us what?"

Again he considered. "No sir," he said finally. "I can't. I won't. But lemme put it this here way." The camera moved in on him, making his already broad face, so sincere and Midwestern and iconic, seem to expand; it now consumed the entire screen. "You best get down on your knees," he said. "Get down on your knees and pray to God up in heaven."

Working her tongue around the far recesses of her teeth and gums to free them of stubborn peanut butter, Laura was not unmoved by the man's message, or by the story as a whole. Like everyone else, she was beginning to wonder what the hell was going on. Was it faintly possible that the planet was in the tightening grip of a genuine threat? Could we be witnessing the first frightful steps of an alien invasion or of some cosmic reckoning wrought by an angry—but very real—God? Frankly, she doubted it. As a reporter, Laura knew from personal experience how nutty people could be, and how, in an age when the media ran rampant, folks chased after public attention, even at the expense of their own dignity. Some of them would say or do anything if they thought they could grab their quarter-hour of fame. The off-screen voices had more questions for Herb Bellview, but, changing channels, she declined to hear them.

But now she encountered the second news story, which jarred her more than the first. Sometime within the past two days, she learned, a man had been shot to death at the home of adult film actress Zoey Zanders. (Here were some exterior shots of the red and white Mediterranean-style house; an orange beach ball drifted lazily across the blue sun-struck waters of the swimming pool.) The victim, identified as one Derek Randolph Wolf, age twenty-six, was said to have been Zanders' business manager and fiancé. (A black-and-white photo of Derek, almost smiling.) No motive for the killing had been publicly released, though robbery had been ruled out, and no suspects had been arrested. Significantly, the whereabouts of Ms. Zanders were unknown, and investigators were referring to her as a 'person of interest.'

Her face ashen, Laura flicked off the TV and resumed pacing, this time at Olympic speed. She remembered the hateful glare Derek had flashed, more than once, at poolside that day. It was a look that suggested he could kill someone— or had it hinted that someone might well kill him? But who would've ... Still pacing, she wrung her hands anxiously. She knew Sarah's cell phone number and thought she might use it within the next minute, if only to make sure the girl was all right. Would it be inappropriate to call her? She didn't know Sarah all that well, but she did know her well enough to think of her as 'Sarah' and not 'Zoey,' and that fact in itself probably meant something, she felt.

Laura crossed the room and seized the phone just as the doorbell began to ring. She knew instantly it was Tammy Spickler out there, and she'd forgotten to tell Laura something, or forgotten her purse, or maybe even forgotten her head. Or perhaps somewhere in her car she'd found that recipe for tuna casserole and refused to go home without turning it over as promised; yes, that one was plausible, for Tammy was honorable about all the wrong things.

No way was Laura going to open that door. But with the

ringing racket of the doorbell, no way could she make her phone call either.

The aggressive ringing continued, and when she could bear it no longer, she strode to the door, pressed her eye to the peephole and saw with a shock that her visitor was Sarah Black.

Twitchy-fingered, Laura overcame the lock and tore open the door, and the two young women confronted each other. Both wore the same slack-jawed wild-eyed expression, making them look almost like a single person staring with wonder and doubt into the silvery depths of a mirror.

"There's blood on your face," Laura said.

"'Tis Banquo's then," Sarah answered, and burst into loud rising laughter.

Laura physically hustled her inside. "You're on the news!" she hissed. "They just showed your house on TV!"

Composing herself, Sarah said: "Yes, yes. No surprise there, given the circumstances." She let her violet eyes scan the tiny apartment's interior, as if there were something here she meant to absorb and savor.

"What happened?" Laura asked.

"At my place?" Sarah shrugged. She was wearing a silky sapphire-blue T-shirt with '69' emblazoned on the chest and her customary sprayed-on jeans. Over her shoulder hung a blue purse. "Something that should've happened a long time ago."

Laura went to the kitchen, moistened a paper towel and began using it to clean up her guest. Dabbing, dabbing. "Where've you been? The incident, the ... whatever you call it, happened a couple days ago."

"I don't know." Very casual. "I been around. Here, there. You know. Freestyling. Just—"

"Hold still."

"Just driving mostly. Thinking. I went to a museum, I went to a play."

Laura squeezed the paper towel into a damp ball and

tossed it into a bin. "Have you slept?"

"A little. In my car. I'd just park along the road somewhere, push back the seat, close my eyes...."

Nodding vaguely, Laura opened a cupboard, took out a cinnamon-raisin bar and handed it to Sarah.

"What is it?" she asked.

"It's food. Eat it."

Sarah picked open the wrapper and tentatively, like a bird, began to nibble. Finding it tasty, she built up speed as she went.

After a careful pause, during which Laura recognized how against the odds it was for her to be less fully clothed than a bona fide porn star, she said: "Sarah, why are you here?"

"I don't know." It was an answer Sarah often leaned on in uncertain times, but even she disliked it here. "I got the impression," she tried again, "that you think the life I lead is ... worth living."

"What do you mean?"

"You know what I mean." Kissing her fingertips, Sarah had made brief work of the breakfast bar. She deposited the wrapper in the same bin that'd swallowed the paper towel. "Take it from me," she said. "It isn't."

"Isn't ..."

"Worth much of anything."

Laura would've pursued this line of conversation further, but Sarah was uncooperative. Slowly the actress circled to the door, again taking in her humble surroundings, virtually inhaling them.

"By the way," she said, "how did your article come out?"

"It didn't. My editor says it's got too much sex. And I need a better ending."

"Well, I can't help you with the sex part." This comment seemed so silly to Sarah that it caused her to grin and then to laugh. "But I might be able to give you an ending."

"Really?"

"I'm going back home now," Sarah said. "My real home.

In Illinois. I'm going to have it out with my father, Johnny Black."

Moving toward the door herself, Laura said: "The baseball player."

"That's right. It's time, and it's past time. I've got a score to settle."

Laura thought of the dead man, the murdered man, in Sarah's foaming wake. "Sarah," she said, "you wouldn't ..."

"Do something crazy? Please. Wherever would you get such a fucking baseless idea?"

Sarah giggled. Laura didn't.

"Come with me," Sarah said.

"To Illinois? *Now?*" Laura was close to the door, but not as close as Sarah.

"Sure. Why not? You come with me, honey, and I'll give your story the ending to end all endings."

Laura frowned, chewed her thin lower lip, stared at the floor. The concept was about as feasible as saying she could sprout wings and fly to Venus.

"Be careful," she offered.

With a nod and a smile, Sarah opened the door, clutching her purse up against her.

"Remember to eat," Laura said. "And get some sleep. Oh, and Sarah—"

"Yes?"

"You were the one that called today to check my address, right? Said you were my sister."

Sarah took Laura's hand, gave it a pat. "Your sister, yes."

13

THE FACE IN THE SKY had told Stallings something important, but at this moment the message eluded him. His thoughts were jumbled. He was still too frightened, too overwhelmed, to think clearly.

Warily, he sat up on his lawn. He had a look around, then had an uneasy look up at the sky. It was as blue and beguiling as the eye of a Siamese kitten. He saw no sign of anything extraordinary. The face had departed, as if blown away by a mighty gust of wind. Everything seemed normal, except for the curious fact that Professor Stallings was sitting like a three-year-old in his backyard.

Feeling ridiculous, he clambered to his bare knees and, with a grunt, stood up. He brushed his hands lightly over his shirt and shorts and had another peek around. To either side of his property was a house that resembled his own—a respectable middle-class rancher. He wondered if his neighbors, all upstanding professionals, had seen him collapse on his lawn, screaming and clawing at the sky, or if they'd seen or heard anything else uncommon. But no one was about.

He moved around a little to see how he felt. Not too bad, surprisingly. His back ached from having fallen on it, but otherwise he felt fine. No dizziness or lightheadedness. Legs felt OK.

So what had just happened to him? Stallings remembered an awful occasion more than twenty years before when he went to a party and ingested a rather potent dose of LSD. It was one of the few times in his staid life that he'd ever deviated from responsibility and convention, and one of the last. But a buddy had half-dared him, half-encouraged him to try the stuff, calling it 'mind-expanding,' and so he had.

It took a while for the drug to hit him, but when it did, it hit him hard. He began to experience what he later learned was synesthesia—a weird mixing together of the senses. For instance, he discovered he could now *see* certain sounds. When his friend spoke to him, depending on the intonation, the sounds would not only register in his ears but erupt across his field of vision as a rolling splash of vivid color. His own name—"Bob? Bob?"—would come at him as a sparkling emerald wave and wash over him coolly. Other sounds produced a particular taste on his tongue—sweet, sour, salty, bitter.... Not only was there synesthesia, but soon his friend's face developed a disconcerting tendency to melt, the features oozing together, sliding down his chest and dripping to the floor like shimmering plops of paint. At the outset, Stallings found these effects interesting and amusing, but when they continued, hour after distorted hour, he felt tormented by them, harrowed and profoundly disturbed. The trip lasted all night and into the next day.

Had he just now suffered a flashback? He didn't think so. A flashback after more than two decades following a single misadventure with acid seemed most unlikely to him. And the nature of the event was so different this time—more compressed, more intense, more lifelike—from how it'd been before. On LSD, Stallings had understood he was hallucinating even as it happened, but the face in the sky seemed real. Terrifyingly real.

As his mind cleared, he began to replay mentally what had just occurred. Not that he necessarily wanted to. There'd been a sound from above, he thought. Nothing definite—a kind of deep thunderous vibration or tremor. There'd also been a change in the light, he was pretty sure. A ghostly flare that he saw not directly but detected in the brief blanching of his general surroundings. Then the black dot, a pinhead at first, falling, falling, and then quickly expanding into a face, the face of a youngish male, mid-thirties maybe, firm and unsparing in its gaze, which happened to be fixed on nothing but Stallings himself. In a matter of seconds, the face filled the sky completely and seemed almost to push down at him, crowding him, pressuring him. The long hair and the smart mustache and beard made the face look contemporary and hip (or to Stallings, left-wing), while its fantastic size and the somber relentless gaze conveyed more authority than the professor could rightly handle.

Then the thing spoke to him. Its words, which ought to've been etched into Stallings' memory, were for some reason gauzy and indistinct. Perhaps his fear had made him less attentive than he should've been. But the face began by addressing him personally and formally. "Mr. Stallings," it said in a voice that was precise, resonant and plenty loud. It noted that things began and things ended, and that people often saw no sense in any of it. Without further ado, it stated that all life on Earth—indeed, Earth itself—was about to be destroyed. No rationale would be forthcoming; annihilation would simply happen. Soon. We should prepare ourselves, the face advised, as best we could. It also said that it would provide a token of good faith involving two of our cities. Soon. (And what could this mean?) It said something else, and then it went away.

What else had it said? What was that final comment?... For now, Stallings couldn't remember.

He noticed a small object twinkling on his lawn and went over to it. It was the glass, unbroken, that had held his iced tea. He picked it up, had one more nervous glance around and went inside his house.

Impulsively, he made a few phone calls. He called his mother, who, along with his father, had retired to the Gulf Coast of Florida. Since he typically talked to her once or twice a week anyhow, calling her now was nothing out of the ordinary. Their conversation today ranged over a variety of subjects, though it didn't touch on the darker aspects of the news since his mother instinctively preferred topics that were wholesome and commonplace. And he certainly didn't mention that he'd just survived a terrifying encounter with a horizon-to-horizon talking face in the sky, and one that spoke of apocalypse at that. When he made the error of bringing up the frustration he sometimes felt from teaching at the college, she chided him. "Oh, Bobby," she said. "It's a job. And a job is a job is a job." Well, he couldn't argue with that, and he wasn't about to. He was pleased that she sounded like her normal self.

Stallings also called some of his old pals and chatted with them about nothing much. They too sounded like themselves, he supposed. Or did they? With them he was less confident in his judgment. If they'd been masking some underlying anxiety just as he was, would he have been sensitive enough to pick up on it, especially over the phone? He frowned in doubt, but nevertheless felt reassured by the mere familiarity of their voices.

Passing through the kitchen, he decided to wash some dishes, including the glass he'd dropped. He didn't enjoy washing dishes but hoped that the very act of doing such a pedestrian task might bring him a sense of day-to-day normalcy. So he turned on the hot water, squeezed some detergent onto a sponge and went at it, his mind active. Even though he was aware that others were claiming to have had a parallel experience with a face in the sky, Stallings wasn't yet willing to acknowledge, even to himself, that what had happened to him outside might actually have happened. For real. As a practical man, he was convinced that there had to be some other explanation. Obviously his imagination, which had never been all that puckish in the past, had played quite a trick on him. But why?

Could be any number of reasons, he deduced. Fatigue, for one. Maybe he was overtired, and his exhaustion had led to a glitch in his mental software. (But he didn't feel fatigued; in fact, he felt as vigorous as ever.) Or maybe he'd fallen victim to work-related tension. His job, dealing with the likes of the bureaucratic Bill Yommer and with all those brain-dead mummylike students, did make him tense. (But then again, he was no more tense than usual. The tension he lived with was continual, predictable and mostly manageable.) Or maybe the swirling stream of alcohol in which he'd been skinny-dipping was beginning to affect him in a serious way. (But in recent days he hadn't touched a drop. Was he being wracked by the pangs of withdrawal?) Or maybe—and this one felt like a genuine possibility—maybe the loss of his wife had torn a ragged hole in his mind that, instead of healing with time, was growing bigger and nastier. Big enough to allow all kinds of nightmares to come bursting through ...

Or perhaps, Stallings speculated, he was in the sorry process of going crazy for no specific reason. Psych hospitals the world over were full of crazy people, and he doubted that doctors could routinely point to a specific reason for why this person or that one had gone psychotic. Most times, he guessed, it just happened.

"Wouldn't hurt me to join a gym," he mused out loud. "Burn off some of this lard, get myself squared away ..."

Finished with the dishes, he found a towel and slowly dried his hands. As he did so, he suddenly recalled with a start the final comment the face had made to him.

*The world will end,* the thing had informed him, *this coming Thursday at 3:00 PM.*

Jesus, Stallings thought. He tossed the towel aside and smiled wanly, his would-be humor bleak and sardonic. What a helluva sendoff. A *See you later* or a *Take care* or even a *Kiss my ass* would've been more to his liking—but then why should the final statement have been any more genial or upbeat than the rest of it?

"I can't even look forward to next weekend," he said, and tried to laugh. But the laugh came out as a garbled choking noise.

Timidly he went outside again, into the warm slanting rays of the sun. Brow knit, hands deep in his baglike pockets, he peered in every direction—even up—and saw nothing unexpected.

Perched on the gray wire fence surrounding Stallings' yard was a handsome purple martin. Standing still, the bird cocked its head one way and another, repeatedly, as if watching or listening for something.

* * *

Next morning, after a restless night, Stallings entertained the idea of visiting a doctor. But physically he felt all right; even his sore back was doing better. He was uncomfortable with the memory of what had happened in the yard, yes, but he simply didn't feel sick. And today, so far at least, he was seeing only the things he was supposed to be seeing, knock on wood.

So he showered, ate some breakfast and got himself dressed for work.

Driving to school, he listened to the news on the radio and took no solace in being reminded that others, a growing number of them, had had their own unsettling dust-ups with a face in the sky. Reports were being filed from all over. Along with the reports came some theories that people were advancing to try to explain matters. One such theory proposed that a chemical agent had either accidentally or maliciously been placed into the drinking water. The notion wasn't too far removed from Stallings' fancy about an LSD flashback, and, to him, it was no more convincing. What chemical was it? Where did it come from? How had it appeared in so many widespread locations? Why had it affected some people and not others? Why, come to think of it, did it always produce the same hallucination and not a vision, say, of pink elephants breakdancing in the streets or of winged pigs clogging the airways?

Other theories had to do with mass hypnosis (which raised the question of who might the mass hypnotist be) and mass hysteria. While the latter possibility was captivating in its way—a groundless belief or absurd behavior could spread through a population like a virus just because people aren't always the most logical—it too failed to persuade Stallings. "Horse hockey," he said. As a man of intellect, he refused to accept that he'd been stampeded into a hallucination. His imagination may've acted up on him, but he didn't think he'd gone hysterical.

Regardless, some psychology professor now came on the radio and claimed that people went hysterical all the time. She began describing the so-called Tanganyika Laughter Epidemic that, in 1962, purportedly saw an outbreak of uncontrollable maniacal laughter spread, mainly among young students, from village to village across Africa, causing schools to be shut down and leaving everyone baffled, scared and ultimately unamused. Equally unamused was Stallings, who considered this the type of claptrap that sometimes gave academics a bad name. Annoyed and impatient, he jabbed at the radio and switched to another station.

More news, only now a woman's voice was speaking in a sober tone about the abrupt surge throughout the nation in violent crime. In the last several days police had been forced to contend with a dizzying spate of robberies, rapes, beatings and murders. Riots had detonated in Detroit, Los Angeles and Miami, and no one could say exactly why. Two men, looting a jewelry store in LA, had been shot to death, not by police but by a random citizen. Using a hand grenade, someone had attempted to assassinate a high-profile Catholic archbishop in Kansas City, but the attempt had failed. The suspect himself, however, had sustained life-threatening injuries....

Dejected with the news, Stallings clicked off the radio just as Harris Community College floated into view before him. He was always struck by how, from a distance, the basic functional cost-effective buildings that made up the school appeared as if they'd wanted to grow taller, nobler, but some unseen power had prevented it, rendering them flat and stunted-looking. Sheer economics, no doubt. Adam Smith's Invisible Hand, descending from above, squashing out a not-too-edible hamburger patty.

The parking lot was emptier than usual—no problem finding a spot—and so were the halls. Black briefcase in hand,

Stallings was headed toward his office when, turning a corner, he saw something curious up ahead.

One of his students, Jamal Jameson, the strapping basketball player, was locked in what was apparently a heated discussion with another, much smaller, student. Though Stallings couldn't quite hear what was being said, both young men were animated, facing each other at close range and gesturing fiercely.

Stallings stopped where he was, watching them. Situations like this always left him stumped and hesitant. Should he step in and try to help out? The John Maynard Keynes approach? Or should he free-market it, just stand back and let things take their own natural course? His role as professor, it seemed to him, really had nothing to do with—

But suddenly Jamal broke down and began weeping openly. He was stooped over, spidery hands on his knees, sobbing. The other student draped a comforting arm across Jamal's broad back and murmured something, words of support, Stallings gathered, in Jamal's ear.

By now Stallings had seen enough, and he began to move toward them, his *in loco parentis* instincts stirring to life. He hadn't gotten too far, however, when a hand from behind him fell urgently on his shoulder, holding him at bay.

The hand belonged to Associate Dean Bill Yommer. "Bob," he said, "I wonder if I might have a word with you."

"Actually, Bill, I just now ... I haven't even ..."

"Only take a minute."

Glancing up the hall, Stallings could see the smaller student gently leading Jamal away; it was as if the muscular power forward had twisted an ankle while battling for a rebound and was being assisted to the bench.

"Bill, honestly, I just now walked through the ... I haven't even—"

"Bob. Please. One minute of your time."

Stallings knew how long 'one minute' with Yommer could last. But with a sigh that could've billowed a schooner's sail,

Stallings surrendered and once more found himself striding along in silence a step or two behind the tall gangly septuagenarian Associate Dean. At one point Yommer reached up to rub his ear thoughtfully, and Stallings noted with distaste how the motion caused those three thin gold bracelets to slide up the older man's forearm. Stallings couldn't help but wonder what the focus of their talk would be today. Had Yommer, or someone higher up, reached a decision concerning that chuckleheaded complaint submitted by the Harvard-bound scholar Amber Glotfelty? Had Stallings violated Yommer's standards by filling out some form in quadruplicate and not quintuplicate? Had Stallings failed to attend some meeting in Springfield or Chicago or Turkmenistan that could've been beneficial to him?...

The answer, to Stallings' surprise, was none of the above. Soon as the two men had seated themselves at the cramped but polished little meeting table in Yommer's office, Yommer leaned straight at Stallings, his aged and hawklike face swooping in all too close, then rocked back away from him, tilting his chair at such an extreme angle that it appeared he might go crashing to the floor. Staring up at the ceiling, Yommer opened his mouth to speak but for the moment said nothing. He seemed energized and paralyzed at the same time. The pause gave Stallings several seconds, though a poor vantage, to study the look on Yommer's uplifted face; it was a look of troubled concentration. Stallings also had a chance to survey once again the three (or was it four?) thin gold necklaces that hung brightly around Yommer's neck, and to assess with disapproval the velvety lemon-colored T-shirt into which they dipped.

"Bob," Yommer said finally, without rancor, "you're not too fond of me, are you?"

Sitting bolt upright to begin with, Stallings straightened his spine another fraction of an inch. "Excuse me?"

"It's all right." Bracelets tinkling, Yommer rocked forward to a more conventional posture. "It doesn't matter. I respect you, and I feel there are certain things I want to say to you."

"Bill, is there a ... If there's a problem—"

"Three items." Elbows on the table, Yommer folded his hands together; he seemed not so much upset as calmly determined to press ahead in the face of some nameless difficulty. "Item number one. Many years ago when I was a young man, I worked in a department store. I stole money from the place that employed me, and I did so on a recurring basis. Wasn't a lot of money, but that's not the point. The point is, I stole the money."

Utterly lost, Stallings started to say something, then checked himself.

"Figured sooner or later they'd catch me," Yommer said, "but somehow they never did. Item number two—and this one's tough." He stood up and drifted across the room to a bookcase jammed full of such crushingly dull titles as *Foundations of the Modern School Movement* and *From Pedagogy to Andragogy: A Guide*. As was often the case, he was wearing blue jeans. "Bob," he said at last, "I once made love to another man."

Uncertain he'd heard correctly, Stallings this time found it easy enough to hold his silence.

"Happened exactly once. When it happened, where, why, who the other guy was—not important. What's important is, it did happen. It did, and may God help me."

Stallings cleared his throat. "Why are you telling me this?" he asked.

"And I don't consider myself gay," Yommer said. "But, well, there you go." He shrugged. "Item number three. Some years ago, my wife left me. Had nothing to do with item number two, by the way; she didn't know about that. She left me because I abused her. Beat her. Knocked her around pretty good. Always felt ashamed of myself afterwards, but then I'd go and do it again, you know? I don't blame Ann one damn bit for leaving me."

Stallings touched a pensive finger to his lip. "You saw it,

didn't you, Bill?" he said quietly.

"Tried going to a marriage counselor, but he was about as useful as Size D tits on a warthog."

"You saw the face. Didn't you."

"What?" For the first time since the discussion began, Yommer gave Stallings his full attention. "What face?"

"The face in the sky. You saw it. And that's why you're telling me all this. You, uh ..."

Yommer stepped toward Stallings and raised his voice with indignation. "I did *not* see any face."

"You feel guilty. Scared. You, you want to—"

"I'm ex-Marine Corps," Yommer said sharply. "Ex-Marines do not see faces in the sky. You hear me?"

"You want to ... confess. It's OK, Bill. I understand. I—"

"Professor Stallings, you'd better curb your tongue."

"I saw it too."

"I don't give a damn what you saw. I *didn't* see it." Yommer was standing right next to Stallings, who gazed up passively into Yommer's strained reddened face. "I *didn't* see it," Yommer said. "And if I did see it, I wouldn't share something as personal as that with you. I told you these things because ... because I wanted to. I wanted to tell someone. And you were it."

Stallings nodded.

"Simple as that," Yommer said.

Closing his grip on the handle of his briefcase, Stallings stood up.

"Bob," Yommer said, pointing his finger at him, "if you repeat one word of this conversation to anyone—to *anyone*—so help me God I'll castrate you and then I'll strangle you."

Stallings opened his mouth, a caustic retort ready and eager to leap off his tongue. Then, reconsidering, he willed his mouth to close. Said nothing. Once again he nodded, and this time      he           went         on          his           way.

14

IT'S DARK IN HERE, even with the lights on, Johnny thought. He was in the Your Town Theatre, dragged here by his pain-in-the-ass semi-buddy Dunkin Helbig. They were standing in front of the stage, Helbig issuing commands to his ragtag troupe of actors, trying to get them marshaled for a rehearsal, and Johnny signing autographs and joking with some of the very players Helbig was trying to marshal. Neither Helbig nor Johnny was enjoying himself much at this moment, though the former ballplayer, with his ready grin and easy manner, was putting up a better front.

"Skeets," Helbig snapped, "I want you up on stage. C'mon. Delbert, you're up there with Skeets. Let's go."

Grudgingly Skeets began moving toward the stage; Delbert stayed where he was.

"Where's Buck?" Helbig demanded. "Where's Buck Winters?"

These questions had been directed more or less toward Emma Winters, Buck's dowdy missus, a poor actress and a worse wife, who was gazing up with limpid puppy-dog eyes at Johnny. "I don't know," she said, not even glancing at Helbig. "I don't know where he is. Still delivering the mail, I suppose."

"We'll work around him," Helbig announced tartly. He held both hands up high like a man under arrest. "OK. Act Two, Scene Two. The hooded figure of Death is warning the villagers of impending doom, but they're all preoccupied with other things."

"You know," Emma said to Johnny, turning her voice into a sultry Eartha Kitt purr, "I've always had an absolute passion for football players."

"I'm baseball, ma'am," Johnny said.

"I like baseball players, too."

"All right!" Helbig said, actually laying his wiry hands on various people around him, urging them one way and another. "Let's go. Let's roll. Let's show Johnny Black the kind of talent—Johnny, why don't you take a seat right here—kind of talent we have at Your Town and the sort of commitment— Delbert, get on up there now—sort of commitment we have to making our community an even better ... Emma?... a place where each and every ... Emma, you sit over here, OK? No, no, over here, away from Johnny. There you go...."

Perfection was content to sit, even though the chair he sat in felt as if it'd been hacked from granite. No theatre buff, he wasn't even sure why he was here, unless maybe Helbig was angling to hit him up for a tax-deductible donation to keep this struggling little enterprise afloat. Yes, that was probably it; what else could it be?

Johnny was feeling pretty strung out. Like many others, he'd become increasingly attuned to, and bothered by, some of the incredible stories being reported in the media. Never one to worry much about current events (he had the notion that Palestinians were Middle Easterners who lived in palaces), he had, however, maintained a longstanding and rather juvenile interest in the paranormal—aliens, angels, space travel, time travel and the like. Hardly the brand of topics that tended to get splashed across the front pages of the nation's newspapers—until recently, that is. Now that they were dominating the news, and in a nerve-tingling way, Johnny felt at once fascinated, vindicated, frightened and well-informed. What did it all mean?

But he had other issues perturbing his mind as well. Earlier today he'd gotten another call from his one-time girlfriend Wanda, the mother of his runaway daughter Sarah. For once, he didn't hang up on her. He didn't say much, but he did do her the courtesy of listening. Her voice had a sad and haunting quality about it—he'd heard the same compelling sounds in certain pieces of country music—and for a while at least it'd held his attention. She reminded him of where she was staying (not too far from Perfection Fitness) and asked him to stop by. Said she simply wanted to see him once again. To spend some time with him. It had nothing to do with money, she claimed; money was the farthest thing from her mind. Of course, Johnny well knew from his past business dealings that when someone insisted it wasn't about money, it was *always* about money.

Nevertheless, he did listen. Those notes in her voice, like the song of a wounded angel ... He wanted to ask about Sarah—had Wanda heard from her lately? Where was Sarah living? How was she living? But pride told him to keep his mouth shut, and, as was usually the case with pride, he obeyed.

Two hours later came a second call, not from Wanda but from someone he'd never heard of. Laura Kennedy. Some reporter out there in La-La Land.

Johnny was at the gym at the time, puttering around, trying to avoid Helbig, taking glum note of how sharply business had fallen off in just the past few days. Yet his bar business was booming—more robust than ever. He gathered that in acutely distressed times people had more faith in alcohol, a short-term investment, than in exercise, a long-term investment. If you were convinced that the world was about to be shattered like a fine crystal goblet dropped on a hardwood floor, what the hell good was fitness? Johnny himself was a strong believer in alcohol, regardless of the times.

The phone rang, and Johnny picked it up. When he understood the young woman's voice in his ear belonged to a West Coast reporter, he bridled a bit.

"Listen," he said, "I got nothing to say about a comeback. Period. That's all just rumors and speculation."

"Comeback?" Laura said. "What comeback?"

"*My* comeback. The one I've been working on now for a coupla months."

"I wasn't—"

"Rumors and speculation."

"I wasn't calling about that."

"Oh."

Laura drew a breath, tried to assert herself. "You know," she said, "you're a hard man to track down."

Beginning to wish he'd let someone else answer the phone, Johnny stared off into the deep recesses of his mostly empty gym. "Not hard enough, apparently."

"But if I can find you, I think your daughter can too."

"My daughter."

"Sarah Black is your daughter, right?"

"Hey, listen, I don't—"

"She's on her way, Mr. Black. To Illinois. She'll be looking for you. And if she finds you—"

"Looking for me." Johnny felt as if he were back in high school toiling to solve an algebra problem on the board. Dark passages, tough going.

"That's right. If she finds you, I don't know what she might do. I don't know what happened between the two of you—"

"Not too sure myself."

"But I spoke to her recently, and I think she may try to ..."

"What."

"Hurt you."

Johnny paused. "Even more, you mean, than she already has?"

"Yes."

He mulled over the possibility. "She say why?"

"No."

"How do you know her?" he said. "Where did—"

But the phone went dead. The voice, which hadn't been at all unfriendly despite its dire message, was gone.

In the theatre, maybe fifteen feet in front of where Helbig and Johnny sat in the dimness, three actors stood close together, scripts in hand. Taking turns, they were reading aloud a segment of Helbig's play that used to be called *Death and Destruction* but now, thanks to Ben Temple, the old son of a bitch, had no title at all. Their voices were dull and inflectionless; whether this was by design or from lack of guidance or talent Johnny didn't know. Occasionally there were long breaks in the dialog during which the actors just stood there eyeing the sparse audience while the sparse audience eyed them back. Helbig seemed satisfied with this feature, so clearly it was deliberate. Yet there were other aspects of the presentation that did draw his unfiltered criticism.

"Speak up!" he might say. "From the diaphragm, from the diaphragm!" Or "Enunciate! Enunciate!"

The dialog itself was anything but transparent. As Johnny sat there, half-listening, half-thinking about those peculiar phone calls, he heard a series of dark, twisted sequences that seemed torn from some fever-induced night terror:

"Pain and suffering. By God. By God."

"What's found is lost."

"Who dunnit?"

"Help. Help me. I can't, I—"

"Sez you!"

"What's life anyway? Fatuity! The F-word."

"I got blisters on my fingers!"

"John Lennon."

"Vladimir Lenin."

"We need to end all this ... termination."

"We need to ... terminate this ending."

"Hold my head. I'm going to vomit."

"All right, OK. Here's what. Let's hoist this bloody body, men, and we'll carry it athwart the heath ..."

But at this point the actor who'd spoken last—it was Delbert, who ran an unsuccessful dollar store—abandoned his character, took an exasperated step toward Helbig and said: "Man, I can't say that word."

"What word?" Helbig asked.

"Athwart."

"You just said it."

"But it sounded artificial," Delbert protested, "when I said it. I won't say it anymore."

"Don't think about it," Helbig said with some weariness. "Just say it."

"Man, I can't. It sticks to my tongue."

"Just spit it out, Delbert."

"Don't even sound like English, you ask me. Sounds like Martian."

Johnny considered this whole theatrical episode fairly Martian and was debating whether or not to say so when something remarkable happened. A loud banging and clattering noise came from somewhere in the back; it sounded as if someone, in a fit of rage, had taken a wooden chair and flung it viciously against a wall, the chair then making harsh contact with several brittle objects on its explosive rebound. Grumbling and swearing noises came next, the voice deep and guttural, like the grunts of a wild boar. Then Buck Winters, full-time mailman and part-time actor, came storming onstage, eyes aflame, fists clenched, his every movement sudden and threatening.

"You're all lost!" he shouted, his sweeping hand gesture indicating he meant everyone before him. "You're a bunch of lost souls!"

Instantly the audience reacted with a collective gasp, a kind of shrinking back from an assault. Even Johnny felt newly alert and somewhat intimidated.

"We're all gonna die," Buck shouted, "and you just sit there twiddling your thumbs! Playing a game! Theatre! Spectacle! Entertainment!"

Abruptly Helbig sprang up and shouted back at him, his own voice with the high screeching quality of a buzz saw: "You got your nerve! Who the hell do you think *you* are? You come in here spouting your blockhead opinions—"

"Your life's not worth a bucket of fresh cow manure, my friend!" Buck, who had taken several steps toward Helbig, was pointing a thick index finger straight at him. Johnny sat up in alarm. "But you're too damn stupid and self-centered to know it!"

"The hell with you!" Helbig shouted, even louder than before. The cords in his neck were popping out. "You get the hell outta here! Get outta here now, and take your goddam Chicken Little opinions with you! And don't come back!"

For a tense moment, Buck stood fuming on the very edge of the stage as if deliberating over whether or not to plunge physically into the scant shadowy audience after Helbig, who, like a bantam rooster, defiantly stood his ground. Then—suddenly—in the same rough manner that'd marked his entrance, Buck swung away and stalked offstage, disappearing into the wings. Seconds later, ugly concussive noises rang out from back there.

Then silence.

Then a smattering of applause that soon grew fuller and louder. Even Johnny found himself clapping for this bright little gemlike moment in the rehearsal.

Helbig sat down and held his triangular head in his hands. Johnny nudged him with his elbow.

"Dude," Johnny said, "that was terrific. I didn't know you could write like that."

Helbig said nothing.

"Did you hear me? I didn't know you could write like that."

"I didn't write it," Helbig said.

"You didn't! Who did?"

"Nobody wrote it," Helbig said.

"Oh my." Johnny inspected a fingernail on his pitching hand. "So, uh ... so what just happened was ... was for real?"

Helbig stared at the floor.

"Sorry, Dunk." Johnny gave him a light punch on the shoulder. "Hey, I liked some of the play, too."

Having absorbed his fair share of culture for the day, Johnny stood up, and a number of thoughts sparked through his mind. He thought of consoling Helbig further by making an offer of financial support to the theatre. He let that thought pass. He considered advising Helbig that something needed to be done about the stony seats and about the front door that'd jammed on them when they first arrived. He let those thoughts pass as well. In the end, he cordially invited the brooding Helbig to stop by the bar later that evening, knowing of course he wouldn't; he never did.

Making his way toward the exit, Johnny found his path blocked by a slim straw-haired fellow with sincere watery eyes. It was Delbert.

"I gotta tell you," Delbert said. "That game you pitched against the Yankees? I watched it on TV. Man, that was the most beautiful thing I ever seen in my life."

"Thank you," Johnny said.

"Bottom of the ninth, just three hitters to go ..." Delbert's voice, which was usually firm and reliable, had become a little breathless. "What'd it feel like?"

Johnny smiled.

"Three outs from perfection," Delbert said. "From immortality. Yankee Stadium. The Bronx Bombers. What was it like?"

Johnny's smile widened. Goosebumps collected on his forearms. "Well, I'll tell you," he said. "It was like this...."

* * *

That evening Johnny's Place was filled to capacity. As he peered out at the crowd from behind the bar, Johnny was struck by the number of new faces he saw—men and women, young and old, smartly groomed and unkempt. It was as if some special magnet had drawn them in—something beyond the magic of Johnny's personal glow; beyond the companionship of fellow humans and the succor promised by cold beer and premium booze. Then again, maybe some arcane force outside was *pushing* people in—driving them to seek shelter, however flimsy or fleeting, as if from a cloudburst.

It was a quiet crowd, too, Johnny noticed, thoughtful and anxious. Since Johnny's Place had been set up along the lines of Joe Namath's legendary old saloon Bachelors III, a nightspot where gambling, sexual license and all-around loose living were not only tolerated but encouraged, the uneasy quiet was abnormal.

And while Johnny's own mood had improved considerably since his escape from the Your Town Theatre, he too felt subdued. Tomorrow he'd put on a pitching exhibition for pro scout Frank Dutwell; if all went well, Johnny might soon find himself back in the big leagues. He'd just received word that last quarter Hipsley's Iced Tea, popularized by an ad campaign starring Perfection himself, had set a new sales record. And thus far, unlike many around him—some of whom sat in this very bar, huddled mutely over their drinks—Johnny had seen no terrible face in the sky. All these facts should've been making him feel downright giddy, he guessed. But they weren't.

Icy Scotch at his elbow, Johnny let his eyes roam the crowd. He did spy a few regulars. Scattered about were a half-dozen lovely young ladies he'd bedded in recent months; their names were unclear to him just now. Over there was big Bubba Schnitzer, who held a membership to Perfection Fitness. To his credit, Bubba was restricting himself this evening to Michelob Ultra. Over here sat Trevor Null, a local politician; like Johnny, Null was knocking back the hard stuff. At a booth sat Johnny's old pal Bob Stallings, the college professor. Surprisingly, Stallings was in high spirits, having said something about how the stock market, which had collapsed into a screaming nosedive, had made him a pile of money. Even more surprisingly, Stallings was drinking nothing more potent than Hipsley's Iced Tea. On the other hand, the guy seated with him—someone named Jenson, another prof—was swilling Jack Daniels at a pace that might politely be described as 'energetic.' Behind the bar, of course, actively managing what Johnny merely oversaw, was Abdul Abbas. An extremely dependable employee, tall and dark-skinned, the short-spoken Abdul had been in a dour mood since his wife left him four years ago for a fertilizer salesman.

Seated at the bar within close range of Johnny was Frank Dutwell, who would soon bring his aged but expert eye to bear on Johnny's current pitching skills, such as they may be. Dutwell was hunched over, working on an imported beer and a large bowl of honey mustard potato chips (everything on the house, naturally). In his mid-sixties, he had close-cropped white hair, a yellowish stare that could penetrate lead, and a massive beak of a nose, this combination making him look something like a bald eagle. Facially he appeared even older than his years, but he moved around with startling spryness, and would've matched up well in this regard with Associate Dean Bill Yommer.

When Dutwell first arrived at the bar, Johnny introduced him as a pitching scout who was there to evaluate some local talent. Exactly who the local talent was he didn't mention. The crowd, heavily composed of sports fans, was impressed, and Dutwell, sensing a friendly audience, launched into a spiel about what a scout looks for in a pitching prospect.

"Any number of factors," he said, pacing back and forth, talonlike hands in motion. "Course, you wanna see the heater. And it's not only gotta have velocity—ninety-plus, minimum— it's gotta have movement, 'cause what good's any fastball if it's straight as a goddam McDermott pool cue?"

He talked about delivery (mechanics should be smooth, not too much stress on the arm itself), aggressiveness (the great ones are never afraid to work inside) and control ("It's like real estate," he said. "Location, location, location").

"Now, some things you can teach," Dutwell lectured, "and some things you can't. You can teach a pitcher how to field his position. You can teach him how to hold a runner on first." He paused, and swept the crowd with a stare that left them feeling scorched. "But you can't teach a guy how to be talented, OK? You can't teach him how to throw ninety-plus. He either can or he can't; it's God-given." He looped his scrawny arm up and around Johnny's sloping shoulders. "This man right here," he said, "threw *ninety-six* miles an hour—in high school! Ladies and gentlemen, nobody taught him that; I certainly didn't. It was God-given."

While his critics would've said that there were many things Johnny should've been taught but unfortunately wasn't, for now no one spoke. Even Johnny simply bowed his head in modesty. After offering a few more desultory comments, Dutwell retired to his barstool, to his beer and potato chips, and the room became generally quiet and solemn. It was as if a dank and dreary fog had wafted in from outside, muffling all color and sound.

No music was playing; Johnny had unplugged the jukebox. But he did have several huge TVs going, and not a ballgame on any one of them. Instead, most every channel was presenting some sort of discussion and analysis of the weird events— flying lights, vanished buildings and people, claims of a fantastic face in the sky—that had lately aroused such an anxiety among the public. Those in the bar, Johnny included, gave the oceanic TVs some serious attention.

Theories concerning what was afoot were plentiful and easy to come by. Everybody seemed to have one, and everybody was giving them away free of cost. Some of the theories seemed better developed and more plausible than others.

On TV now was a Father Menendez, who, in his priestly garb, was expounding in a thick Spanish accent on religious apparitions and especially on the one known as Our Lady of Guadalupe. It seems that in the winter of 1531 on a hill near Mexico City a man named Juan Diego encountered a teenage girl who was enveloped in a shimmering field of light. When, speaking in the local tongue, she requested that a church be built nearby in her honor, Diego understood she was the Virgin Mary. He reported the event to his superior, Bishop Zumárraga, not the most gullible of men, who asked for proof of her identity. So Diego met with the girl again, and she instructed him to gather some Castillian roses from the top of the hill. Since no such roses grew in the area and since it was

winter anyhow, Diego figured he'd come up empty-handed.
But he didn't—the roses were there. He then delivered them to
the Bishop, at which point they both discovered that an image
of the Virgin had somehow become emblazoned on Diego's
tilma, or cloak. That cloak, still bearing the miraculous image,
exists to this day, Menendez said.

The implication was clear: the face in the sky was a
religious apparition. It wasn't unthinkable. Yet the two types of
apparition, then and now, were so strikingly different that most
of those in Johnny's Place seemed even more skeptical than
Zumárraga had been. But since no one wanted to be seen as
rude or disrespectful when it came to religion, no one had
much to say.

Switching the channel with his remote control, Johnny
came to another accented man (German, this time) who,
pressing his fingertips together pensively, was arguing that the
face in the sky was a 'volumetric display.' In other words, a
three-dimensional image artificially projected. The man, a
physicist according to the caption at the bottom of the screen,
had a knowledge of volumetric displays that seemed
monumental, and he sprinkled his talk with references to depth
cues, voxels, rotational and translational motion, and, most
disturbingly, 'dead zones.' The man to whom he was speaking,
the host of the program, wanted to know if the technology
existed to bring off such a spectacular and convincing trick as
an immense moving face in the sky—and to do so repeatedly
in countless locations.

"Well," the physicist hedged, "who knows what's possible?
Who really knows?"

"And what agency would be responsible for this ...
mischief?"

The man just shrugged as if to say his previous answer was
still in effect.

"People are claiming," the host said, "that the face talks.
How do you account for that?"

A shake of the leonine head, another shrug, a shift in the

cushioned chair. "I'm interested in visuals. I don't know about audio."

At this, a sizable portion of the crowd in the bar began to jeer openly.

"Some people are saying they could *feel* the face's breath when it spoke to them. Any explanation?"

The physicist scratched the back of his neck for a moment. "The wind?" he suggested.

People in the bar erupted into catcalls and obscenities, and before somebody was tempted to fire a shot glass at one of his top-of-the-line TVs, Johnny once again changed the channel.

Another scientist, this one a woman, rimless glasses, hair tied back in a severe bun, and she was giving voice to what many already suspected and feared—that the planet Earth was in contact with extraterrestrial life. Or vice versa. Obviously this contact did not seem to be unfolding in a manner that favored Earth.

"We may be dealing," she said grimly, "with a K2 or K3 civilization."

Echoing the puzzled murmurs in the bar, a voice onscreen said: "K2? K3? I'm not sure I ..."

"I'm alluding," she said, her voice with more ice in it than Johnny's Scotch, "to the Kardashev Scale. It's a way of measuring how technologically advanced a civilization is. A K2 civilization would be capable of harnessing all the power available from a single star. Think of it. A K3 civilization could harness all the power of a galaxy! By comparison, of course, Earth is not yet at K1."

After a pause, her questioner said: "But surely any civilization so advanced would be friendly toward us. In a ... a grandfatherly way. Sensitive. Respectful. Caring."

"Not necessarily," she said crisply. "Such aliens may have nothing in common with us at all. They may not even be life as we would recognize it."

"Not ... I'm sorry. As we would ...?"

"Who's to say they're even carbon-based, as we are?"

When she turned her narrow head at an angle, light flared from her glasses as if shot from a ray gun. "It's been speculated," she said, "that plasma life, composed of magnetic forces, could live *inside a star.* Millions of degrees! Think of it. At the other extreme, on a super-chilled wasteland of a planet, it's conceivable that life could emerge that's based on hydrogen and helium."

"Really."

"Yes. So what would any of these creatures look like? How would they think and behave? I have no idea, but something tells me they may not have the same values we have."

"You mean they may not relate to democracy, for example. Or Christianity ... or baseball ..."

The woman chuckled. "They may not relate to Earth."

Johnny could've done without that vaguely insulting mention of his sport, and indeed without the rest of it. He felt depressed; probably the others did too. He toyed with the idea of replugging the jukebox and cranking up some rock 'n' roll but wasn't confident that this tactic would accomplish anything. Instead, he kept the TVs on but squelched the volume, giving people a chance to process—or forget—what they'd just heard. Most of it was probably hot air anyway.

"Next round's on me," he called out. "If we're gonna get invaded, we best be fortified."

Nobody laughed or even brightened up. In fact, over by the booth occupied by Stallings and Jenson, two young guys were standing almost nose-to-nose, snarling at each other and apparently ready to fight. Now a third guy came hurrying over—Johnny knew none of them—and tried to intercede. Suddenly a punch was thrown and then a couple more.

"Hey!" Johnny yelled. He was stunned. No one fought in his bar; people got shellacked, but they did so with decorum.

The three guys had seized hold of each other, and more joined in; a mass of bodies lurched one way and another. Feisty old Frank Dutwell jumped into the mix while the burly Abdul hurtled toward the trouble spot like a torpedo. In the booth,

Stallings seemed confused and flustered; Jenson, much more relaxed, was doing everything he could to shield his drink from harm.

Recovering himself, Johnny leaped over the bar in one athletic bound and landed square amid the brawlers. People pawed at him, and he pawed back.

"HEY!" he bellowed with all his strength. "THAT'S ENOUGH!" Had everyone gone mad? "THAT'S ENOUGH, I SAID! HEY!"

15

FOR SARAH, a journey of two thousand miles began with a single peal of the wheels. The trip figured to take thirty hours if she drove nonstop, but the way she was streaking along she might get there yesterday. Six hundred and fifty rambunctious horses lived beneath the hood of her cherry red Corvette, and she had most of them galloping hard most of the time. She drove 60 mph in town, 120 mph on the freeway, and 200 mph in her raucous pounding heart.

Happily for her, the cops so far all seemed to be somewhere else; these days reckless drivers were the least of their worries. While she had no drugs in the car for a change, she did have the gun. She also carried with her the damning label 'person of interest' following the shooting death of Derek Wolf. So blazing across the country like a roaring red UFO did not reflect careful conservative thinking on her part. But then being careful and conservative weren't qualities she'd ever been known for anyhow.

Though they weren't foremost in her thoughts as she drove, Sarah knew about the stories and far-fetched rumors that had the public in a tizzy. She'd glimpsed some headlines, caught some news on the radio, heard some people talking. Lotta weird shit, all right. She also had the scary intuition that society, in her view not too stable to begin with, was being pressured in ways that might tilt it or even topple it. Glancing left, she saw a blue-and-white high-rise wrapped in shuddering orange flames. No fire trucks, no police.

Personally, she hadn't seen any face in the sky; somehow she doubted she would. On the other hand, if she did see such a face, it wouldn't be all that far removed, she judged, from some of the other outlandish sights she'd seen in her day. When you make a career of porn, you see things routinely that are a tad outside the ordinary. She wondered what she might say to the face if it appeared to her and began making all kinds of harrowing pronouncements. Though she'd listen for a while out of curiosity and courtesy, eventually she'd feel obligated to say something back. It was her nature.

But she didn't think the face was real; it was all a hoax or a myth. People liked to tell stories. They liked to be amused and entertained—hell, if they didn't, there'd be no porn. She didn't believe in ghosts or apparitions, and didn't have much faith in aliens either (except the illegal kind that sneaked across the Mexican border; she'd worked with some of those). She'd read about the Fermi Paradox, which stated basically: If the universe is full of life—as exobiologists would have us believe—then where's the supporting evidence? There really wasn't any—no TV or radio signals from above, no artifacts down below. Nor was she convinced that God was behind it all, or that God even existed. If He did exist, He ran a pretty loose ship, from what she could tell. Why had He made such a gunky mess of things?

As she was exiting California, plowing into Nevada, she received a call from her lawyer, Ernesto Cruz. She considered it unwise to take the call, but she did listen to his recorded message.

"Zoey," he said, "my God, where are you? What happened?

"I would've called you before this, but I was upset by the ... the disturbance at your place. Knocked down and out, you might say.

"And I was hoping you might call *me*, or stop by.

"Listen," he said, "I know more about that guy than I let on. Eric ... Derek. I know the kinda trouble he was. Whatever happened, however it went down, I know who's to blame.

"Don't do anything you'll regret, OK? Or anything more, if you already have. Christ, you know what I mean.

"Take care of yourself, Zoey. And remember I'm here if you need me.

"*Adios* for now, *mi chica. Mi rayito de luz.*"

Dropping the phone on the leather-trimmed seat next to her, she nearly smiled. That Ernie, she thought. He was quite a character. And a very sweet guy. A father figure to her.

Too bad her actual father hadn't been more of a father figure to her. The bastard.

Truth was, she hadn't seen either of her parents in close to four years. But while she'd cut off contact completely with her father, she'd kept up a dribble of communication—sporadic, dutiful, unfulfilling—with her mother.

In some ways Wanda had been more of a challenge and a mystery to her than had her father. Not truly trained or educated for anything, Wanda had zigzagged through a series of middling jobs, none of which had much to do with any of the others. She'd been a beautician, a cook, a real estate rep, an aromatherapist, even a fully made-up clown at little kids' parties. Sometimes she'd been unemployed for long stretches, and Sarah, without being asked, had sent her money. Certainly Wanda's health issues had been a factor there—the diabetes, the depression. Of course the habitual relocations, which had slowed in recent years but hadn't ceased, made her difficult to track. Doubly so when she forgot or refused to pay her phone bill, which did happen.

Finding Wanda by phone was one thing; actually talking to her was another. For if Sarah's father felt Wanda was too ungrounded, too ditzy and too open-minded, she was still old-fashioned enough to be displeased with the reality that her cherub of a daughter, so pure and innocent, had grown up to be not just an adult film actress but the notorious Princess of Porn. Sarah had told her straight out, and Wanda had told her straight back that she didn't like it. Told her with some emphasis. So having a conversation about Sarah's work was risky, painful and pretty much impossible.

Another potentially rich topic of conversation would've been Johnny 'Jet' Black. Perfection, who cast such a long and dark shadow across both their lives. But while each woman craved to discuss him, and in minute technicolor detail, neither could bear the thought of allowing him any more space in her world than he'd already arrogated. Each of them would've said vehemently that he was the main reason she was what she was, and it wouldn't have been high praise. As he did with everyone else, Johnny drew intensely mixed reviews from his own family, but they generally went unspoken.

So what then did Sarah and her mother talk about when they decided to talk? Not much, as a rule.

Strangely, she'd always loved her father more than she did her mother, and, later on, she hated him more too. When she was a toddler, everything was ideal—or that's how she remembered it now. Sometimes, goofing around, he'd pick her up by her ankles and swing her in circles, gently, carefully. Though the game unnerved her mother, Sarah delighted in it. She liked being upside down. Down was up, left was right, all the blood rushing to her little head, making it feel tight and full like a water balloon. Then she might climb on his back and play horsey for a while, Johnny's long strapping body making him seem as big as an actual thoroughbred. When she got older, he'd play catch with her and occasionally take her to the ballpark where she met his friends, grinning dark-skinned men with names that sounded like miniature songs unto themselves: Aurelio, Santiago, Alejandro, Julio, Orpheus, Zyshonne.... They picked her up and held her, much as Johnny did, and she liked it.

But the older she got, the less she saw of her father, and when puberty transfigured her, she began seeking him out in the form of other boys, other men. Many of them physically resembled Johnny  tall, handsome, dark-haired, athletic. Yet some of them didn't. Looking back on those years, she saw that the pattern wasn't as perfect as she wanted it to be.

Certainly the pattern didn't apply to Mr. Rutter, the high school guidance counselor with whom Sarah was required to meet once a week after being busted for Ecstasy. (She never liked the name 'Ecstasy' for MDMA, which made her feel warm and calm but never ecstatic, and would've therefore supported a name change to either 'Warm' or 'Calm.') Mr. Rutter was a shrimpy gentleman with a full mane of lawless pewter hair, a pinched florid face and the sex drive of someone three decades younger. He kept a large color photo of his wife and kids on his cheap metal desk, and kept his hand on Sarah's knee even as he counseled her in his soft gravelly voice about the dangers of drug use. Sarah paid more attention to his hand than to his words, and, to her amazement, found herself becoming aroused right there in his out-of-the-way office, which, in all honesty, could've been even more out-of-the-way than it was for what she—they—had in mind.

How would Mr. Rutter react, she wondered, if she placed her hand on *his* knee, and then slowly slid it up his inner thigh, farther and farther, until ...? Only one way to find out.

She expected she might get caught, expected she might get into trouble, expected she might even go to jail. She didn't expect (and neither did he, one would bet) that she'd get pregnant, though she did. Some deep rattling aftershocks all around on that one. Thank God that three months into the pregnancy she miscarried. Blood, blood, blood—but given the impropriety of it all, it was better than having the baby.

By the time Sarah got to Harris Community College, she saw her father only now and then. He was there but not there (not all that different from her mother, actually, whose skittering movements were starting to build a distance between Wanda and her newly independent daughter). The only person Sarah could count on with some confidence was her friend Kayla.

She met Kayla in high school about the time word was being whispered through the classrooms and hallways that Sarah was pregnant and that the father-to-be was not a student. With her cascading blond curls and lithe delectable body, Kayla was almost as attractive as Sarah and perhaps even less inhibited. Which was saying something. They shopped together, studied together (exactly once), and partied together.

In the absence of other diversions, they would talk to each other for hours on end, usually about guys. Since both girls had proven themselves to be adventurous with the opposite sex, they had a wealth of material to discuss. Kayla admitted that she had a thing for older guys, and she could understand why Sarah had gotten involved with Mr. Rutter, even if Sarah never could. From what Sarah could tell, Kayla had a thing for *most* guys—old, young, tall, short, white, black. Even the disabled. She was an equal opportunity slut. But Sarah had little room to criticize, so she didn't.

She didn't, that is, until one evening when Kayla showed up to a bluegrass concert at HCC in the company of Sarah's own father, Johnny Black. Attending the show by herself, Sarah was speechless when she first saw them in the lobby purchasing tickets and acting for all the world like a 'couple.' When speech finally came to her, it was the stricken appalled oh-my-God type, and she flounced right over to them.

"What the hell do you think you're doing?" she shrilled at them both. They were surrounded by knots of people.

Arm in arm, Johnny and Kayla blinked at her innocently.

"You can't do this!" Sarah hissed. Though it was unclear which person she was addressing, it was Johnny who spoke up.

"Do what?" he said.

"This!"

"Why not?" he asked.

"She's my best friend!"

"So?"

"She's eighteen years old!"

"So?"

Surreally, banjos were beginning to twang merrily in the distance. Sarah leaned as close to Johnny as she could and spat out her next words ferociously.

"She's a slut!" Sarah said. "And I think my father can do better."

"Now, hold on just a second," he came to life, poking his finger at her. "You got no business insulting the woman that

I— Come back here! Any woman that I choose to date
deserves a little more, a little— Sarah!"

But as the banjo music accelerated, so did Sarah—through
the oppressive stares in the lobby, out into the dappling
moonlight, and off soon enough to the deliberately
nondescript film studios that pepper the hot dry San Fernando
Valley.

Never once did she think *He can spend time with my sleazy
friend but not with me.* Nor did she think *If he wants a slut, I'll give
him a slut all right*, but she could have.

She could have.

Whipping eastward in the 'Vette, the car eating up miles as
a shark would devour teeny fish, Sarah supposed she must be
somewhere in the broad vicinity of the Bonneville Salt Flats. It
was a place where, just for the hell of it, high-spirited men and
women came to drive sleek rocketlike cars at world record
speeds. To her, right about now, it sounded like a great idea. So
she cranked up the radio—the Doors were playing
"Roadhouse Blues"—and pressed her right foot clear to the
floor. The ZO6 roared as if in orgasm, and the scarlet speed-
needle fell to the right like a tree collapsing in a forest.

\* \* \*

Much later.

Not especially tired but hungry and restless, Sarah pulled
into the dirt parking lot of a plain-looking roadside diner. In
the lot she noted two pickup trucks and one mud-spattered
jeep. Yes, a bustling place. It was early evening (or was it early
morning? She'd lost track of the time), and the sky was gray
and lifeless. A lone arc light, very old, hung above her, offering
minimal illumination, while a splash more light, this the color
of a cheese omelet, shone from the window at the front of the
small rickety wooden building. The sign above the door read
Winer-N-Diner.

She parked her car and sat back in the bucket seat and

smiled at her own contrariness. All the restaurants she passed along the way, some of them quite nice, and she winds up at the Winer-N-Diner! Well, she wasn't in the mood for *haute cuisine* anyway, she guessed, and Jack Kerouac would've approved her selection.

Opening the car door, Sarah discovered that a young man was standing next to her, just inches away.

"How do?" he said mildly.

The man's face was abstracted and yet focused at the same time; his stare, which he'd locked on Sarah's face, seemed to be coming from a great distance away. His hair was long, dirty-blond and greasy, and his gray muscle shirt was streaked and spotted with random black stains.

She tried to yank the door closed, but in one swift movement he blocked it with his hip and leg.

"Nice ride you got here," he said. His voice, like his stare, was intimate but seemed to be coming from far away.

"I like it."

"*Real* nice ride." He licked his lips. "You're a good-lookin' girl," he said.

She glanced around. They were alone. If she screamed, no one would hear.

"Thanks."

For a while he said nothing, just held his position. Motionless. He seemed, silently, to be engaged in some crude calculation, weighing one possibility against another.

"Say," he started again, "you wouldn't ... you wouldn't ..."

"No," she said. "I wouldn't."

He nodded, apparently neither pleased nor displeased. Probably it was the answer he'd anticipated.

"I want you to gimme somethin'," he said. "I ain't particular about what it is. But I want somethin'."

Like him, Sarah didn't move much. Her violet gaze was as steady and remote as the gaze that pressed down on her.

"What," she said.

With an effort, his eyes swung away from her to the blue

purse on the seat next to her.

"What's in that there pocketbook?"

She looked at it without expression. "Nothing."

"Open it up. Lemme see."

She nodded, reached over slowly and picked it up.

"Open it," he said.

Carefully she unzipped it, reached in and brought out the Beretta. She flicked off the safety with her thumb and pointed the weapon at his face, causing his mouth to slacken with dull surprise.

Without a word he backed away from the car as Sarah emerged from it, still holding the gun at his face. She motioned for him to go around to the other side of the vehicle, its cooling metal ticking like a clock. He went where he was directed, and she went with him. Here, they were even less conspicuous than they had been.

"Get down," she told him.

"How's that?" He looked bewildered.

"Get down," she said. "On your knees."

He tried to laugh; it was a sick little snorting sound, devoid of cheer. "Listen, lady," he said. "Ma'am. I was just funnin' with you, OK? Just ... They ain't no ... you got no call—"

"Get down," she said. "Or I'll kill you where you stand."

Something in her voice told him she was dead serious, and, after taking a second or two to choose the precise spot, he dropped to his knees in the dirt.

She stood in front of him. To him, the gun's maw looked so big he could've fallen down inside it.

"Sing me a song," she said. He raised his eyebrows slightly. "And not just any song, either. I want something wholesome and happy. Quintessentially American. How about 'Take Me Out to the Ballgame'—do you know it?"

He shook his head no. On the road, a garbage truck drove by.

"I'll help you then," she said. "Follow my lead." She lifted her clear voice in melody. "Take me out to the ballgame ... Sing it."

He sang the line. Not very well.

"Take me out to the crowd ..."

Again he sang. Part of his ravaged mind was beginning to recognize even now that he'd never experienced anything like this before; that even if he lived through it, he would never know anything like it again. The recognition brought with it a kind of wonder.

"Buy me some peanuts and crackerjack ..."

This time, before he could respond, she pushed the gun's muzzle deep into his mouth. "Sing," she said.

Cautiously he moved his head left and right, no more than half an inch, and grunted to indicate that he was unable to do what she wanted.

"Sing," she repeated. "You can do it if you try. I want you to try."

He paused, collected himself and did as he was told. The quality of his singing, well shy of operatic before the gun penetrated his mouth, was even less impressive now. Yet Sarah seemed to appreciate it.

She prompted him: "I don't care if I never come back!"

"I boam pare ib I bebber pum bap...."

In this manner they completed the rest of the song.

She removed the gun from his mouth. "Get up," she said, and he rose. "Now—I want you to walk down the road. That way." She gestured with the gun. "Walk until you're sure I'm not here anymore. If you're not sure, keep walking until you *are* sure."

His breath coming in shallow gasps, he nodded, brushed off his pants at the knees, and began to walk, hands floating somewhat at his sides.

But he hadn't gone ten steps when suddenly he wheeled around, his eyes lit with an excited, almost crazed, defiance.

"Who the hell do you think you're foolin'?" he shouted, his voice high and desperate. "Huh? I know better. I know ... That damn gun ..."

"Excuse me?" She hadn't moved, and didn't move now.

"That gun ain't even loaded. I knew that. I knew that all along, goddammit. You think ..." His hands were raised like those of a frenzied preacher in mid-sermon. "You think you can fool somebody, but lemme tell you," and he took a step toward her.

"One of these trucks belong to you?" she asked.

The question, unexpected as it was, stopped him, confounded him. "Why?" he said.

"That one, maybe?" She bobbed her head at an old rusted-out Dodge.

"Mebbe."

Her first shot blew out the right headlight. Glass tinkled. Once again, the man seemed surprised and displeased. Her second shot destroyed the left headlight. Then, without comment, she put the gun back on him.

His entire body slumped as if in formal surrender. "Yes, ma'am," he said simply. "Yes, ma'am." He bowed his head, turned away very slowly and began to walk into the ashy grayness. This time he kept on walking.

After the ruckus, Sarah expected to receive company, but no one appeared. All was quiet. She climbed back into her Corvette and fired it up, its gruff rumble a welcome sound. A different eatery might suit her better after all, she decided. She threw her 'nice ride' into gear, backed up and pulled out fast, sending up a cloud of dust.

Her hunger gnawed at her.

16

"KEEP YOUR SHIRT ON, dude," Johnny said by cell phone to Frank Dutwell, who was already at the HCC ball field awaiting the pitcher's arrival. "In fact, keep all your clothes on. I'll be there in five minutes." Johnny gave his black pickup some extra gas, not that it needed any, just as he slammed over a series of craterlike potholes in the road.

Bang bang bang bang bang bang *bang!* BOOM!

Yeah, buddy, Johnny thought. Keep that double-wishbone suspension and those heavy-duty shocks from getting flabby.

He was pretty sure he'd detected a trace of impatience in Dutwell's scratchy old voice just now, and it saddened Johnny. Because whose fault was it that the three of them—young Danny Pepper too—were going to arrive at the diamond at three distinct times? Not Johnny's, certainly. He'd offered to chauffeur them, but Dutwell had booked a room right next to the school, and Danny, a student, was on-site anyhow. It just wouldn't have worked. So it was very likely, then, that three different guys, given three different starting points, would show up at three different times. And one of them, Johnny for example, would have to be last.

Still, he did feel fretful and guilty at running behind schedule. In the modern world everything, even baseball, had a political dimension, and you ignored it at your own peril. Years ago when he'd retired from the sport, he hadn't been forced out so much by diminishing skills (even though they *were* diminishing) as by politics. At long last, after one untoward incident on top of another and another, Johnny's bad boy reputation had made him too hot to handle; he had to go. Nowadays, even he reluctantly admitted he could see Major League Baseball's point of view, staid though it might be. What the hell had he been thinking that night he mooned the home plate umpire at U.S. Cellular Field, and then mooned the entire crowd, many of whom had supported him over the years?

He fed his truck some more gas. No, showing up late this morning for the pitching demo wouldn't help his cause any.

But there was a whole side of life, the subtler side, that Johnny had never quite been able to master. Academics, for instance, had never been his forte. He recalled being a student in high school and how even the supposedly easy subjects, art and music, left him feeling defeated and humiliated. He couldn't draw; he couldn't sing. And the tougher subjects, God help him, like math and biology, left him groping miserably to understand why they'd ever been conceived, much less taught.

The only time he'd known something in class that his peers didn't ended in disaster for him. The biology teacher, a tall reedy man with ears the size and sensitivity of two radar dishes, had just announced to the class that 'sumac' is the only word in the English language that begins with the letters 'su' but may be properly pronounced with a 'shh' sound. Johnny, who said nothing, sat there frowning, and it was as if the teacher, with those monstrous ears, had overheard his thoughts.

"You think I'm mistaken, Mr. Black?" the teacher said.

"I do," Johnny replied.

"You sound positive."

"I'm just as sure as sugar," Johnny said and began to cackle.

The eruption of outlaw laughter from his classmates felt delicious to him, though the ensuing trip to the principal's office followed by a week in detention hall made him wonder if he shouldn't have answered the question with a brisk "No sir."

Indeed, he might not have passed biology that year if it hadn't been for his old buddy Bob Stallings. A good guy—and a smart guy too—Stallings had partnered with him in the lab and had helped him study for the tests, which couldn't have been much harder had they been written in hieroglyphics. Secretly, Johnny envied Stallings at times for knowing things

Johnny didn't, and for being able to do things Johnny couldn't. Stallings, who'd gone on to become a college professor, must be some sort of genius, Johnny gathered.

Yet Johnny had been blessed with talents of his own, physical talents, that those around him could barely fathom. Even as a kid, he was stronger and quicker than most of his playmates, and his coordination was off the scale. He could do things easily that some guys couldn't do at all. The first time he tried to dribble a basketball, he did so with confidence and authority. He felt no need to look at the ball in order to control it. Why bother? It was a big enough ball; you could tell from the feel, from the rhythm, where it would be at any instant. A few years later he tried his hand at bowling and rolled a strike on his first attempt. His friends were impressed—but what was so hard about bowling? The pins were large easy-to-hit targets; nail the pocket, and they'd all go flying. Now, if the pins had been designed to move around as you tried to hit them, well, that might make it a challenge. But they didn't. They just stood there. Easy.

Of course, no sport came to him more quickly or more naturally than baseball. He was a force in Little League at nine years old and its premier player at eleven. At thirteen he showed up to observe a high school practice session expecting to be dazzled by the superior skills these older guys were bound to display but instead felt disappointed and disillusioned. Standing near the bleachers along the first base line, this gawky pimple-faced kid that no one knew soon began harassing established players with a blend of basic advice and acid criticism. To make matters worse, his remarks were delivered at deafening volume and in a cracking high-low adolescent voice that thrashed the nerves of anyone within a hundred yards of its origin. Finally, if only to shut him up, one of the coaches invited him to take the field so they could see if he played as well as he yapped.

Turned out he did. Johnny went straight to the mound, declared he was a pitcher and declared further that he had yet to see the hitter (on this field, at least) who could touch him. And he began to throw. Even then the raw essentials of his sinewy overhand turbocharged delivery were in place, and the players and coaches, most of whom loved to gab almost as much as Johnny, found that suddenly they'd been robbed of speech. Though they moved their lips, no words came out. The ball seemed to roar off the kid's fingertips like a ... like a fighter jet, and the most lethal hitters on the team were reduced to flailing at Johnny's offerings as if swinging a scimitar at some invisible ogre. "Fastball, up and in," Johnny might announce cockily prior to a pitch, or "Curveball, down and away." But it didn't matter what warning he gave; no one could touch him.

Obviously, when he was old enough, he had no problem making the team. The only ones who had problems with him were the hitters, who couldn't hit him; the catchers, who couldn't catch him; and the coaches, who couldn't coach him.

After somehow graduating from high school, Johnny spent a year in the minors—just one year. Even at that, it was a difficult period, both for him and for those around him, since he didn't care to be in the 'bush leagues' and since those in charge of him weren't quite sure what to do with him or how to do it. Supposedly their job was to teach him command—not only of his pitching repertoire but of himself. They wanted the flighty young phenom to learn something about discipline, responsibility and maturity, so that soon he'd be able represent professional baseball in a professional fashion and, just as importantly, be able to lead his own life with grace and aplomb. Despite their most genuine efforts, his handlers fell short of their goals.

Inevitably, and with a sunburst of publicity, Johnny 'Jet' Black made his major league pitching debut. His opponents were the Baltimore Orioles, several of whom claimed they knew nothing about this Black youngster and described the upcoming contest as 'just another game.' It was anything but. In the seven innings he lasted, Johnny fanned twelve Orioles, humbling them with a fastball that seemed to trail smoke and a curve that broke downward so sharply it made onlookers think of a peregrine falcon diving for prey. But he also walked six, hit a batter, booted a ground ball and yielded five earned runs. And he took the loss. Still, even the doubters agreed he'd given fans plenty to talk about.

They had even more to talk about when, after the game, Johnny and some teammates went out to mark his coming of age (though he was still underage) with a night on the town. Before the long night concluded at a bar featuring pastied pole dancers, a scuffle broke out, police were called, and a woman named April May accused Johnny of groping her. While denying to investigators that any 'groping' had taken place, he did admit to 'copping a feel.' He also denied drinking, a denial that was supported by his teammates though not by Ms. May.

And so his roller coaster career was off and whistling down the tracks.

Now, many years after his career had lurched off the tracks and gone crashing to earth, Johnny was hoping to get things fixed. Always an optimist, even he knew what he hoped to do would test him severely.

Parking his truck, he saw in the distance that Dutwell and Danny were chatting amiably with each other near home plate; this was good. From what he could tell, no one else was around—also good. Johnny checked his gold Cartier watch and shrugged. He was thirty minutes late. Not good, but not bad either. No, not too bad, especially for him. He grabbed his cleats and his Wilson glove, adjusted his black and silver Sox cap and strode toward the field, feeling tight but ready.

They all greeted each other warmly, with Johnny and Dutwell exchanging one-liners about last night's barroom brawl ("You shoulda fined 'em," Dutwell said. "I would've had to fine myself," Johnny came back. "I was in the middle of it") and Danny chiming in that they were lucky the face in the sky hadn't made the whole bar disappear.

But the small talk was kept even smaller than usual. They all knew why they had assembled. Johnny laced up his cleats,

and Danny took a ball from a burlap bag he had nearby and
flipped it to his battery mate. After studying it briefly, rotating
it with his long sentient fingers, Johnny made his way to the
mound, his manner serious. Dutwell drifted over toward first
base; he was holding a device known as a Jugs gun, used for
measuring a pitcher's velocity.

Per habit, Johnny kicked some dirt away from the rubber
and fondled the rosin bag, casting it aside with something like
contempt. Then he began loosening up, lobbing the ball lightly
to Danny, who would snap it smartly back to the mound and
hammer his mitt with his right fist.

Johnny understood the deal. At this early stage of the
comeback process, he would not be expected to demonstrate
full-fledged major league form. Having left the game before
young Danny had left grade school, he figured to be rusty. But
he had to demonstrate the *potential* to recover his major league
form. Specifically, his mechanics should be sound. He should
appear fit and healthy. Most of all, his arm should be 'live'; that
is, he should still possess major league 'stuff.' Regardless of
where his pitches went exactly (since control could be honed
later), his fastball should hop and his curveball should crackle.
If they did, Perfection could well earn himself a ticket to Triple
A, and from there back to the limelight—to The Show.

The mound felt comfortable, and so did Johnny's arm. He
was throwing harder now, working up an agreeable sweat. As it
still did from time to time, his memory began to reach back to
that one brilliant afternoon at Yankee Stadium when Johnny,
facing the best team in baseball, laid claim to the loftiest
nickname in all of sports: Perfection. It was the day he threw
not just a no-hitter, a sparkling precious gem in itself, but a
perfect game. Twenty-seven up, twenty-seven down. It was a
feat so rare and fantastic that only a handful of men had ever
accomplished it. Men like Cy Young. Don Larsen. Catfish
Hunter. Sandy Koufax.

And Johnny 'Jet' Black.

There are special days in sports (and in life, one supposes) when the gap between aspiration and achievement shrinks and then disappears. Miraculously, you do precisely what you'd set out to do. For Johnny, that day against the Yanks was one of those wondrous unicorn days. His heater was pushing for triple digits; the deuce was biting like a hungry Siberian tiger. Even the control—up, down, in, out; never his specialty—was crackerjack. By the seventh inning he felt as if he were pitching in a brightly lit tunnel; his whole world consisted of four people: himself, the catcher, the hitter and the ump. Nothing else mattered. Nothing else existed. The only negative he felt was the fact that periodically he had to stop pitching so his own team could bat. He would've preferred to pitch straight through, mowing the hitters down like so many blades of grass.

Already in flight, his confidence rose to a new level in the eighth inning when he disposed convincingly of the cleanup hitter, Alex Romero, who would go on to be named the American League MVP. Ahead in the count 0 and 2, Johnny knew that Romero would be expecting him to waste one—to entice the rawboned power hitter to chase a pitch outside the zone. Instead, Johnny decided to challenge him with some hot spicy mustard right down Broadway. Romero started to swing, checked himself, then recoiled in disgust and disbelief as the ump called him out on strikes. Called him out flamboyantly at that, pivoting and windmilling his thumb as if he too were a pitcher. Romero tossed his bat high in the air where it twirled in slow motion like a space station in a Stanley Kubrick movie. The ump said something to the slugger, who said something back, and someone rumbled out of the dugout, and there was a prolonged and spirited rhubarb. But Johnny stayed away from it and above it; it didn't concern him. He had just five hitters to go.

Then he had just one. Just one man standing between him and baseball immortality, and his name was Donnie 'Scooter' Richards, the second baseman. Richards was a mediocre Punch and Judy-type hitter, but he had a shrewd eye and a decent history against the lanky fireballing lefty who peered down at him now. Johnny knew that the final out of his chef-d'ouevre would not be a gimme.

Yet it was. To his amazement and to that of everyone in the ballpark, Richards swung at a bad pitch and bounced it back to the mound where Johnny snared it and took off toward first. Big Orpheus Johnson was ready to accept the underhand toss he knew would be coming, and Johnny was ready to make the toss. But on impulse (something Johnny could seldom resist), he just kept on running and made the putout himself, outscooting Scooter to first by half a step.

Pandemonium. His teammates poured from the dugout like beer from a keg. Flashbulbs and jubilation. Indecipherable shouting. The cover of *Sports Illustrated* caught the celebration artfully, with Johnny riding on the broad shoulders of his joyful buddies, both arms raised overhead, fingers spread, his mouth open as if he were trying to comprehend what he had just done. Beneath the shot, the caption screamed a single emphatic word: 'PERFECTION!'

Adrenaline pumping, juices flowing, Johnny could feel the triumph of that long-ago day even now as he kicked and fired toward Danny Pepper. The kid's mitt looked as wide as the bed of Johnny's truck, and he thumped it consistently. Abruptly he realized he was destined to pitch again in the major leagues; he was on the verge of authoring one of the great comeback stories in baseball history. And this time around he might even conduct himself with class, restraint and gentlemanly manners. It would befit his years, he felt.

Off to the side, Dutwell called out: "OK Johnny, lemme see you *bring* it!" He was holding up the Jugs gun.

Bring it? What the hell did that mean? He *was* bringing it. He'd *been* bringing it.

Johnny fingered the rosin bag, wiped some sweat from his face with his glove and really reached back with his next pitch, rocking into it and following through extravagantly.

"C'mon, Jet!" Dutwell squawked. "Lemme see the number one! The cheese! The gas!"

Johnny wiped his face again and walked over to him. "What the hell you talking about?" he asked, more curious than annoyed.

Dutwell showed him the numbers on the gun. They made no sense—72 mph.

After a moment Johnny said: "Your gun's broken, Frank."

"I don't think so. I got the kid throwin' it back harder than you're throwin' it in. No offense."

Blank-faced, Johnny returned to the mound and fired a couple more, launching them with such an exaggerated motion that he almost went airborne. No verbal reaction from Dutwell, however, who merely rubbed his old white head, hitched up his sagging pants and crossed the infield to home plate.

"You got a bat?" he asked Danny. Danny found one, and Dutwell took it. "You got a mask? A chest protector?" He did. "Put 'em on," Dutwell said.

When Johnny, still atop the mound, grasped that Dutwell meant to bat against him, he became indignant. "You gotta be kidding," he said.

Dutwell didn't answer him immediately. He went to the batter's box, dug a small trench with his right foot, tapped the plate with the head of his bat and took a few flexing half-swings. Then he settled into a closed crouching stance, fists cocked at his right shoulder. "Bring it," he said.

Johnny did, or he tried to, and Dutwell blooped the first offering foul, watched it carom loudly off the grungy tin roof of a concession stand. Then, after sending Danny to the burlap sack for more balls, Dutwell, who looked as if he should've been reclining in an easy chair with the sports page and some graham crackers and milk, began to connect. He laced one sharply to left and lined two more into right-center. Wordless, Johnny seemed entranced, benumbed. Another shot to left, and another to right-center. The horrific exercise finally ended, not too mercifully, when Dutwell reached outside for a split-finger fastball and ripped a wicked one-hopper off Johnny's knee, causing him to swear and hobble around in wincing pain as if he were two decades older than Dutwell.

Tactfully, the old scout waited till Johnny finished hobbling before he slowly approached the mound. (Devastated, Danny moped around home plate, his head drooping.) Neither Dutwell nor Johnny talked for a while, the solemn sweat-faced pitcher poking at the ground with his toe. Then Dutwell, speaking in a quiet measured voice, delivered a brief speech. He said that in this life things begin and things end, and we as human beings often see no sense in any of it. So it was with Johnny's career, which had been extraordinary in more ways than one. But like everything else, it began and it ended, and now it was over for sure. Over. And there was no disgrace in that; it was the way of things. Johnny would have to see the facts as they were and, when he could, accept them.

Johnny started to say something about how maybe he'd strained himself in that melee last night; maybe if he had another opportunity—

"Johnny," Dutwell said simply, looking up at him. "Johnny."

Still poking at the earth beneath him, Johnny seemed inclined to mutter something more but didn't. Dutwell offered to buy him lunch, but Johnny just shook his head.

"I'll give you a call," Dutwell said, and then he and Danny faded away—faded like the bits of a dream that seem so real and vivid when you first awaken but soon slip off to oblivion.

The pitcher appeared rooted to the mound. It was where he belonged and where he didn't belong. If Danny's mood had been bleak, Johnny's was abysmal. His dream had been shattered. The gift he'd had for most of his life, an uncanny ability to throw a baseball, had finally and unquestionably deserted him. Had he been a different person, he might've wept. As it was, he spat.

His arm had deserted him much as his daughter Sarah had deserted him years before. Damn her. He picked up the rosin bag and slammed it back down. Come to think of it, Sarah was supposedly on her way home, but if the scouting report could be trusted, he didn't anticipate a bubbly reunion. Plus his ex-girlfriend Wanda was up to something; who knew what? Plus there was all that crazy shit on TV and in the newspapers....

Ah, my. Life could be so ... Well, it just wasn't ... He was staring off steadily, silently, at the pointed roof of a very dark house beyond center field....

For no particular reason he began to stare straight up. Had there been a noise from up there? A flash of light?

After a moment he began to see something—a black dot in the sky, directly overhead. The dot was growing larger, drawing nearer. Changing.

Johnny staggered slightly. What he was seeing couldn't be happening. It couldn't be.

Oh my God.

His glove dropped from his hand as he continued to stare.

17

ONCE AGAIN, Dunkin Helbig was in a foul mood, and this stupid China business was doing little to buoy him. He had plenty of work to do, but most of his obligations lay elsewhere, not here at Perfection Fitness where his job required him to be. So he walked without direction across the rubberized floor of the gym, his gray eyes shifting in a surly way, his thin lips finding creative new methods of scowling. Occasionally his wanderings caused him to pass beneath one of the numerous TVs that were suspended throughout the gym, and he heard fragments of the China reportage.

Apparently something major had happened in or to the Chinese city of Korla. As Helbig gradually came to understand, Korla was a good-sized metropolis in northwest China, the capital of a large prefecture. It had a healthy economy, based in part on the production of fragrant pears, and, like most of China, a very long history. At this moment, where Korla was in its history was a matter of intense speculation and debate— many were claiming that the city had come under an attack of some kind. Without being too specific, officials at the Pentagon were confirming that a significant and unfortunate event had occurred there, and, as a result, the U.S. military had been placed on alert. Chinese news sources, not normally known for their openness, had gone so far as to acknowledge a 'crisis.' Given these scant facts, a worldwide rumor factory had sprung into furious action.

Of course, none of this aroused Helbig's sympathy or concern, or not for the folks in China anyhow. He did feel sympathy and concern over any consequences this latest development might have for him. But he had little interest in Chinese people, most of whom lived so far away, and none of whom had done anything to earn Helbig's favor. Now and then he ate Chinese food, but it always left him feeling unsatisfied and vaguely cheated. And he considered the Chinese language (not that he knew beans about it) unthinkably complex, with its singsong sounds and alien symbols that looked like chicken scratchings. Could you imagine being born in China and having to learn that infernal gibberish? And then trying to write a *play* in it? Good God. On the other hand, Helbig had to concede it was China that had given the world Chairman Mao, who *had* written in Chinese and who, like Helbig, hadn't thought well of Western society— so maybe the Chinese weren't totally off-base after all.

Regardless, Helbig was beginning to fear that all this tabloid journalism would eventually have a harmful effect on his dreams—on his theatrical project. If things got turbulent enough, who would want to go see his play? Would he even be able to get it mounted? Already he was seeing spotty attendance at the rehearsals, and difficult behavior from some of the actors who did show up. The sheer cheek of Buck Winters yesterday, stomping around like a gorilla in heat, stirring up trouble and dissension ... Helbig'd had a good mind to lift his hand against Buck, and the only reason he didn't was the sour knowledge that Buck would've beaten him silly. But still, Helbig worried about where things were headed—worried about *Death and Destruction*, or whatever it might finally be called. He'd read somewhere that the Irish writer James Joyce had opposed war on the grounds that it would distract people from reading Joyce's work, and he knew where the great man was coming from.

Talentwise, Helbig and Joyce had much in common, Helbig would've argued.

No sign of Johnny so far today. Man, Helbig mused, what a soft life that guy must live. *La dolce vita*. Out all night, in bed half the day. Fame, women, clout, money. Money seemed to fall on Johnny the way pigeon crap fell on Helbig—with surprising regularity and quantity. Yet how much of that moolah had Johnny donated to the financially downtrodden but culturally aglow Your Town Theatre? Thus far, not a penny. And despite all Helbig's crass hints, Johnny had given no sign that his tightfistedness was due to change anytime soon. To Helbig's critical eye, Johnny was like all the rest of the moneyed class—self-indulgent, self-centered. The slim little trainer would've told him as much too, but Johnny paid his salary, modest though it was, and Helbig therefore tried not to antagonize him any more than was absolutely necessary.

From overhead, a man's voice coming from a TV was saying: "... by both the Secretary of State and the Secretary of Defense. It's a thorny question, no doubt about it, because plainly the satellite images do exist. But what do they reveal, and at what point does John Q. Public have a right to see them? Every day our intelligence people collect untold mountains of data, virtually all of it classified. Obviously, these data are classified for a reason, and they can't be declassified purely on the basis...." The voice became inaudible as Helbig moved along.

Johnny wasn't the only one missing today. As always of late, the gym was nearly empty—just two customers. To the rear of the spacious room a big blowsy woman, Gladys Nieberding, was lying on a mat doing crunches, and in a remote corner a pumped-up tattooed man known only as the Beast was doing seated concentration curls with a dumbbell that outweighed Helbig's car, the one he'd kept hidden away for the past year. In his camouflage do-rag and black string tank, the Beast was a shredded mass of tanned rippling veiny muscle, a fanatic who never missed a workout for any reason and who clearly had a host of psychological issues. Helbig, who found him intimidating, never spoke to him and kept his distance now.

Why was the gym even open? Helbig grumbled silently to himself. He ought to just close the place down and go home. Then again, closing down would involve telling the Beast that he had to leave before he was ready, and that might prove a poor way to initiate communication with a man who was a dues-paying member and, more to the point, might decide to eat Helbig as a between-meals protein snack.

As he meandered along, slyly watching himself in the vast mirrors that covered the walls, Helbig brooded for a bit about the dark foreign-looking man he'd met in the coffee shop a couple of days before. Abdul. Why had Helbig ever agreed to meet with him? Why, having agreed to, did he run his mouth so foolishly, babbling on about his upbringing, his writing, even about ... about his running over that woman in the parking lot, killing her? By being reckless with his words—unforgivable for a writer!—he'd put himself in a position of weakness and jeopardy. Abdul was surely a domestic spy or an undercover cop who would move against him with a vengeance. It wouldn't surprise Helbig if he got busted any minute now and then sent to some secret overseas prison to be stripped and flogged and waterboarded for months on end. Or at the very least, he guessed, he would lose his job and have his masterful play be suppressed forever.

But while Abdul was a problem for Helbig, a young man named Chance Smathers was an even bigger and more urgent problem. Rapping his knuckles against a Nautilus machine as he passed it, Helbig turned his thoughts to Chance, whom he'd met at the theatre. For a period of three or four months roughly a year ago, he had been Helbig's lover. Helbig had rarely been close to anyone in life, and he wasn't a believer in either friendships or relationships. But Chance was a bright witty fellow, charming when he chose to be, and adept at playing to Helbig's ego and his various insecurities. And with his curlicued blond hair, pale blue eyes and perfectly aligned white teeth when he grinned, Chance was easy enough for Helbig to look at. He was much more attractive than Helbig, at any rate. So after some hesitation (probably not enough hesitation, Helbig would later conclude), the would-be playwright decided to ... take a chance.

Since the relationship had been built on the flimsiest of foundations—Helbig found Chance cute; Chance found

Helbig talented—it couldn't last. And especially since Helbig was part of it in the first place. He himself had given it two weeks at the outside, and when it went longer, he called it a resounding success. Then he ended it. He saw his life as a starship, and he wanted to fly it solo.

One small kicker, however. On the evening when Helbig set fire to the bank and then drove his Spectra into and over a woman in the parking lot as he made his frantic escape, Chance was staying at Helbig's apartment. After securing his car in the garage out back, Helbig rushed into his kitchen white-faced and breathing fast. Chance, who was sitting at the table eating a plate of quiche Lorraine, stared up in alarm. "My heavens," he said, putting down his fork, "you look as if you just killed someone." His state of shock addling what sense he had, Helbig blurted: "You know what? I did."

In the tense minutes and hours to come, Chance said all the right things. He did his best to calm his partner and to elicit the facts. He advised Helbig, quietly but decisively, that Helbig must go to the police and tell them what had happened. He would be swamped with trouble—he could count on that—but far less trouble than if they banged on his door five minutes hence with a warrant for his arrest on a charge of manslaughter. He had to do what was decent and responsible and moral.

For his part, Helbig said all the wrong things, starting with "Bull*shit!*" Accent on the second syllable. Distorting the circumstances to make himself seem as innocent as possible, he explained that the accident was just that: an accident. The woman, God rest her unlucky soul, happened to be in his way as he was driving. And she got clobbered. He was certain she was dead, so reporting what'd transpired wouldn't help her in the slightest. All it would accomplish would be to get Helbig flung into some dark dingy cell with one or more priapic felons who were bigger and stronger than he was, and infinitely filthier and more perverted than he could imagine. What's done was done, he said. A tragic accident. It was time to let the dead rest in peace.

Not long afterwards, Helbig and Chance went their separate ways, and that, in Helbig's mind, was the end of it.

But then just this morning, a second kicker. After a year, an unshaven Chance, looking as if someone had doused him with water and then dried him with a large industrial fan, showed up at his door and said he needed money; said he'd lost his job as an insurance agent and was growing desperate. Chance felt confident, he said, that Helbig would help him out in his time of need. It was an odd word to use, Helbig thought—'confident.' Not 'hopeful' or 'optimistic' but 'confident,' as if he knew Helbig would be unable to refuse him. Helbig, who wasn't flush himself and who didn't typically handle stress with a lot of poise, gave Chance what cash he could and didn't say much about it. Didn't raise his voice or even an eyebrow. Chance thanked him and went away.

From the instant Chance had mentioned money, Helbig realized he was being blackmailed. He realized too that Chance would now become a recurrent and unwelcome part of his life—that the blackmail would continue. And he realized as well, with a faint sharp thrill, that the time would come when he would have to murder Chance Smathers.

All these realizations, the last one especially, bothered Helbig. They meant, obviously, that he would have to siphon some of his creative juices away from his play and apply them to the task of murdering Chance. Unavoidably, the play would suffer. Already Helbig was considering different scenarios whereby he could dispose of his former lover. He could push him down a flight of stairs; he could put poison in his quiche.... Whatever was cost-effective and efficient. On a more personal level, the fact that he was contemplating murder brought grief to his self-concept. As one who'd always deemed himself a leftward-leaning man of the people, his current aggressive train of thought suggested he was perhaps more right-wing, more Nietzschean, than he'd ever suspected. Maybe he didn't know himself as well as he believed, and this possibility pooled in his gut like acid.

Through the window at the front of the gym Helbig saw a white sedan pull up and park. A customer maybe?

Overhead, from one of the TVs, a woman's voice was saying: "... no troop movements in the area. Nor apparently is there any evidence that ballistic missiles were launched with China as the target. One other theory that has yet to be ruled out conclusively is that the Chinese themselves were constructing a weapon at or near the site, and, through either accident or sabotage, the thing—whatever it was—detonated. We are trying to get word from the International Seismological Centre as to whether ..."

\* \* \*

Out in the parking lot Bob Stallings, after parking his pearly white Chevy Malibu, just sat behind the wheel for a while. He'd made up his mind to continue his self-improvement program by joining a gym, and what better gym to join than Perfection Fitness, owned by his pal Johnny Black? Maybe Perfection himself would be in there working out.

But, as he knew he would, Stallings was feeling some last-minute heebie-jeebies. Unlike Johnny, he'd never been too gifted at anything physical, and he wasn't sure how comfortable he'd feel in a gym. As a kid, having no quickness and only so-so strength, he'd been forced to use his ample bulk to achieve even minimal success in sports. In wrestling, for example, he'd simply grab the other guy and fall on him like a human avalanche. Sometimes this technique would work; sometimes it wouldn't. In football, he was used mainly as a blocker. All he had to do was stand here, his chubby forearms held up in front of him, and he presented opposing players with a hell of an obstacle.

When he tried out for Little League baseball, the coaches took one look at his round heavy-footed body and decided to make him a catcher. Put on the 'tools of ignorance,' they told him. God, how he'd hated that expression. But what he'd hated worse was trying to catch Johnny, whose fastball was absurd even then. It was like trying to reach out and snare a flash of light. But a baseball, deflecting savagely off a bat or kicking unpredictably off the dirt, hurt worse than your everyday stream of photons ever could. Actually, when the coaches saw how limited Stallings was, they didn't let him catch too often; for his own safety, they kept him on the bench.

"Time to get off the bench, Bobby." It was his wife's voice, speaking to him. Sometimes Jenny spoke to him from the grave, giving him guidance, urging him along. "C'mon," she seemed to murmur in his ear. "Get off the bench and get in the game."

With that, Stallings took a deep breath, got out of his car and walked over to the gym.

Once inside, he discovered that no one was at the desk to greet him. In fact, not too many people were around anywhere. Understandable, he supposed, with all the hubbub going on in the world. Awkwardly, he stood there waiting for several minutes.

In what would qualify as a bold move for him, he decided to go find someone who could assist him. First person he saw was a prehistorically large man, heavily tattooed, sitting on a bench doing something with a dumbbell. The man, whose fantastic muscles seemed to have a presence and a personality of their own, was wearing a do-rag and a black string tanktop with a message across the chest in bone-colored gothic letters: 'Bang Yo' Head.' Whether the message referred to a type of music or to what the man might do to anyone who bugged him was unclear to Stallings, who, in his neat gray LL Bean sweatsuit, suddenly felt overdressed or underdressed or misdressed or something. Politely, he waited for the man to finish whatever it was he was doing.

"Excuse me," Stallings said. "Do you work here? I was trying to ... What I was ... I was wondering ..."

The man stroked his Fu Manchu and gave him the neutral

analytical look a customer might display in appraising a used car.

"You need to talk to the twinkie," the man said.

"Excuse me? I need ..."

"The twinkie." He nodded toward the far side of the room where Dunkin Helbig dithered.

"Yes. Right. Thank you," Stallings said. "Thank you very much."

Approaching Helbig, who remained where he was, Stallings saw a runty young man—short, spare—with an expression that was both acute and detached. His movements were quick and almost birdlike—a twitch here, a twitch there. Rather wide across the brow and narrow at the chin, his head was triangular in shape. He had clipped dark hair, shifty gray eyes and a taut mouth that hinted he'd seen all species of disagreeable sights and was trying, with a certain dignity, to rise above them. He was wearing an *Angels in America* T-shirt—the allusion baffled Stallings—and a pair of floppy white gym shorts. For some reason, the professor, who'd learned to accept just about all types at the college, felt a shade creeped out by this guy.

Nevertheless, Stallings walked up to Helbig and told him he wanted to join Perfection Fitness.

"Join the gym, eh?" Helbig said. He sounded dubious, as if Stallings had boasted he was building a time machine in his basement. "Name?"

"Bob Stallings."

Since Helbig had never learned the identity of the woman he'd killed—he'd done everything he could to avoid learning it—the name meant nothing to him. Or hold on just a sec; perhaps the name *was* somehow familiar to him, and in an unpleasant context. Was there a Stallings employed at the bank Helbig had tried to torch? Possibly ... Or might this be one of the elusive members of Your Town's governing board that was insisting his play be 'adjusted'? Perhaps ... Or was he something else entirely? A professor, maybe, out at HCC, teaching in some discipline that Helbig, when he was there a few years before, couldn't stomach—chemistry or accounting or ... or business ...

"Dunkin Helbig," the young man introduced himself coolly.

Signing some papers that Helbig extracted from a pocket in his shorts—how disgusting!—Stallings was having similarly eerie feelings about him. Sometime in the recent past, he would've bet, his own life had crossed with Helbig's, and in a regrettable way. What had happened? Probably, though Stallings couldn't quite place him, Helbig had been a student at HCC—either one of his, or one he'd heard about from someone else. Wait a minute. Hadn't there been a Helbig kid who'd gotten involved in the school's drama program and wanted to stage *Oh! Calcutta!*? Everyone was agreeable till they belatedly looked into the play's content and learned it was shot through with nudity and sex. Loads of it! Administrators at the college, with support from Stallings and other faculty, managed to stop the play on moral grounds before it ever started, but not without a long and acrimonious discussion of academic freedom, freedom of speech, censorship and the like.

Could this be the same Helbig?

Since it was apparent that Stallings would've been more at home in a spacecraft probing the rings of Saturn than exercising in a gym, Helbig offered to show him around and—for a price—to train him.

"But first," Helbig said, "let's have you do some cardio. Get you warmed up."

He led Stallings to the raised platform where assorted cardio machines stood like Dadaist architecture, all gray and black and stark. Helbig gestured for his trainee to climb on board a treadmill, and, not exactly oozing confidence, Stallings did.

"You want me to run on this?" he asked, instinctively gripping the handlebars though the machine was not yet in motion.

Helbig laughed rudely. "No, my God," he said. "You're in no shape to run; you're a beefball." To Stallings' surprise, Helbig poked him sharply in the belly with his finger. "I'm afraid you've got a passel of work to do before you'll be running or lifting much or otherwise impressing anyone around here. Now—let's get you started with a nice slow grandmotherly walk."

He pushed a button, and the rubber beneath Stallings' spotless Nikes quivered to life and began to roll toward him. Very slowly.

"You're lucky you got your big fat butt in here when you did," Helbig said. "All that pork you're packing—you look like a pregnant sow. That's unhealthy as hell, you know? Ugly too. I'll be back."

Like a leprechaun, Helbig vanished, leaving Stallings to walk and walk and walk. But the pace was leisurely, and, after a moment, Stallings fell into a smooth easygoing rhythm. Walking was one thing he could do. He began to relax. Frankly, he wasn't too fond of this Helbig character, who'd come across as condescending and even insulting toward him. But he knew that his wife, who'd always been more patient than he could ever be, would want him to show some restraint. "Don't judge him too quickly, Bobby," he could almost hear her saying. "Not everyone's had your advantages in life, and there may be more to this young man than you're aware." Shrugging, Stallings decided not to dwell on Helbig and guessed that maybe others at the gym would prove more congenial.

Eventually he gave some attention to the TV that hung in the air before him. As he would've expected, the set was tuned to a news channel—or maybe he was seeing yet another news special that had preempted something else; could be either. By now, coverage of current events had basically taken over TV and most other forms of the media. So grimly fascinating and darkly urgent was the news that few people were interested in anything else.

The ticker crawling across the bottom of the screen told Stallings that stocks were plummeting once again, like an elevator falling freely down its shaft. Wow. He felt a dizzying excitement. In less than two days he'd made more money in the market than he'd made in the twenty years previous. And all because he'd gone short, wagering on a market collapse, which was now happening. Millions of investors—clever ones, seasoned ones—were losing their asses, but not Robert Earl Stallings. He was becoming rich. Rich! The backhanded way he was becoming rich did make him feel a trifle guilty, but he could cope with it easily enough. Besides, he told himself, sooner or later the market, the economy and everything else would bounce back to rosy health. They always had before.

Of course, one of the reasons stocks were diving today was the gloomy uncertainty surrounding the situation in Korla, China. While no one was willing yet to come out and say just what had happened there, Stallings gathered from all the dire whisperings and rumors that it was something pretty bad. Maybe truly bad. But then again, who really knew? As a professor, a man of empiricism, he needed clearer evidence than what he presently had before he exercised his human right to run off screaming in panic. Same with the lights in the sky (that he hadn't personally seen); same with that terrifying face (that he *had* seen). There had to be some ordinary down-to-earth explanation. To this point, it simply hadn't been uncovered. Most people tended to overreact when confronted with the unknown; they let their emotions sweep them along in a torrent. Stallings liked to believe he was different.

As he strolled slowly ahead, going nowhere, a thought came to him. Hadn't the face said there'd be a token of good faith involving two cities? Korla was definitely a city, and something had happened to it. Or apparently something had. Could this be in keeping with the message? A fulfillment of what could only be called a prophecy? But Korla was just one city; the face had mentioned *two* cities. Stallings scratched the side of his moist shapeless nose, ruminating. It all seemed unlikely to him, and within minutes he'd put the thought aside.

Another thought came to him: he was not only warmed up, he was bored. Whatever had happened to Helbig?

Idly, Stallings let his gaze drop from the TV to the front door, down in the distance. Someone had just come in—a young woman. And my goodness gracious, what a young woman it was. Her lustrous black hair framed a face so alluring and sensuous it belonged in the movies. Elizabeth Taylor in her youth perhaps. The body was no less sensational, packaged in a tight purple top and even tighter lavender pants. When she turned, he saw she had the word 'WISH' sewn across her bottom—'WI' on one voluptuous buttock and 'SH' on the other. Well, she wasn't the most conservative of dressers, Stallings thought, but he wasn't about to complain.

She also sported a nifty blue purse slung over her left shoulder.

He continued to watch her and saw that she seemed as hesitant and lost as he'd been when he first came in. (Where was Helbig? Stallings wondered.) Very soon, Stallings began to sense something familiar about the woman, as if he knew her from somewhere. Knew her from ... Well, how about that. Was it possible? His face lit up. Though he was some distance away from her, he spoke her name out loud.

"Sarah," he said. Johnny's daughter.

To stop the treadmill, Stallings pressed the same button Helbig had used and found to his dismay that the machine now went faster. He pressed the button again, and the machine went faster still. Holy hell. Not too gracefully, he was able to hop down off the rolling rubber just as it appeared he might lose his footing, fall and cripple himself.

Goofy grin on his face, he went straight over to Sarah and said: "Hey, stranger!"

Turning toward him, Sarah bloomed with delight. "Mr. Stallings!" she said.

Impulsively they hugged each other.

"Call me Bob," he said. "You're not my student anymore.

So. Sarah." He drank her in. "You look ... You look ..." He groped for words that flitted away from him like butterflies.

"Yes," she said.

"So you're back in town. Gee, it's good to see you."

"Good to see you ... Bob." Did she really mean it? She seemed to.

"What brings you back?"

She tossed her hair. "Family. Haven't seen them in a while."

"Your old man know you're here?"

"No, no. I haven't told him."

"You haven't! Gonna surprise him, huh? Won't that be great."

Her huge violet eyes, when they landed full on his, struck him with a force that was almost physical. "I intend to surprise him," she said.

18

IT WAS THE CRAZIEST STUNT she'd ever pulled, not that she'd pulled many. Laura Kennedy had jumped on a jet and flown to Illinois.

Her timing, if not her logic, had been excellent because soon after the 747 touched down, all commercial flights in the USA were cancelled indefinitely. No reason given. For the foreseeable future, the airways would be open only to birds, military planes and the inexplicable clusters and ribbons of swirling multicolored lights that danced in the sky night and day, without sound but with greater and greater frequency.

Those same airways would also be open, of course, to that giant freakish living face, which had appeared now at various times to perhaps a third of the populace but, unlike the lights, had never once been photographed or taped.

Laura had no compelling reason to be in Illinois, but she saw no compelling reason to be in California either. And that was the gist of it. At first she thought she might simply take Sarah up on her invitation to join her—Sarah, whom she found so funky, nonconformist and (though she would've rejected the word) inspiring. She assumed she'd track down the true and definitive ending to the story she'd written for the *Times*. Maybe she could prevent something bad from happening, too, something the impetuous actress might try with her father. If Laura saw a bright side to that black-edged fallen angel, she understood there was a dangerous side as well.

Probably Derek Wolf, if he weren't dead, could offer a helpful comment here.

But then as she drove away from O'Hare Airport in a subcompact rented car, traveling down I-55 at five mph *under* the speed limit, Laura came to recognize that she was in fact working on a much bigger story than the one on porn. She was covering the biggest story any reporter ever could: the end of the world. Because it did seem, to her and to many others, that the planet Earth might just be teetering on the brink of a cosmic precipice. Soon they would know. If all those shivering instincts out there proved correct and the world ended, well then, any project she might undertake wouldn't have much value. Everyone would be dead. But if the spooky signs that people had fixed on turned out to be a false alarm and the world managed to survive, she might wind up with a captivating—and saleable—piece of journalism. Something special.

What she wanted, what she envisioned, was a tapestry of in-the-moment reactions and opinions taken from average people in a typical mid-American city. She wanted their thoughts on the world's predicament for sure, but she'd also take their thoughts on most other topics that came along. She would create a naturalistic word-picture of what they were thinking, saying and doing as the moment of reckoning drew near. To do so, she would fire up her trusty voice recorder and visit a cross-section of the community—a luncheonette, let's say, a school, a tavern—and talk to anyone who was willing to talk. She was genuinely curious to know if and how most people were bearing up.

Along the way, she hoped to get together with Sarah, who either didn't have her phone with her or wasn't answering it.

Arriving in town, Laura opted to hit Perfection Fitness first since she'd contacted it once before and since she guessed Johnny might be there, or Sarah, or both. As it happened, neither was there, and exploring the facility was like walking through a ghost-ridden mausoleum. The quiet, the inactivity, weighed on her.

In all, she found just one person inside, a balding rotund man wearing a sloppy white T-shirt and sloppy white gym shorts. Aside from standing next to a flat bench, he seemed to be doing nothing and appeared graceless in the mere act of standing. Not too eagerly, she went up to him and started a conversation.

His name, he said, was Anthony Schnitzer; most people called him 'Bubba.' At this moment he was waiting for his trainer to show up and guide him through his workout. The trainer's absence stirred mixed feelings in Bubba, who wasn't fond of the guy ("a real prick," as he put it) but who wasn't sure what to do if left to his own devices. "You'd think after six months of workin' out I'd have a clue," he said. "But I don't. This whole fitness thing ... I do it, but I don't wanna have to think about it. Doin' it's bad enough." He said he'd be willing to talk to Laura for a while on the record.

Bubba sat himself on the bench, and she was tempted to sit down beside him. But she didn't; she stood.

LK: So where is everybody today?

BUBBA: Damn if I know.

LK: I have to believe the gym's usually a little busier than this.

BUBBA: I believe so too.

LK: You think people are staying away because they're scared?

BUBBA: Could be. Yeah, I'd say so.

LK: What are they scared of, would you say?

BUBBA: Well, all kinds of stuff. You know.

LK: Tell me.

BUBBA: Crime, for one thing. People gettin' mugged. Houses set on fire ...

LK: What else?

BUBBA: I don't believe most folks cares too much for all them lights in the sky.

LK: What do you suppose they are?

BUBBA: I set out on my porch last evening, ate some buttered popcorn, watched 'em for about twenty minutes.

LK: What d—

BUBBA: Real pretty, I thought. Kinda reminded me of the Fourth of July. But quiet.

LK: What do you suppose they are?

BUBBA: The lights? Hell, I dunno. Part of the scare tactic, I guess.

LK: Scare tactic?

BUBBA: Sure. Just like that big ol' face.

LK: You've seen the face?

BUBBA: Damn straight I seen it. Ain't you?

LK: No. Not yet.

BUBBA: Well, I sure as hell did. Last weekend. I was out back changin' the oil in my truck. Goddam face came down at me—I made a helluva mess with the oil, lemme tell you.

LK: It scared you?

BUBBA: Scared me! I liked to piss myself. Thing took up the whole friggin' sky, you know?

LK: Did it speak to you?

BUBBA: That ain't no way to start off a Saturday morning, I'll guarantee you.

LK: What did it say to you?

BUBBA: Aw, you know. Usual stuff. But it never scared me as much as they wanted.

LK: As much as who wanted?

BUBBA: The ones behind it.

LK: And they are?...

BUBBA (pause): I'd say the federal government. They're behind *all* this stuff. The lights, the crime wave ...

LK: *Our* federal government?

BUBBA: All these rumors the world's gonna end ...

LK: I want to make sure I understand you. You're saying our own government has somehow ... crafted the face?

BUBBA: That's right. Everything else that's goin' on, too; they cooked it up. That bushwa over there in Coral, China ...

LK: How?

BUBBA: Whadaya mean, how? How they doin' it?

LK: Uh huh.

BUBBA: Hell, I dunno. But they got people, qualified people. Scientists, spies. Specialists.

LK: Specialists?

BUBBA: Not just anybody can make a goddam face in the sky, seems to me.

LK (pause): Why do you suppose they're doing these things?

BUBBA: Well, I—

LK: You said something about a scare tactic.

BUBBA: That's right. See, the whole idea here is for the government to keep control of the people. They can do that by scarin' 'em.

LK: So this is all just a—

BUBBA: Scarin' the bejesus out of 'em.

LK: It's all just a trick, a fabrication.

BUBBA: That's it.

LK: But it appears to me, Mr. Schnitzer—

BUBBA: Bubba.

LK: Bubba, it appears to me that things have gotten *out* of control. Society is breaking down.

BUBBA: No. That's what they want you to think.

LK: But you said yourself, just a moment ago—

BUBBA (shakes his head): Just another part of the scare tactic.

LK: The muggings, the fires?

BUBBA: Yep.

LK: People dying?

BUBBA: Yep.

LK: Hmm.

BUBBA: Federal government's a terrible thing.

LK: Are you afraid to die, Bubba?

BUBBA: Me? Afraid? No. (pause) Not as much as they want me to be. But it ain't gonna happen anyways.

LK: Never?

BUBBA: No time soon. And the world ain't gonna end neither.

LK: Never?

BUBBA: Not for a good while. And you can take that to

the First National Bank and earn some dough on it.

Finished with Bubba, Laura left the gym and walked in the direction of a coffee shop she'd driven by earlier. Though the streets were mostly empty of people and traffic, she felt uneasy walking; maybe the emptiness itself disturbed her. A young black man, either angry or frightened to judge by the look on his face, ran toward her and by her at full speed. Across the street, another man, this one white, ran by in the opposite direction. Somewhere, someone was howling—a pained plaintive cry without meaning. Squeezing her voice recorder, nerves beaten flat from the travel and yet buzzing anxiously from everything else, she ducked hurriedly into The Daily Grind.

A handful of customers in there—better than the gym. But a table of three stood up to leave even as Laura was pushing through the door. She went to the counter and ordered a vanilla iced coffee. Briefly, she considered questioning the freckle-faced redhead who'd waited on her but decided that this might be poor form. Cradling her tall plastic cup, she let her eyes settle on an elderly man whose tousled white hair resembled the foam atop a serving of dry cappuccino. He was wearing a sky-blue sport shirt and staring meditatively out a window.

His name, she would soon learn, was Ben Temple. Though long retired, he kept active in the community by volunteering his time at the hospital and by serving as artistic director of the Your Town Theatre. He enjoyed spending time with his family, but at this moment, except for Laura, he was by himself.

LK: So you're an artist?
BEN: Oh, no. Being artistic director of a small theatre doesn't necessarily make you an artist.
LK: You're being modest.
BEN (smiles): Truthful. But I've been fortunate enough to've worked with some very talented people over the years.

LK: Anything interesting going on at the theatre now?

BEN: Oh my. That's an understatement.

LK: Good stuff?

BEN: Well—interesting. I don't know quite what to say about it other than that.

LK: You've piqued my curiosity.

BEN: Didn't mean to. Tell you the truth, I can't focus too much on the theatre with all these other things going on, you know?

LK: The face, you mean?

BEN: The face, the whole whoop-de-doo.

LK: Have you seen it?

BEN (shakes his head): Feel kinda left out. But then again, I don't need to see it. I've seen enough strangeness for one lifetime.

LK: What do you think it means?

BEN: I don't know. Can't be anything good.

LK: Are we all going to die?

BEN (laughs): Sooner or later. I've got a friend named Trevor Null—the County Commissioner?

LK: Haven't met him.

BEN: You're not from around here; that's right. Anyhow, Trevor claims that God is gonna zap the planet the same way He zapped Sodom and Gomorrah back in the day.

LK: Do you agree?

BEN: Again—I don't know. But over the years Trevor's been right more often than not. He says—

LK: Let me ask you— I'm sorry.

BEN: He says we're all up Shit Creek with a turd for a paddle.

LK: I ... Let me—

BEN: Ms. Kennedy, I beg your pardon. Please don't quote me on that. Or Trevor. That's impolite for him to say and impolite for me to repeat.

LK: It's OK.

BEN: But you get my drift.

LK: I do. (pause) Let me ask you about China. Do you think that whatever's happened there—

BEN: Have you heard the latest?

LK: What.

BEN: They're saying now that the city—what was it? Korla?—is gone. It doesn't exist anymore.

LK: Oh my God.

BEN: Heard it on my car's radio not ten minutes ago.

LK: What happened?

BEN (crosses his legs): They're not saying.

LK: Nuclear weapon?

BEN: They're not saying. But it's as if someone took an enormous eraser to the city and just wiped it away.

LK: We live in interesting times. It's not *there* anymore?

BEN: Gone.

LK (pause): Do you suppose there's any connection between that and ... all the other stuff?

BEN: The face, the lights ...

LK: Right.

BEN: Well, you know, we've had these disappearing buildings. I guess it's not that grand a leap to go from having a restaurant disappear to having an entire city disappear.

LK: Uh huh. I'm told that the face, when it talks to people, says something about a city or two cities or some such.

BEN: Yes, I've heard the same thing.

LK: A 'token of good faith.'

BEN: Ironic, isn't it? That phrase a 'token of good faith' sounds so positive.

LK: So what do you think's going to happen?

BEN (uncrosses his legs): There's no precedent. How do you make a judgment when, uh ...

LK: What's your gut tell you?

BEN: My gut's not much good. I can't even drink my coffee.

LK: We're in for it, aren't we?

BEN (laughs): You sound like my wife. If we *are* in for it, what are we supposed to do about it?

LK: What *are* we supposed to do?

BEN: Pray, maybe. I've been doing a lot of that. Doesn't seem to help much.

LK: Should the government be doing more?

BEN: What should they do? What do you do in a case like this?

LK: Should we open a line of communication?...

BEN: To whom? To what? How?

LK (pause): One more question. Where will you go? Today. When you're done your coffee—

BEN: I'm done with it.

LK: Where will you go next?

BEN: My wife hasn't retired yet; she still works for a living, God bless her. She's at work now. I'm gonna go get her, take her home with me. I don't care what they say.

LK: It's been good talking to you.

BEN: Joan and I'll stick close together till this thing's over.


Ignoring two other potential interviewees—they were spaced-out druggie types, unpromising—Laura left when Ben did and made it back to her car without incident. She locked the doors and took off, listening to the radio as she drove. Ben's startling synopsis of Korla was borne out by the sober professional voices delivering the news—according to the latest accounts, the city could now be referred to in the past tense. While no one could explain how or why, Korla simply wasn't there anymore; even the tight-lipped Chinese were admitting as much. Its inhabitants, buildings, streets, traffic, culture, attractions and shortcomings were all gone. Whatever plans its citizens may have harbored, whatever their fears, hopes, hobbies, complaints, principles, passions, guilty pleasures and secret musings on life in this universe or some other—all had been mysteriously expunged. As a result, countries around the globe were issuing a sputtering stream of accusations and denials.

Driving ahead, no exact destination in mind, Laura tried to call her parents in Minnesota; she couldn't reach them. She tried to call Sarah; couldn't reach her.

Before long, she found herself on a gently bending parkway along the outskirts of town. Picturesque trees, mown grass. A sign advised her that she was drawing close to Harris Community College, whose squat functional buildings now began to hover like a mirage in the distance. Shaky but determined, Laura decided to take the exit and discover who on campus might be available for a recorded chat.

Not many, from the looks of the parking lot, which was dotted with no more than ten or twelve cars. On her way up the sidewalk she ran into a gaggle of four female students headed away from the school. She spoke to them briefly and learned that two of them believed classes had been canceled for the day and two believed they hadn't been. Since, regardless of their beliefs, all four were clearly in a rush to go somewhere else, Laura made no attempt to interview any of them.

Inside, she saw that the classrooms and halls were vacant. Many of the lights had been turned off, and the halls were filled with a gauzy gray gloom that made her think of twilight. Her footsteps echoed hollowly off the bare floors. She was about to turn and leave when she spied a trickle of pallid light seeping out the open doorway of a narrow office.

Peering through the doorway, Laura saw a man of considerable years seated at a desk studying some documents. Beneath his deforested scalp he wore a mild frown and a pair of reading glasses. To her puzzlement, he also wore a tangerine-colored T-shirt made of some chic velvety material, several thin gold necklaces and several thin gold bracelets on his right wrist. The sturdy brass nameplate on his desk identified him as William J. Yommer, Associate Dean of Academic Affairs.

So immersed was Dean Yommer in his lucubration that thirty seconds passed before he realized he had a visitor. When he finally did become aware of her—"Hello," she called;

"Ahem, hello!"—he listened carefully to her proposal to interview him and then bluntly expressed his resistance. She'd made no appointment with him, and he'd had no time to organize his thoughts properly for any kind of formal discussion; these facts ran counter to his personal policy. Besides, he was very busy. But when the young lady persisted—she was not without charm, this Kennedy girl, and she did represent a *national* newspaper—he gradually gave in, agreeing to talk for a few minutes. Though he never would've said so, sharing his views with what could be a wide audience had a rather intoxicating appeal for him.

LK: You seem to be buried in work.

YOMMER: It's a common misperception that those of us in academe belong to the leisured class. But it just isn't so, and I can testify to that.

LK: What is it you're working on?

YOMMER: Now?

LK (nods): If you don't mind my asking. I see you're going through a hefty stack of papers.

YOMMER: I'm preparing for a series of meetings with specific members of our faculty. Performance evaluations, and I'll leave it at that. As a rule, anytime I go into a meeting, I try to be thoroughly prepared.

LK: You have a lot of meetings, I take it?

YOMMER: Meeting with people—discussing the relevant issues—is crucial to our success at HCC. It's called 'communication.' Unless we communicate with each other, and do so on a regular basis, we're left to flounder in the dark.

LK: I notice a lot of people are missing today.

YOMMER: I can't speak to others' whereabouts.

LK: I just talked to some students outside. A couple of them told me classes have been canceled.

YOMMER: That's correct. Classes have been canceled for the remainder of the day.

LK: Why?

YOMMER: I'm not authorized to address that question. It's an internal matter.

LK: Is it because there's a general panic underway?

YOMMER: Ms. Kennedy. Please. As I suggested, some issues I can address; some issues I cannot address.

LK: Let me ask you this. If classes have been canceled and most other people are gone, why are you still here?

YOMMER: Why am I ...

LK: With all respect.

YOMMER (firmly): Do you remember my observation about not being a member of the leisured class?

LK: Yes.

YOMMER: Well, I think it applies to your question. My position requires that I adhere to my duties regardless of whether or not classes are in session. I get paid to achieve results, and it doesn't matter how many hours I have to spend in achieving them.

LK: I under—

YOMMER: Would it surprise you to know that I often come in and work on Saturdays and Sundays?

LK: No, it wouldn't.

YOMMER: It's called a 'work ethic.'

LK: I understand.

YOMMER: I'm glad you do.

LK: Let me ask you, sir, if I could, about China.

YOMMER: Certainly. My background is in International Relations, and I do have some expertise in China.

LK: It's being reported that the Chinese city of Korla has been ... eradicated. No one seems to know how it happened or who's responsible. What's your reaction?

YOMMER (pause): I would say this. The People's Republic of China is a very significant player in world affairs. It's an economic powerhouse. This is a nation that's been sadly overlooked for far too long, and sooner or later we'll have to sit down with her and go eyeball-to-eyeball.

LK (long pause): What, uh, what about Korla?

YOMMER: What about it?

LK: What do you think might've happened there?

YOMMER: The news reports?

LK: Yes.

YOMMER: We're assuming, of course, that those reports are accurate.

LK: Yes.

YOMMER: You're asking me to speculate.

LK: Well—yes.

YOMMER: I don't like to speculate, Ms. Kennedy, unless there's a very solid foundation in facts. And then it's called 'extrapolation,' not 'speculation.' At this stage, I don't believe we have a solid foundation in facts.

LK: Well ... OK. How about this then: have you ever seen the face?

YOMMER: Which face?

LK: The face in the sky.

YOMMER: I'm an ex-Marine. Does that tell you anything?

LK: Uh—no.

YOMMER: Ex-Marines do not worry about alleged faces in the sky.

LK: But did you see it?

YOMMER (stares up at the ceiling): No. And I have nothing further to say about that damn face.

LK: Are you concerned about what's happening? Because *something* seems to be happening.

YOMMER: I think 'concerned' is an appropriate word. Not 'scared,' and certainly not anything stronger than that. But 'concerned'—because it implies a thoughtful and contained response to a situation that asks our attention.

LK: Do you believe in an afterlife?

YOMMER: I do.

LK: Do you think we'll be seeing that afterlife sooner rather than later?

YOMMER (smiles): You keep trying to get me to speculate. But I'll tell y—

LK: No, I just—

YOMMER: I'll tell you what. Just this one time I'll break my rule. I'll speculate.

LK: Please do.

YOMMER: Because this is something I've turned over in my mind. (pause) I don't know if we'll be seeing the afterlife anytime soon. (pause) But I suspect when we do see it, we'll notice certain commonalities with the life we have here.

LK: Such as?

YOMMER: I think, for example, we'll *work*—not just sit back on a cloud and do nothing. People draw satisfaction from purposeful work.

LK: Uh huh.

YOMMER: Working, of course, means we'll be communicating with each other.

LK: Right ...

YOMMER: And communication implies meetings. I can picture the afterlife as entailing an infinite series of vigorous well-structured meetings.

LK: Well, that's—

YOMMER: And you know what? I plan to be right in the middle of them.

LK: I believe you.

YOMMER: Right in the middle.

LK: I believe you.

YOMMER: Oh—before you go, let me have you sign this sheet acknowledging that you and I met today.

Leaving the office, Laura felt wearied. She'd met people like Yommer before, or somewhat like him—stiff, programmatic, their very brains beribboned with red tape—and conversation with that sort always sapped her energy. They were like black holes deep in space, sucking up all the light around them. Don't dare wander too close or you'll spiral down inside that gravitational vortex and never escape....

She was scared too, having hurtled by 'concerned' a long

time ago. And she was hungry.

She didn't know what she could do about her fear except push right through it—try to be assertive, forward-leaning; stay engaged. But her hunger was a problem with a clear-cut solution.

Casting a final glance at the campus, Laura swung her car around the barren lot and headed back toward the downtown. Maybe she could find a cozy little bistro where they served low-cal beers and low-fat burgers.

19

THE FEELING—it was a premonition—descended on Helbig quite suddenly. It was like the first prickly chill, the first throbbing ache, that precedes a long and hellish bout of the flu.

He had just turned away from the roly-poly new guy, Bob Stallings, whom he had set in klutzy motion on the treadmill. Neither man had taken more than a dozen steps before the cold clammy feeling floated down on Helbig and left him trembling in abject misery. There was a very real chance, it struck him, that his play wouldn't be performed in front of a paying audience anytime soon. No, and if conditions deteriorated further, resulting in some genuine damage to society (he didn't count China as 'society'), the public's interest in theatre might be next to zero for longer than he could bear.

All around him, the TVs with their godawful news reports bedeviled him. Every syllable of every report was one more ounce of adversity weighing against him and his blockbuster drama. By now a tremendous glut of words had been bandied about, tons and tons worth, with truckloads more sure to come. How many of the words were even true? It didn't matter; they were all hurting him deeply.

Helbig needed some reassurance that the plan to put on his play was absolutely still in place, and he needed it quickly. Without even a minute's delay, he would call Ben Temple and get the reassurance he craved and deserved.

Or would he?

Goddammit, how many times in his star-crossed life had he been in a situation similar to this one—having been promised something only to have it yanked unfairly away from him? Too many times to list, though he did take the time to list some of them. To begin with, he *should've* had his parents, and

for a few short years he did. But then they got into a terrific
row and decided they didn't want each other and didn't want
him either; neither one would have him. So he was left to be
raised by a pair of indifferent aunts, one after the other, each of
whom had her hair arranged into a rigid upright column that
looked like a monolith honoring some Assyrian god. Martha
and Edna. He hadn't spoken to either lady in years, and he
wondered dully if they were still around, still singing in church
on Sundays, or if they'd gone off to that finer-tuned and much
more selective choir in the sky. (Not that Helbig believed any
such celestial choir existed.)

In high school, he was a finalist for a literary award to be
presented to the student who, in the teachers' estimate, had
written the best essay. It had come down to a choice between
his piece and one written by a student named Daryl Dodge.
Daryl wasn't as flashy a writer, but he did have the advantage
of being a brown-nose, a company man and a shrewd
politician—before Helbig had ever given politics much
thought. Helbig's essay took on the local educational system,
mocking its alleged flaws, while Daryl's essay lavishly praised
that same system as being the ideal tool to foster learning. One
of the teachers, something of a malcontent himself, confided
to Helbig that based on sheer literary merit he should win the
award easily. Naturally, he didn't. Nor did he accept the news
with equanimity. At the awards ceremony, he jabbed his finger
at the committee and at his rival and screeched at them:
"You're all afraid of the truth! Chick chick chick chick chick
chick chick!"

Then, at HCC, he suffered the *Oh! Calcutta!* fiasco. Helbig
was hopeful that in this post-Sexual Revolution age, a play with
a dab of sexual innuendo could be staged in a college setting
and no one would have a cow. To his delight, when he first
announced his intentions, no one did object. He might've
guessed it was because no one at this provincial school had
even the foggiest idea of what the play was about. In time, the
facts tumbled out, and people were having cows all over the

place. The most common sound on campus became a loud laboring MOOOOOOOOOO! Chief among Helbig's adversaries was an overweight business professor who, working quietly but tirelessly behind the scenes, kept insisting that HCC's reputation was on the line—that decent people had to stand up for clean wholesome American values and not allow 'dirt' to be presented on stage. In the end, their side won, and Helbig, who dropped out of school, gravitated to the Your Town Theatre, where kindly old Ben Temple, with his snow-white hair and snow-white scruples, also refused to let him do *Oh! Calcutta!*.

The old son of a bitch.

The question now was, would Ben let Helbig do his *own* damn play?

Mumbling to himself, Helbig scurried off to Johnny's private office where no one was supposed to go except Johnny (but where Helbig often went when Johnny wasn't around) and called Ben.

"Ben," he said, trying to hold his voice in check, "I've been watching the news, and I don't like what I see."

"Nobody likes it," Ben said.

"I don't know where all this stuff's gonna come out."

"I don't either, Dunk."

"It's got me worried, Ben."

"Same here," Ben said. "The world's never seen anything like it."

"The world!?" Helbig yawped. "The hell with the world; I'm worried about my play! We gonna stick to the schedule or what?"

Across the miles, he heard Ben exhale. Then he heard him exhale again; he sounded as if he might be climbing a long flight of stairs. "Listen," Ben said, "I can't talk right now. I'm tied up. I'll call you back, OK?"

"Ben, dammit, what I ... Hey, Ben? Dammit, all I want ... Hello?"

But Ben had hung up.

Fuming, Helbig tried repeatedly to call him back but couldn't reach him. Afterwards, he stayed awhile in Johnny's office, pacing to and fro, attempting to calm himself. It didn't work; he felt as if he had a Harley Fat Boy revving inside his chest. So he stepped outside into the parking lot, continued pacing, continued trying to come down a notch. He thought the open sunlit spaces might help, but they didn't—not much. Finally he decided to go in search of Ben, talk to him face-to-face. Obviously this tactic would mean abandoning his post at the gym and could definitely get him fired if Johnny found out. But job security wasn't at the forefront of his unstrung mind just now, so he hopped on his Schwinn bicycle and started pedaling.

Knowing that Ben did volunteer work at a hospital, Helbig thought of calling there and asking if that's where he was. But he didn't want to give his quarry a chance to flee. So he rode his bike some distance to the site and began snooping around for Ben's 'Your Town'-decorated van. The hospital, however, was surrounded by multiple parking lots—and a parking garage—and before long the effort became too much. It also occurred to Helbig that Ben wouldn't necessarily have brought the van anyway, but might be using his everyday car. Whatever that was. After thirty minutes and not even entering the hospital, he turned tail and pedaled off to the Your Town Theatre. No vehicles there, no activity—no surprise. Shining with sweat, panting with fatigue, he went next to Ben's home, which Helbig had visited on theatre business more than once over the years. It was a smart-looking gray stone house in a better neighborhood than Helbig's. Though he did see the van parked in the drive, he still couldn't be sure Ben was home.

Helbig laid his bike down on the trim grass, walked over to the front door and rang the doorbell. No answer. He rang again, pressing on the button till the tip of his finger began to pulse with pain. Nothing. He beat on the door with the meat of his fist and added to the racket by bawling: "BEN! BEN TEMPLE! I KNOW YOU'RE IN THERE, BEN! OPEN

THE DOOR! BEN TEMPLE!"

Meanwhile, behind him, a Volvo driven by Joan Temple pulled up and parked. A moment later, Ben, driving a second Volvo, parked behind her. The two Temples got out, and Ben escorted his wife up the walkway. Seeing Helbig—and hearing him; "I KNOW YOU'RE IN THERE, BEN!" he roared, hands on hips—Ben held Joan's hand and interposed his own not too rugged body between her and the agitated little man at the door.

"I'll be with you in a second, Dunk," Ben said, causing Helbig to flinch in surprise.

A regal woman, tall and stately, Joan peered down at Helbig with withering distaste as she passed him; one would've thought she'd just noticed some mutant and especially repugnant weed spoiling her manicured lawn—an extraordinary weed that moved around, perspired, glowered and even, after a fashion, communicated.

"Ben—" Helbig began.

"In a second, Dunk." Ben unlocked the door and made certain his wife was safely inside before turning to Helbig.

"Ben—"

"Dunk, are you daft?" Ben's tone was one of carefully restrained exasperation. He wanted to convey the fact that he *was* exasperated, but he didn't want to do so in a pitched way that could cause the problem to escalate. It was an artful tone that he'd practiced with Helbig frequently. "You rode your bike all the way out here? For God's sake, why?"

"Ben, I need some reassurance."

"Don't we all."

"I'm talking about my play. We're gonna go ahead with it, aren't we? On schedule?"

"Dunk—"

"Ben?" Helbig was standing maybe two feet in front of Ben, eyes fixed and glittering, face bathed in sweat, breathing rapid and shallow. His manner seemed partly pleading, partly menacing.

Ben selected his words with a discretion so fine it would've impressed a high-voltage electrician. "Dunk," he said, "the way things look now, quite honestly, we may—*may!*—have to adjust the schedule. Somewhat."

" 'Adjust' it?" Helbig snorted. "The way you're 'adjusting' my script?"

Granting the point with a wry smile and a half-shrug, Ben held his ground, held his tone. "There's a lot going on these days, you know? Some of it's not so good. Look, I'm as devoted to theatre as anybody—"

"Not as devoted as I am."

"—but these are tough times. We've got to put things in their proper persp—"

"Art is long, Ben. Life is short."

"People are afraid, Dunk, that life may be all *too* short. So let's keep things in their proper perspective, shall we?"

"Perspective!" Helbig sneered. He hated the word. Artists didn't get to be artists by having perspective; artists lived like haughty princes inside the palace of their work.

"You heard about China, didn't you? That city over there? They're saying now it's gone. If that's true, a bunch of people are gone with it."

Helbig waved his hands. "But that's *China*, Ben. China's half the world away!"

Ben took a step toward his door. "We all live in the same world."

"Aaaaaaaaaah."

"And their troubles are our troubles, unless I misunderstand." He had his hand on the doorknob.

"Ben, I need some reassurance. I've worked too long, too hard—"

"We'll wait and see what develops," Ben said. "That's the best I can do for you. If you'll excuse me, I need to be with my wife."

"No."

"What?"

"No—I won't excuse you. I want your word, Ben, that we're gonna move ahead with the play come hell or high water."

Eyeing Helbig warily from his doorway, Ben said: "Dunk, you've been a ..." He couldn't locate an acceptable word or phrase. "... a guy I've worked with. I have a ... regard for you. But you'll need to go away now." He dipped his white head at Helbig, trying to suggest finality, and closed the door behind him. Locked it.

For much longer than Ben would've liked, Helbig remained outside the door, beating on it and yelling at Ben to show his face. Then Helbig began to chant. "*Ars longa, vita brevis!*" he cried like some Keatsian cheerleader. "*Ars longa, vita brevis!*"

He stopped only when Ben appeared in the window holding a phone and apparently calling somebody—calling the cops maybe. Never mind that phone service was becoming sporadic and that police (and firefighters) had been hard to find lately. The gesture was enough.

Resentfully Helbig backed away. He picked up his bike, climbed aboard and eased down the walkway. He was muttering bitterly to himself.

* * *

Pedaling home—it never occurred to him he might return to work—he had no conscious thoughts. He was alert to what was happening around him, and he responded correctly to challenges such as moving vehicles and pedestrians, but there was no thought process of which he was aware. Just action and reaction. Yet on a deeper level some mentation must have taken place because he had already formulated a plan. It wasn't a great plan; indeed it was as primitive as a plan could be. But it was there, before him, ready to be carried out.

When he arrived home, he showed no emotion in discovering that his former lover and current blackmailer

Chance Smathers was hanging around outside the apartment waiting on him. It wasn't completely unexpected since, if the guy needed more money, where the hell else would he go? At the same time, Helbig couldn't help but feel his huffing growling outrage beginning to rear up on its thick hind legs. Damn, he'd just doled out a fair chunk of change this morning. If this was to be the typical turnaround time, he'd be bankrupted by nightfall.

"Chance," Helbig said dryly, "I didn't expect to see you back so soon."

"Didn't expect to be here. But Dunk, I've been thinking."

"Dangerous activity, that."

Helbig put his bike aside and breezed right by Chance on a beeline for the garage. Chance, who'd cleaned himself up a smidgeon, trailed after Helbig as if attached to him by an invisible cord. When Helbig entered the garage, his blond shadow followed. Moving almost automatically, Helbig snapped on a feeble overhead light that revealed a haze of cobwebs, a stockpile of red plastic jugs along the wall, and his car—the midnight blue Spectra, undriven in more than a year.

"Here's what I think," Chance said. In sum, he felt that he and Helbig should get back into an intimate relationship. They'd been a fabulous couple, adding immeasurably to each other's life, and Chance couldn't recall a reason for their separation anyway—other than Helbig had decreed it was necessary. "Let's be special again," Chance said. "Give it some real thought at least, won't you, the way I have."

Though the car had been undriven, it had not been unstarted. Every few days Helbig had started it and let it run for five or ten minutes. Long enough to keep the battery charged, but not long enough to risk carbon monoxide poisoning. (He would've contended, however, that there were worse ways to go than to slip off into a warm embracing CO sleep—plenty of worse ways.) It was time to check the car again, so he swung open the door, sat down inside and turned the ignition. Vroom! Nice. After a moment he cut the motor.

"You'll be happy to know, I think," Chance said, "that I've reconsidered that whole unfortunate episode with the woman. The woman in the, um, parking lot. I can see your side of it now. It was just one of those things. An accident. Tragic but unavoidable."

" 'Ineluctable,' Joyce would say." Helbig went around to the trunk and opened it.

"And nothing that needed to be reported."

"You *would* have to mention that business, wouldn't you."

"I didn't have to," Chance said, "but I wanted to. To put your heart at ease."

"Uh huh."

Moving precisely and unemotionally, Helbig began loading the red jugs into the trunk of his car.

"I also felt," Chance said, "that your offer to help me this morning was very sweet and very generous. Later on, when I thought about it, I was moved."

"Great." Still hauling the jugs.

Hands in his pockets, Chance watched Helbig—watched the flitting avian movements.

"What, uh ... what're you doing?" he asked.

"What's it look like?"

"Looks as if you're loading up the trunk of your car with gasoline."

"That's it."

Chance nodded. "Need some help?"

"No."

Chance nodded again. "There's something else," he said. "Today, a short while ago, I saw the face. That face everyone's talking about? In the sky? It scared me, Dunk. It scared me way down deep where I live."

Bending over the trunk, rearranging the jugs, his expression hidden, Helbig said nothing.

"I think we're all up to our neck in shit," Chance said. "If the world's going to end—and I think it might—I'd like to spend my last hours with you, Dunk."

Still with his back to Chance, Helbig slowly straightened up. He held his silence, and may well have been processing a set of complex ideas or a tangle of deep-rooted feelings.

"That face," Chance said, "was the face of Death. I'm convinced of it."

Without a word, Helbig wheeled around and struck Chance's newly shaven jaw with his fist. A vicious blow that connected solidly—*whap!*—it spun the unguarded victim's head ninety degrees and dropped him to a crawling position. In fact, Chance tried to crawl but couldn't, collapsing to his belly and then rolling over dazedly on his back. He looked narcotized—but he also looked like a man who was beginning to grasp just how skewed his judgment had been.

"Here's another scary face for you," Helbig said, looming over him, bringing his own frightful mug, livid and hateful, down to where it hung no more than a yard above Chance's unfocused eyes. "You ass."

Then he pulled away, went back to hauling jugs.

When he finished, he shut the trunk and debated what to do about Chance. A part of Helbig wanted to beat his one-time companion to death; if he used a tire iron, the task could be accomplished quickly and simply. For good measure, he might then douse the body with gasoline and set it afire.

But he sensed he was on the verge of doing something rash and foolish. Bludgeoning Chance to death would stain the garage with telltale blood. A fire, if he set one here, could spread; he might actually burn down the garage, his own apartment and half the neighborhood. Besides, he didn't want to waste the gasoline. At length he calculated that Chance, who was still semi-conscious on his back, would keep till later. Helbig could lock him inside this dark enclosure and deal with him at his leisure.

Ready to roll, Helbig gave Chance a kick in the head in hopes it would keep him horizontal for a while longer. He raised the bay door and once again started the car, pulled it out into the alley. Then he went back inside, found a padlock, kicked Chance in the head again, lowered the door and locked it. Moving with the same deliberate speed, he went around to the other side of the garage and secured the lock there.

The flat line of his mouth set even more grimly than usual, he got in the car and drove away.

* * *

Not having driven a car recently, Helbig appreciated the feel of the seat, the acceleration, the steering. Though drawing undue attention to himself might've worked against him today, he didn't care. He drove recklessly, aggressively; he leaned on the horn, ran stop signs, trashed the speed limit. Helbig on a bike would not have enjoyed meeting Helbig in a car.

One small subunit of his mind wanted him to return to Ben's house and torch it. But the half-baked notion wouldn't have worked. The house was stone, and Helbig remembered with disappointment the skimpy damage he'd done to the bank. No, though the little subunit howled its protest, especially at sparing that tall snooty wife of Ben's, he understood that the house was the wrong target.

The correct target was the Your Town Theatre, which was no more than a big dry wooden box, extremely combustible. He pulled up with a squeal of rubber directly in front of the building. People might see him, but he was unconcerned. (Did he actually *want* to be witnessed?) What he was about to do wasn't a crime, he would've argued, but an act of righteous resistance, a cri de coeur. He was standing up boldly for the dignity and worth of the everyday working American, who, down through the deckle-edged pages of history, had been kicked around far too often. *Keep your promises, bossman*, he thought to himself. *Keep your promises to me and to all of us or pay the price.* If he got caught, Helbig guessed he might have to pay the price himself, but he had a hunch no one would nab him.

He fought his way through the sticky door and lugged the gasoline inside, two jugs at a time. Most of them he took to the stage area; others he dropped off at various strategic points. The theatre was honeycombed with crooked corridors and hidden-away rooms, the majority of them tiny—a cloak room, restrooms, dressing rooms, storage rooms, closets.... They would all receive their share of low-octane. If they'd had the power to speak, they would've expressed dismay, but probably not surprise, at what was about to happen. *C'mon, we know him,* one of them would've chided. *The surprise would've been if he'd stayed true to us, saluted our heritage, protected us from harm....* Helbig meant to saturate the place, and then to destroy it, as completely and spectacularly as he could.

A man who could be strikingly meticulous in his behavior, Helbig wasn't too meticulous now. He tore the cap off a jug and slung the gasoline every which way; some of it splashed on his T-shirt and shorts—on his bare skin. He seized another jug and, grunting with his exertions, sent more gas sloshing all around. Then another jug, and another. The rich smell of the stuff—its heavy wetness too—stimulated him more than any musky cologne or ice-cool aftershave worn by some hunky stubble-faced stud could ever do....

One might've supposed that at a crossroads like this Helbig would've been inclined to revisit a sampling of the memories he'd made here—the theatre had provided him with some of his semi-happiest times. But his thoughts refused to tilt in that direction. Instead, he found himself growing increasingly excited about the monstrous fire he would soon ignite. While no delay was possible, of course, he wished it could be night so the brilliant dancing flames could be showcased in all their vivid glory. Rippling orange against bottomless black! His penis stiffening—not beneficial to his work—he hurried through the theatre, emptying the jugs and recalling a piece he'd memorized for his first acting class, John Evelyn's signal description of the Great Fire of London:

> *Oh the miserable and calamitous spectacle! such as haply the world had not seen since the foundation of it, nor be outdone till the*

*universal conflagration thereof. All the sky was of a fiery aspect, like the top of a burning oven, and the light seen above 40 miles round about for many nights. God grant mine eyes may never behold the like, who now saw above 10,000 houses all in one flame; the noise and cracking and thunder of people, the fall of towers, houses, and churches, was like an hideous storm, and the air all about so hot and inflamed that at last one was not able to approach it.... Thus I left it this afternoon burning, a resemblance of Sodom, or the last day.*

Well, Helbig would give the world a Great Fire too, or die trying. With the last of his jugs he'd drawn a trail of gasoline out to the front door. Having some fuel left over, he splattered it all around the foyer where he stood. The crystalline moment held no room for hesitation, for nostalgic reflection. Instantly he produced his Bic lighter and, kneeling down next to the exit, set the floor—the entire room and beyond—aflame. There was a soft crackle, which expanded into a much louder crackle, and red-orange tongues of fire stood up like so many demons jabbering and crowding all around him.

The heat came at him with a surprising fury, and he backed into the door, causing it to close. Knowing he had just seconds to bolt, he fumbled for the doorknob, found it and turned it. He was feeling an eddying mix of exhilaration, awe and sexual arousal. A rush. But when the knob turned and the door stayed stubbornly in place, Helbig began to feel something different: grave disappointment, and the slashing ripping assaults of the fire. Wildly, he jerked at the doorknob to no avail, then threw himself at the impassive door again and again, thumping against it, hands and arms in a flutter. The sounds he made were squawking and birdlike, and he resembled a terrified parakeet trying to escape its cage.

But the door wouldn't budge.

"Goddam!" he squawked.

To his horror, he saw that the door itself was on fire. Even worse, *he* was on fire—his clothes, his skin, his very flesh. The pain was intense beyond words; he felt as if some predator were eating him alive, razor teeth tearing him apart. He banged helplessly on the door with his fists, but it remained immobile. Then, almost on instinct, he whirled around to confront his destroyer. The wall of fire roared at him, pressed against him, cooked him. While he was still able to see, he lifted his eyes toward the ceiling; something had caused him to lift his eyes. In the pit of his heart he fully expected to see a face, an uncompromising face that would loom down at him fiercely, call him by name and speak to him in a way that would magnify his torment.

Would it be a man's face? he wondered. The same face others had seen? Or in his special instance, would it be the face of the woman he'd killed? Wearing the same gargoyle expression as when the car had smashed into her ... It seemed to him the second alternative would be far worse.

Staring upward, he was astonished to see no face at all— only a blazing mass of fire.

Then he saw nothing.

20

STANDING WITHIN ARM'S LENGTH of Sarah at Perfection Fitness, Bob Stallings recognized once again what a lucky guy Johnny was. A storied career as a baseball player, enduring fame, more money than Stallings could ever dream of (even with the stock market getting clipped as if by a cross-eyed barber)—and then *her* for a daughter. Beauty and brains together in the kind of priceless package that came along all too rarely. Character, too. From teaching her at HCC, Stallings knew what a hard worker Sarah was; when she made up her mind to do something, by God, she did it. No, she and her father hadn't always enjoyed a super-smooth relationship, but so it often went with parents and their kids. And surely Johnny was at least partly to blame for the friction between them. Stallings liked him, but Perfection—let's be honest—had been known to gall even the most tolerant of people.

Whatever the case, Sarah had come home to Illinois, and she wanted to surprise her dad. Pretty cool, Stallings thought.

"But first I need to find him," she said. "I don't suppose you know where he is?"

"No, but he's like a bad penny," Stallings smiled. "He'll turn up."

They had a cursory and unsuccessful look around the gym. The Beast couldn't help them, but didn't harm them either. Since Helbig was still nowhere in sight, Stallings used the gym's phone to give Johnny a call. On the first two attempts, he had no dial tone. Then he got one and made the call, but Johnny didn't answer.

"It's all right," Stallings said, warming to the challenge. "We'll find him. Did you check his condo?"

"He's got a condo?"

Boy, he thought, you *have* been out of touch. "Real ritzy

place," he said. He started to give her directions, then rethought himself. His dorky trainer was MIA; school would be shutting down early (a technicality, since few students or college employees were showing up anyway). What else did he have to do? "I'll take you there," he said.

They decided to go in one vehicle—his, since he doubted he could even function in the low-slung close-quartered Z06 'Vette that, glistening in the sun like a ruby, held him mesmerized for several seconds.

"That's a sweet car," Stallings said as they drove off in his sedate Malibu. "How much did that baby set you back, if you don't mind my asking?"

"Actually," she said, "I didn't have to pay for it. It was part of a package deal that my people worked out with ... somebody else's people."

"Really!" Stallings didn't have any 'people.' "What sort of work do you do? Maybe I should get into it myself."

"Oh ... well ..." Though the sights beyond her windshield were as ordinary as a bowl of oatmeal for breakfast, Sarah seemed to find them more captivating than she did this thread of conversation. "I'm in the media."

"Yeah? TV? Movies?"

"Uh huh."

"You work in front of the camera? 'Cause if you don't mind my saying so, you're a very pretty young lady."

"Thank you, Bob."

"So ... so ... do you work in front of the camera?"

She nodded. "I have."

Stallings had seen so many of his students drop out of school after a semester or two to wind up pumping gas at a service station or serving fries in a fast-food joint. By contrast, here was a girl who'd gone on to achieve success—maybe notable success. But she didn't want to talk about it.

"Sarah," he said, "you're modest."

At this, she had to laugh—her trademark rising infectious laugh that sounded like music. "That's something no one's ever called me before." She became serious. "I've made some money in the business," she said, "but right now I'd prefer not to think about my work."

"Sure."

"I mean, I'm a little discouraged with how things have gone lately."

"I understand." He really did understand. "Work gets on my nerves all the time," he admitted. He thought of Bill Yommer; of the hapless students who resembled extras in *Night of the Living Dead.*

"So why don't you move on?"

"Oh, I'd like to, Sarah. I would. Step up to a university ... That'd be great."

"Why don't you?"

"Well ..." He glanced over at her, feeling less dashing than he wanted to. "To teach at a university these days, you pretty much need your doctorate. I didn't get mine."

"Mm."

"I started on it...."

Their eyes were drawn to a bearded one-armed man, his silver nose-ring throwing off sharp bursts of sunlight. He was shaking his one fist and cursing at them from the sidewalk. He seemed angry. He seemed crazy. It looked as if he might run out into the street and try to tackle the car. Then they were past him.

"Why didn't you keep after it?" she asked.

The question was valid. "I don't know." Stallings searched his memory. "You get older, you get responsibilities. I needed income more than I needed a degree."

"You had a wife."

He looked at her. "Excuse me?"

"You got married," Sarah said. "Which might've been a complicating factor. I remember you talked about Jenny all the time in class."

"Oh. Right. Did I?" The comment pleased him, and he smiled distantly. "I guess I did."

"So how's she doing?"

The question, so predictable, somehow caught Stallings off guard. "Sarah," he said after a moment, "she passed away. About a year ago."

Shocked, she placed her hand lightly on his arm.

"An accident," he said.

"Bob, I'm sorry." She let him know she'd be willing to listen if he wanted to talk about what had happened. But he didn't. Still too painful. And just that quickly, they'd each learned something new about the barbed wire fences people were prone to erect in their conversations.

Soon Johnny's condo, or the palatial building in which it was housed, rose before them. The towering structure seemed at once old and new, traditional and modern, reverent of the past and yet comfortable with the future—more comfortable with it than much of the public was, at any rate. Though he'd been here several times before, Stallings always felt humbled by the pricy elegance and refinement that brooded down at him from above; he was a lowly professor at an obscure community college, after all. For her part, Sarah kept her violet eyes wide open—Stallings gathered she didn't miss much, here or anyplace else—but appeared unruffled.

He parked the car and they got out and went inside. The ground floor, very clean and softly lit, featured a sprinkle of small but posh boutiques. Sarah window-shopped at the jewelry store while he went to the reception desk and spoke to the security guy; the two men shared a nodding acquaintance that Stallings figured might give him a useful edge in the search for Johnny.

It gave him no useful edge at all. As soon as the uniformed man (Reinhard Belzec, by his nametag) asked Stallings if Johnny was expecting him and Stallings said no, the contest was over. Belzec declined to say if Johnny was home, declined to take a message and declined to cooperate in any way. In fact, he rounded out his side of the terse exchange by noting that no part of the building, including the ground floor, was open to those without explicit and legitimate business there, and that loiterers and intruders were subject to prosecution under the law. Stallings thanked him and retreated hastily to Sarah, who'd been eyeing up a sapphire ring.

When he told her what had happened, she said: "Let me have a go at it," and walked over to the desk herself, each bumping stride a minor aphrodisiac, the word 'WISH' across the curved seat of her pants tilting abruptly one way and then the other and then back again like some teasing hormonal seesaw, the entire display transporting Stallings not to a different place but to an earlier time—to his teen years when even the shape of a girl's calf or the sound of her voice could redirect his blood flow. Ashamed of himself, he tore his gaze away from Sarah and put it on the floor, allowing it to return only when she got close to the stern-faced Belzec.

Except now he didn't seem quite as stern-faced as he had before, when under the spell of Stallings' urbane charm. As the professor looked on with open-mouthed amazement, the two fell into a friendly animated discussion, both of them smiling, gesturing, even laughing once or twice. Taking less of his time than Belzec might've preferred, Sarah wrapped up and walked back to Stallings. "C'mon," she said, and they left together.

Outside, Sarah said: "My father left this morning about ten o'clock. He was wearing a baseball cap and carrying a glove. He was on his way to the HCC ball field; we don't know why. Probably driving his black Ford pickup. Not expected back at any particular time."

Stallings, who'd taught Sarah some lessons in the classroom, felt as if he'd just been taught one himself. "How did you find all that out?"

"I asked."

"Well, I asked too. The guy didn't tell me anything."

"It's all in *how* you ask," she said.

Stallings nodded, frowned, rattled his keys and drove her to the ball field.

It was deserted—no cars, no people. Nothing but a

whispering breeze beneath a clear sunny sky. Still, they parked, got out, had a half-hearted walk around. Stallings spotted an object on the mound, and they went over for a closer look. Turned out to be a glove, big, cocoanut brown, and finely made. Sarah reached down and picked it up.

"It's left-handed," Stallings noticed.

"It's a Wilson," she said. "It's his."

They stood there for most of a minute, turning one way and another, seeing nothing unusual, and trying to imagine what had happened with Johnny earlier that day. Why had he come here? Was he alone? With others? Was he OK? Why had he left his glove behind? Perplexed, Stallings had let his eyes settle on the pointed roof of a very dark house beyond center field.

"Let's go sit down," he said.

Taking the glove along, they sat in the stands near third base.

"I played some baseball myself when I was a kid," Stallings said. "I was a catcher. Actually caught your dad a couple times."

"I caught him a couple times myself," Sarah said. He had the feeling they may've been referring to different activities.

He waited awhile and tried again. "Baseball must've been a huge part of your life when you were growing up, huh?"

"Huge is right," she said. "Didn't leave much room for anything else."

Something other than wisdom urged Stallings to set about softening the spotlight that was trained on his pal. "Listen. Sarah. I know you and Johnny weren't always on the best of terms—"

She made a loud dismissive sound, an angry exhalation: "Hunh!"

"But sometimes families simply don't communicate the way they should. It's not uncommon. You take my family. About five years ago, my parents retired to Florida—*without telling me*. They just took off!"

"In my case—"

"Next thing I knew, they were kicked back in Naples. Lousy communication, but so it goes."

"In my case," she said, "I took off on my father. And I did it for good reasons, OK?" Her words had a firmness to them that implied she didn't care to elaborate.

Stallings slipped his right hand into Johnny's glove. Absently, he opened and closed it, admiring its texture. Though Stallings was larger than most men, the glove felt too big for him.

"Have you seen the face?" he asked suddenly.

"In the sky?" She shook her head, causing her flowing black mane to scintillate. "No. I don't believe in it. I think it's all bullshit," she added, and the vulgarity surprised Stallings.

"Why?"

"Well, think about it," she said. "A face that comes from where? Outer space? And fills up the sky? How's it possible? And why haven't more people seen it? If it's that humongous, why hasn't everyone seen it? Why no pictures? Has it been caught on radar? When it comes pushing down, does it knock airplanes out of the way? Does it make them crash?"

She sounded indignant, as if the mere conceit of a doomsday message from the heavens were a personal affront to her. Her questions were well-founded and thought-provoking, even if most planes were no longer flying. But there was one small problem....

"Sarah," he said, "I saw it. I saw the face."

"You did." She turned to scrutinize him, her own expression inscrutable.

"Two days ago. I was in my yard. Thing came down at me and bowled me over."

"It was real?"

"Whether it was real or not, I don't know. But I saw it." Stallings cast his eyes skyward now in apprehension. All was blue, peaceful and normal.

"Did it speak to you?"

"Did it ever." He told her how the face, after a brief philosophical prelude, announced almost matter-of-factly that the world was about to end. Soon. No rationale was supplied. Sometime prior to Earth's destruction, there would come a 'token of good faith' involving two cities. Again, not much detail. "When the face spoke to me," Stallings said, "I could feel its breath. Like gusts of wind from a great big propeller. But warm. Humid."

"So you believe in it. You must."

"Depends on what you mean by 'believe,' " he said. "Do I believe the face represents God, or death, or some extraterrestrial hit squad? I sure don't know. But I believe I experienced *some*thing."

"Hmm." She crinkled her smooth brow. Was she still convinced it was all bullshit? She gave no clue. "Where can we look?" she asked.

He didn't follow. "For what? The face?"

"For my father."

"Ah. Well." He stood up, extended his hand to her. "Come with me."

Their ultimate destination was Johnny's Place, which Sarah did know about from phone conversations with her mother. But between the ball field and that popular downtown purlieu sat any number of other bars and restaurants that Johnny had been known to frequent. Stallings and Sarah stopped by some of them, the ones that were open, and asked around. They found no trace of Perfection.

Driving on, Stallings recalled another place Johnny had mentioned recently, the Your Town Theatre. Why Johnny, who was no sophisticate, might have some interest in a local playhouse was unclear to Stallings, but he decided to swing by anyhow. Some years ago Stallings and his wife had seen *Death of a Salesman* performed there; both had judged it skillfully written if terribly depressing in its message. Cruising up the street, Stallings was taken aback to see the theatre, the front half especially, devastated by a fire that might not have completely burned out yet; a pall of charcoal smoke hung over the site like a storm cloud. The building's remains were charred and jagged, heavy wooden beams twisted and reduced to blackened stumps. The smell of destruction hit Stallings' nostrils with a raw pungency that almost sickened him.

"Look at that," he said.

"My goodness," Sarah murmured.

"Hope no one got hurt."

By the time they got to Johnny's place, afternoon was shading into evening. Another thirsty crowd was on hand—but again, very hushed, very oppressed-looking. The faces in here could've belonged to people whose spouses had been wheeled off to delicate surgery hours ago and who were hoping desperately for a favorable outcome but fearing the worst—suspecting, in fact, that for them only the worst had been deliberately reserved. After nosing here and there and checking with dark taciturn Abdul behind the bar, Stallings and Sarah accepted that tonight's gathering did not include Johnny.

They slid into a booth along the wall. At this point, both were a little subdued. Stallings was tired from all the running around, while Sarah was even more fatigued from her long journey and from not having slept much in days. He ordered a tall glass of Hipsley's Iced Tea. Disdaining her fatigue, she ordered a double shot of Wild Turkey on the rocks. When she drank off half of it in one gulp, not batting an eye, Stallings was forced to conclude that maybe she'd lived life a pinch more fully and rebelliously than he'd reckoned.

As always, the TVs were on, and, as always, they were delivering the news. Most of the coverage concerned the strange fate that had befallen Korla, China; video footage showed the scene where, until earlier today, the city had stood. Now there was nothing but a vast grayness, as if the city—buildings, cars, half a million people—had been pulverized into a layer of fine soot. Still no clear explanation for how or why this had happened, or who or what was behind it. Reactions from around the world were pouring in unabated, and the tone of the comments ranged from sympathy and caution to bluster and belligerence. At home, the White House had issued a statement offering condolences to the families of anyone hurt or killed, and pledging to work alongside China to identify the perpetrators and bring them swiftly to justice. Sipping his tea, rounded jaw propped on his cupped hand, Stallings absorbed these reports glumly.

Some sketchy coverage was also being devoted to a new disturbance that had allegedly occurred in Iowa, but the facts here were so thin as to be almost nonexistent. Stallings took in what he could of this nebulous story with more of the same glumness.

Meanwhile, Sarah, invigorated by her Wild Turkey, decided to do something she hadn't done of late—review her cell phone messages. Tapping through them with a practiced finger, she was impressed with how many she had. A boatload, even considering she was the notorious Princess of Porn and did tend to be more of a magnet for communications than the average person. A high percentage of the messages appeared to be from lawyers and police. These she ignored. She ignored all the others as well, except for a handful of calls from Laura Kennedy, the newspaper reporter for whom Sarah had developed a fondness. She had it in mind that if she used her phone, maybe the authorities could get a fix on her location. (If they even cared, with everything else that was happening.) Regardless, she was going to give Laura a call; the hell with it.

Laura picked up, and her voice was so crisp and clear she might've been sitting in the same room. "Sarah!" she squealed.

"Laura!"

"Sarah!"

"Laura!"

Grinning, Stallings watched Sarah's juvenile excitement with good-natured amusement; it certainly beat what was on TV.

"Where are you?" Laura shouted.

"I came home. Like I told you."

"But where exactly are you? I made the trip too. I flew east. Maybe we can—"

"You did? Oh my God! Where're *you*?"

"I'm in a bar," Laura said. "Place with really juicy hamburgers. It's, uh ..."

"I'm in a bar too. My father's. It's ..."

At precisely the same instant they both said: "Johnny's Place."

Both of them screamed happily, which was discomfiting to Stallings, but he went with it. Sarah sprang to her feet, and not far away another young woman jumped up, phone pressed to her ear. When they saw each other, both screamed again. Sarah tossed her phone in the general direction of Stallings, who plucked it out of the air with a Johnny Benchlike ability he'd never evinced in Little League. Gushing and giggling, the two women threw themselves at each other and embraced. Stallings had another sip of his tea, wondering what the funereal crowd must've thought of all this gaiety.

Laura joined them at the booth. Introductions were made, and Stallings took an instant shine to the plain-faced modestly attired reporter from the West Coast. With her affable straight-ahead style she reminded him, just a speck, of his deceased wife. Plus, she was obviously tight with Sarah, and, as a journalist, she could certainly outwrite and outthink Stallings' students. She was OK. Like their favorite uncle, he beamed at the ladies, letting them do most of the yakking, of which there was plenty.

But ever the academic, Stallings stayed tuned at least in part to the words and images raining down on them from the TVs. The focus of the news broadcast was changing, slowly at first, then radically, heart-stoppingly. The Iowa piece, so vague at the outset, was now clarifying into something very definite and simple, if not quite believable.

According to reports originating from within the state, the city of Des Moines *no longer existed*. Like Korla, Des Moines had suddenly, inexplicably and yet totally vanished from the planet.

Amateur video (the networks hadn't arrived there yet) supported the claim. Grainy and jerky, the tape, apparently shot from just outside what used to be the city, revealed a far-reaching prairie of silent featureless gray. Pan left, pan right, zoom in—nothing but gray. The shots from Iowa and those from China were almost identical—but different enough, when the camera turned away from the awful desolation, to spark a thrill of terror. Two cities—two—had now been obliterated.

Stallings and Sarah and Laura and everyone else sat motionless with their eyes stuck to one of the scattered TVs. Uneven and uncertain, a single voice, a man's, emanated from all the sets:

"... still attempting to get confirmation of that. But the event seems to've happened roughly forty to forty-five minutes ago. Eyewitnesses, some of them frighteningly close to the edge of this ... this ungodly circle of destruction are all basically saying they saw and heard the same thing: nothing. No blinding burst of light, no thunderous explosion. No mushroom cloud. The city of Des Moines, whose name means 'of the monks,' I'm told, capital of Iowa, located near the very heart of North America, has simply, my God, ceased to exist. Just ... it's ... And we now have word, we're receiving word, that the Governor of Iowa, who we understand is ... Where is he? He's in Washington, DC, he was very fortunately traveling out-of-state, the Governor is preparing to make a statement...."

They cut to a shot of an empty podium. Now a bespectacled man wearing a goatee, a technician perhaps, wandered in front of the camera and signaled to someone off-camera. He pointed at something, then waved his hand sideways as if indicating that the thing, whatever it was, needed to be repositioned. Realizing he was on-camera, he stepped briskly out of view.

The same voice from before intoned: "Waiting to hear from the Governor of Iowa ..."

The shot of the empty podium continued. And continued.

Then the TVs all went dead.

For a long while everyone in the bar just sat there, waiting nervously for the TVs to come back on. They didn't. Behind the bar, Abdul held up the remote control, poked at it. He poked at it some more. No response. Dead silence.

Faces even more stricken than they had been, people began to mumble and move around. Some of them got up and left. One of the customers closest to Abdul said something to him, and Abdul, not liking what he'd heard, pivoted toward the customer and said something back. Voices rose.

To command his friends' attention, Stallings reached out and placed one hand on Sarah's hand, and one on Laura's. "Listen," he said.

"Oh, dear God," someone wailed.

Somewhere nearby, a glass or a bottle smashed violently.

"Listen," Stallings said to the two women. He stood up. "You're both gonna spend the night with me, you hear? C'mon."

Numbly Sarah and Laura got to their feet. Two panicky young men rushed by the booth, almost colliding with them.

"Watch now," Stallings said, guiding his charges along. "Over this way. C'mon."

Again the sound of smashing glass. Overhead, the lights began to flicker. An older man wearing a suit and tie, seated at a table, hung his head and began to weep. Loudly. Another man, younger and not as well dressed, stood at his elbow shouting abuse at him and pushing him. "You're a coward," the aggressive man said. "You're a wimp."

Stallings was trying to shield the women and hurry them along at the same time. "C'mon," he said.

Then they pushed through the doorway, bursting outside into the darkening spring air, the openness. People ran by them.

"Up here," Stallings said. "The white Malibu."

They fell into the car, Laura in the back, and Stallings started the engine, stepped on the gas.

As they sped off into the gray light of the evening, almost

the same color as the fallen cities, he felt himself trying to come to terms with a problem larger, stranger and less tractable than any he had ever known. He couldn't do it. His heart beat rapidly.

For several minutes no one spoke.

"I live out this way," he said at last with a nod, gripping the wheel. It was a pointless remark, but he'd felt the need to say something.

"Toward the college," Laura put in.

Sarah said nothing, and Stallings imagined he could feel the terror that lay upon her and kept her silent. It blanketed her and everyone else, the whole world. It covered them all like a shroud, he thought.

21

"SO WHAT DO YOU THINK of that stuff, huh?" Ernesto Cruz was speaking to his friend Peter LeMan, the porn star. The 'stuff' to which he referred was cognac, which both men were sipping contentedly from snifters. "Not too shabby, huh?"

Recumbent in a white deck chair, LeMan had another small sip and smiled. He was gazing out at the blue-gray water.

After a delicious steak dinner cooked by Cruz on his grill, they were relaxing on the elevated redwood deck of his beach house in Manhattan Beach, California. The view of the empty sands and the ocean beyond was excellent and, both would've agreed, conducive to philosophical thinking. Wearing a peach-colored guayabera shirt, khaki shorts and old flip-flops, Cruz was up and moving around, but not in an agitated way. His shirt was unbuttoned, and the sun, sinking slowly toward the flat line of the Pacific, glinted off the grizzled hair on his chest. The younger LeMan, in a white tanktop and white linen pants, almost blended in with the creamy chair that held him. A light breeze, cool and pleasant, caressed their hair and skin with a touch that felt womanly.

"All cognac is brandy," Cruz observed, "but not all brandy is cognac. Did you know that? No? In order to qualify as cognac, the brandy has gotta be made in or pretty damn close to the town of Cognac, which sits on the Charente River in France. Gotta be—that's French law.

"I made a trip over there a few years ago—vacation with a little fact-finding thrown in, OK? Before that, I thought the only acceptable way to drink a truly sublime cognac was straight, at room temperature. Found out that the French themselves—and you know how persnickety *they* are—mix their cognac with all kinds of stuff. Tonic water, ginger ale, club soda, juice, ice, you name it.

"Ever been to France? No? My friend, you should've gotten out and about a bit more when you had the chance. Emerson said that traveling is a fool's paradise, but in that instance Emerson was the fool. Travel can broaden your perspective, make you more cosmopolitan. The word 'cosmopolitan' literally means 'citizen of the world'—but you probably already knew that, right?"

LeMan smiled faintly and kept his eyes on the water. Like the water, his eyes were blue-gray. While his brown hair was full and shaggy, his mustache was thin—a wisp of dark smoke blowing across his angular face. He appeared utterly serene, and he accepted everything Cruz said with the same mellow spirit in which it was offered. Then again, perhaps LeMan heard only a fraction of the words coming his way, his own mind conceivably delving into a boundless treasure house of memories, both happy and sad.

"Anyhow," Cruz went on, strolling around the deck, "I did some experimenting, and I discovered I like my cognac mixed with fresh lemonade." He held up his snifter in the slanting light, studied the golden hue. "Would the French approve? I don't know. I guess we'll never know. But I like to think they wouldn't disapprove." He treated himself to another sip.

"That's a helluva view out there, isn't it?" Cruz asked. "Love the view. I think anytime we're close to the water, it has a soothing effect. It unjangles our nerves. Unless maybe we're caught in a whirlpool," he laughed. "Or a tsunami. Then it'd be too much of a good thing.... But there's something inside us that responds to water. Probably because it was the ocean that spawned us all those millions of years ago. Land life was originally sea life, and a part of us still yearns, I believe, to go back to our beginnings, to go back home. We feel a tug, a kind of wonderful ache down deep in our heart...

"Course, what I like to do when I'm looking out there is watch the people. People on the beach, people in the water. Volleyball, surfing. I tell you, if this place didn't invent volleyball and surfing, it sure as hell should have; they're part of the scenery. Or most times they are; you've seen it yourself....

"But what I really like to do is watch people who aren't doing anything in particular. Maybe they're just sitting there in their swimsuits on the beach, admiring the waves as they break, or they're walking along, maybe holding hands. Conversing. Eating an ice cream cone. Just being themselves. From a distance, I'll try to imagine their lives, you know, figure out who they might be, what they might do for a living, how they might relate to one another. Ever do that? No? I do it all the time. Hopeless voyeur, right? But it makes me feel better, more complete as a human being. It fills in some missing pieces of the puzzle known as Ernesto Cruz. Or it almost does...."

LeMan smiled and sipped his cognac. A solicitous host, Cruz asked him if he needed a refill. Maintaining his ghost of a smile, LeMan moved his head very subtly from side to side. Cruz shrugged and continued to perambulate the deck, his shirt fluttering.

"One more note on the cognac," Cruz said. "The brand is Martell—VSOP. I've read that every January, on the birthday of Edgar Allan Poe, this mysterious guy, this figure dressed in black, shows up at Poe's gravesite and drops off some roses and a bottle of Martell cognac. An enchanting story in itself. But I figure if Martell is good enough for Poe, even though he's dead, it should be damn well good enough for us, huh? Say, you *are* familiar with Poe, aren't you? 'The Raven,' 'The Masque of the Red Death'? Yes? Good. Good. I do consider it ironic, however—and I'm sure you do as well—that, given our current circumstances, the lost cities and all, we find ourselves enjoying a beverage that's associated so intimately with the American Poet of Death....

"Well, *ayuda tener un sentido de humor,* as my mother always used to say, bless her soul. It helps to have a sense of humor....

"And speaking of the French, as I just was and often do, I suppose I'm what they would call a bon vivant. I relish fine food and drink, and I make no apologies in that regard. In LA you can get almost any kind of food you want, even food that more or less resembles what I used to eat in Costa Rica. But here, what passes for Costa Rican food isn't nearly as delectable. It's never cooked the way my mother used to cook it; something is missing. Hmm. Yes, I know what you're thinking, amigo—what's missing is my mother. Huh? And once again, you're correct. My God, you should've tasted her *arroz con pollo*. Just rice with chicken, but you should've tasted it. To die for, and I'll tell you why. Because it was cooked with love."

As he did periodically, Cruz laughed a little, displaying the gap in his front teeth. It was a laugh that featured both mirth and melancholy. "Doesn't matter how long I live in America," he said, "I'll always be a Tico in here." He thumped his chest with his fist. "And I'm proud of it."

Reclining in the deck chair, the smiling LeMan moved not a muscle. All that moved was a lock of his hair, and that was lifted by the breeze.

"Food and drink," Cruz said. "The sensual pleasures of life ... When I was just a hoptoad, a *chico*"—he held out his hand at thigh level—"food and drink were practically all we had. And we didn't have much of them, you know? I never had a new shirt till I was sixteen. Always the hand-me-downs, from brother to brother. So at an early age, I came to appreciate life's little things, because the big things were all out of reach. I understood the value of a pat on the back for a task well done. A comfortable bed to sleep in. A piece of poetry. A piece of pottery. A song. A flirtatious smile directed at me by an otherwise intelligent redhead who sat next to me at school. Most of all, the loving support of my family, including my brothers, one of whom, Felipe, God rest him, passed away three years ago this November. Hey—if you're poor but don't know it, then how poor can you be?...

"In my country we have a saying, a slogan if you will: *Pura vida*. We put it on T-shirts, billboards, bumper stickers ... but it has worth nonetheless. You've heard of it? Yes? The literal translation is 'pure life,' but in fact it means much more than that. It means something like 'Life is great,' and we sometimes use it to say hello or goodbye or simply to express satisfaction in the way things are—even if they're not as satisfying as we'd like." He let the phrase roll off his tongue with grandiloquence, like an orator: "*Pura vida* ... It's not just my country's credo, my friend, but one I've adopted as my very own. Take whatever satisfaction life may afford you and savor it."

He leaned back against the rail surrounding the deck, taking care not to obscure his friend's view.

"I was born and raised in San José," Cruz said. "Wait a minute," he laughed. "That sounds like a song—the one Dionne Warwick used to sing. Remember that one? No? Just as well, because I'm not talking about that place up the road in Silicon Valley; I mean the capital of Costa Rica. *My* San José." He gave his cognac a swirl. "Busy-ass town. One big traffic jam sometimes. But a happening town too—lively, diverse ...

"Just outside the city proper, up on a hill, is the suburb of Escazú. Lovely community—pretty as a sunset. It's where the Americans come to retire. When I was a teenager—about a thousand years ago—I wangled a part-time job in Escazú, and I came to know the Americans. Frankly, I liked them. And not everyone did, because the Americans had money while most of us, the homeboys, were broke. Yes, some class envy, some xenophobia. But where others may have cultivated resentment, I began to build a dream.

"I vowed that one day I would travel to America and make my home here. Why? You remember what Willie Sutton said when they asked him why he robbed banks. ''Cause that's where the money is,' he said. From a distance, and from talking to the rich retirees in Escazú, I had become a believer in the American Dream. So when the time came, I broke the news to my family, and I vamoosed. Well, they had a fit, you know, especially my father." Cruz made his voice deep and rough—or more so than it already was. " 'Whatsa matter?' he said. 'Costa Rica not good enough for you?' " More laughter. "But in the end, as you might have surmised, they all backed my decision. And backed it even more when I started sending home some money."

He had a sip of his cognac and pushed away from the rail, began to move again. Even when standing still, Cruz was more active than LeMan, who, from his chair, continued to smile and gaze out to sea.

"Now, you may be wondering," Cruz said, "why did I choose California? Why not Minnesota? Why not—I don't know—why not Illinois? All right, let me tell you. One thing we did have when I was growing up was a TV. Sometimes I'd watch movies on TV, and most often they were made in the USA. Movies fascinated me, even the old black-and-white ones. Flicks from the thirties, the forties. You ever watch that old stuff? No? Amigo, you don't know what you've been missing. This one picture sticks in my mind even today. *The Public Enemy*, starring Jimmy Cagny. There's a scene when Cagny takes a grapefruit and shoves it in a woman's face—just for spite! Shocking moment. But I'll tell you, seeing it made me sit up and say: 'Wow. In America, anything is possible. Even a grapefruit to some poor woman's kisser. Anything at all.'

"I made up my mind to live and work where they made these enthralling movies. I would go to California.

"And soon enough I wound up in the midst of a movie-making machine—the San Fernando Valley porn industry. Not exactly the kind of movies I'd envisioned, but here I am. The work is real and so are the people. And so is the compensation, as well you know. At this stage in the game I wouldn't change my career, even if I could. I have found my métier, and it's been good to me."

Apparently remembering something, Cruz placed his snifter on a wooden table. He withdrew a Cuban cigar—a Punch Punch—from his shirt pocket and walked over to LeMan, offered it to him. When LeMan politely declined, actually raising his hand an inch or two in demurral, Cruz shrugged and lit the cigar for himself. He stood in place for a few seconds, blowing dense gray clouds of smoke that vanished swiftly in the breeze. Then he strolled back to his drink. Though his mood of contentment deepened as he puffed on the cigar, he continued to feel restless, oddly energized.

"Make no mistake," he said, "America has been good to me too. The only major adjustment I had to make was switching from being a soccer fan to being a baseball fan. Not as easy as you might assume. In Costa Rica, you see, soccer is a religion, and I followed my own favorite team, Herediano, with a holy passion. Around here, you've got some soccer, sure, but men don't follow it. Not real men, men with cojones." Cruz frowned slightly, as if he'd just stumbled across some minute but bothersome flaw in the universe. "Around here, real men follow football, baseball, mixed martial arts. When I considered my options, well, baseball felt about right for me. It has its partisans back home, so I thought what the hell. Give it a shot, huh?

"It took a while," Cruz said, meaning it took a while for him to become a baseball fan. "I tried rooting for the Dodgers, but they were too glitzy for me. Tried the Angels, even the Giants, the A's. Nothing clicked.

"Then one evening I was watching TV, and I came across a White Sox game. Out on the mound was this big tall southpaw named Johnny Black. 'Jet,' they called him. Later on, they called him 'Perfection.' Well, I'd heard of him before, but this was the first I'd ever seen him in action.

"By the way, you a baseball fan? Huh? Are you? Good. I thought you were....

"So there I sat, OK, watching this Jet guy pitch like I'd never seen it done in my life. High leg kick, straight over the top delivery, 97, 98 mph. The hitters may as well have been swinging at smoke." He blew a long gray stream of smoke to illustrate his point. "Struck out a dozen or so, gave up three or four hits—all bloop singles. Then he lost the game; don't ask me how.

"But here's what brought me over," Cruz said. "What

converted me, so to speak. There were these two college-age girls, really luscious, looked like something *you'd* hook up with in one of your Triple-X movies, and they were sitting behind first base holding up a sign. Sign said: 'WE LOVE YOU JET,' and they were shaking it at him, you know? Shaking everything at him. So in the bottom of the fifth inning, between hitters— there's a guy standing at the plate waiting to hit!—ol' Jet jogs over past first base, climbs into the box seats and takes both these girls in a big hug, and they're giggling and jiggling and loving every second of it, and he kisses them both. Repeatedly. They kiss *him*. Cameras flashing, announcers tongue-tied. Then he climbs out of the seats, jogs back out to the mound and starts pitching again as if nothing had happened.

"*Caramba!* How can you not love a guy like that? From that time on, I've been a fan of the Pale Hose, probably the only Costa Rican-born, California-based, porn industry-connected White Sox fan in existence."

Cruz laughed in bemusement at the renegade ballplayer and also at himself—at his own eccentric tastes.

"Curious thing is," Cruz said, scratching his dark jowl soberly, "Johnny Black reminds me of somebody. Somebody I've worked with. But I can't quite think of who it might be. All that incredible talent, but the unpredictability too—pushing the envelope till it rips apart ..."

He scooped up his snifter with his left hand, had a sip and then drew lightly on his cigar, which he held in his right. Returning the snifter to the table, he resumed pacing.

"That guy was a piece of work, all right," Cruz allowed, "but I've met some unforgettable characters in porn as well. You, for one, my friend. I don't know how you do it. The prospect of making love to a strange but beautiful woman—or a whole bed full of them at once—does have its allurements. But to do it on command—the director says 'Go' and you perform—and to do it under bright lights with all these rubberneckers ten feet away watching your every move ... the cameras rolling ... I don't know. At the very least, the romantic in me would rebel....

"I can guess what you're thinking: 'If you had a schlong the size of your forearm the way I do, you'd tell the romantic in you to shut the hell up and then you'd put that schlong to work'—huh?"

Cruz laughed, and LeMan, supine in the chair, increased his smile—or maybe he didn't. Maybe it was only an optical illusion produced by the fading reddening light.

"Zoey Zanders is another one," Cruz said, his shirt flapping in the breeze. "That's not her real name. I've seen her real name on contracts; can't remember what it is. But she's absolutely without peer, that one. Smart as a ... as a college professor, but with a face and body that would've made Helen of Troy suicidal with envy. Course, I don't need to describe Ms. Zanders' assets to *you*, now, do I? You had a pretty good time with her in *A Boff in the Woods*, if my worn-out memory still serves me at all....

"First time I met her, she sat across a table from me in my office—couldn't have been more than eighteen, nineteen years old. And she looked me straight in the eye, and she said in this firm level voice: 'I plan to be a star in this business.' What could I say to that? I'd never encountered anything like her before—the beauty, the bravado. 'That's good,' I said. She said: 'I plan to be a superstar.' I said: 'Well, that's even better.' 'Before it's over with,' she said, 'they'll be calling me the Princess of Porn.' And she was just as serious as the IRS. I looked at her and said: 'Would you care to join me for lunch?' I waited one beat and threw in: 'Your Royal Highness.' Oh, she got a kick out of my playful jab. Laughed like hell— as if she hadn't laughed in a while. Right away she started calling me 'Ernie,' which normally I can't abide, but with her it's OK, you know? *Está bien.* With her, I kinda like it.

"So we had lunch. Just a friendly lunch. And that was fine...."

Cruz blew another long aromatic plume of cigar smoke and had another sip of cognac. The wheels in his head were turning.

"But I can recall another occasion with Zoey, another lunch, that wasn't nearly as congenial. This time she brought that guy with her, Eric or Derek—I can never remember his name, even though he's been in the news. Wolf. You met him. What a jackass! Well, this was my first experience with him, and we were having lunch—Armenian place over in Glendale—and everything was OK, and then suddenly, from out of the blue, he leaned into my face and said: 'Are you afraid of me?' I didn't answer him. I couldn't; my mouth was full of shish kabob. He said: 'Some people are afraid of me. Are you?' I still didn't answer him, though I did start to chew a good deal faster. Up to then I *hadn't* been afraid of him, but at that moment—I'll be honest—I was beginning to feel a lot less comfortable....

"Here's what happened. Zoey gave him a slap on the shoulder and said to him: 'Hey. Are you afraid of *me?*' He shot her a look, and then he broke out laughing. He laughed for a minute solid, laughed like a loon."

Cruz flicked some ashes from his cigar. "It dissolved the tension. Or let me put it this way: it dissolved the tension around *me.* But there was still something at work at that table. A sort of discord, you know? A disharmony. It was ugly. Because all the time he was laughing, she didn't so much as smile. She just glared at him with an animal ferocity. As Queen Victoria used to say: 'We are not amused.' I'll tell you, amigo, when I saw that icy stare on Zoey's face, I not only refused to laugh, I refused to blink or swallow. My mother, God love her, may not have raised a genius for a son, but she didn't raise a goddam idiot either."

Drink in one hand, cigar in the other, Cruz walked over and stood beside LeMan. Lowering his voice, the older man said: "I can't believe she killed him. And yet I do believe it. What's more, I believe he had it coming. What the exact provocation might've been, I don't know. But the big bad Wolf got what was coming to him."

Almost imperceptibly, LeMan nodded in agreement.

"May God have mercy on us all," Cruz said, and he turned to gaze out at the water, which had acquired a resplendent golden shimmer with the proximity of the setting sun.

"First thing this morning," he said, "I went for a walk along the beach. You can guess what happened. I was poking along, musing to myself, minding my own business, when the apparition came down at me. The giant face. It ballooned until it filled the sky completely, and it pressed down at me until I thought we would touch noses. I've been informed I have a big nose, but you know what? That face has a bigger one, my friend. Much bigger.

"And it spoke to me. The same message you've read about, heard about. Get ready to die, the face advised me, because death is coming, coming to all of us. The entire planet. Soon."

He held up his Martell cognac and his Punch Punch cigar. "So as you can see," he said, "I'm getting ready." Again he laughed, and again the laugh conveyed a plexus of emotions, merriment not necessarily chief among them. LeMan smiled.

"I spoke back to the face," Cruz said. "Perhaps it was impertinent of me, but I meant no disrespect. Quite the opposite. I told it: 'Whatever you say. You're the boss. If we're bound to die, then we're bound to die.' "

Cruz shrugged, had a sip, took a puff. "Sometimes in life we're overmatched, you know? Checkmate. That was one of those times for me, and it still is. I believe it's one of those times for all of us."

For several minutes they kept their squinting eyes trained on the sunset, which was reaching its fiery climax. Half the sun had already sunk from view, but the rich red half that remained seemed doubly bright, reflecting off the wide glassy plane of the water. To the north and south, a band of warm-looking light spanned the horizon, and a narrow path of the same light skimmed the ocean in ripples from the edge of the world to the empty shore, where the waves shattered with a repetitive rumble both soothing and unsettling. Well above the blaze, a rack of clouds drifted peacefully along, and they shone with a dazzling range of colors that held the men spellbound: pink and violet and salmon and gray.... Farther up, the sky was indigo and then black. A blackness was silently but inexorably building from all sides, and more so now that the sun had finally fallen from sight.

Cruz had a sip of his cognac. "It's been a good ride," he said. "But all rides, no matter how good, must come to an end. Right? You know that from all your sexcapades."

LeMan too had a sip of his cognac.

"Amigo," Cruz said, "it's been an honor to know you. *Pura vida.*"

Each man made a fist, and they tapped their fists together.

"But you need to hear something," Cruz said, "and I may as well be the one to tell you. No offense, but you talk too damn much." He kept a straight face for one second, then he bent over with laughter, roaring and shaking.

LeMan smiled and peered out at the darkening water.

22

ONE TIME, when he was still in the minors, Johnny awoke, painfully hungover, to find himself in a jail cell. The inside of his mouth tasted as if it'd been coated with turpentine and sprinkled with sawdust. At first he didn't know where he was. Beneath him was a hard cot, and all around him the ambience was bleak and institutional: the naked walls, the cramped size of his cubicle, even the close leaden air that seemed to prickle his skin. Then he saw the crisscross of the iron bars, and a chill seized at his entrails.

When he saw his cellmate, who was lying propped up on his elbow in a cot alongside his, the chill spread from his gut throughout his sickened body. The filthy-looking man—his whiskered face was splotched with either grease or blood—had one eye closed and the other half-open. His toothless mouth was also half-open, a slimy bead of spittle dangling from his chapped lip. The half-open eye was fixed on Johnny. Forty years old or sixty, the man lay motionless, staring silently, smelling of stale alcohol, dried urine and hovering death. What thoughts, if any, were generating behind that unblinking eye were beyond Johnny's ability to guess, not that he had the strength or the will to try....

Because the young ballplayer had powerful friends that the other man lacked, Johnny was promptly released into the world of relatively free people. For this he was grateful. But neither before his release nor after could he remember just what he'd done to earn a stay, however brief, in a cage. He recalled being at a boisterous roadhouse in some Podunk town somewhere in the vast directionless Midwest, and he recalled drinking with men he didn't know and with women he barely knew. Loud music, heavy kidding. Where had his teammates been? Probably misbehaving as well, but in a more civilized way, and probably closer to home. For Johnny that night, the alcohol had cascaded down on him like a waterfall, pounding him senseless, washing him away to oblivion.

The charges against him were dropped the same day he was released, before he could become clear on what they even were. If the police had informed him of the accusations—and he was pretty sure they had—he'd forgotten overnight what he'd been told. Since the incident had occurred before he was famous, there was no coverage in the newspapers or on TV; he couldn't learn from them what he might've done. He supposed he could read the police report or consult with the attorney who'd acted on his behalf. But he didn't. He could've even contacted the woman (it *had* been a woman) who'd sicced the police on him, assuming he could figure out who she was. But he made no effort to identify her or communicate with her.

He took none of these steps, because he was afraid. He was afraid to find out what he'd allegedly done—even though, with the charges being dropped, he might not have done anything. Yet the mere fact that his memory of the night's final hours had been wiped clean, like a hard drive that'd been scrubbed, had shaken him terribly, made him wonder if he hadn't done something so shameful that his conscious mind had suppressed the damning images in a desperate act of self-defense.

Afterwards, he even stopped drinking for a solid week.

It had been one of the hairiest misadventures of his life. But by comparison, what happened today had been worse. Way worse. The pitching fiasco—72 mph! Ol' Frank Dutwell tearing the cover off the ball!—followed by that nightmarish encounter with a colossal disembodied face in the sky ... A face so huge that, during its visit, Johnny could see nothing else. A face that had told him bluntly to prepare himself for the end of the world, an event supposedly scheduled for just two days hence. At the peak of the episode, Johnny could've traced the individual hairs, big as sequoias, in the thing's mustache. Rattled to his core, he was inclined now to stop drinking not just for a week, but for the rest of his natural life. Of course, if the face could be trusted, the rest of his natural life wouldn't amount to a week.

Timidly he picked himself up off the mound where he'd collapsed and, leaving his glove behind, staggered the fifty yards to his truck.

He needed to talk to someone. Rooting around inside the cab, he located his phone and set about the task of deciding whom to call. He knew so many people, so many women especially, but at an extraordinary moment like this, he struggled trying to determine where his call would best be placed. In something of an upset, he settled on the young woman who, about a week before, had shown him and the entire crew at his bar how to do the latest dance craze—what was it called? The Countdown, right—and then afterwards had entertained him further at his condo. She'd struck Johnny as a worthwhile girl, fun and empathetic. And he'd promised he'd be in touch with her, hadn't he? Remarkably enough, she actually *was* a dance instructor, who worked as a stripper on the side. Her stage name was Fanny Dujour; he didn't know her real name, perhaps because he hadn't asked.

He tried to call her and discovered his phone wasn't working. He tried again and connected.

"Fanny?" he said. "Johnny. Perfection," he added, in case she knew more than one Johnny.

Speaking in a voice that sounded like someone else's, he told her that he'd been thinking of her and wondered if they might not get together again—soon. He indicated that life hadn't been going too well for him lately and, in fairness, doubted that many folks these days could claim to be riding in a boat that hadn't sprung a few leaks. Maybe Fanny herself had been feeling out of sorts? She admitted as much and, noting that the dance lesson business was hardly thriving, invited him to come over to her place that very second.

As he drove, he tried to recollect more exactly this colorfully named woman with whom he'd spent a grand total of eight or ten hours. She'd danced with him—and with everyone else—sated his sexual desires and generally made him feel buoyant with her peppy patter concerning topics he seldom if ever thought about: the beauty of horses, the attractions of Ireland, the heroines of modern dance. (On this last subject, Johnny recalled putting in a word of praise for Jennifer Lopez.) Physically, Fanny was long and blonde, with fireworks in her green eyes and a cute little mole down near the corner of her mouth.

So when he showed up at her house and she opened the door, he was unnerved to see she was of medium height, with brown hair, brown eyes and no mole. Moreover, she was a crinkle or two older than she rightly should've been. Had he found the correct address?

"Fanny?" he said.

"Johnny, whadaya know?" she said and waved him in. "Helluva note, ain't it? All this scary shit that's going on ..."

"Fanny?" he repeated, and went inside.

"I'll make you a drink."

"No, thanks."

But she went to the kitchen and made him a drink anyhow; she'd already made herself one. As she bustled around, Johnny surveyed her as closely as he could without being offensive. She was well-built and—she was wearing shorts—had the lithe curvy legs of a dancer, a stripper. She was also wearing a trim ice-blue T-shirt depicting an exotic little (four-armed!) man in mid-dance; the caption read *Nataraja: The Cosmic Dancer*. This offbeat reference to dance seemed to seal it all right—it was Fanny—and Johnny gathered that, like many another barroom hustler, he'd been fooled by the play of artificial lights that one evening, or by the trickery of alcohol, or by the heat of his own lustful excitement.

Or did he have this woman confused with someone else entirely? He felt uncomfortable.

"Here," she said, handing him the drink. He set it on a countertop and didn't touch it again.

"I saw the face today," he said softly. "It's got me a little messed up."

"*You!*" she shouted in a voice so piercing she sounded as if she were miked. "You think I haven't seen it?"

"I dunno. Have you?"

"You're goddam right I have!" She snatched up her tumbler and took a ferocious slurp. "Two days ago I stood here in this same kitchen, and that freaking thing came down and nailed me through that window right there behind you." She used her drinking hand to gesture, and the ice cubes clacked against each other.

"Through the window!" He turned and had an uneasy gander up at the baby blue sky. "I never heard of that before."

"You think I had? Hell, that's not even *legal*, is it? Peeping in someone's window."

Johnny tried to picture the visual effect. It seemed to him that the face, in order to approach the window, would've had to swoop down at an angle, and then at the point of contact it would've been unable to wallop her with the same sky-filling size and impact that he and so many others had experienced. Not enough room. He had to conclude that Fanny (if that's who she was) had been let off easy, but he wasn't about to share that conclusion with her.

"Could you hear it through the windowpane?" he asked.

"CAN YOU HEAR *ME?*" she shrieked.

He said he could.

"I'll tell you what the hell I was doing," she said. "I'd just gotten a pop tart—it was frosted strawberry—out of the refrigerator, and I was about to stick it in the toaster." Johnny's eyes followed her clacking gesture to the Sunbeam toaster. "Suddenly, Johnny, I got the feeling that I didn't want frosted strawberry after all, but rather frosted brown sugar cinnamon, OK? So I started to reconsider." She held up her free hand as if thoughtfully manipulating a pop tart.

"I like chocolate myself."

"Right about that time," she said, "I heard a rumble, like a stock car firing up its engine. Except this stock car would've been flying straight overhead, way up there. There was a flash of white light. I came over here to the window"—she reenacted her movement—"looked up at the sky and man oh man, that was all she wrote." She had another, somewhat less vehement, slurp of her drink.

"I know," he said. "I been there. I was—"

"Johnny, when that thing talked to me, I could not only hear the words, I could *feel* 'em, down in here." She tapped her tumbler against her breastbone. "Every syllable a goddam vibration, you know?"

"Yeah. I was—"

"Dropped the pop tart right on the floor. Took a step backward and squished it. I was in my bare feet. Disgusting."

Sighing, Johnny had a long wistful gaze at his drink but restrained himself. "So what do you think it means?" he asked.

"What's it mean?" She came toward him, eyes open, both hands grasping her drink as if she thought it might try to jump down and run away from her. "The face? The, uh ..."

"The message, the lights in the sky ..."

"The whole kit and kaboodle."

"Yeah."

"Only one thing it could be." He braced himself. "We're looking at the Second Coming," she said.

"Of ... of Jesus?"

"Who the hell else?"

He knitted his fingers together, touched two of them to his chin and, since she'd drawn closer to him than he wanted, took the opportunity to roam about the kitchen with a troubled contemplative look on his face. Her theory was as likely as any he'd heard, he supposed, and she proceeded to buff it up with some fancy talk about the Tribulation, the Rapture, and several other terms that didn't often get used in dugouts, bars or gyms. Johnny didn't know what to think.

"So that giant face we saw," he tried to pin her down, "was the face of Jesus?"

"Yep. Him or His spokesperson." She shrugged. "Today, if you're big, you got a spokesperson."

He ran his hand over his chin. He'd bet on a long shot in coming here, and he was once again piling up evidence that gambling wasn't something he excelled at. "So what do we do?" he asked.

"Do?"

"About the whole screwy situation. I don't mind telling you, Fanny, I feel pretty doggone anxious, and I'm open to any advice, any wisdom, you might wanna share."

"I thought you'd never ask." She took another slurp from her drink and set it down on the countertop beside Johnny's.

"By the way, you *are* Fanny, aren't you?"

"Here's what I think," she said, and this time she drew so close to him he could feel her whiskey breath warming and tickling his bare stubbled throat. "I say we get naked. I say we make love like we've never done it before and like we'll never do it again. Animal love. Kinky love. The kinda love that makes your eyeballs roll back in their sockets." She pressed up against him. "Starting in about two minutes. One minute."

He took a step backward. "Do you ... do you figure Jesus would approve?"

"Honey," she said, "in my case, I don't think it matters. Some of the things I've done in my life ... When the time comes, Jesus is gonna kick my ass no matter what I do or don't do now. So I say why not go out on a high note, doing something I love and enjoy? Be like riding a comet straight into the sun ..."

By this point Johnny was backing up with real dedication. "I can't do this," he said.

"Sure you can. You've done it before."

"Not now," he said. "Not today."

He kept backing up till he backed into a door that happened to lead outside. Showing the quickness and coordination of a former pro athlete, Johnny threw open the door and catapulted himself out into the breezy sunshine.

"I'm sorry," he said.

* * *

His black truck barreling through the streets like a cruise missile, Johnny sat behind the wheel attempting to drive and use his cell phone at the same time. Never a great combination—but if the world was about to end anyway, he reasoned, where was the harm? He had a thousand numbers he could call, and one of them might just hook him up with somebody who could bring him some comfort. Trouble was, service was out. He couldn't reach anybody. He dropped the phone between his legs and asked himself what was he doing, where was he going.

Then, to his surprise, the phone rang. The ringtone was a snippet from the blues classic "Hip Shakin' Mama," and the caller—another surprise—was his longtime agent Buzzy Bilkman. Johnny took the call.

"Hey, dude," he said. "What's up?"

"Johnny, Johnny," Buzzy wheezed. He sounded distraught.

"Whatsa matter?"

"Aah, you know. Life. For Chrissake. How you doin'?"

"I been better."

"I hear you. Listen. Jet. I gotta tell you. No easy way, you know? I just ..."

"Yeah?"

"There was times ... Ah, Johnny. I didn't always get you the best possible deals, OK?"

"Well, I wouldn't—"

"I thought you should know. I mean sometimes—not always—I was cuttin' myself a bigger slice of the pie than I shoulda been, and cuttin' you a smaller slice, you know? Moneywise."

"Yeah, well, I wouldn't—"

"The Hipsley's deal, for one."

"I wouldn't worry too much about it, Buzz. I've done OK. People starving in Africa, but I've had food on my plate."

"I'm just ..." Buzzy paused, apparently taking a prolonged drag on a Camel. "... so ashamed, Jet. For Chrissake. I shouldn'tna done it, I shouldn'tna done it."

"You see the face?" Johnny guessed.

"Yeah, I seen it. And it seen me, too. Seen right through me."

"Don't worry about it, dude." A motorist honked angrily at Johnny, who then jammed his own horn in response. "The money thing, I mean. The rest of it, the end of the world and whatnot, I'd say go ahead and worry about that."

"For Chrissake. Incidentally, you do your show and tell with Dutwell yet?"

"Yeah."

"How'd it go?"

"It went."

"That's how life is," Buzzy said. "Things go. They just go."

Wishing Buzzy the best, Johnny parked his truck at Perfection Fitness and got out. No sooner had he closed the door than a teenage boy, sixteen, seventeen years old, crept up to him in a hesitant and yet vaguely hostile manner. Goggle-eyed, the kid stood maybe fifteen feet in front of him, mouth open, hands open at his sides, lean and whippetlike, staring tensely at Johnny as if sizing him up. Did he mean to mug the celeb? Ask for an autograph? Standing still, Johnny returned his gaze, but much more calmly, gently.

"What?" Johnny finally said.

As if stung by the word, the boy darted away, sprinting down the street with the frenetic choppy stride of one trying to escape. Smiling sadly, Johnny shook his head.

And shook it again when, turning to face his gym, he saw that someone had put a gaping hole in the wall-size window out front. Shards of broken glass glistened up at him. So big was the hole that a man could step through it, and Johnny did, without emotion. His outward reaction to Buzzy's call, to the peculiar kid, and to the current unfortunate state of his window was nearly invisible.

The gym felt weird inside, cavernous and empty, with the fluorescent lights overhead flickering, the electricity erratic. It was like watching an old-time movie, not a very happy one. Johnny moved around listlessly. From one of the room's far recesses came a noise, the unmistakable jarring clank of an Ivanko dumbbell striking the rubberized floor. So the gym wasn't empty after all. With no particular purpose in mind, Johnny headed back to see what was doing.

What he saw was the do-ragged and tattooed bodybuilder dubbed the Beast, back for his second workout of the day. Or maybe he was still laboring manfully through his first marathon workout. The guy was known to spend many a sweat-soaked hour in the gym, and the results showed. His physique—huge, hard, sensationally bedecked with blue-veined muscle—bore only a faint resemblance to the body of a regular adult male. He seemed to like it that way, and Johnny, while he didn't understand it, was OK with it too, and with the man himself.

Respectfully, the proprietor lingered at a certain distance while the Beast, seated on a bench, completed a set of one-arm triceps extensions using a dumbbell that most people couldn't have budged with a crane. Johnny had no idea what drove bodybuilders to do what they did, and he especially had little insight into the Beast, though from time to time they did chat. Yet watching the brutish man train, raising the dumbbell again and again from the back of his head to a position well above his head, Johnny did perceive here a definite work ethic, and one almost frightening in its crystalline purity. How much better a pitcher might Johnny have been, he wondered, had he brought to his own sport even a sliver of the focused discipline that the Beast, in his own way, demonstrated daily? Was demonstrating this very instant ... Damn, he thought.

When the dumbbell clanked to the floor at last, Johnny came closer. "Beast," he said, "what's happening?"

"Hey, bro." In the weight game, Johnny had noticed, the

hardcore types usually addressed you as 'bro,' 'bra,' 'brother' or 'man'; first names scarcely existed.

"So who broke the window?" The question was delivered in a polite tone, very nonaccusatory.

"I dunno," the Beast answered. "I was here when it happened, but I was in the middle of a set. Didn't wanna fuck up my concentration by lookin'."

"Cool. Cool." Again, the work ethic, Johnny thought. "Seems like *everything's* breaking," he suggested with a frown. "Don't you think? Not just the window. Everything. Everywhere."

"Whole damn world, bro, I'm with you."

It occurred to Johnny that he was probably interrupting the man's routine, and he had no wish to be a burden. "You got a minute?" he asked.

Hospitably, the Beast held his gargantuan arm toward another bench, inviting his guest to sit. "When you own the place," he said, "and you got a Cy Young trophy on your mantel, I always got a minute."

Johnny thanked him and plopped down.

"Question," he said. "Day after tomorrow, 3:00 PM, is the world gonna end?"

The Beast stroked his Fu Manchu lightly, reflectively. "Can't say for sure. But that's how I'd bet, yeah."

"That being the case, dude, why're you in here working out? Why bother? And I don't mean to pick at you; I'm just curious, is all."

No need to stroke the mustache this time. "'Cause I want to," came the reply. "It's what I do. It's me bein' me." Still seated, the Beast abruptly straightened one massive arm, the fist down close to the floor. His grainy triceps was so engorged it looked as if it might explode. "And I like bein' pumped," he said.

"I can accept that." And indeed Johnny could. In fact, he detected a broad similarity between the Beast's attitude and the one expressed by the sexually liberated woman who may or may not've been Fanny. *Why not go out on a high note*, she'd said, *doing something I love and enjoy?* "Kinda like riding a comet into the sun, huh?"

"Well, I wouldn't—"

"Lemme ask you this," Johnny said. "A while ago I talked to somebody that told me we're facing the Second Coming of Jesus. You buy that? I'm just curious."

Shrugging, the Beast turned his trapezius muscles into a pair of scaled-down Alpine mountains. "Eschatology," he said.

"Excuse me?"

"It's the study of how the world is supposed to end. Every religion has its own opinion, see. Muslims, Hindus, Buddhists ... even your Zoroastrians."

"Huh."

"Sounds like you got a servin' of the Christian version," the Beast said. "My own favorite scenario comes from Norse myth. Twilight of the Gods. Appeals to the Wagner in me. There you get a raft of natural disasters, followed by a battle among the gods, and then the whole fuckin' world gets dunked in seawater."

Johnny was peering at the Beast the way he used to peer in from the mound to read the catcher's signs. "How do you know all that?" he asked.

"I read."

Rubbing his forehead, Johnny silently acknowledged the mystery and the might of the written word. "Is there some religion somewhere that talks about a face in the sky?"

"Not that I know of, bro." The Beast stood up and stretched, began to prowl, putting his tattoos and his otherworldly muscularity into motion. Though not nearly as tall as Johnny, he was twice as wide. "But I sense," he resumed, "we may be off-track with all this religious razzmatazz."

"Yeah?"

The Beast nodded. "Personally, I suspect the Earth may be up against a goddam *berserker*."

"A berserker!" Johnny stood up too. "What the hell's that?

Hey, I don't even like the sound of that."

"Doomsday machine," the Beast said, explaining that such a sobering device, engineered by an alien civilization, could've been built as a weapon of war and then gone astray, wandering throughout the cosmos, destroying life wherever it found any. Or it could've been designed as an innocuous instrument of exploration, a probe, but then mutated into a planet-killer. This certainly could've happened if the device was self-replicating— a form of von Neumann machine. Something could've gone horribly amiss in the replication process, even as it sometimes did with human beings.

"A doomsday machine," Johnny murmured despondently, staring up at the ceiling lights flickering above him like a cold distant galaxy. He wished he could pick up a rosin bag and fondle it, but there was none to be had. "Wow. A berserker ..."

"Course," the Beast admitted, "it'd have to be a pretty goddam courteous berserker, givin' us time to get ready and all...."

"Hey. You scared of dying?"

"Ain't lookin' forward to it, bro. But it's like the poet says: 'Death, a necessary end, will come when it will come.'"

"I guess so." Johnny glanced around. Empty. "You all done? The workout, I mean."

Like a hungry T. rex, the Beast hulked over the dumbbell. "One more set," he said.

Johnny smiled. With this guy there was always one more set. He'd probably be doing one more set when the world got snuffed.

"When you're finished," Johnny said, "turn out the lights, OK?" On their own, they went out for a moment, then came back on. "If they need it."

"No problem."

Suddenly the Beast began to chuckle, and then to laugh heartily. Since Johnny had never seen him do either before, he paid attention. "What is it?" he asked.

"Can you imagine," the Beast said, "the triceps God must

have? Son of a bitch! Make Mr. Olympia look like a pencil-neck."

"Probably so."

The bodybuilder sat down on the bench, hoisted the dumbbell. "Make Mr. O look like Barney Fife."

\* \* \*

Johnny had known for some time that he would eventually get together again with his ex-girlfriend Wanda, his daughter's mother. He just hadn't known when. Now he did know when.

He would do it immediately.

Unless she'd moved again, he knew where she was staying. The apartment wasn't far, and he decided to leave his truck behind and walk. As he strode along, the purposeful long-legged gait the same one that'd taken him to and from major league mounds so many times, he began to reminisce. In her younger days, Wanda's personality had been as wacky and fun-loving as Johnny's; it was their shared zaniness that'd brought them together.

In spite of everything, he found himself grinning at the memories. Wanda, who'd always had Earth Mother tendencies, once persuaded Johnny to visit Costa Rica on the spur of the moment so he could appreciate the spectacular wildlife of the teeming rainforest (or the 'jungle,' as he called it). While he received no special thrill from the plants or animals, he did delight in the capital city of San José, and especially the Americanized suburb of Escazú, where he sipped Imperial beer and developed a taste for rice with chicken....

On his thirtieth birthday Wanda presented him with a frosty white cake the size of an igloo, out of which she jumped. Nude. The event occurred at a chic Lake Michigan restaurant packed with friends, players, team officials and—inevitably—the media. Her thinking was that bits and pieces of the cake would cling to her body and obscure her essentials. Nothing clung but the bulging eyes of the onlookers, and for one of the rare occasions in his life Johnny knew the feeling of cheek-reddening embarrassment....

Years later, Wanda and an all-too-young Sarah decided to go skydiving together. The idea had been Wanda's, but his daredevil daughter took to it eagerly. Since Johnny was loudly opposed to this dangerous nonsense, the two became doubly determined to go ahead with their jump. And they did. He was there to witness the spectacle, and as he stared up into the blue, shading his eyes with his hand, heart hammering, he would've sworn that nothing that might descend from the sky could ever frighten him half as much as those two tiny twirling silhouettes....

Now, he had to ask himself: Why had he and Wanda gone their separate ways? It'd been so long that he couldn't dredge up much of a rationale. He really had nothing against her except she was just one woman, and he'd craved more than one woman. Why put yourself on a diet when you could turn every day, and every night, into a banquet?

But sometimes Johnny's logic seemed illogical even to him.

Wanda's apartment house was a tall, narrow wooden container, rather frail, of which she occupied the second floor. After rubbing his hands together a few times to psyche himself up, he climbed the dim stairs and knocked on the unmarked door. When the door swung open, he was stunned that he could look inside and see himself in there already. Or rather, he saw a blown-up color photo on the wall of Johnny Black wearing his Sox cap and uniform and laughing at the camera—laughing at the viewer, himself—as if he hadn't a care in life.

Then his eyes fell on the woman who'd opened the door. It wasn't Wanda, not even close, and for the second time in the same day he thought that perhaps he'd arrived at the wrong address. This woman was dark-haired, dark-complected, with a decidedly ethnic stamp. Stout, but vigorous. Commanding. She was wearing sea-green scrubs and a nametag that read *Maria Castillo*.

"I'm sorry," Johnny said. "I'm ... Could you ... I was ..."

Dourly, she studied his face, turned and studied the photo, then turned back to him. Unsmiling, she said: "Come in."

Trailing her into the living room, he said: "I'm ... Ma'am, I may be mistaken. I was ..."

The distance to the couch was only a few short steps, and when they arrived there, he gazed down at a woman he didn't recognize. Eyes closed, she was lying on her back, her lower half covered by a dirty gray sheet. She looked sick and old, and was either asleep or unconscious. Or dead.

Then he recognized her.

"Wanda," he said. "Oh my God. What happened? Oh my God."

23

BOB STALLINGS PULLED INTO his wide slanting driveway and parked the Malibu. Before them, his streamlined rancher seemed to crouch in the dimness. He climbed out of the car and made his way around to the other side, intending to open each lady's door for her. But by the time he got there, both Sarah and Laura had already gotten out on their own.

"Over here," he said with a flick of his hand, and they headed for the breezeway that led from the garage to the house. As they moved quietly along, Stallings had a glance up at the sky, not knowing what to expect—some of those dancing angelic lights that'd been in the news?—but he saw nothing. A thick bank of clouds must've slid in toward evening, he guessed, for there was nothing above but darkness. Not even a star.

"*Mi casa es su casa*," he said, keys jangling as he pushed open the door.

Sarah, who hadn't spoken in a while, piped up: "That's what Ernie always says."

"Who?"

"A friend of mine," she said. "In California."

Stallings locked them in and tried to offer some reassurance. "We'll be OK here," he said. Even as he made the statement, he wondered if it had any basis in fact. He clicked on some lights. "C'mon," he said. "I'll show you around."

So he took them on an impromptu tour, calling their attention to this and that and making comments. On some level, he liked serving as tour guide, since it felt like a normal enough activity, and being 'normal' was important to him just now. Moreover, he'd developed a genuine fondness for his home and took a gentle pride in noting its better qualities. He hadn't always felt so confirmed. Perhaps to prop up his ego, he'd originally aspired to a house much grander, more imposing. But his wife had pushed for the rancher, with its simple, rustic trim, its large windows, its exposed wood beams here and there. "It'll be comfortable," Jenny had said. "It'll be peaceful." As usual, she'd been right, and over the years he'd come to appreciate just how right she was.

He showed the two women where the light switches were and, in the bathroom, showed them how to jiggle the handle after flushing the commode. "I oughta have someone come by and take a look at that," he supposed. "You shouldn't have to jiggle that handle." In the kitchen, he showed them where the glasses and dishes were, and warned them about the drawer that held the silverware. "Don't pull it out too far," he said, "or it'll just come flying outta there and land on the floor. Spoons and forks all over the place." It'd happened to Stallings on more than one occasion. "I probably oughta have someone take a look at that drawer, too."

The women nodded silently, distractedly.

"Now," he said. "Anybody hungry? Thirsty?"

No one was.

But sooner or later someone *would* need something to eat or drink, most likely Stallings himself, so he figured he'd better check his supplies. He opened the cupboard and saw, stacked rather neatly, peanut butter, tuna, soup, canned vegetables, crackers, cookies.... Plenty for one person, he judged, but what about three? Furrowing his brow, he turned to the refrigerator, opened it and peered in as if he were a surgeon studying an X-ray. Milk, orange juice, eggs, strawberries, sliced ham, American cheese, leftovers from last night, additional leftovers from the night before ... more stuff up in the freezer. Did he have enough? Probably—but how much was enough? How long would they be holed up here? Would the stores be open? What if the electricity cut out?

Of course, if the world ended on schedule, having an impressive stockpile of food wouldn't matter much.

"Lots of vittles," Stallings announced, closing the door.

"I've got food to make you fat—butter pecan ice cream—food to make you thin—Lean Cuisine—and food that has no effect on your shape one way or the other. Whatever you like. When you want something, just help yourself."

He sat down at the kitchen table, and the others sat down with him. No one spoke. After a moment Stallings stood up and went to the living room to see what was on TV. He found nothing but static, and a very harsh static at that—a stormy battlefield of tiny gray and white explosions erupting angrily at him, and a steady mindless roar as if an anxiety-seeking missile were powering straight at his puttylike nose. He turned off the TV and checked the computer in his office—no Internet. He even tried his bedroom radio, but it blasted him with an ugly noise much like what'd blared from the TV. Discouraged, he went back out to the kitchen to find Sarah and Laura seated in exactly the same attitude as before. Neither had budged. Both were mute, staring down at the table.

Stallings located a short glass and, delving into the fridge once again, poured himself a splash of Hipsley's Iced Tea. He had no idea what secret ingredients might've been swimming around in it, but the tea always seemed to fortify him, to brighten him. He waggled the jug at his guests, but they had no interest.

Exhaling, he sat down between them, sipped his elixir. "So what do you think?" he said to them both.

Neither spoke.

After a moment, he said: "So, Sarah," and shifted toward her. Even after the rigors of her past few days, her unlined face still appeared fresh and lovely, pretty much in defiance of physical law. Her rich dark hair was tousled, and fatigue shone in her violet eyes, but she was holding up almost supernaturally well. The magic of youth? Stallings wondered. Force of will? Freaky genetics? "You still think that face in the sky is bullshit?" he asked her.

"I do," she said. "But that doesn't mean nothing's happening."

Laura, whose skin was so pale her blood might've been drained from her svelte body and replaced with tap water, grunted vaguely.

"Most times," Sarah said, "whatever happens is bullshit. But it happens anyway, you know?"

"Mm," Laura grunted again. "Those poor people in Des Moines ..."

"Dead," Sarah said.

"Korla too," Stallings said. "Don't forget about them."

"Ashes," Sarah said.

"Korla too, right," Laura acknowledged.

"Ashes to ashes," Sarah said.

"My God," Laura said. "Just ... just ..."

"Just bullshit," Sarah said, "is all it is. Hateful, cruel ..."

"Nothing like it before," Stallings allowed. "Not like this. Wars, yes. Bombs. But nothing like—"

"All those poor people," Laura said.

"Nothing like this," Stallings said.

"Someone oughta be ashamed," Sarah said bitterly. "For doing all this. Someone really oughta ..."

"We're gonna catch it, aren't we?" Laura said.

"Sure we are," Sarah answered. "What the fuck else—"

"Well, now," Stallings hopped in, reaching for a fatherly tone, "let's just—"

"What else would you expect?"

"Well, now," he said, "let's just try to stay calm, OK? Try to stay—"

"Pretty fucked up world, you ask me," Sarah said.

"—stay rational," Stallings went on, sounding a trifle irrational even to himself. "If we knew for certain what the future was going to bring, we'd all be zillionaires, right?"

The women looked at him as if they expected him to follow through now with some sort of trenchant insight that would bathe everything in a more hopeful glow, but he just sat there, his chunky fingers forming a fence around the squat glass of tea that rested on the table.

"That face," Laura said, "warned us that the world was about to end. But first—"

"First," Sarah broke in, "there'd be a 'token of good faith' involving two cities. And we—"

"We've had that," Laura said. "Korla, one. Des Moines, two."

"Des Moines, two," Sarah said. "So it's happening. It's bullshit, but it's happening."

"It is," Laura said softly. "It really is."

"Happening right *now*, goddammit," Sarah said with some heat.

Very thoughtfully, Stallings pushed away from the table, stood up and began slowly pacing around the kitchen. His lips were pursed, and his expression was one of deep concentration, as if he were engaged in a chess match with a crafty player who was just slightly stronger than himself. Without even being aware of it, he was beginning to move in the same unrushed peripatetic manner he often used in the classroom (though now, still clad in his LL Bean sweatsuit and carrying a glass of bourbon-colored tea, he gave off a vibe not often felt in a community college).

"Korla," he said at last. "You ever been there?"

"It's in *China*," Laura said, as if that answered the question.

"Do you know what it looked like?" he asked.

Laura shrugged. "Looked like a city, I guess."

"Mm hmm." Stallings sipped his tea. "What's it look like now?"

"It looks like ..." Laura glanced over at Sarah, who, as a former student, wore the wary mien of one who'd encountered this type of sly probing inquiry before. "... like nothing," Laura said. "Like a big gray nothing."

"How do you know that?" Stallings asked.

"I saw it on TV."

"You saw what on TV?"

"A big gray nothing."

Stallings permitted himself to smirk a little. "How do you

know," he asked, "that what you were seeing was in fact Korla? Somebody said so?"

"The people on TV, yes."

"So you don't know what the city looked like before—"

"And the people on the radio said the same thing."

"You don't know what it looked like before—probably never even heard of it—and you're taking someone's word for what it looks like now. Is that it?"

"Well, I wouldn't, I don't—"

"Same deal," Stallings said, "with those disappearing buildings. I've not heard of anyone yet who actually witnessed a building disappear. Have you? We're being shown photos—which can be doctored—of scenes that represent—supposedly!—the aftermath of some *alleged* event." He set down his tea so he could move his hands more freely and dramatically.

"So you're saying," Laura began.

"Same way with Des Moines," Stallings said, jabbing a finger.

"Not quite," said Laura, who stood up and launched herself into orbit around the room in the direction opposite that of her host. "I've been to Des Moines. I know what it looked like."

"Uh huh. Did you see it on TV tonight?"

"Yes."

"What'd it look like?" Stallings asked. "Did it look like Des Moines?"

"It looked like a big gray nothing."

Stallings bounced on the balls of his feet and flung open his arms aggressively as if he meant to body slam someone—maybe Laura. "If Des Moines didn't look like Des Moines," he cried, "then how do you know you were looking at Des Moines?"

Stopping in front of him, Laura stared up at his rounded cheeks, his bright blinking eyes. "Let me get this straight," she said. "You're saying this whole thing is what? A deception? A hoax?"

Stallings hesitated. He wasn't exactly sure *what* he was saying. He took a breath. "A hoax, possibly," he said. "Who knows? Perhaps a test of some kind."

Sarah, who had held her silence during this exchange but who had watched and listened carefully, stirred to life. "A test?" She tossed her remark at him like a dart.

"That's right," he said. "A test, a psychological test. Of our resources, our resilience ..."

"But who would the test-giver be?" Sarah asked. "And what the hell would he be hoping to gain?"

Stallings walked over to the table, picked up his tea and had a sip. "I don't know."

"How could anyone coordinate something like this?" Sarah asked.

"I don't know. I'm just saying ..." The zest he'd felt for his own set of ideas was already fading. "Hey, all I'm saying—"

"Bob," Sarah said, "the lights in the sky have been videotaped."

"So?" He strode over to a window, had a look up above. As before, he saw a perfect blackness—no lights, no stars, no moon. He could've been gazing up into an infinitely deep hole. "I've never seen them myself," he said, "except on TV. But let's say they're objectively real. So what? Lights in the sky. So what? What do they prove?"

Now Sarah stood up too. Seated, she was easier to contend with, it seemed to Stallings, both visually and rhetorically. But when she rose like this, putting that incomparable body on display and in motion, her sheer physical oomph tended to fluster him.

"What about the face in the sky?" she asked. "An awful lot of people have seen it, including you."

Stallings put his eyes on the white bulk of the refrigerator, said nothing.

She came near him. "You did see it, didn't you?"

"I, uh ... I had an experience," he hedged. "But sometimes,

if you're tired, if you're stressed ..."

When the apparition swooped down at him that day, it seemed almost to press against him, though no actual touching occurred. Its hard brown eyes were trained on Stallings' eyes in a personal almost intimate way, yet so enormous was the face that it blocked out everything else—every sight, every thought. *Mr. Stallings*, the vision said in a grave voice, *things begin and things end*, and sprawled on his back, pinned between the face and the earth, he could feel the warm moist puffs of breath as they washed over him like an unwelcome surf. He recalled his screams as they leaped up out of his chest and throat, separate from his own volition, and watched in wonder as his hands clawed wildly at the sky, at the fearsome face. *Prepare for the end*, the thing told him, pushing down at him, and he'd screamed some more.

Though he would later try to deny the knowledge, rationalize it, shunt it aside, Stallings knew instantly and absolutely that he and everyone else were in a heap of trouble.

"If you saw the face," Sarah said, "and if you listened to its words, you must have some sense of what it means." She was just beneath him, peering up at him, plumbing his eyes. "So tell us the truth, Bob. What's it mean?"

He ran his hand backward through his brown thatch of hair, then ran it through again. "Hell, I don't know," he blurted. "It probably means we should switch rooms, OK? Let's go in the living room where it's more comfortable, OK?"

The others were agreeable, and he led them to the living room, whose lights he extinguished, a certain dimness seeming to suit the mood. Sarah and Laura sat on different sections of the L-shaped sofa while Stallings went to a plush leather La-Z-Boy chair and sat not in it but on the carpeted floor in front of it. Since his youth, anytime he felt tense he preferred to sit—if sitting was required at all—on the floor; it helped him relax. So keen was this preference that he had to be careful he didn't yield to it in formal situations.

Having succeeded in changing the scene, Stallings now

succeeded in changing the subject. He began talking about how much simpler and better life seemed to be back when he'd been growing up. He mentioned Boy Scouts, the Muppets, pet rocks, men on the moon and a faddish dance called the Hustle. "Along the lines of the Countdown," he said, "but tougher to do. I never could figure it out." At this moment nostalgia obviously had its attractions, and Laura told about how she'd once won a blue ribbon for having perfect attendance in grade school. Not to be outdone, Sarah remembered how her mother once bought her a small gift, a charm bracelet, when Sarah managed to go two full weeks without causing either a teacher or the principal to call home with a complaint. "I wasn't necessarily better behaved," she said. "Just sneakier."

Even in those days, they conceded, they knew something about fear, though the fear then tended to be more mundane, more commonplace. Sarah said she became scared every time her mother announced they'd soon be moving to a new apartment or town. "I was always just getting used to where we were," she said. "Then I'd have to go to a whole different environment. New people, new places. Everybody judging me all over again. Happened all the time. It made me cry." She rubbed her arms. "It gave me hives."

Laura's biggest fear, she said, was more abstract. She was afraid she'd have no discernable impact on the world; that she'd be a cipher, a nobody. She claimed to see it everywhere—people were born, they grew up, they made some babies, they worked a pedestrian job, and they died. Hideous. The possibility that she too could have such a colorless meaningless life—and she hadn't avoided it yet!—terrified her. It explained why she'd moved from Minnesota to California, and why she'd come now from California to Illinois. She was seeking something. Or seeking to escape something. To escape the banal.

Listening to these confessions, Stallings felt he should chime in as well. He said that his worst fear had always been financial; he'd been afraid he wouldn't be able to secure a decent-paying job, or if he did land one, he wouldn't be able to keep it. "People always downplay the importance of money," he said with an air of wisdom. "Idealists. They say: 'Give me love, give me happiness.' But I'll tell you something. You ever want to buy a car or a house"—he waved his hand at the house they were in—"you try to pay for it with love or happiness. See how far you get."

Stallings smiled without conviction. "I'll tell you something funny," he said. "Recently I did some maneuvering in the stock market. Called things exactly right for a change, OK? These last couple days, I don't know how much money I've made, but it's been a bundle. A small fortune, I guess. But my perception is, Wall Street's in ruins—a freaking train wreck. It's gotta be." He chuckled ruefully. "I doubt if I ever see a dime. Then again," he said, "if that face is right, it really doesn't matter, does it?" He crossed one leg over the other. "Nothing matters."

He chuckled again, and this time his chuckle escalated into a high-pitched uncontrolled titter. When it went on awhile, the women stared at him, and he forced himself to stop.

In fact, Stallings had misled his friends somewhat. He had told them one of his fears, yes, but not the worst one. His very greatest fear was that something bad might happen to the person he felt closest to in life. And, to his devastation, that fear had already been realized. Anything further would be, in his terms, a kind of surtax; in Sarah's terms, it would be bullshit. (But this hardly meant that nothing more could happen, to him or to others—whatever its intentions, Fate never seemed to consult with Stallings before taking action.)

A thought occurred to him, and he clambered to his feet. "You'll need something to sleep in," he said. "You'll need some pajamas." Both women tried to object, but, a man on a mission, he went off to see what he could dig up.

Since Laura was about the same size his wife had been, finding something for her proved easy enough. All of Jenny's clothes, every stitch except for the outfit she was buried in, still hung obediently in her closet, still rested peacefully in her dresser drawers; he hadn't been able to bring himself to get rid of them. Quickly he selected a fine cottony mid-length nightgown, mint green, Jenny's favorite color.

Now the voluptuous Sarah, of course, presented Stallings with a problem—he doubted she would fit into anything Jenny had owned. But, he reckoned, she *would* fit into a pair of his own pajamas. Trouble was, the decorous conservative taste that marked his daily wardrobe was nowhere to be seen in his sleepwear; most of his pajamas, brightly hued and often adorned with humorous slogans, would've given pause to Ronald McDonald. Eventually he settled on a baggy silk top and bottom covered with scarlet broken hearts and the phrase PRISONER OF LOVE printed all over, countless times.

Well, Sarah was tired, he figured, and the lighting was weak. Maybe she wouldn't notice.

When he went back to the living room, the women were up and moving around, preparing to turn in. He handed them the pajamas without ado and decided that Sarah could have his bedroom, Laura could have the guestroom, and he would remain in the living room. He would bed down either on the sofa, as he had the night of his final drinking bout, or on the floor in front of the sofa. It would depend on his mood. They all said their goodnights, had some hugs and went their ways.

Yawning, Stallings sat himself on the L-shaped sofa. Within minutes he had relocated to the floor. Still sitting, he let his eyes go to a window whose drapes had not been fully drawn, and through the open space he saw in silhouette the black shape of a lilac bush. So cheerful-looking during the day, at this late hour, the plant looked alien and forbidding. His mind was active with a jumble of thoughts and feelings, most of them unpleasant, and he doubted he would sleep much tonight. He doubted his guests—or anyone else—would sleep much tonight. Had two cities truly been destroyed? Was more destruction on its way? Facing the window, his back to the sofa, he heard strange noises from outside. Somewhere in the dark a siren was wailing, up and down, in a pained febrile ululation. What message was it trying to convey? And he heard the popping sound of firecrackers as well—or was it the sound of gunfire?

The sinister lilac loomed at him.

As they often did, his musings went to his dead wife, and he wondered what Jenny would think of him at this instant. He had brought not just one woman into their home but two. Two women at once! Lord have mercy. *Robert!* he could almost hear her saying in disbelief, *Robert Earl Stallings, what in the name of God ...?* Now *Jenny,* he might come back at her, *this isn't quite what it looks like. Let me explain, I can explain....* And probably he could've.

But he would've had a harder time explaining what was happening now. Someone was in the room with him. It was Sarah. They saw each other in the dimness, and she came straight to him, padding along softly in Stallings' outlandish pajamas.

"Sarah," he said. "You OK?"

She sat down on the floor next to him and snuggled against him. "I don't know," she said.

In a natural and automatic reflex he put his arm around her shoulders and held her against him. "Sure you are," he said.

"I don't know."

Neither the thrill nor the guilt he might've been expected to feel in these circumstances was there. Only a surprising but genuine calmness. A calmness that couldn't quite dispatch the heavy chains rattling ominously in the dank dungeon of his soul, but did make them sound smaller, farther away, less frightening. He kept his arm around her, and she stayed pressed against him.

As time passed, he felt more than just a sense of calmness; he felt—there was no getting around it—a flush of sexual desire. It had been a long time since Stallings had been with a woman, and Sarah was a woman who, whether she wanted to or not, simply exuded sexuality. But Stallings was a gentleman who knew where to draw the line, he told himself, and Jenny could've been proud of that much. Besides, Sarah was his friend's daughter, a former student, and a girl at least two decades his junior. She was scared, and she deserved to be protected, not abused.

He squeezed his arm around her. Such sweetness, he thought. Such innocence. A salty tongue, no question, but innocence nonetheless.

Stallings dozed a little, and he believed Sarah did too. Two or three times he awakened, felt the warm astonishing flesh molded against him and became momentarily confused. What the ... Then he remembered. Once, he was sitting there half-asleep and half-awake, fantastic chimeras roaming among his fuzzy thoughts, when suddenly Sarah started and gasped as if escaping, or trying to escape, from a nightmare. Stallings tightened his grasp on her slightly and whispered: "It's all right. It's all right." Knowing that it wasn't all right, but believing in the lie anyway.

Outside, the popping noises continued at intervals, and the siren, off somewhere in the night, continued its nonstop plaintive wailing. When it reached a certain pitch, something like a desperate cry for help, he couldn't help but shudder....

Jenny Jenny Sarah Mom you OK corn on my foot but don't worry about it shoot a rocket up that monster hairy nostril incredible boobs ashes to ashes were you ready for this gotta hand it to that Invisible Hand dead and more dead castrate you then strangle you theatre smells like a cooked rat wait for the Governor with all that pork you're packing but poor pathetic Earth not yet at K1 and how many forms am I gonna have to sign for all this no never never never ...

Gradually the black turned into gray, and the gray became a softer gray.

No pink, just gray.

Dawn.

* * *

Later, Sarah awakened to find herself alone on the floor. She took a few minutes to gather herself.

That last dream of hers had been horrid, though by now, she thought, she should be getting used to it. It was always the same. A young man, Derek probably, quivering with anger, stands just in front of her. Menacing her. She has a gun. And she shoots him not once, but multiple times, blood geysering from the wounds in his face, throat and chest. Now the young man transforms into an older man—her father, Johnny Black—who, spouting gallons of blood, looks down at her with an aloof but palpable scorn. Not a word spoken. Blood is filling the room as if it were a bathtub, jetting into her face, swirling around her legs. Nothing but blood, blinding her, choking her, pushing her one way and another ...

Ouch. Though the carpet was soft and full, her back was stiff from spending the night on such an otherwise unforgiving bed. She stretched and yawned, rolled over, sat up and had a long quizzical stare at the weird pajamas she was wearing.

From the kitchen came the aroma of coffee and muffins, and she heard the sound of running water, as if someone might be taking a shower.

A moment passed, and her eyes settled on her blue purse and her cell phone, both of them perched on a low glassy table before her. Dutifully she'd tried to call her mother in recent days, but with the erratic service she hadn't been able to get through. Why not try again?

This time she had service. The phone at the other end rang a few times, and someone answered. But not her mother. A man's voice, hauntingly familiar, said: "Hello?" Only after three or four beats of her heart did she recognize the voice as her father's, and then she sucked in her breath sharply and hung up.

24

EVEN MORE THAN MOST MEN, Johnny disliked being shocked. To his chagrin, he was now being shocked on a regular basis.

Standing over the limp motionless form of his ex-girlfriend Wanda, who seemed unaware of him and of everything else, he was able to make out faint traces of her one-time young and perky face in this current older and not so perky face. The nose was still there, the cheekbones.... But mostly her features had changed, and changed for the worse. It was as if Johnny were viewing the sad end-product of some devilish time-lapse photography.

"Oh my God," he said.

Wanda's chestnut hair, which, long and beautifully flowing, had always been one of her physical highlights, was now greasy, matted and streaked with gray; it produced a witchy effect. Her closed eyes were surrounded by a webwork of little lines, and beneath each eye was a purplish bruised-looking bag. Her mouth was drawn and pinched. Her skin was sallow, and her breathing barely noticeable. In all, she appeared not just sick but markedly aged—yet she was two years younger than the still handsome and vibrant Johnny.

He turned to the nurse—in those scrubs she had to be a nurse, right?—and searched her face. Searched her nametag once again too—Maria Castillo.

"Whatsa matter with Wanda?" he asked, his voice taut.

Maria was lingering next to the large color photo on the wall of a grinning lighthearted Johnny Black, the bill of his Sox cap raised at a jaunty angle. "She's not well."

"I can see that, Ms. Castillo." It cost him some effort to keep his voice in check. "But whatsa matter with her? Is it the diabetes, or the depression, or ...?"

"Those problems," Maria said, "plus some others. Ms.

Lease is resting. You should let her rest."

Turning back to the inert Wanda, Johnny thought *Yeah, she's resting all right; doing a helluva job of resting.* "Listen," he said. "I'm no medical expert, but shouldn't she be in the hospital?"

"No."

"No?"

Maria shook her head somberly. "I just came from there. Let me assure you, it's not the place to be. These last few days ..." Again she shook her head, implying that the hospital at this point wasn't capable of doing what it was meant to.

Johnny sat down beside Wanda, held her skinny hand, stroked it. He seemed hopeful of imparting some of his own nervous energy to her.

"She hasn't been eating much lately," Maria said, "but I got her to eat a cookie a while ago. It should help."

"She gonna be all right?"

The nurse pressed her hands together in front of her. "Well, that's certainly what we're hoping for, isn't it."

Johnny took this comment as both compassionate and evasive. "It certainly is," he said.

Maria went to a table where a laptop computer rested. She shut it down, closed it and placed it in a soft black carrying case on the same table. As she zipped the case shut, a realization smacked Johnny in the head like a foul ball.

"Hey, you aren't leaving, are you?" he said.

She scooped a pair of vials off the table and held them up so he could see. "In two hours," she said, "give her three white tablets"—she jiggled a vial—"and one yellow capsule"—she jiggled the other vial.

"Wait a second." He stood up. "Where you going?"

"She can take them with either juice or water."

Maria lifted the slim case and picked up a fat black bag, her medical bag, and began moving toward the door. With two athletic strides Johnny cut in front of her.

"You can't just run off," he said.

Unflappably, she tilted her head back and locked onto his

glazed eyes, which hovered a foot above hers. "Mr. Black," she said, using his name for the first time, "I have other places I need to be, other patients I need to help."

A reasonable enough position, Johnny would've admitted, but he didn't care for it regardless. "Ma'am," he stammered, "I don't ... You see, I can't, I'm not ..."

When she continued to push her own steady gaze deep into his eye sockets, he reluctantly stepped aside, and she passed to the door.

"Do your best," Maria said. "I'll try to come back." After a moment she added: "Ms. Lease told me sooner or later you'd be here. I must confess, I didn't believe it." She held him briefly with her eyes, opened the door and left.

Johnny couldn't believe it himself. He couldn't believe a lot of things. Couldn't believe where he was, what he was doing, the conditions under which he was doing it. The whole loopy state of affairs. He had the stunned disoriented look of a traveler who'd just climbed down from a Greyhound bus to find himself not in Portland, Oregon, where he'd expected to be, but in Portland, Maine.

Not knowing what else to do, he sat down again with Wanda, held her hand, stroked it. He tried talking to her in a soft cooing voice—"Wanda? Wanda? How you doin', babe? Huh? Hey, Wanda?"—but she didn't respond. She just lay there looking sick and old. Next door to dead.

Then suddenly, her eyes still closed, she spoke. "Johnny?" she said in a feeble voice. "Johnny?" It was at once a question and a statement. Heartened, he tried to get her to talk some more—maybe just say his name again—but she either wouldn't or couldn't. Sleep wrapped a massive tentacle around her and dragged her down.

"Wanda?" he said. "I'm here, babe. Hey, Wanda?"

After a while he got up and stretched his long legs, walked in a ragged circle. Though he didn't want to, he took in some of the apartment's meager details. The living room was miniature; Johnny had closets this size. No curtains hung on the windows; instead, sheets had been tacked up, dirty gray, like the one on Wanda. A cane-back chair, missing a leg, sat lopsided, and next to it were several cardboard boxes. Actually the boxes were heaped and scattered here and there, everywhere. Most of them were empty. A couple or more mousetraps had been positioned along the cracked and peeling walls. In the air hung a sour odor—garbage? the miasma of a sick person?—along with a warm heavy stuffiness. Johnny searched for an air conditioner; couldn't find one. Searched for a fan; couldn't find one.

But in the kitchen he did find some paper towels. He tore one off the roll, wet it with cool water and took it to Wanda. After folding it into a small rectangle, he dabbed it gently against her forehead, hoping to make her more comfortable.

When the time came for her medicine, she began to stir restlessly as if she knew some task awaited her. Doubtful that she could swallow anything substantial, Johnny crushed the tablets with the butt of a steak knife and used the same knife to saw open the capsule. He dumped the resulting powder into a small cup of orange juice and carried it to Wanda solemnly as if presenting the Holy Eucharist.

"Johnny?" she said weakly, eyes closed.

"Wanda, hey, I've got something for you." He slipped one hand behind her head and delicately raised it two inches. With the other hand he held the cup to her lips. "Drink up," he said.

Surprising him, she drank. Not as quickly or neatly as he would've preferred, but she drank. When she finished, he cleaned her with another paper towel.

Sitting next to her, he wondered what he'd just given her—wondered what exactly it was supposed to do. How it worked. Blessed with near flawless good health himself, he'd had little contact with medicine in the past, his own therapies having been limited to aspirin, diathermy, whirlpool baths, the occasional icepack, B-12 injections, fine liquor and vigorous massage (sometimes administered in a professional setting, sometimes not). But he had faith in Nurse Castillo, and he hoped Wanda would soon get better.

Hungry, he went to the kitchen and nosed about for food. Aside from a handful of vanilla wafer cookies, he found nothing edible. The bread was moldy, the milk curdled; not much else.... The cookies, of course, he needed to save for Wanda. Deciding that now would be an excellent time for him to tighten up his usually liberal and scattershot diet, he sighed and poured himself a glass of water and took it into the living room with him.

He checked on Wanda, then sat down on the floor next to her. Sometimes when he felt edgy, he liked to sit on the floor. It was an oddball habit, and for several minutes he tried in vain to recall where he'd acquired it. One of his buddies maybe?... He let his eyes go to a window. He studied it. Here was a twist. He could remember a time—it hadn't been all that long ago— when, in order to beat the team's curfew, he would leave and enter his room through the window, sometimes using sheets that'd been knotted together. Now the sheets were tacked up in front of the window.

At last he became drowsy, and he slept fitfully. His slumber was in no way assisted by the mousetraps that, every hour or two, banged abruptly and loudly. The snapping traps sounded like gunshots, and the first time one went off it startled him to such an extreme that he knocked his glass of water halfway across the room. In the distance, a siren rent the night air with a mournful quavering cry. When he slept, he dreamed (as he often did) of a gorgeous young woman. Except this gorgeous young woman was stalking him, aiming to hurt him, to kill him. He thought maybe he knew her, but he couldn't be positive. Perhaps she was a stranger.

BANG! went a mousetrap.

Morning's light seeping in through the gray sheets, he roused himself and spent more time with Wanda, sitting beside her, holding her hand, talking to her. As before, he got little or no response. Not much change in her condition that he could tell. It crossed his mind that she should probably receive her medication not just once but at recurring intervals—the nurse hadn't actually said. So he picked up one of the vials and held it in the dull light, had a close look at the directions.

Just then the phone rang, and Johnny debated whether or not to answer it. Thinking it might be someone important— Nurse Castillo, for instance—he lifted the receiver and said hello. A lengthy pause, and then whoever it was hung up. He shrugged. People these days and their crummy manners. Probably someone expecting to hear Wanda's voice, not his.

Forgetting the phone, he held the vial in the light again, reading and rereading the directions. He told himself he had to be careful here; this was no time to boot one. A person's life might well be at stake....

* * *

Later that morning, the white Malibu pulled up and parked outside Wanda's apartment. Bob Stallings was driving, and Sarah and Laura were in the car with him.

Sarah had said she'd like to visit her mother, and the professor immediately offered to drive her. She told him where she thought her mother was staying, and he said that yes, Johnny had mentioned how Wanda had supposedly rented a place not far from the gym. Stallings knew the neighborhood.

"Your mother'll be glad to see you," he said, thinking wistfully of his own parents, trusting they were hanging in there. "Shame you were never able to track down your old man." He chuckled impishly. "Hey—maybe he's hiding from you."

"Maybe," she said.

Hearing the reference to Sarah's father, Laura pricked up her ears. "Mind if I come along?" she asked. She didn't want to stay by herself in the house, she said.

Still clinging to her journalist's mission, Laura brought her voice recorder with her in hopes of interviewing Stallings or Sarah or someone else along the way. But she saw she'd have to wait for the opportunity.

The streets were quiet, but so was Sarah—decidedly so—and Stallings was going on and on about how when the time came for him to retire, he planned to move not south as his own parents had, but up north, possibly to Maine. The Pine Tree State. "You gotta love pine trees," he said. "All fresh and green and Christmassy." For the moment, the very real chance that the world might not exist beyond tomorrow, let alone during his retirement years, seemed irrelevant. "Besides," he insisted, "warm weather's not all it's cracked up to be. It can make you feel sluggish. Half-dead. Now brisk weather, a nice sharp chilly breeze—that'll make you feel alert, see. Make you feel *alive.*"

"Maybe you should move to the North Pole," Sarah said dryly as they reached their destination.

They agreed that she should go inside and spend some private time with her mom. Afterwards, she would come and fetch her friends, bring them in for introductions. While they waited on Sarah, Laura would ask Stallings some questions as part of a project she was working on.

They all stepped outside into the drab light of an overcast day.

"An interview?" Stallings asked. "Really?" He was flattered; the only interviews he'd done before this were job interviews. "Heck, I don't know anything. What'll we talk about?"

Meanwhile, Sarah adjusted the strap of her blue purse, which lately was a guaranteed accessory to every eye-candy outfit she wore. She made her way to the ramshackle entrance.

"Hey, sister," Laura called after her in a voice that was playful but serious as well. "Don't do anything I wouldn't do."

Sarah paused and looked back over her shoulder. "Honey," she said, "I won't do anything that shouldn't be done."

She closed the door behind her and ascended the stairs slowly ... inexorably. They were wooden stairs, old and splintery. Shadows. Cobwebs. An unidentifiable foul odor, not overpowering but not easily ignored either, floated around her like a nasty memory. The steps groaned every time she placed her weight on them.

At the top of the staircase she came to a landing. Above her hung a dusty 60-watt lightbulb, and before her rose an unmarked door. She stood there for half a minute. Then a minute. Several minutes. Silence. Her cold violet eyes immobile, she appeared to be trying to see right through the door—or to see perhaps into the future, if only for a short distance.

Now she took a breath. Her hands crept to her purse, and she unzipped it. Smoothly and deliberately she reached inside....

STALLINGS: What, uh ... what is that?

LK: What's what?

STALLINGS: That thing there. That device.

LK: It's a voice recorder.

STALLINGS: Really? You're gonna record us?

LK: If you don't mind.

STALLINGS: Huh. No, that's fine, that's ... Yeah. Wow. Is it on?

LK: Is it ...?

STALLINGS: Is it running? The recorder. Hello, hello.

LK: It's on. See that little light?

STALLINGS: Ah.

LK: So here we go. Professor Bob Stallings, I'd like to hear some of your thoughts today. Some of your impressions.

STALLINGS: OK. Concerning ...

LK: Concerning anything. Everything.

STALLINGS: Sure. Point me in a direction.

LK: Let's start with Sarah Black. When did you first meet her?

STALLINGS: Oh, gee. Well, I first met her when she was just a little kid. Ages ago. I'm pals with her dad.

LK: Johnny Black.

STALLINGS: Perfection, right. The one and only. (chuckles) And then Sarah became a student of mine at HCC.

LK: Good student?

STALLINGS: By the way, HCC stands for 'Harris Community College.'

LK: Was she a good student?

STALLINGS: Sarah? Oh, my. Yes. Anytime she learned something, it stayed learned.

LK: Are you familiar—

STALLINGS: Wish I had a bunch more like her.

LK: You familiar with her work? Her work since college?

STALLINGS: Not really. Said she was in the media, but that's about all she said.

LK: Uh huh.

STALLINGS: And that's one of the things I respect about her, you know?

LK: What's that?

STALLINGS: She's reserved.

LK: She's ...

STALLINGS: Reserved. She is. No, she is. And what I mean by that—OK—yes, she *is* kinda outspoken. OK? Dresses ... I dunno ... unconventionally. Drives a hot car. But I'll tell you what, she doesn't go around boasting about her accomplishments the way a lot of people do.

LK: Right.

STALLINGS: Her philosophy seems to be *Just do your job. Do your job, do it well, and pretty soon people'll sit up and take notice.* Am I right?

LK: I think so.

STALLINGS: Which is a refreshing throwback, I'd have to say, to what we used to call the 'old school.' Old-fashioned values. Conservative values. Same values that made this country great.

LK: Spoken like a Professor of Business.

STALLINGS: There you go.

LK: Old school and rock-ribbed himself.

STALLINGS (smiles): There you go.

LK: Bob, you're an educated man. What do you make of our ... predicament these days?

STALLINGS: Our predicament—you mean our living hell? The face in the sky, the fate of Des Moines, so on and so forth?

LK: Yes.

STALLINGS (nods, then folds his arms): I honestly don't know. Sometimes I think I know, and then I think I don't know. You know? Right now I don't know if I know or not.

LK: Is there any—

STALLINGS: You don't have to quote me on that, OK? Half the time I don't like what comes out of my own mouth.

LK: Is there anything in your field of learning—business, economics—that might shed some light on what's ... what's ...

STALLINGS: What's happening to us? That's an interesting question. (pause) I'm not sure. Companies go bankrupt, go out of business. Entire governments have been known to collapse. Could the same thing happen to the planet Earth?

LK: Could it?

STALLINGS: Well, there was a famous economist, John Maynard Keynes—you familiar with him?

LK: A little.

STALLINGS: Keynes once said: "In the long run we're all dead." He might've misjudged the time frame. Maybe we're all dead in the short run.

LK: Are you ready to die?

STALLINGS: No.

LK: Tomorrow afternoon, if it happens—

STALLINGS: Not sure it matters whether I'm ready.

LK: If it does happen—if the world ends—who or what's behind it?

STALLINGS: No idea.

LK: Is it going to happen?

STALLINGS: No idea. Like I said last night, if we could tell the future, we'd all be zillionaires.

LK: But if you had to venture a g—

STALLINGS: Hey. If I were John Jacob Astor, maybe I could tell you. He *was* a zillionaire.

LK: John Jacob Astor.

STALLINGS: Familiar with him?

LK: I don't—

STALLINGS: Waldorf-Astoria?

LK: Oh yes.

STALLINGS: Astor was a guy who definitely had a feel for the future. Late 1700s, he made a mountain of money in the fur trade, but he also bought and developed a number of properties in Manhattan. And this was Manhattan long before it was really Manhattan, OK? But he seemed to have an ability ...

LK: An ability to ...

STALLINGS: To look ahead. To see what was coming. I'll tell you something else he did. He was a pioneer in the drug trade. Opium.

LK: Opium! Here? In the USA?

STALLINGS: Overseas. He was smuggling shiploads of Turkish opium into China.

LK: He was a drug trafficker.

STALLINGS: He was. Talk about being ahead of the curve! But he knew something about mankind, and he sensed where we were going. So maybe a guy like that ... with his prescience, if John Jacob Astor were standing with us right here today— (jumps) What was that? What was ...

LK (turns and stares upward): It sounded like ...

STALLINGS (stares up): Like gunfire.

LK: Oh no.

STALLINGS: That was gunfire.

LK: Oh no. Oh Lord. Oh no.

Sarah reached inside her purse and drew out the gun,

flicked off the safety. She held the muzzle straight up in the air while she considered what to do. Or how to do it. Did she even have the right apartment? She'd seen no name on the mailbox or anywhere else that would give her confidence. If she did have the right apartment, how did she know her mother hadn't rendered it wrong by moving on to some new location days or weeks ago? Or maybe her father, after answering the phone ninety minutes before, had gone off somewhere himself.

Her father. He was the real point of this singular visit, the only point. He was the point of everything....

She turned the doorknob, and the door, which was unlocked, began to open. She gave it a push, and it swung wide open.

First thing she saw was her father's face, bigger than life, angling down at her. She leveled the gun and strode through the doorway, firing as she went. The gun made a barking noise, erupting with the same fearful rhythm and crazed aggression as a rabid dog. All the shots struck the defenseless target in a tight cluster—right eye, forehead, nose, mouth.... She was shouting something and weeping at the same time, making no sense. When she felt she'd done enough, she broke off the attack, lowered the weapon and started to tremble all over. Her tear-streaked face was ghostly white.

Over on the couch, seated alongside Wanda, Johnny had watched with more than mild disapproval as his daughter, whom he hadn't seen in years, barged in unannounced and blasted to bits the large framed photograph of himself that'd hung with complete innocence on the wall.

He uncrossed his legs. "Well, this is a fine how-do-you-do," he said. "You wanna wake up your mother? Your mother's sick over here."

Sarah turned and hit him with a high-beam glare that was meant to blind him. She raised the gun, pointed it at him and then flung it down hard against the floor where it discharged once again, the bullet puncturing another hole in the wall.

"You self-righteous bastard," she said.

Johnny stood up. "You freaked-out simple bitch."

"You're worth about two cents."

"And you're worth less than that."

For several seconds they held their positions, and neither knew what would happen next. Then they both knew.

Sarah rushed at her father and threw her arms around him, embracing him. At the same instant, he embraced her. They held each other fiercely, as if they might never let go—as if they never should have let go years before. Weeping against his chest, Sarah said nothing. Johnny, his expression mingling pain and joy, murmured: "It's all right, it's all right. Hey. Sweetheart. It's all right."

About this time Stallings came charging into the room, his head lowered, his hands raised, resembling the mediocre high school football player he once had been.

"Get down!" he yelled. "We heard shots! We heard gunshots! Get down!"

Neither Johnny nor Sarah moved. On the couch, Wanda lay motionless.

A grim-faced Laura appeared in the doorway.

Gradually Stallings straightened up. He looked around; looked at Johnny and Sarah. "We heard shots," he repeated, his voice losing some of its authoritative punch.

"It's all right," Johnny said.

Still uneasy, Stallings nodded, though the message hadn't been directed to him. Laura came in and stood beside him. Bemused, the professor scratched his head.

25

IT WAS THURSDAY, very possibly the Final Day for Earth, and Stallings was still scratching his head. He was driving his Malibu to Des Moines, Sarah sitting up front with him and Laura somewhere in the back with her voice recorder, laptop and spiral-bound notebook.

Or he was driving to where Des Moines used to be; was the city still there?

He was scratching his head because he wasn't quite sure why they were making this journey. The idea had originated with the women. Ambitious Laura had hatched the notion that by going to Des Moines, she could better pursue her story of the world's end—or its survival, as the case may be. Whatever was happening to the planet was tied in with the fate of that city; she should go there and see first-hand what she could, talk to people in the area. Sarah's motives were less clear, but she seemed to feel there was some powerful karma at the site that probably ought to be explored. Maybe she also wanted to give her parents some time together, what with Wanda improving slightly. As for Stallings, he simply had nothing better to do, including his job.

The sky was very dark, though flecked in places with little silver forks of lightning. Thunder rumbled down at them, but not too harshly—not yet. Untold tons of rain floated above them, but none fell. Not yet. As he drove west beneath that charcoal sky on I-74 and west again on I-80, crossing the vast openness of Middle America, Stallings felt almost as if he were piloting a craft through the black measureless voids of outer space.

Once they got underway, they had some discussion about when exactly the world was scheduled to end, if indeed it was. The face in the sky had told Stallings 3:00 PM; Sarah and Laura had heard 1:00 PM. Then they realized that the women had been in California when they received their information, while Stallings had been in Illinois. Since the difference between the time zones was two hours, in effect they'd been given the same time. This consistency did not cheer them.

After that piece of conversation, they hadn't much more to say, and they pushed ahead in silence. Soon Stallings found his own thoughts trailing back to the day before—to Wednesday.

Standing there in Wanda's apartment watching Johnny and Sarah caught up in that long embrace, Stallings and Laura decided to let the family reunion play out on its own. They would make themselves scarce for a while to afford the others some privacy. Which they did. But in the meantime, they needed to come up with something to do, since just loitering outside the door didn't seem too appealing.

Stallings had a suggestion. "I'd like to visit my church," he told Laura. "Would you care to join me?"

To his delight, she said yes, and the two made their way to the New Covenant Church. It was small and made of brick, rather old-fashioned, and located in a quiet sylvan neighborhood. Stallings hadn't been there since the funeral service for his wife. He wondered if his absence had been noticed. He also wondered if anyone would even be there at this odd juncture of the week. But when they pulled into the tree-fringed parking lot, they were encouraged to see a number of vehicles.

They were less encouraged to see a bearded man with long frizzy hair, a fanatical gleam in his eye and a hand-painted sign that bore a single blood-red word: REPENT! The man, who was well past his college years, was wearing a purple-and-white toga and sandals.

When they got out of the car, the man came straight at them. He pointed his finger at them and said in the keen screechy voice of a quarterback calling signals over the din of a hostile crowd: *"The end is coming! God is watching! Where will you spend eternity?"*

"Did you make that toga yourself?" Stallings asked. "Or did you buy it?" He reached out and felt the material. "Where would you go to buy a toga?"

"*The end is coming!*" the man screeched.

"He's not usually here," Stallings informed Laura, who looked jumpy. "Never used to be, anyhow."

"*The flames of hell are exceedingly hot!*" the man screeched.

"Get a job," Stallings said, taking Laura lightly by the arm and maneuvering around him. "Shave off that beard and be productive."

Stallings escorted Laura inside, and they went to the sanctuary. The room was far from full, but a scattering of people were present—clusters of two or three, plus some lone individuals. Shoes clacking against the hardwood floor, the newcomers found a pew, sat down. Most of the scant crowd were seated, Stallings observed, though some were kneeling in prayer.

Not far away, the pastor, a young man named Larry LaHood, was moving about, speaking quietly and earnestly to one person or group and then another. And another. The Reverend took his job seriously—almost too seriously, Stallings sometimes felt. Soft-spoken but strikingly intense, LaHood had a disconcerting tendency to come across as a prosecuting attorney. He was tall, gaunt and pale with a hard narrow ax blade of a face. His sandy hair was recently barbered, and his cold gray sparkling eyes called to mind a Norwegian fjord. At this moment LaHood was wearing a black clerical shirt with a clerical collar and black slacks. A former smoker, he nowadays chomped habitually on a big wad of Bubblicious gum, usually Blue Blowout. Now and again he'd blow a bubble the size of a grenade, then pop it loudly, almost violently. Every time he did, something deep inside Stallings' chest would quail and quiver. POW!

In short order the Reverend joined them, stood beside them, peered down at them. "Robert," he said softly, "we haven't seen you in quite some time."

"No," Stallings said.

LaHood peered down at him, working his gum, contemplating. He then shifted his attention to Stallings' companion. "Welcome," he greeted Laura. "You two are ... together?"

Laura said yes just as Stallings said no.

"We're together," Stallings fumbled, "but we're not really *together*." He moved his hand back and forth in a gesture that added nothing at all to his words.

The Reverend peered down at them dourly, remotely. Suddenly he blew a bubble and popped it. POW! After a moment he said: "And you've come here today because ..."

"We're afraid," Laura said. Stallings bowed his head in assent.

The thin face that loomed down at them permitted itself a thin smile. "What was it Dr. Johnson once wrote? 'When a man knows he's to be hanged in a fortnight, it concentrates his mind wonderfully.' " LaHood belabored his gum. "In point of fact," he said, "you've come to the right place. Because I'm here to tell you there's nothing to be afraid of."

"The world's not gonna end?" Stallings looked up hopefully. "We're not gonna die?"

"Robert," the Reverend replied, "that's not what I meant. That's not what I said, and that's not what I intimated."

Stallings blinked a few times, said nothing.

"In point of fact," LaHood continued, "I believe that the end of the world —this world—is imminent, and that Death is staring down darkly at all of us. These are the End Times." He nodded solemnly, and went on in a voice that was barely more than a whisper, more than a hiss. "But should this circumstance be a cause of fear ... or a source of joy and jubilation?"

Neither Stallings nor Laura was able to supply an answer.

Without warning, the pastor sat down next to Stallings— sat so close that the outer edge of their thighs pressed together. The cold gray eyes came down nearer than ever; the mouth, when not speaking, punished the blue gum with a speed and regularity that was machinelike.

"Listen to me," LaHood said softly. "Both of you. I'm going to quote from the Holy Scripture, from the sacred word of God almighty. Listen."

He leaned in still further, gum in motion, the sharp gray eyes stabbing at them like bayonets, and the two visitors did their best to listen.

"But in those days," he intoned in his soft penetrating voice, "after that tribulation, the sun shall be darkened, and the moon shall not give her light. And the stars of heaven shall fall, and the powers that are in heaven shall be shaken. And then"—here the Reverend actually reached over and took hold of Stallings' round shoulder—"then shall they see the Son of Man coming in the clouds with great power and glory. And then shall He send his angels, and shall gather together his elect from the four winds, from the uttermost part of the earth to the uttermost part of heaven." He broke off his recitation. "Do you know what a parable is?" he asked.

Stallings made no sound.

The Reverend turned to Laura, who said: "Yes—it's a story used to illustrate a moral or spiritual lesson."

Chewing rapidly, he held her in his gray gaze for several seconds. "Very good," he said finally. To Stallings' horror, LaHood then blew a big bubble and popped it explosively at close range.

POW!

His voice at once soft and cutting, almost hypnotic, the Reverend resumed his quotation. "Now learn a parable of the fig tree," he said. "When her branch is yet tender, and putteth forth leaves, ye know that summer is near; so ye in like manner, when ye shall see these things come to pass, know that it is nigh, even at the doors."

Though it seemed impossible, LaHood brought himself even closer to Stallings—to his moist cheek, his tense ear. He was grasping the professor's arm with both hands.

"Verily I say unto you," the Reverend declared, "that this generation shall not pass, till all these things be done. Heaven and earth shall pass away, but my words shall not pass away. But of that day and that hour knoweth no man, no, not the angels which are in heaven, neither the Son, but the Father."

Releasing his grip, LaHood backed away a few inches—no more—and lifted his index finger.

"Take ye heed," he concluded. "Watch and pray; for ye know not when the time is."

A sustained silence. Eventually the Reverend allowed: "Now I'm not normally one to quibble with the wisdom of the Holy Bible, but I submit to you that today, even as we speak, we *do* know when the time is. We do know. We do know."

He took notice of Laura. "You wish to say something."

"Just ... it's a beautiful passage. The Book of Mark. King James version."

With the same measured but very real intensity that imbued his voice, he studied her clear everyday face. He scanned her eyes as if trying to read something inscribed within them. He did not seem displeased. He pounded his gum. "Very good," he said. "Very good."

Stallings gave her a look of approbation himself, but his eyes were abruptly drawn back to the Reverend, who had stood up and spread his hands over them.

"A moment ago," LaHood said, "I told you there was nothing to be afraid of. And I spoke the truth. For death holds no fear for those who are right with God." He bent over and poked his finger at Laura. "Are you right with God?" he asked.

She met his gaze. "I believe so," she said.

"Feel free to exult, my child, because very soon you'll be able to touch the loving face of your almighty maker, God in heaven." Still bent forward, he jabbed his long finger at Stallings, who flinched as if the finger had scraped his eyeball. "Are you right with God, Robert?"

Stallings hesitated. "Well," he said, "I don't know. I mean ... I'm not sure."

Slowly and calmly, the Reverend straightened himself. His severe face betraying no emotion, he assaulted his gum from various angles. At last he bent over again, lowering his face till it floated just six inches from Stallings'.

"Get right with God," LaHood advised, "and God'll get right with you. Soon as that happens, you'll be able to face death as God would wish—in the soaring spirit of exuberant celebration." Then, deliberately—almost sadistically—he blew an enormous bubble, comic-book blue.

Stallings wanted to pull back, to turn away, but felt that doing so would be disrespectful. He held still.

POW!

* * *

Behind the wheel of his car, closing in on Des Moines, Stallings stretched his back. It was a four-hour drive, and his back tended to stiffen up when he sat motionless for too long. Should've brought some Tylenol, he told himself.

He checked the odometer and checked the gas gauge. They'd be able to get there, he judged, though coming back (assuming they were to come back) would be a whole different story. So far, all the gas stations they'd passed had been closed save one. Cars and trucks, even an ATV, had descended on that facility like so many outsize metal locusts, and five or six customers were engaged in a fistfight next to one of the pumps. Stallings shot by without slowing down or commenting.

To dispel the glum mood in the car, he was inclined to say something about the weather (which was threatening) or the traffic (which was light) or their location relative to Des Moines (which was pretty close). But he couldn't find the strength to vibrate his vocal cords. Maybe someone was hungry or thirsty? They'd packed a small Coleman cooler with ham sandwiches and Hipsley's Iced Tea. But his passengers were well aware of the cooler, and they would certainly speak up if they wanted something....

He let his fingers go to the car's radio where they played briefly over the 'on' button. He'd turned the radio on a couple times before only to be disappointed by the same obnoxious static that seemed to've taken over all electronic devices. Actually, he did discover one station that was still broadcasting—it was a bluegrass station—but Sarah objected to that option with something like anger. Now, he decided to let the radio alone.

Almost against his will, his thoughts circled back to the Reverend LaHood. The man's attitude, his beliefs, troubled Stallings. People who were zealous with their faith always seemed to place their emphasis on the hereafter, not on the already here. *My kingdom is not of this world*, and so on. But such an approach, Stallings would've argued, unfairly diminishes the importance of the current world. The things that make up this life—our adventures and misadventures, our victories and defeats, our loves and losses—must count for something, he felt. Otherwise, why go through the exercise?...

It occurred to Stallings that, during their years together, he and Jenny had never talked much about the Big Issues: the meaning of life, the meaning of death, the existence and nature of God, the prospect of an afterlife.... Well, they'd been relatively young and practical and not too fascinated with anything metaphysical, except maybe the economy. If Jenny now existed in some other dimension—heaven, let's call it—what was it like there? he wondered. Did she look the same? Did she, as a spirit, have an appearance at all? What did she do there? Did she have a daily routine? Did she even have 'days'? Did she ... did she think about him? If she was in the company of others, was she part of a society, as it were, with rules? A government?...

Stallings winced in annoyance. He certainly hoped there were no bureaucratic meetings in heaven; he'd had enough of them to last him for the rest of this life and throughout eternity. Bureaucratic meetings belonged in hell....

Beside him, Sarah's voice intruded on his reverie. "Isn't that odd?" she said.

"What," he roused himself.

"The traffic."

There'd been a dribble of highway traffic, some vehicles zipping along, others just putt-putting. He'd seen nothing remarkable in it.

"What about the traffic?" he asked.

"It's all moving in the same direction. *Toward* Des Moines."

He thought about it. She was right. He hadn't seen anything coming at them for at least thirty minutes. One would guess that if Des Moines had been destroyed—razed by some unfathomable cosmic force—traffic would be racing in just the opposite direction as people scrambled to get away. And yet ...

"That *is* odd," he said. "Maybe ..."

"Everybody's probably doing what we're doing," Laura said from the back seat. "Making a pilgrimage."

The word struck Stallings' ear in a curious way. "A pilgrimage," he said.

"That would explain the hitchhikers," she added.

Stallings both had and hadn't noted a sprinkle of hitchhikers, more of them than he might've expected, along the route. Physically he'd seen them, but mentally he'd disregarded them. He hadn't picked one up since he was eighteen and didn't know any better. The last one he stopped for back then was a hirsute young man who looked like maybe the sound engineer for the Grateful Dead; within five seconds the guy threw up in the car. Not a word spoken to that point. The car, of course, belonged to Stallings' father, which made it a fine mess all around.

No, Stallings wasn't a huge fan of hitchhikers.

"We should pick one up," Laura said.

"No, no," Stallings said.

"Why not?" Sarah asked.

"No room."

"I've got room back here," Laura said. "We could help someone get where he's going."

"I'm not running a taxi service." He was remembering the last couple guys they'd passed. Drifter types, dirtball types. Perennial hitchhikers. Not too far removed, come to think of it, from that joker who'd upchucked in his father's Buick.

"Bob," Sarah said, "one of them might be able to give us some news—about what's going on."

He glanced over at her, caught a whiff of her perfume, and immediately felt himself weakening.

"I dunno, Sarah," he said. "These guys, they all look like, like ..."

"Not all of them," she said. "Not that guy." She tossed her smooth black mane of hair at another hitchhiker standing ahead of them alongside the road.

Stallings zeroed in on him and saw in the distance a young fellow with just a nap of blond hair on his head and none whatever on his face. What's more, he was wearing a well-cut suit, dark gray, about the same color as the moiling sky. Carrying no bags, he could've been someone's grandson on his way to a job interview with the FBI or IBM—though Stallings doubted that either firm was hiring just now.

Before he knew it, he'd pulled over, stopped and allowed the young traveler to hop in the back seat with Laura. Then they were off again.

"Where you headed?" Stallings asked, trying without success to find the guy in the rear-view mirror.

"The fallen city," he said. "Des Moines," he threw in, perhaps in case someone thought he was referring to Las Vegas or Tijuana.

"I'm Bob Stallings."

"Call me Harrison."

An easy enough name, was Stallings' opinion. But ambiguous—was it his first name or his last name?

"What do you hear, Harrison," Sarah asked, "about the world? What's going on out there?"

"Well, I dunno, you know?" His blond head resembled an onion bulb. His eyes were close-set, and his mouth seemed too small for his homely face. "Some crazy-ass shit out there."

"Like what."

"Just heard this morning," he said in a singsong voice, surprisingly carefree, "the United States has declared war. We're officially at war."

"Who with?" Laura asked.

"With the enemy."

"And who would that be?" Stallings asked.

"Nobody seems to know," Harrison said. "But we're definitely at war with 'em. And once we figure out who they are, we'll squash 'em like bugs."

"That's how we do it," Sarah said.

"Damn straight."

Stallings noticed that they'd lately passed from a wide-open rural area into more of a suburban setting. Convenience stores, a car dealership, another gas station or two—everything apparently closed.

"So why're you going to Des Moines?" he asked Harrison, still unable to locate him in the mirror.

"I dunno," Harrison said. "Why not?"

"Figure it'll still be there?" Laura asked.

"I dunno. Probably not. Probably just dust and ghosts. Be cool to see it, though, don't you think?"

Stallings, who couldn't have produced a much stronger answer himself, nodded. "I like the suit," he said.

"Thanks," Harrison said. "First time in my life I ever wore a suit. Not even my goddam suit. My uncle's."

"Why're you wearing it?" Laura asked.

"Wanted to see what it felt like. Might not get another chance, you know?"

"Might not," Sarah agreed.

Harrison's small sensitive mouth bent itself into a contented smile. "Today's a day of firsts," he said. "For me, anyways."

"Might be a day of lasts," Stallings put in wryly.

"Past three years," Harrison said, "I never got outta bed before 10 o'clock. Today I did." He stared down at his hands. "Never told my mother I love her, you know? But today— well, I didn't, but I thought about it, OK? Another goddam first."

Laura was inspecting her voice recorder. "This might be one more first for you," she said. "How about if I ask you some questions?"

He frowned at her. Then his frown went away as he gave her a once-over. "I dunno," he said. "Questions—what kinda questions?"

"Easy ones. Let me just ..."

"Them's the kind I like."

"If I can just ..." Recorder ready, she jotted something in her notebook.

Far ahead, Stallings spied a caution light, and he eased up on the gas. Even as he attended to the duties of driving, a portion of his mind was curious about the questions Laura might put to this smartly dressed, but not too smart, passenger. Her first question, when it finally came, baffled the professor.

"What are you doing?" she said.

Hmm. *What are you doing?* Stallings repeated the words silently to himself. Meaning ... what are you doing, uhhhhh, professionally? He rubbed his chin. Academically? Existentially? What are you ...

Then, directly behind him, Laura started to speak again but cut off her comment and screamed so piercingly that the tiny hairs on Stallings' forearms stood erect. In the next instant, Sarah had flung off her seatbelt and launched herself halfway into the back seat even as Stallings, reacting instinctively, jammed on the brakes and then fought with both hands to control the car as it swerved from the right lane to the left and back to the right again. Grunts, shouts and curses from everywhere. A wrestling match in the back seat. Slowing down, the car ran off the road and sideswiped a guardrail before grinding to a halt.

"Goddammit!" Stallings said in shock and confusion.

Grabbing at his seatbelt, he heard a door open and turned to see Harrison scampering away. So long and good riddance, Stallings thought. Awkwardly, he got out as well. He opened the door next to Laura and saw no visible damage to her, though with her hair mussed and her face white and her hands fluttering like percale sheets in a stiff wind, she didn't look too nonchalant. Sarah had crawled into the back seat with her and was tending to her.

"Laura," Stallings said, "you OK? You're OK. You OK?"

He turned and watched the gray suit, much smaller now, run toward a 7-11, open the door and dart inside. Stallings was surprised the door hadn't been locked; the store was dark and the lot deserted. He debated what to do. Go after him? Call the cops? Things being the way they were, neither alternative made sense. He turned back around to Laura, who was still jittery but still OK, then turned around again and stared in frustration at the 7-11.

Then something extraordinary happened. The store and everything in it disappeared.

One second it was there; the next it was gone. No lights or flames or erupting debris—no noise, for that matter. The building simply ceased to exist. A flat layer of gray sooty substance much like a shadow marked the site.

Stallings swallowed, took a step backward and began to hyperventilate. He took another step backward and almost tumbled down inside the open doorway and on top of the women.

Righting himself, he started to babble. "Did you see that?" he cried. "Did you see that? Store just ... just ..."

The others climbed out and stared in the direction of his pointing shaking finger.

"I was standing here," he said. "That guy, that—that Harrison ..."

"Where'd he go?" Sarah asked.

"In the store."

"There isn't any store," Laura said.

"That's what I'm *saying*," Stallings tried again. "My God, it just ... just ..."

Timidly they all advanced toward the site. They didn't advance too far. A breeze came down from the dark ominous sky and stirred the bed of dust, lifted some of it, scattered it about. A black minivan, headed for Des Moines, approached, slowed down and then sped on while they stood there.

Pulling himself together, Stallings said: "C'mon. Let's get outta here."

No one argued.

But when they drew near the car, there was a second extraordinary event.

The sky, which had been flashing and rumbling all day, now blanched completely for half a breath. It was as if some titanic photographer, armed with a monstrous camera, had taken a snapshot of the entire scene. Soon after came a deep booming noise, like the rattle of thunder. And yet it was *different* from thunder, or so it seemed to Stallings, who'd had an experience like this once before. Sarah and Laura froze in place and looked uncertainly at each other. By contrast, Stallings, slowly and unwillingly, began to tilt back his head, to lift his gaze fearfully to the awful sky straight above.

When the black dot appeared, zooming down at them, it was hard to discern against the murky backdrop. But as it grew larger, it became easier to see, and then impossible not to see. Suddenly, as Stallings had known it would, the black dot blossomed into a human face—the same one he'd seen before. There were the same gimlet brown eyes, the flowing brown hair, the neatly groomed brown mustache and beard. If anything, the face's expression was even more sober and more critical than on the first occasion, as if it belonged now to a hanging judge, and Stallings and company were manifestly guilty of the worst treason, many times over, against all that was true and just and holy.

The face expanded in size, like an image on the surface of a balloon, until it covered half the sky. Then it took up the whole sky. It seemed to push down at them even farther, crowding them, pressuring them. As he had earlier, Stallings collapsed on the ground, hands held up; Laura went down next to him. Bracing herself against the Malibu, Sarah stayed upright.

A moment passed as the thing's tremendous eyes twitched minutely from one person to the next to the next. It seemed alive. All three could feel its breath pouring over them warmly. Moistly. Though nothing touched them, they felt pinned in place, puny and helpless.

Now the eyes settled on Stallings, and he squirmed beneath them. The gigantic lips parted as they prepared to speak. Stallings had rarely been less comfortable in his life.

"Mr. Stallings," the face addressed him. The enunciation was crisp; the volume ringingly forceful. "Your thoughts."

"My ... my ..."

Concise and direct, the request, if that's what it was, had a certain economical beauty to it. But Stallings would've preferred something fuller, clearer, less Delphic. He would've preferred almost anything.

"My, uh ... oh jeez," he said. "If I ... my thoughts ... they, uh ... oh Lord, I ... I really don't ..."

Showing little emotion apart from sternness, the face continued to glare down at him.

Then Sarah spoke up. Spoke up sharply, directing her words at the thing above her.

"So who the hell are you?" she said. "*What* are you?"

Bottomless black pupils the size of moons turned toward her, locked on her.

"You what's behind all the trouble?" she demanded. "The missing people? The missing cities?"

"Uh, Sarah?" Stallings tried to head her off.

"If you are," she said, "you oughta be ashamed of yourself."

Pressing down at her, the face in the sky seemed attentive but utterly unfazed and regally aloof.

"You've got the power to do good," Sarah said, "but you don't. You do evil."

Sprawled on her back, Laura managed to make a sound. "Sarah?" she said. "Hey, Sarah?"

"You're immoral and you're cruel."

Its mien unchanging—still neutral—the face spoke a single word to her. "Indeed," it said.

" 'In*deed*,' " she mocked it. "You're a ... a self-righteous bastard!" It was the same phrase she'd thrown at her own father.

At this, both Stallings and Laura turned toward Sarah, who was still braced against the car, and gave her a glazed look of astonishment and despair. But when they turned back to the face, they saw only the dark flickering sky.

The apparition had vanished.

As Sarah began stalking around resentfully, muttering to herself, kicking at the dirt, Stallings and Laura decided to stay put for a while. Horizontal. Pulse returning to semi-normal, Laura was already berating herself for not finding the nerve to've confronted the face with a series of incisive journalistic questions. She'd probably just missed out on the greatest interview of all-time!

She sat herself up.

Stallings' thoughts weren't quite as high-flown. He rolled over to his hands and knees and, with a sigh, stood up. He brushed at his clothes and moved around some to see how he felt. He rubbed his back.

"I'm getting too damn old for this," he said.

26

ONCE AGAIN at the helm of his now scratched and dented Malibu, foot on the gas, Stallings tried to calculate what effect, if any, Sarah's little outburst might have on the state of things. Probably not a good effect, he guessed.

Straining his imagination, he attempted to place himself in the position of that preternatural face in the sky, wherever it came from, whatever it represented. So there the thing was, looming down magically and majestically at the planet Earth. Obviously its intention, minutes ago, had been to communicate with someone special, someone whose ideas carried exceptional weight and value—a college professor. Robert Earl Stallings. But for what purpose? Well, to collect additional data that might solidify—or perhaps undercut—the stated plan to wipe out everybody and everything. Yes, that had to be it. The face was having second thoughts, it seemed to Stallings. And it wanted to be sure of what it was about to do before it did it.

Simple enough.

But then what'd happened? Temperamental Sarah had leaped uninvited into the fray and bad-mouthed the vision with a series of fairly personal criticisms, winding up by calling it a 'self-righteous bastard'! Goodness gracious sakes alive. Here Stallings glanced over at her in pure wonder; gazing moodily out the side window, she didn't notice him. Though he didn't know for sure, he frankly doubted that the face had been pleased; the professor, who'd suffered similar verbal attacks from disgruntled students, certainly wouldn't have been. If the fate of the world hinged even in part on that rocky exchange between scary apparition and scary former student, he figured that the home team had lost some valuable points.

Or had it?...

The first step Stallings had taken upon climbing back in his car was to crack open a cold bottle of Hipsley's Iced Tea and begin thoughtfully sipping. He reached down now and had another restorative sip.

It was possible, he supposed—and this was a long shot—but it was distantly possible that the face might actually respond positively to Sarah's moment of brutal candor. Maybe, thanks to her, the thing was already developing a new respect for Homo sapiens as a feisty lot, full of a bumptious and fiery spirit that simply couldn't accept bullying or defeat. Maybe Sarah, who was by no means a dummy, had employed a sly impromptu form of reverse psychology, hoping to achieve that very result. Maybe everything was on its merry way to turning out fine and dandy after all!...

Or maybe not. When he recalled the face's firm no-nonsense manner, its brusque comments and its sheer size and implied destructive power, whatever optimism he'd tried to muster fled like a cat burglar before whirling lights and a wailing siren. The fact that a sky-filling apparition was hanging around at all didn't build confidence. Stallings had been in better situations, he judged, and so had everyone else. And this particular situation could well turn worse before the day was through.

At this hour, the sky still so gray it was almost black, they were following Route 6 down into Des Moines. The city, Stallings was relieved to see, still seemed like itself. He spotted a few pedestrians, all of them moving in the same direction as the Malibu, many with their thumbs out, and the flow of traffic, which had picked up, was reassuring. (All vehicles, his included, were streaming southwest into the core of the city.) Most importantly, though, everything still appeared as it should; there were buildings, streets, traffic lights, even a large billboard featuring a color portrait of his pal Johnny Black holding up a glinting glass of the same tasty beverage Stallings was now nervously sipping.

"You know," he said vaguely, "I think maybe we're gonna

be OK. I think maybe ..."

The others said nothing.

But soon traffic had slowed till it was barely moving, and then it *wasn't* moving; they'd come to a dead halt. Stallings grimaced as he checked the gas gauge—almost empty. Craning his neck, he saw that their route up ahead had been clogged by abandoned cars. Dozens of them—hundreds—blocked the thoroughfare, turning it into a very disorganized parking lot. Just in front of him, a determined-looking man in a Cubs cap got out of his Camry, swung the door shut and walked ahead. Behind Stallings, people who seemed more focused and concerned than impatient or exasperated were likewise leaving their cars and hurrying ahead on foot.

He cut the engine. "C'mon," he said, and they all climbed out of the Malibu.

They pressed ahead with a tingling urgency, as did others, but the blockade of abandoned cars made progress difficult.

"This way," Stallings might call out as he led them along, or "Over here, c'mon."

"Thirty minutes!" a bald hook-nosed man announced from the cab of his parked Dodge Ram. He was eating a pastrami sandwich.

Stallings checked his watch; it was 2:30.

"Say, what happened up there?" he asked the man, gesturing to where they were headed. "Anything?"

"Up there?" the man repeated.

"Yeah. What's up there? What'll we see?"

The man smiled. His teeth looked like the yellowed porcelain of an old urinal. "Why—everything," he said. "And nothing." He leered at Sarah. "Hey babe," he said. "I seen you. I know you. You're, uh ... what the hell's your name? You're Zoey Zanders!"

"I'm Sarah Black," she said, and she and her two chums moved on.

As they made their way, the number of orphaned cars decreased, but the size of the crowd swelled. No one was saying much—just staring ahead, moving ahead. They were approaching an intersection, and even from a distance something about it looked peculiar to Stallings. What was it?... A throng of people had gathered there, forming a line, almost a cordon, that stretched left and right as far as he could observe. It was as if they'd assembled on a dock and were sadly watching a ship sail away—or were waiting sadly for one to arrive.

"'Scuse me," Stallings said, nudging people aside. He'd taken Sarah by the hand; Sarah had grabbed Laura's hand. "Pardon me," he said.

Even before reaching their destination, he'd figured out what was wrong with the scene, and he didn't like it. There was no skyline ahead of them. No buildings. When at last he'd shouldered and elbowed his way to the front of the crowd, he saw with dismay that what lay before them was essentially nothing—nothing but a great gray sea of soot that seemed to extend forever. In fact, the gray of the sky and the gray of the soot were indistinguishable, and he would've sworn he was staring down into the dark pit of a forgotten coalmine or a forsaken well. For an instant, he lost his balance and staggered backward into someone. Then he lurched forward into the hideous powder. Fortunately, it was only a few inches deep, and the ground beneath it felt solid. Uneasy, he stepped back to where he'd been, which was the middle of a street that'd been split in half.

"Over this way," Stallings said to his friends, and they began to slide rightward along the edge of the desolation.

Something had caught his eye over there, and he felt compelled to investigate. A young guy with his hair drawn back in a ponytail, pink granny glasses and a pink diamond stud in his left ear was selling T-shirts. He'd set up a wooden table and stacked the shirts neatly on top of it. One of the shirts bore a cartoon image of a smug-looking Earth flexing its biceps; the caption read I SURVIVED THE FINAL DAY. Another shirt, not quite as optimistic, featured an unsmiling smiley face and

the message FACE IT—YOU'RE DOOMED. Still another
shirt depicted a white spiral galaxy, possibly the Milky Way,
spinning elegantly against a wash of black. Beneath the picture
was the statement THERE'S A HELL OF A GOOD
UNIVERSE NEXT DOOR; LET'S GO. The words were
attributed to ee cummings, a name Stallings didn't recognize
and whose lowercase letters he found affected.

When he saw that several people had not only bought T-
shirts but were wearing them, he was astounded. Capitalism
was wonderful, but hey, let's be real! He walked over to the
merchant and said in disbelief: "T-shirts?!"

"Twenty bucks a pop," the guy said. "And I do have
double extra large."

"You've gotta be kidding."

The guy shrugged. "OK, fifteen bucks. I like you; you
remind me of a professor I once had."

"You have *got* to be," Stallings insisted, "kidding me!" He
was holding his mouth open as far as it would go.

"All right, OK. You drive a hard bargain. Twelve bucks,
and that's my limit."

But Stallings had a limit too, and he turned indignantly
away from the T-shirt salesman.

"Twenty minutes!" someone announced.

Pushing ahead with his arms held out stiffly, his face blank,
his stride unsteady—he looked like a mummy—Stallings
discovered that other entrepreneurs had also set up shop. He
came next to a stand where a woman was selling homemade
jewelry: lapis lazuli rings, turquoise necklaces, silver-and-jade
bracelets.... Some of the baubles were rather attractive. Farther
along, a man was grilling hotdogs, and the tempting aroma had
drawn a long line of hungry customers. Stallings didn't join
them. Elsewhere a magician was entertaining people with card
tricks, many of which involved the ace of spades. Donations
could be placed in an upturned top hat on the corner of his
wobbly table. In spite of himself, Stallings, who'd always
admired sleight of hand artists, put a five-dollar bill in the hat.

He wasn't so generous with the escape artist. This guy was hanging upside down in a straitjacket from what looked like a chin-up bar. Wriggling furiously, he seemed to be getting nowhere. "I can do this!" he yelled, his face flushed. "I can do this!"

As Stallings wandered along, someone bumped into him roughly, knocking him sideways. Two men were fighting, not very skillfully. The one who'd blundered into him drew back his fist, preparing to throw a punch at the other man. Impulsively, Stallings wrapped his arms around the first man and pulled him away from his opponent. "That's enough!" Stallings scolded. "Both of you! That's enough!" He held the man in a heavy bear hug that was meant to calm him, or at least control him. Then, when it felt right, he released him.

The man spun around, his eyes blinking and splashing like rain puddles, and said: "Where'd he go?"

"Forget it," Stallings said.

"You don't know what he did to me."

"Doesn't matter. For God's sake, man, where's your sense of perspective?"

Unimpressed, the man tore off into the horde, hell-bent.

"Ten minutes!" came the announcement.

The crowd eddying around him, Stallings began to focus on a woman who'd knelt down along the shoreline of the ugly gray sea. Her head was bowed, and she was obviously in prayer. From this angle, she bore a strong resemblance to his mother—the permed silver hair, the stout (but not too stout) body. She was wearing a robin egg blue top and white slacks. When he came closer to her, he saw that she'd sunk her knees into the filthy soot.

He stood beside her and rested his hand on her shoulder. For a moment she remained motionless; then she looked up into his eyes. To his amazement, she still resembled his mother. She smiled at him, and he tried to return her smile. He hoped that whatever expression he'd conjured would bring her some consolation, some support. When she lowered her head to resume praying, he kept his hand on her shoulder for what seemed like many minutes but was probably no more than a few lines of a cherished psalm. A tear welling in his eye, he stepped away from her.

Standing by himself, Stallings realized that he was in fact by himself. He'd become separated from Sarah and Laura. Where had they gone? He pivoted one way and another but didn't see them. Anxiously, he tugged at his fingers. So dense was the milling crowd that he feared he might never find them, yet they had to be somewhere nearby. He began to retrace his steps, squinting, fretting.

Suddenly he began to doubt his eyes. The gray gloom to which he'd become accustomed now began to brighten and undulate with a play of multicolored lights. It was as if he were standing beneath one of those mirrored disco balls. When he lifted his eyes, he saw that the sky, which was still angry, had become filled with moving lights. He'd seen them before on TV, but until now he'd never appreciated their exquisite beauty. Bronze and burgundy, orange and orchid, salmon and sienna, they circled and zigzagged, soared and dipped. They were absolutely soundless. Some of them moved in patterns; others didn't. Some moved swiftly; others just floated along. Each light was about the size of a human, and—strangely— some of them were shaped a hint like humans. Here were projections that might be arms; that could be legs....

One of the lights, this one a shimmery mint green, slowly descended until it hovered about five feet over Stallings' head. Unmoving, he stared up at it and marveled, as did others. It seemed to possess a kind of translucent skin, and its glow wasn't uniform but was composed of countless lesser lights in slightly different intensities, all of them throbbing and trembling. Did the thing have an intelligence about it? An awareness? Stallings couldn't have said, but a part of him wanted to reach out to it, to invite it to come closer, perhaps even to touch it....

On some level, he understood that what was happening

now—this business with the lights—didn't bode well. But he also understood there wasn't much he could do about it.

Besides which, time was expiring.

"Two minutes," someone said.

The green light flitted away from him, rose to an altitude far above the gray sea and blended in with a host of other swirling lights.

Dropping his eyes, Stallings saw two people standing together in the wasteland. Though they were some distance away, Sarah's profile was unmistakable, and the woman next to her had to be Laura. He began moving toward them, slowly at first, then more quickly. He felt a need to join them before ... before ... His feet squished clumsily in the soot—it was like trying to hurry across a soft silky beach—and the lights dancing above him caused him to feel disoriented. Behind him, many in the crowd had launched into a loud chanting countdown. TWENTY, they roared, NINETEEN, EIGHTEEN, SEVENTEEN....

So fast, he mused to himself. It had all come crashing down so fast....

As he approached the women, he opened his arms, and they opened theirs. None of them spoke. Somberly they pressed together and held on, their heads down-tilted, their eyes closed. From behind Stallings, the chant continued: TEN, NINE, EIGHT, SEVEN....

Even with their eyes closed, they could tell that the mysterious lights had disappeared and the sky had reverted to that churning darkness, interrupted only by short quick stabs of lightning.

They held their breath.

THREE, TWO ...

They held each other.

ONE, ZERO! ...

Nothing happened.

They held on some more.

Still nothing happened.

Still ... and still ...

Stallings straightened up, concentrated on his watch. It was hard to read.

"The count," he said, "the, uh, the time, may've been off. Half a minute fast maybe, a minute ..." They stood there.

Other people stood there. Heads were turning, hearts beating.

A minute or two passed, and nothing much changed.

Growing restless, people began to move, to speak. They were trying to break out of the tight little spheres of dread and bewilderment that contained them, like baby birds trying to break free from their eggshells.

"Well, what do you know?" Stallings said. A timid smile lit his fleshy face, and the smile turned into a grin, and the grin became laughter. "Well, what do you know?" he said again, this time louder.

Sarah and Laura clasped their hands together and looked with relief and gratitude toward heaven. Here and there, people began to celebrate. Some cheered and clapped, some pumped their fists in the air, and more than a few collapsed to their knees. Many wept. Kids ran every which way, laughing, shrieking and making noises that couldn't be categorized. Stallings, who'd become more pessimistic lately than he ever would've admitted, surprised the women by erupting into a giddy and completely random jig, twirling around in the sea of soot like a dervish on amphetamines. Dark clouds kicked up beneath him.

* * *

Back in Illinois, an open-mouthed Johnny Black, satisfied that his gold Cartier watch had told him the truth, held his arms overhead in a big V. He felt as if he'd just pitched another perfect game.

Pacing the floor of his beloved downtown office, Johnny's agent Buzzy Bilkman, hands quaking, managed to light up a

Camel. "For Chrissake," he said.

Professor Jeff Jenson poured himself a straight shot of Jack Daniels and drank it off. Then he took the bottle to his kitchen sink and, without regret, dumped what was left of the whiskey into the basin.

And Ben Temple felt his breath ease from his lungs in a long and much-needed exhalation. He turned to his wife and twined his arms around her, held her close. "Joanie," he said. "Oh Joanie, Joanie ..."

But out in California, Ernesto Cruz had a different reaction. Years of doing battle within and against the American legal system had taught him exactly how tangled and ironic life could be. When the deadline came and went, he began to frown. It was a frown that refused to pass even as time did, instead becoming deeper.

Almost a scowl.

Yes, he was a cynical man, but his cynicism, he would've maintained, had been founded on hard experience.

Irritably, he continued to wait.

27

FROM THE COLD black soundless depths of space, the planet Earth looked something like a blue eyeball—one that might wink shut and never open again. But the eyes that saw Earth from that vantage were extremely acute, able to home in if necessary on the most minuscule of facts.

As they did. Over time, an impressive volume of research, visual and otherwise, had been carefully accumulated.

Yet even at the topmost levels of thought and action, delays could and did occur. The evidence, which was constantly in flux, had to be measured and remeasured, analyzed and reanalyzed. When the stakes were high—even middling high, like now—deadlines were sometimes reluctantly but unavoidably pushed back a bit. Just a bit.

Such was the case here.

Of course, a decision finally did come down, and it wasn't the one that most earthlings would've applauded.

The pulse of energy, unimaginably potent, struck the planet as soon as it was generated, and the globe broke apart like a dry wafer. Bob Stallings was caught in mid-pirouette, and everyone and everything else were caught in mid-something. So immediate and overwhelming was the blow, like the slicing impact of a guillotine's massive blade, that no one felt a thing.

All was ended. In a microsecond, bits of the planet and everything that comprised it went hurtling in a billion directions.

And in that microsecond, Earth came to know, with an intimacy usually reserved for lovers, the true meaning of death and destruction.

28

IN A PARALLEL UNIVERSE, a somewhat different version of Professor Bob Stallings was sitting in a classroom at Harris Community College. He wasn't teaching; he was taking in a physics lecture being presented by one of his colleagues. Stallings had read that elite Wall Street firms often went out of their way to hire people with a background in physics, and he didn't understand why. Why not a background in business? Or economics? Now, after 45 minutes of perhaps the most abstruse lecture he'd ever heard or even imagined—it might as well have been coming at him in Mandarin Chinese!—he still didn't understand why.

He wondered if the students seated around him, all four of them, were as lost as he was. (Unlike MIT or Cal Tech, HCC didn't attract a lot of students who were cut out for physics.) Since none of the four ever asked a question or made a comment, Stallings had no way of measuring whether his ignorance was larger or smaller than anyone else's. Reminding himself that they were actual students in the class and he was just a one-time visitor, he had to assume they all knew more than he did.

Of course, his brainpower wasn't being helped any by the physical discomfort he'd been feeling from the moment he first sat down. He had wedged himself gamely into a wooden desk that'd been designed, decades ago, for a much smaller person. Another five pounds, he admitted to himself, and he couldn't have squeezed in here at all. Maybe he should consider joining a gym.... Shifting his weight one way and another did nothing to solve the problem, but he tried it anyway. My God, he thought, this is awful!...

The cryptic lecture was being delivered by Professor of Physics Jeff Jenson. Slim and intense-looking, with hard little proton eyes and a trim gray-flecked beard, Jenson prowled back and forth in front of the class, speaking fluently, gesturing precisely. He was wearing a white T-shirt bearing the emblem of a black swan, and a pair of faded blue jeans. Some of these facial and sartorial details didn't sit too happily with the clean-shaven Stallings, who, as always, was wearing a button-down Oxford shirt and a Donald Trump silk tie. But he forgave his colleague, since Jenson was clearly passionate about his field and since he chose his words and shaped his sentences with such meticulous care. In another reality, it seemed to Stallings, Jenson might've made a competent English professor.

He definitely wasn't talking about nouns and verbs today. Instead, he was talking about the nature of the universe, or the 'multiverse,' as he sometimes called it. The names he was dropping were mostly unfamiliar to Stallings, but he gathered they belonged to mathematicians or scientists of some stature: Karl Gauss, Georg Bernhard Riemann, John Wheeler, Richard Feynman, Alan Guth. Much worse than the exotic names were the exotic—and incomprehensible—terms: dark matter and dark energy, symmetry and supersymmetry, decoherence, the anthropic principle. The words crawled into his head like a procession of earwigs. Worse still was Jenson's reference to a man named Schrödinger, who had apparently owned a cat that was half dead and half alive, or dead and alive at the same time, or something. No sense at all to that one. The only concept that appealed to Stallings even minimally was the Heisenberg uncertainty principle, since everything Jenson was saying left him feeling profoundly uncertain.

"So I think we can agree," Jenson declared, "that string theory, superstring theory and M-theory are all one and the same." He paused, eyes twinkling. "Except they're all different."

Stallings sneaked a sideways glance at his classmates (who nodded sagely at this last remark), thought about asking for clarification, then decided to keep his mouth shut.

Probably should've said something, Stallings realized too late, since Jenson had already plunged into yet another off-the-wall topic. Quantum theory.

"Now," he challenged the group, "according to quantum theory, what would you say the chances are that you could suddenly dematerialize—poof! just like that—and then rematerialize, I don't know, let's say on the planet Mars?"

Stallings waited patiently for someone to answer this insane question, and when no one did, he spoke up himself.

"Well, I can help you with that one," he said.

"Bob?"

"Zero. There's zero chance, Jeff, that I'm gonna disappear from this desk"—it seemed to have pretty firm grip on him—"and reappear on Mars."

Jenson stroked his beard, within which an amused tolerant smile was starting to glimmer. "Actually," he said, "according to quantum theory, there *is* some chance it could happen. An infinitesimally small chance, but a chance nonetheless."

"Not possible," Stallings said.

"Highly unlikely," Jenson corrected him. "But possible. In fact, electrons do that sort of thing all the time."

"I'm not an electron."

"Doesn't matter." Jenson had put himself in motion, cruising about the room like a subatomic particle himself. "Quantum theory is one helluva theory," he said. "It supposes that any event—listen to this, now—*any* event, regardless of how incredible or illogical it may be, could possibly occur."

"Any event."

"That's correct."

Though unconvinced, Stallings wouldn't have objected too much had he dissolved from the room this second and safely reassembled in his own office where he might then be able accomplish something productive. He never would've said so, but he rather regretted his decision to attend the lecture. If this was physics, his colleague, not to mention Wall Street, could have it. It was the stuff of fantasies and dreams.

Unwilling to let it go, Jenson positioned himself directly in front of Stallings, hands up, fingers spread. "I want you to

think of something crazy," Jenson urged him. "Some event
that you believe simply could not occur. Ever."

Stallings inferred that this meant something in addition to
the trip to Mars already mentioned. Well, OK. He'd play along.
Drumming his fingers on his vise of a desk, he thought first
about the Cubs and how they didn't seem destined to win a
World Series anytime soon. But 'anytime soon' was weak; give
them enough time, a thousand years maybe, and the Cubbies
would probably come through.... Then he remembered a
bizarre short story he'd read as an undergraduate about a man
who, for no apparent reason, abruptly transforms into an
insect. An insect! Sick stuff. Also, most unlikely to happen in
real life. But since some mentally ill writer thought the idea up
long before Stallings did, he didn't want to suggest it now due
to lack of originality.

Veering off in a new direction, he considered his wife
Jenny. How he loved her! But what if he'd never met her? Or
what if they'd gotten together, only to have fate uncaringly
separate them? What if something unfortunate or tragic had
happened to her? What if—God forbid—what if she'd gotten
sick or injured and then died? He could hardly bear to think of
it, and to have suffered that crushing a loss would've been
impossible for him, Stallings felt.

(Yet it had nearly happened. Little more than a year ago,
Jenny had been walking across a parking lot when some
speeding jackass just missed running her over and killing her
for sure. She escaped without a scratch, thank God. But what
if?... Oh, he shuddered to think of it.)

"OK, how about this," Stallings said.

Jenson and the others gave him some close attention.

"One day," Stallings went on, "this humongous face
appears in the sky. Human face, OK? And it tells people that
the world is about to end. And the world does end, OK?
Everybody dies. How about that? Could that happen?"

Jenson seemed taken aback. He gave his colleague a
protracted stare—a neutral stare, not too impolite—of the sort

perfected by psychiatrists. The students at whom Stallings had cast sidelong glances now cast sidelong glances at him.

"Well," Jenson cleared his throat, his beady eyes unblinking. "Where'd you come up with that?"

"I dunno."

"You're sketching out what? Some type of alien invasion?"

"I dunno. I just made it up."

"Some type of doomsday scenario?"

"I dunno. Could it happen?"

"Let's hope it doesn't," Jenson said sincerely. "But, according to quantum theory, the answer is yes, it could happen." Tapping at the air with a mechanical pencil, he once again began to pace. "And I'll take it one step further than that. It probably already *has* happened."

Stallings and the students sat up.

"How's that?" Stallings said.

"Chances are, it's already happened."

"It's ... it's ..." Stallings chortled. "Well, pardon me, Jeff, but I must've missed that one. Maybe I was looking the other way?" He chortled again.

"We all were. Because if it happened, it happened in another universe."

"In another ..."

"More and more," Jenson said, "physicists and cosmologists believe that our universe is just one of trillions, each one—"

"Oh, come on, Jeff!"

"Each one embodying new and different possibilities. Like revised drafts of the same script—"

"Aw, Jeff."

"—written by the Master Author."

"Aw, please. Jeff. Really." Fidgeting in his desk, Stallings was convinced that Jenson had drawn his information not from a textbook but from a comic book. "My goodness, if this is the sort of moonstruck malark—"

But just then Associate Dean Jonathan ('Please don't call

me John') Black opened the door and stuck in his handsome thick-coiffed head. Instantly everyone relaxed at the sight of his easygoing grin. "So how we doing in the world of the very small and the very large?" he asked jokingly. Oftentimes Jonathan came around just to banter for a minute with the instructors and the students; it was another reason for his campus-wide popularity. Noticing his old friend Stallings, Jonathan said: "Bob, what's up? You taking some remedial?"

Stallings chuckled and conceded that maybe he was.

"Hey," Jonathan said. "Have you gotten to Haldane's quote yet? No? 'The universe is not only queerer than we suppose, it's queerer than we *can* suppose.' Right, Jeff? First time I heard that, I took it as a comment on alternative lifestyles."

Laughter from everyone.

Hand held up next to his face as if he were taking an oath, Jonathan said, not too seriously: "I didn't say that. You didn't hear me say that."

More laughter.

With a wink and a wave, he stepped back into the hallway, closing the door behind him.

It was the excuse Stallings had been hoping for. He fought his way out of the medieval desk and, hustling toward the door, made his apologies. "Sorry," he said. "I, uh ... I just remembered that, um ..." Like Jonathan, he waved to the class, but without the same suave style or rich effect.

In the hall, his friend hadn't gone too far. "Hey, guy," Stallings called to him. "So whadaya think of all that physics stuff, huh?"

Jonathan turned toward him and offered him a white gleaming smile that would've made Gatsby's seem chintzy by comparison.

"Physics!" he said. "I dunno, man. Too deep for me."

Stallings understood that the Associate Dean was being modest. The two men had grown up together, and if there'd been a brighter kid in the neighborhood, Stallings didn't know who it could've been. In fact, if not for his pal's kind-hearted tutoring, Stallings might not have conquered high school Biology. With that tall, rangy physique of his, Jonathan probably could've done OK as a scholar-athlete, Stallings guessed. A basketball player maybe. But he'd had no interest in sports—always with his head poked in a fat book, always studying, always laboring to grow his mind.

He was a born educator, and a super guy.

"So how'd it go out there in the Golden State?" Stallings asked him.

Last weekend, Jonathan had gone to California to see his daughter Sarah get married.

"Great, great. Beautiful ceremony, nice reception. You should've been there."

Stallings had been invited, of course, but he'd begged off. Although he'd taught Sarah a few years before, he didn't really know her that well, and going clear to California to see a wedding had seemed burdensome. Now, talking to his buddy, he felt selfish, wrongheaded and guilty. If their situations had been reversed, he figured, Jonathan would've made the trip; he was that kind of guy.

"Sarah's a sweet girl," Stallings said. "And the fellow she married—what'd you tell me his name was? Ernesto ..."

"Cruz. Ernesto Cruz. Works for Disney."

"He's a lawyer?"

"Yeah, but I like him anyway." They both laughed. "Tell you the truth," Jonathan said, "he's a good egg. Couple years older than my baby, but a real 'bon vivant,' as he puts it. He had all this Martell cognac and these Cuban cigars. We were partying like there was no tomorrow."

Stallings tried to paint a mental picture of the festivities, with Jonathan somewhere in the middle of them. Music and dancing, no doubt, convivial people, tons of mouth-watering food ... Dammit, yes, Stallings should've been there!...

"Listen, Jonathan," he said, feeling for the right tone. "Jenny and I were talking the other day—it's been a while since we've had you and Wanda over for dinner."

Jonathan clapped his hand down on Stallings' shoulder. "Just say the word, brother. I'm a big fan of that lovely lady's cooking."

"How about this Saturday. Six o'clock."

Jonathan pointed his finger at him. "You got it."

"Make it five o'clock. We'll have a drink or two. I'll get Jenny to whip up some of that pot roast you like, you know, with the, uh—"

"The new potatoes ..."

"New potatoes, baby carrots ..."

"Some of those pearl onions ... *Mais oui! C'est magnifique*," Jonathan said, kissing his fingers and strolling down the hall. "Bob, I'll be ringing your doorbell at four."

"Bring your appetite."

Smiling to himself, Stallings walked over to a window, had a gander out at the rolling greenery of the quad. Life was pretty good, he thought. Yes, it had its ups and downs, but overall it was pretty good. At this moment, just being alive felt pleasantly satisfying.

A twanging bouncing noise was coming up the hall. Turning, Stallings saw big Jamal Jameson, one of the school's basketball players, dribbling a basketball as he approached.

"Jamal—hey!" Stallings said. "Not in here, OK? You want to practice your dribbling, do it in the gym or do it outside."

Impudently, Jamal held out the ball one-handed in the professor's face. Stallings took the ball and balanced it on the tip of his right index finger. Never an athlete, he had, however, taught himself one modest trick. Slapping the ball—whap! whap!—with his left hand, he got it to spin in place rapidly, under superb control. Carefully, he lifted it, twirling like the globe itself, up before Jamal's popped-out eyes. With a show of petulance, the youngster seized it back and went on his way, trying and failing to duplicate Stallings' feat; the ball kept flying off his finger. But at least he'd stopped dribbling it.

Smiling again, Stallings shook his head and had another

look out the window. A handful of students were sitting in a gazebo talking; others were crossing the campus in various directions, their pace unhurried. A college campus in clement weather was always so tranquil, he thought. So tonic.

On impulse, he inclined his gaze to the mild blue sky and saw a train of cumulus clouds drifting slowly along. The first one looked like a camel, he supposed, and the next one, mmmmm, like a weasel. That third one looked like a white sperm whale....

And here was another cloud that resembled a human face. How about that. He could make out the eyes, the Roman nose, even the mouth. The face seemed to be peering straight down at him, smiling.

Buoyant as a cloud himself, Stallings returned the smile.

Yes, he thought, life was pretty doggone good.